STON

'I do not fear you,' said Thuro evenly. 'You are a man of little worth. Come then, child-killer, earn your salt!'

The man tensed and raised his sword, but then his eyes flickered to a point behind Thuro. 'Who are you?' he asked and Thuro turned his head. Behind him, seeming to appear from nowhere, was a man in a white bearskin cloak. His hair was black and silver shone at the temples; his face was square-cut and clean-shaven, his eyes grey. He was dressed in a dark leather tunic over green woollen leggings and he carried a silver staff with two ebony grips – one at the top, the second halfway down.

'I asked who you were,' repeated the assassin.

'I heard you,' answered the newcomer, his voice deep, and colder than the winds of winter.

'Then answer me.'

'I am Culain lach Feragh, and you have attacked my ward.'

By David Gemmell

Legend
The King Beyond the Gate
Waylander
Quest for Lost Heroes
Waylander II
The First Chronicles of Druss the Legend
Drenai Tales: Omnibus One
Drenai Tales: Omnibus Two·

Wolf in Shadow
The Last Guardian
Bloodstone

Ghost King
Last Sword of Power

Lion of Macedon
Dark Prince

Ironhand's Daughter
The Hawk Eternal

Knights of Dark Renown

Morningstar

Hawk Queen: The Omnibus Edition
Stones of Power: The Omnibus Edition

DAVID GEMMELL

STONES OF POWER

This omnibus edition includes

Ghost King
Last Sword of Power

orbit

www.orbitbooks.net

ORBIT

First published in Great Britain in 2014 by Orbit

3 5 7 9 11 12 10 8 6 4

Typeset in Bembo by Hewer Text UK Ltd, Edinburgh
Printed and bound by CPI Group (UK) Ltd, Croydon, CR0 4YY

Papers used by Orbit are from well-managed forests
and other responsible sources.

Orbit
An imprint of
Little, Brown Book Group
Carmelite House
50 Victoria Embankment
London EC4Y 0DZ

An Hachette UK Company
www.hachette.co.uk

www.orbitbooks.net

Principal Characters

(in alphabetical order)

ALHYFFA – Daughter of Hengist, wife of Moret

BALDRIC – Warrior of the Pinrae

CAEL – Son of Eldared, King of the Brigante

CULAIN LACH FERAGH – Warrior of the Mist, also known as the Lord of the Lance. Master of weaponry.

ELDARED – Brigante King and Lord of Deicester Castle. Betrayed his brother Cascioc twenty years before to help Aurelius gain the throne.

GWALCHMAI – King's retainer. Cantii tribesman

GOROIEN – The Witch Queen, immortal and ruthless

HENGIST – Saxon king, father to Horsa, the warlord

KORRIN ROGEUR – Woodsman of Pinrae, Brother to Pallin

LAITHA – Ward of Culain

LUCIUS AQUILA – General of the Romano-British forces

MAEDHLYN – Lord Enchanter to Aurelius

MORET – Son of Eldared

PALLIN – Half-man, half-bear, tortured by the Witch Queen

PRASAMACCUS – Brigante tribesman

SEVERINUS ALBINUS – Roman legate of the Ninth Legion

THURO – Son of High King Aurelius Maximus and the Mist Maiden, Alaida

VICTORINUS – King's retainer and First Centurion

Roman Names of British Settlements

ANDERIDA – Pevensey

CALCARIA – Tadcaster

CAMULODUNUM – Colchester

CATARACTONIUM – Catterick

DUBRIS – Dover

DUROBRIVAE – Rochester

EBORACUM – York

LAGENTIUM – Castleford

LINDUM – Lincoln

LONDINIUM – London

LONGOVICIUM – Lancaster

PINNATA CASTRA – Inchtuthill

SKITIS ISLAND – Isle of Skye

VENTA – Winchester

VINDOLANDA – Chesterholm

VINDOMARA – Ebchester

Ghost King

This book is dedicated with love to Stella Graham, to Tom Taylor and to Jeremy Wells for the gift of friendship.

Also to the ladies of the Folkstone Herald – *Sharon, Madders, Susie and Carol – for Rocky. And to Pip Clarkson who cast the pearls anyway.*

Foreword

Ghost King is a fantasy novel and not intended as historically accurate. However the cities of Roman Britain, as named, did exist in the areas suggested, as did certain of the characters who appear in these pages.

Cunobelin was certainly a powerful warrior king, who earned the title Brittanorum Rex from the Roman writer Seutonius. Cunobelin reigned for forty years from his base at Camulodunum, possibly giving rise to the Arthurian legends.

Paullinus was also a true man of history, and did defeat the Iceni of Boudicca during the ill-fated uprising. During the same period the Ninth Legion did indeed disappear. Some historians claim they were ambushed and destroyed, others suggest a mutiny that the Romans covered up.

The manoeuvres of Roman military units are detailed as accurately as research and the needs of drama allow.

The language used is relatively modern, and undoubtedly there will be some students who find it jarring to read of arrows being 'fired', when of course the expression evolved only after the introduction of matchlock muskets. Similarly 'minutes' and 'seconds' appear ahead of their time.

Such arguments as may be offered can be overcome by pointing out that since the language being spoken is not English, but a bastardized form of Latin-Celtic, some licence in translation should be allowed.

Of the life of Uther Pendragon, little is known. This is not a history of the man, but a fantasy.

In other words it is not the story as it was – but as it *ought* to have been.

David A. Gemmell
Hastings, 1988

1

The boy stared idly at the cold grey walls and wondered if the castle dungeons could be any more inhospitable than this chill turret room, with its single window staring like an eye into the teeth of the north wind. True there was a fire glowing in the hearth, but it might as well have been one of Maedhlyn's illusions for all the warmth it supplied. The great grey slabs sucked the heat from the blaze, giving nothing in return save a ghostly reflection that mocked the flames.

Thuro sat on the bed and wrapped his father's white bearskin cloak about his own slender shoulders.

'What a foul place,' he said, closing his eyes and pushing the turret room from his mind. He thought of his father's villa in Eboracum, and of the horse meadows beyond the white walls where mighty Cephon wintered with his mares. But most of all he pictured his own room, cosy and snug away from the bitter winter winds and filled with the love of his young life: his books, his glorious books. His father had refused him permission to bring even one tome to this lonely castle, in case the other war leaders should catch the prince reading and know the king's dark secret. For while it might be well-known in Caerlyn Keep that the boy Thuro was weak in body and spirit, the king's retainers guarded the sad truth like a family shame.

Thuro shivered and left the bed to sit on the goatskin rug before the fire. He was as miserable now as he had ever been. Far below in the great hall of Deicester Castle his father was attempting to bond an alliance against the barbarians from across the sea, grim-eyed reavers who had even now established settlements in the far south from which to raid the richer northlands. The embassy to Deicester had been made despite Maedhlyn's warnings. Thuro had not wished to accompany his father either, but not for fear of dangers he could scarce comprehend. The prince disliked the cold, loathed long journeys on horseback and, more importantly, hated to be deprived of his books even for a day – let alone the two months set aside for the embassy.

The door opened and the prince glanced up to see the tall figure of Gwalchmai, his brawny arms bearing a heavy load of logs. He smiled at the lad and Thuro noted with shame that the retainer wore but a single woollen tunic against the biting cold.

'Do you never feel the chill, Gwalchmai?'

'I feel it,' he answered, kneeling to add wood to the blaze.

'Is my father still speaking?'

'No. When I passed by Eldared was on his feet.'

'You do not like Eldared?'

'You see too much, young Thuro; that is not what I said.'

But you did, thought Thuro. It was in your eyes and the slight inflection when you used his name. He stared into the retainer's dark eyes, but Gwalchmai turned away.

'Do you trust him?' asked the boy.

'Your father obviously trusts him, so who am I to offer opinions? You think the king would have come here with only twenty retainers if he feared treachery?'

'You answer my question with questions. Is that not evasive?'

Gwalchmai grinned. 'I must get back to my watch. But think on this, Thuro: it is not for the likes of me to criticise the great. I could lose the skin from my back – or worse, my life.'

'You think there is danger here?' persisted the prince.

'I like you, boy, though only Mithras knows why. You've a sharp mind; it is a pity you are weakly. But I'll answer your question after a fashion. For a king there is always danger; it is a riddle to me why a man wants such power. I've served your father for sixteen years and in that time he has survived four wars, eleven battles and five attempts on his life. He is a canny man. But I would be happier if the Lord Enchanter were here.'

'Maedhlyn does not trust Eldared; he told my father so.'

Gwalchmai pushed himself to his feet. 'You trust too easily, Thuro. You should not be sharing this knowledge with me – or with any retainer.'

10

'But I can trust you, can I not?'

'How do you know that?' hissed Gwalchmai.

'I read it in your eyes,' said Thuro softly. Gwalchmai relaxed and a broad grin followed as he shook his head and tugged on his braided beard.

'You should get some rest. It's said there's to be a stag-hunt tomorrow.'

'I'll not be going,' said Thuro. 'I do not much like riding.'

'You baffle me, boy. Sometimes I see so much of your father in you that I want to cheer. And then . . . well, it does not matter. I will see you in the morning. Sleep well.'

'Thank you for the wood.'

'It is my duty to see you safe.' Gwalchmai left the room and Thuro rose and wandered to the window, moving aside the heavy velvet curtain and staring out over the winter landscape: rolling hills covered in snow, skeletal trees black as charcoal. He shivered and wished for home.

He too would have been happier if Maedhlyn had journeyed with them, for he enjoyed the old man's company and the quickness of his mind – and the games and riddles the Enchanter set him. One had occupied his mind for almost a full day last summer, while his father had been in the south routing the Jutes. Thuro had been sitting with Maedhlyn in the terraced garden, in the shade cast by the statue of the great Julius.

'There was a prince,' said Maedhlyn, his green eyes sparkling, 'who was hated by his king but loved by the people. The king decided the prince must die, but fearing the wrath of the populace he devised an elaborate plan to end both the prince's popularity and his life. He accused him of treason and offered him Trial by Mithras. In this way the Roman god would judge the innocence or guilt of the accused.

'The prince was brought before the king and a large crowd was there to see the judgement. Before the prince stood a priest holding a closed leather pouch and within the pouch were two grapes. The law said that one grape should be white, the other black. If the accused drew a white grape, he was innocent. A black grape meant death. You follow this, Thuro?'

11

'It is simple so far, teacher.'

'Now the prince knew of the king's hatred and guessed, rightly, that there were two black grapes in the pouch. Answer me this, young quicksilver: How did the prince produce a white grape and prove his innocence?'

'It is not possible, save by magic.'

'There was no magic, only thought,' said Maedhlyn, tapping his white-haired temple for emphasis. 'Come to me tomorrow with the answer.'

Throughout the day Thuro had thought hard, but his mind was devoid of inspiration. He borrowed a pouch from Listra the cook, and two grapes, and sat in the garden staring at the items as if in themselves they harboured the answer. As dusk painted the sky Trojan red, he gave up. Sitting alone in the gathering gloom he took one of the grapes and ate it. He reached for the other – and stopped.

The following morning he went to Maedhlyn's study. The old man greeted him sourly – having had a troubled night, he said, with dark dreams.

'I have answered your riddle, master,' the boy told him. At this the Enchanter's eyes came alive.

'So soon, young prince? It took the noble Alexander ten days, but then perhaps Aristotle was less gifted than myself as a tutor!' He chuckled. 'So tell me, Thuro, how did the prince prove his innocence?'

'He put his hand into the pouch and covered one grape. This he removed and ate swiftly. He then said to the priest, "I do not know what colour it was, but look at the one that is left."'

Maedhlyn clapped his hands and smiled. 'You please me greatly, Thuro. But tell me, how did you come upon the answer?'

'I ate the grape.'

'That is good. There is a lesson in that also. You broke the problem down and examined the component parts. Most men attempt to solve riddles by allowing their minds to leap like monkeys from branch to branch, without ever realising that it is the root that needs examining. Always remember that, young prince. The method works with men as well as it works with riddles.'

Now Thuro dragged his thoughts from the golden days of summer back to the bleak winter night. He removed his leggings and slid under the blankets, turning on his side to watch the flickering flames in the hearth.

He thought of his father – tall and broad-shouldered with eyes of ice and fire, revered as a warrior leader and held in awe even by his enemies.

'I don't want to be a king,' whispered Thuro.

Gwalchmai watched as the nobles prepared for the hunt, his emotions mixed. He felt a fierce pride as he looked upon the powerful figure of his king, sitting atop a black stallion of seventeen hands. The beast was called Bloodfire and one look in its evil eyes would warn any horseman to beware. But the king was at ease, for the horse knew its master; they were as alike in temperament as brothers of the blood. But Gwalchmai's pride was mixed with the inevitable sadness of seeing prince Thuro beside his father. The boy sat miserably upon a gentle mare of fifteen hands, clutching his cloak to his chest, his white-blond hair billowing about his slender ascetic face. Too much of his mother in him, thought Gwalchmai, remembering his first sight of the Mist Maiden. It was almost sixteen years ago now, yet his mind's eye could picture the queen as if but an hour had passed. She rode a white pony and beside the warrior king she seemed as fragile and out of place as ice on a rose. Talk among the retainers was that their lord had gone for a walk with Maedhlyn into a mist-shrouded northern valley and vanished for eight days. When he returned his beard had grown a full six inches and beside him was this wondrous woman, with golden hair and eyes of swirling grey like mist on a northern lake.

At first many of the people of Caerlyn Keep had thought her a witch, for even here the tales were told of the Land of Mist, a place of eldritch magic. But as the months passed she charmed them all with her kindness and her gentle spirit. News of her pregnancy was greeted with great joy and instant celebration. Gwalchmai would never forget the raucous banquet at the Keep, nor the wild night of pleasure that followed it.

13

But eight months later Alaida, the Mist Maiden, was dead and her baby son hovering on the brink of death, refusing all milk. The Enchanter Maedhlyn had been summoned and he, with his magic, saved young Thuro. But the boy was never strong; where the retainers had hoped for a young man to mirror the king, they were left with a solemn child who abhorred all manly practices. Yet enough of his mother's gentleness remained to turn what would have been scorn into a friendly sadness. Thuro was well-liked, but men who saw him would shake their heads and think of what might have been.

All this was on Gwalchmai's mind as the hunting party set off, led by Lord Eldared and his two sons Cael and Moret.

The king had never recovered from the death of Alaida. He rarely laughed and only came alive when hunting either beasts or men. He had plenty of opportunity in those bloody days for the Saxons and Jutes were raiding in the south and the Norse sailed their Wolfships into the deep rivers of the East Country. Added to this there were raiders aplenty from the smaller clans and tribes who had never accepted the right of the Romano-British warlords to rule the ancient lands of the Belgae, the Iceni and the Cantii.

Gwalchmai could well understand this viewpoint, being pureblood Cantii himself, born within a long stone's throw of the Ghost Cliffs.

Now he watched as the noblemen cantered towards the wooded hills, then returned to his quarters behind the long stables. His eyes scanned the Deicester men as they lounged by the alehouse and he began to grow uneasy. There was no love lost between the disparate groups assembled here, though the truce had been well-maintained – a broken nose here, a sprained wrist there, but mostly the retainers had kept to themselves. But today Gwalchmai sensed a tension in the air, a brightness in the eyes of the soldiers.

He wandered into the long room. Only two of the king's men were here, Victorinus and Caradoc. They were playing knucklebones and the Roman was losing, with good grace.

'Rescue me, Gwal,' said Victorinus. 'Save me from my stupidity.'

'There's not a man alive who could do that!' Gwalchmai moved to his cot and his wrapped blankets. He drew his gladius and scabbard from the roll and strapped the sword to his waist.

'Are you expecting trouble?' asked Caradoc, a tall rangy tribesman of Belgae stock.

'Where are the others?' he answered, avoiding the question.

'Most of them have gone to the village. There's a fair organised.'

'When was this announced?'

'This morning,' said Victorinus, entering the conversation. 'What has happened?'

'Nothing as yet,' said Gwalchmai, 'and I hope to Mithras nothing does. But the air smells wrong.'

'I can't smell anything wrong with it,' responded Victorinus.

'That's because you're a Roman,' put in Caradoc, moving to his own blanket roll and retrieving his sword.

'I'll not argue with a pair of superstitious tribesmen, but think on this: if we walk around armed to the teeth, we could incite trouble. We could be accused of breaking the spirit of the truce.'

Gwalchmai swore and sat down. 'You are right, my friend. What do you suggest?'

Victorinus, though younger than his companions, was well respected by the other men in the King's Guards. He was steady, courageous and a sound thinker. His solid Roman upbringing also proved a perfect counterpoint to the unruly, explosive temperaments of the Britons who served the king.

'I am not altogether sure, Gwal. Do not misunderstand me, for I do not treat your talents lightly. You have a nose for traps and an eye that reads men. If you say something is amiss, then I'll wager that it is. I think we should keep our swords hidden inside our tunics and wander around the Keep. It may be no more than a lingering ill-feeling amongst the Deicester men for Caradoc here taking their money last night in the knife-throwing tourney.'

'I do not think so,' said Caradoc. 'In fact, I thought they took it too well. It puzzled me at the time, but it did not feel right. I even slept with one hand on my dagger.'

15

'Let us not fly too high, my friends,' said Victorinus. 'We will meet back here in an hour. If there is danger in the air, we should all get a sniff of it.'

'And what if we find something?' asked Caradoc.

'Do nothing. If you can, walk away from trouble. Swallow pride.'

'No man should be asked to do that,' protested the Belgae.

'That may be true, my volatile friend. But if there is to be trouble, then let the Deicester men start it. The king will be less than pleased if you break the truce; he'll flay the skin from your back.'

Gwalchmai moved to the window and pushed open the wooden shutters.

'I do not think we need to concern ourselves about hiding weapons,' he said softly. 'The Deicester men are all armed.'

Victorinus swept up his blanket roll. 'Gather your gear now and follow me. Swiftly.'

'There are about a dozen of them coming this way with swords in their hands,' said Gwalchmai, ducking down from the window. Gathering his belongings, he followed his two companions to the rough-carved wooden door leading to the stables. Drawing their swords they stepped through and pulled the door shut behind them. Swiftly they saddled three horses and rode out into the yard.

'There they are!' someone shouted and soldiers rushed out to block the riders. Victorinus kicked his mount into a gallop, crashing into the crowding warriors, who scattered and fell to the cobbles. Then the trio were thundering under the beamed gateway and out into the snow-swept hills.

They had not travelled more than a mile when they came upon the bodies of their comrades, lying in a hollow by a frozen stream. The retainers had been armed only with knives, but at least eleven of the seventeen had been killed by arrows. The rest had been hacked to death by swords or axes.

The three men sat their horses in silence. There was no point in dismounting. They gazed at the dead faces of those who had been their friends, or at the least their comrades in war. By a gnarled oak lay the body of Atticus, the rope-walker. Around him the snow was

16

stained with blood, and it was obvious that he alone of all the retainers had managed to inflict wounds upon the attackers.

'At least three men,' said Caradoc, as if reading the thoughts of his companions. 'But then Atticus was a tough whoreson. What do we do now, Victorinus?'

The young Roman stayed silent for a moment, scanning the horizon. 'The king,' he said softly.

'And the boy!' said Gwalchmai. 'Sweet Juno! We must find them – warn them.'

They are dead,' said Victorinus, removing his bronze helm and staring at his own distorted reflection. That is why the retainers were lured away and murdered, and why the king was invited on the stag-hunt. It was a royal stag they hunted. We must get back to Caerlyn and warn Aquila.'

'No!' shouted Caradoc. 'This treachery cannot go unpunished.'

Victorinus saw the pain in the Belgae's eyes. 'And what will you do, Caradoc? Ride back to Deicester and scale the walls to find Eldared?'

'Why not?'

'Because it would be futile – you would die before getting within a yard of Eldared. Think ahead, man. Aquila does not expect the king back until spring and he will be unprepared. The first sight he will see coming from the north is the Deicester army and any allies Eldared has gained. They will seize Eboracum and the traitor will have won.'

'But we must find the king's body,' said Gwalchmai. 'We cannot leave it for the crows; it is not fitting.'

'And suppose he is not yet dead?' offered Caradoc. 'I would never forgive myself for leaving him.'

'I know what you are feeling, and I grieve also. But I beg you to put aside emotion and trust Roman logic. Yes, we could bury the king – but what of Eboracum? You think the king's shade would thank us for putting his body before the fate of his people?'

'And if he is not dead?' persisted Caradoc.

'You *know* that he is,' said Victorinus sadly.

2

Thuro was lost. It had happened soon after the riders left the castle, when the dogs had picked up a scent and raced into the dark wood with the hunters thundering after them. Having no intention of galloping into the trees in hot pursuit, he had reined in the mare and followed at a sedate canter, but somewhere along the trail he had taken a wrong turn and now he could no longer even hear the hounds. The wintry sun was high overhead and Thuro was cold through to his bones . . . and he was hungry. The trees were thinner here, the ground slowly rising. The wind had dropped and Thuro halted by a frozen stream. He dismounted and cracked the ice, dipping his head and sipping the cold fresh water. His father would be so angry with him – he would say nothing, but his eyes would show his displeasure and his face would turn away from the boy.

Thuro cleared the snow from a flat rock and sat down, considering all the options open to him. He could ride on blindly in the hope of stumbling upon the hunters, or he could follow his own tracks back to the castle. It was not hard to find the right course of action with options such as these. He mounted the mare and swung her back to the south.

A large stag stepped lightly on to the trail and stopped to watch the rider. Thuro reined in and leaned forward on the pommel of his saddle. 'Good morning, prince of the forest, are you also lost?' The stag turned contemptuously away and continued its leisurely pace across the trail and into the trees. 'You remind me of my father,' Thuro called after it.

'Do you often talk to animals?' Thuro turned in the saddle to see a young girl, dressed like a forester in green hooded woollen tunic, leather leggings and knee-high moccasins fringed with sheepskin. Her hair was short and a mixture of autumnal colours – light brown, with a hint of both gold and red. Her face was striking, without a hint of beauty and yet. . . .

Thuro bowed. 'Do you live near here?' he asked.

'Perhaps. But obviously you do not. How long have you been lost?'

'How do you know that I am lost?' he countered.

The girl stepped away from the tree beside the trail and Thuro saw that she was carrying a beautiful bow of dark horn. 'You may not be lost,' she said, smiling. 'It may be that you found your tracks so fascinating that you decided you just had to see them again.'

'I concede,' he told her. 'I am seeking Deicester Castle.'

'You have friends there?'

'My father is there. We are guests.'

'A fortune would not induce me to be a guest of that foul family,' she told him. 'Continue on this path until you come to a lightning-blasted oak, then bear right and follow the stream. It will save you time.'

'Thank you. What is your name?'

'Names are for friends, young lordling, not to be bandied about amongst strangers.'

'Strangers can become friends. In fact, all friends were at some time strangers.'

'All too true,' she admitted. 'But to speak more bluntly, I have no wish to strike up a friendship with a guest of Eldared's.'

'I am sorry that you feel this way. It seems a great shame that to sleep in a cold and draughty castle somehow stains the spirit of a man. For what it is worth, my name is Thuro.'

'You do speak prettily, Thuro,' she said, smiling, 'and you have a wonderful eye for horses. Come, join me for the midday meal.'

Thuro did not question her sudden change of heart but dismounted and led his horse away from the trail, following the girl into the trees and up a winding track to a shallow cave under a sandstone rock face. Here a fire had burned low under a copper pot perched on two stones. Thuro tied the mare's reins to a nearby bush and moved to the fire where the girl joined him. She added oats to the boiling water, and a pinch of salt from a small pouch at her side.

19

'Gather some wood,' she told him, 'and earn your food.' He did as she bid, gathering thick branches from beside the track and carrying them back to the cave.

'Are you planning to light a beacon fire?' she asked when he returned.

'I do not understand,' he said.

'This is a cooking fire. It is intended to heat the oats and water, and to give us warmth for an hour or so. The wood you need should be dry and no thicker than a thumb-joint. Have you never set a cooking fire?'

'No, I regret that is a pleasure I have not yet encountered.'

'How old are you?'

'I shall be judged a man next autumn,' he said, somewhat stiffly. 'And you?'

'The same as you, Thuro. Fifteen.'

'I shall fetch some more suitable wood.' he said.

'Get yourself a platter at the same time.'

'A platter?'

'How else will you eat your oats?'

Thuro was angry as he left the cave – an emotion he rarely felt and with which he was exceedingly uncomfortable. As he had followed the forest girl he had become acutely aware of the rhythmic movement of her hips and the liquid grace of her walk. By contrast he had begun to feel he was incapable of putting one foot in front of the other without tripping himself. His feet felt twice their size. He longed to do something to impress her, and for the first time in his young life wished he were a shade more like his father. Pushing the thoughts from his mind he gathered wood for the fire, finding also a round flat stone to serve as a platter for his food.

'Are you hungry?' she asked.

'Not very.' Using a short stick, she expertly lifted the pot from the flames and stirred the thick milky contents. He passed her his rock and she giggled.

'Here,' she said, offering him her own wooden plate. 'Use this.'

'The rock will be fine.'

20

'I am sorry, Thuro; it is unfair of me to mock. It is not your fault you are a lordling; you should have brought your servant with you.'

'I am not a lordling, I am a prince: the son of Maximus the High King. And doubtless were you to be sitting in the hall of Caerlyn, you would feel equally ill at ease discussing the merits of Plutarch's *Life of Lycurgus*.'

Her eyes sparkled and Thuro realised they echoed the russet tones of her hair – light brown with flecks of gold.

'You are probably correct, Prince Thuro,' she said with a mock bow, 'for I was never at ease with Lycurgus and I agree with Plutarch in his comparison with Numa. How did he put it? "Virtue rendered the one so respectable as to deserve a throne, and the other so great as to be above it".'

Thuro returned the bow, but without mockery. 'Forgive my arrogance,' he told her. 'I am not used to feeling this foolish.'

'You are probably more at ease chasing stags and practising with sword and lance.'

'No, I am rather poor in those quarters also. I am the despair of my father. I had hoped to impress you with my knowledge, for there is little else I have to brag of.'

She looked away and poured the cooling oats to her platter, then passed the food to Thuro. 'My name is Laitha. Welcome to my hearth, Prince Thuro.' He searched her face for any hint of mockery, but there was none.

He accepted the food and ate in silence. Laitha put down the pot and leaned back against the cave wall, watching the young man. He was handsome in a gentle fashion and his eyes were grey as woodsmoke, softly sad and wondrous innocent. Yet for all the gentleness Laitha saw, she found no trace of weakness in his face. The eyes did not waver or turn aside, the mouth showed no hint of petulance. And his open admission of his own physical shortcomings endeared him to the girl, who had seen enough of loud-mouthed braggarts vying to prove their strength and manhood.

'Why do you not excel?' she asked him. 'Is your sword-master a poor teacher?'

'I have no interest in sword-play. It tires me and then I fall ill.'

21

'In what way ill?'

He shrugged. 'I am told I almost died at birth, and since then my chest has been weak. I cannot exert myself without becoming dizzy – and then my head pounds and sometimes I lose my sight.'

'How does your father react to all this?'

'With great patience and great sadness – I fear I am not the son he would have preferred. But it does not matter. He is as strong as an ox and as fearless as a dragon. He will reign for decades yet – and perhaps he will marry again and sire a proper heir.'

'What happened to your mother?'

'She died two days after I was born. The birth was early by a month and Maedhlyn – our Enchanter – was absent on the king's business.'

'And your father never remarried? Strange for a king.'

'I have never spoken to him of it . . . but Maedhlyn says she was the still water in his soul and after she had gone there was only fire. There is a wall around Maximus and his grief. None may enter. He cannot look me in the face, for I am much like my mother. And in all the time I can remember he has never touched me – not an arm on the shoulder nor the ruffling of a single hair. Maedhlyn tells that when I was four I was struck down with a terrible fever and my spirit was lost within the darkness of the Void. He says my father came to me then and took me in his arms, and his spirit searched for mine across the darkness. He found me and brought me home. But I remember nothing of it and that saddens me. I would like to be able to recall that moment.'

'He must love you greatly,' she whispered.

'I do not know.' He looked up at her and smiled. 'Thank you for the oats. I must be going.'

'I will guide you to the ford above Deicester,' she said.

He did not argue and waited while she cleaned her pot, platter and spoon. She stowed them in a canvas pack which she slung to her shoulder and then, taking up her bow and quiver, she set out alongside him. The snow was falling thickly now and he was glad she was travelling with him. Without tracks to follow, he knew he would have been lost within minutes.

They had gone but a little way towards the trail when they heard the sound of horses riding at speed. In the first second that he heard the horsemen, Thuro was delighted – soon he would be back at the castle and warm again. But then he realised it would mean saying goodbye to Laitha and on an impulse he turned from the path, leading the mare deeper into the trees and behind a screen of bushes below the trail.

Laitha joined him, saying nothing. There were four men all armed with swords and lances. They drew up a little way ahead, and were joined by three riders coming from the opposite direction.

'Any sign?' The words drifted to Thuro like whispers on the wind and he felt ashamed to be hiding here. These men were out in the cold searching for him – it was unfair of him to put them to further trouble. He was just about to step into view when another man spoke.

'No, nothing. It's incredible. We kill the father in minutes, but the beardless boy causes more trouble.'

'You are talking nonsense, Calin. The father killed six men – and that was with an arrow deep in his lungs. The boy is costing only time.'

'Well, I intend to make him pay for wasting my time. I'll have his eyes roasting on the point of my dagger.'

Thuro stood statue-still until long after the riders had moved on.

'I do not think you should go back to Deicester,' whispered Laitha, laying a gentle hand on his shoulder.

Thuro stood unmoving, staring at the empty trail, his thoughts whirling and diving from fear to regret, from panic to sorrow. His father had been murdered and Thuro's world would never be the same again. This morning he had been miserable and cold, seemingly alone within a cheerless castle. But now he knew he had not been alone, that the giant strength of Aurelius Maximus, the High King, had covered him like a mantle and the companionship of men like Gwalchmai and Victorinus had shielded him from grimmer realities. Laitha was right; he was a spoiled lordling who did not even know how to set a cooking fire. Now the world was once more in turmoil. Eldared, as Maedhlyn had feared, was a traitor and a regicide. The prince was now a hunted animal, with no chance of escaping his hunters. Of what use would be his learning now? Plutarch, Aristotle and Seutonius were no help to a weakly boy in a perilous wood.

'Thuro?'

He turned slowly and saw the concern in Laitha's eyes. 'I think you would be wise to leave me,' he said. 'My company will bring danger to you.'

'What will you do?'

He shrugged. 'I will find my father's body and bury it. Then, I suppose, I will try to make my way back to Caerlyn.'

'You are now the king, Thuro. What will you do when you get there?'

'I shall abdicate. I am not suited to govern others. My father's general, Lucius Aquila, is also his second cousin. He will rule wisely – if he survives.'

'Why should he not?'

'Eldared has the equivalent of five legions and four hundred horsemen. At Caerlyn there are only two legions; the rest of my father's army is made up of militia men who return to their homes in winter. The killing of my father will see the start of a war no one can afford. With the Saxons invading the south, Eldared's ambition is lunacy. But then the Brigantes have always hated the Romans, even before Hadrian built the wall to torment them.'

'I was taught that Hadrian built the wall because he feared them,' said Laitha.

'If that were true, there would have been few north-facing gates. The gates were sally points for raids deep into Brigante territory.' Thuro shivered and noticed that the snow was quickening beneath a thunder-dark sky. 'Where is the nearest village?' he asked.

'Apart from Deicester Town there is Daris, some eight miles to the south-east. But Eldared will have men there looking for you. Why not come to my home? You will be safe there.'

'I will be safe nowhere. And I do not wish to place you in peril, Laitha.'

'You do not understand. I live with my guardian and he will allow no one to harm you.'

Thuro smiled. 'I have just told you that Eldared has five Legions. He is also the man who murdered the High King. Your guardian cannot be as powerful as my enemies.'

'If we stand and debate, we will freeze to death. Now, let your horse go and follow me. Trust me, Thuro, for I am your only chance for life.'

'But why release my horse?'

'It cannot go where I will lead you. And, perhaps more importantly, your hunters are seeking a boy riding and will not search the paths we will walk. Now come on.'

Thuro looped the mare's reins over her head and draped them over the saddle pommel. Then he followed the lithe form of the forest girl ever deeper into the trees, emerging at last at the foot of a high hill in the shadow of the northern mountains. Thuro's feet were cold, his boots wet through. A little way up the rise he stopped – his face white, his breathing ragged as he sank to the snow. Laitha had walked on maybe twenty paces when she turned and saw him beside the trail. She ran lightly back to him and knelt. 'What is the matter?'

'I am sorry – I cannot go on. I must rest for a while.'

'Not here, Thuro, we are in the open. Come on, just a little more.' She helped him to his feet and he staggered on for perhaps ten paces. Then his legs gave way beneath him. As Laitha bent to help him, she saw movement some two hundred paces back along the trail. Three riders emerged from the trees, saw the travellers and kicked their horses into a gallop.

'Your enemies are upon us, Thuro!' she shouted, dropping the pack from her shoulder and swiftly stringing her bow of horn. Thuro rolled to his knees and tried to stand, but his strength had fled. He watched as the riders drew their swords and saw the gleam of triumph in their eyes, heard the malice in their screams. His eyes flickered to Laitha, who was standing coolly with her bow stretched, the string nestling against her cheek. Time seemed to slow and Thuro viewed the scene with detached fascination as Laitha slowly released her breath and, in the moment between release and the need for more air, loosed the shaft. It took the lead rider between his collarbones and punched him from the saddle.

But the remaining riders were too close to allow such perfect timing again and Laitha's next shaft was loosed too swiftly. It glanced from the second warrior's helm, snapping back his head; he almost lost his balance and his horse veered to the right, but the last man hurled himself from his saddle to crash into the forest girl as vainly she strove to draw another arrow from her quiver. Her hand flashed for the hunting-knife in her belt, but he hammered his fist into her jaw and she fell to the snow, stunned. The other horseman, having gained control of his mount, stepped from the saddle and approached Thuro with his sword extended.

'Well, little prince, I hope you enjoyed the hunt?'

Thuro said nothing, but he climbed slowly to his feet and met the assassin's eyes.

'Are you not going to beg for life? How disappointing! I thought at the least you would offer us a king's ransom.'

'I do not fear you,' said Thuro evenly. 'You are a man of little worth. Come then, child-killer, earn your salt!'

The man tensed and raised his sword, but then his eyes flickered to a point behind Thuro. 'Who are you?' he asked and Thuro turned his head. Behind him, seeming to appear from nowhere, was a man in a white bearskin cloak. His hair was black and silver shone at the temples; his face was square-cut and clean-shaven, his eyes grey. He was dressed in a dark leather tunic over green woollen leggings and he carried a silver staff with two ebony grips – one at the top, the second halfway down.

'I asked who you were,' repeated the assassin.

'I heard you,' answered the newcomer, his voice deep, and colder than the winds of winter.

'Then answer me.'

'I am Culain lach Feragh, and you have attacked my ward.'

The man glanced at the unconscious girl. 'She is only stunned – and she killed Pagis.'

'It was a fine effort and I will compliment her when she wakes. You, boy,' he said to Thuro softly, 'move behind me.' Thuro did as he was bid and Culain stepped forward.

'I do not like to kill,' he said, 'but unfortunately you and your companion cannot be allowed to leave here alive, so I am left with no choice. Come, defend yourselves.'

For a moment the two assassins simply stood staring at the man with the staff. Then the first of them ran forward, screaming a battlecry.

Culain's hand dropped down the shaft to the central ebony grip and twisted. The staff parted and a silver blade appeared in his right hand. He parried the wild cut and reversed a slashing sweep to the assassin's throat. The blade sliced cleanly free and the man's head slowly toppled from his shoulders. For one terrible moment the body stood, then the right knee buckled and it fell to rest beside the grisly head. Thuro swallowed hard and tore his eyes from the corpse.

The second assassin ran for his horse and, dropping his sword, vaulted to the saddle as Culain stepped over the corpse and retrieved Laitha's bow. He selected an arrow, drew the string and loosed the shaft with such consummate skill and lack of speed that Thuro had no doubt as to the outcome even before the missile plunged into the rider's back. Culain dropped the bow and moved to Laitha, lifting her gently.

After a while her eyes opened.

'Will you never learn, Gian?' he whispered. 'Another doe for your collection?'

'He is the son of the king. Eldared seeks to kill him.' Culain turned and as his eyes fastened on the prince, Thuro saw something new in his gaze, some emotion that the boy could not place. But then a mask covered Culain's feelings.

'Welcome to my hearth,' he said simply.

3

Eldared, King of the Brigantes, Lord of the Northern Wall, sat silently listening to the reports of his huntsmen. His sons Cael and Moret sat beside him, aware that despite his apparent tranquillity their father's mood was darkening moment by moment.

Eldared was fifty-one years of age and a veteran of dark intrigue. Twenty years before he had switched sides to support the young Roman Aurelius Maximus in his bid for the throne, betraying his own brother Cascioc in the process. Since that time his power had grown and his support for Maximus had earned him great wealth, but his ambition was not content with ruling the highlands. During the last five years he had steadily increased his support amongst the warring tribes of the high country, and solidified his power base among the Britons of the south. All he needed for the throne to fall was the death of Aurelius and his weakling son. After that, a surprise raid on Eboracum would leave him in an unassailable position.

But now a plan of stunning simplicity had been reduced to ashes by simple human error. Three retainers had escaped and the boy, Thuro, was at large in the mountains. Eldared kept his face calm, his hooded eyes betraying no hint of his alarm. The boy was not a great problem in himself, for he was by all accounts spineless and weak. However, if he managed to get back to Caerlyn then Lucius Aquila, the canniest of generals, would use him as a puppet to rally support against Eldared. Added to this, if any of the survivors lived long enough to warn Aquila, then the raid on Eboracum would become doubly perilous.

Eldared dismissed his huntsmen and turned his gaze to his elder son Cael, a hawk-eyed warrior just past his twentieth birthday.

'Suggestions?' invited the king and Cael smiled.

'You do not need me to state the obvious, Father.'

'No. I need you to show me you *understand* the obvious.'

28

Cael bowed. 'At present the boy is of secondary importance. He is hidden somewhere deep in our lands and we can deal with him at leisure. First we must find the three who escaped, most especially the Roman Victorinus. He is a man Aurelius had chosen for future command and I believe it was he who stopped the others from returning to seek the king.'

'Well and good, boy. But what do you suggest we *do*?'

'Concentrate our efforts in the south-west. Victorinus will cross the Wall at Norcester, and then cut east and south to Eboracum.'

'Why would he take the long route?' asked Moret. 'It only increases his danger.'

Cael's eyes showed his contempt for the question, but his voice was neutral as he answered it. 'Victorinus is no fool, brother. He knows we will send men south-east and he gains time by such a manoeuvre. We need to use Goroien.'

Moret cleared his throat and shifted nervously in his seat. Eldared said nothing.

'What choice do we have, Father?' Cael continued.

'Choice?' snapped Moret. 'Another dead Brigante babe for that foul woman!'

'And how many dead Brigante men will fall before the walls of Eboracum if we do *not* use the Witch?' replied Cael. 'If I thought it would guarantee victory, I would let Goroien sacrifice a hundred babes.'

'Moret has a point,' said Eldared softly. 'In this deadly game I like to control events. This Mist Magic of hers can be a boon, but at what price? She plays her own game, I think.' He leaned back in his chair, resting his chin on his steepled fingers. 'We will give the huntsmen another two days to catch the retainers. If they fail, I will summon Goroien. As for the boy . . . I believe he could be dead somewhere in a snow-drift. But send Alantric into the high country.'

'He will not like that,' said Moret. 'The King's Champion sent out after a runaway boy?'

'His likes and dislikes are mine to command – as are yours,' said Eldared. 'There will be many opportunities in the spring for Alantric to show his skills with a blade.'

29

'And what of the Sword?' asked Moret.

Eldared's eyes flashed and his face darkened. 'Do not speak of it! *Ever!*'

Victorinus sat near the narrow window of the alehouse tavern staring out at the remains of the Antonine Wall, built far to the north of Hadrian's immense fortifications and stretching from coast to coast over forty miles. It was a turf wall on a stone foundation and, as he stared, the young Roman saw the ruins as a vivid physical reminder of the failing Roman Empire. Three hundred years ago three legions would have patrolled this area, with a fortress every Roman mile. Now it was wind-swept and mostly deserted, except in remote villages like Norcester, on the well-travelled trade roads. He sipped his ale and cast a covert glance across the room to where Gwalchmai and Caradoc were sitting together, just beyond the six Brigante tribesmen. The three had been journeying for nine days; they had managed to buy provisions and a change of clothing from a Greek merchant on the road south. Victorinus was now dressed in the garb of an Order Taker: a long woollen robe and a fur jerkin. Across his shoulders hung a leather satchel containing stylus parchment and a letter from Publius Aristarchos naming him as Varius Seneca, an Order Taker from Eboracum.

The innkeeper, an elderly Romano-British veteran, moved on to the bench seat alongside Victorinus.

'How soon can delivery be made if I order goods from you?' he asked.

'They will be here in the second week of spring,' answered Victorinus, acutely aware of the Brigantes who sat nearby. 'Depending of course on what you need,' he continued. 'It's been a bad year for wine in Gaul and supplies are not plentiful.'

'I need salt a deal more than I need Gallic wine,' said the man. 'The hunting is good in these hills, but without salt I can save little meat. So tell me, what does your merchant charge for salt?'

Victorinus drew in a deep breath; he was no quartermaster and had no knowledge of such dealings.

'What are you charged currently?' he asked.

'Six sesterces a pound. Five if I take the bulk shipment and then resell to the tribesmen.'

'The cost has risen,' said Victorinus, 'and I fear I cannot match that price.'

'So what can you offer?'

'Six and a half. But if you can secure orders from surrounding villages, I will authorise a payment in kind. One bag in ten sold will come to you free.'

'I do not know how you people have the nerve to sell at these prices. It is not as if we were at war. The trade routes are as safe now as they have ever been.'

'Your thinking is a little parochial, my friend. Most of the trade routes in Brigantes territory may be open, but there is a war in the south, and that has cut our profits.'

A tall Brigante warrior with a deep scar across his cheek rose from his table and approached Victorinus.

'I have not seen you before,' he said.

'Is there any reason why you should have done?' replied Victorinus. 'Do you travel much to Eboracum?'

'You look more like a soldier than an Order Taker.'

'I earn more salt this way, friend, with a great deal less danger.'

'Are you travelling alone?'

'Even as you see. But then I carry little money, and there are few who would attack an Order Taker. They would much rather wait until I have fulfilled my duties and then raid the wagons on their way back.'

The man nodded, but his keen blue eyes remained fixed on the young Roman. Finally he turned his back and rejoined his comrades. Victorinus returned to his conversation with the innkeeper, while keeping a wary eye on the Brigantes. The scarred tribesman looked across at Caradoc and Gwalchmai.

'Where are you from?' he asked.

'South,' said Caradoc.

'Belgae, are you?'

Caradoc nodded.

'I thought I could smell fish!' The other Brigantes chuckled and Caradoc coloured, but tore his eyes from the warrior. 'I had a Belgae woman once,' continued Scarface. 'She charged a copper penny. She looked like you; perhaps it was your mother.'

Gwalchmai reached across the table and gripped Caradoc's arm, just as the tribesman was reaching for his sword. 'It could well have been his mother,' put in Gwalchmai softly. 'As I recall, she had a fondness for animals.'

The Brigante rose from his bench. 'Not wise to be insulting so far from your homeland.'

'It's my upbringing,' said Gwalchmai, rising smoothly. 'I was taught always to silence a yapping dog.'

Iron blades slid sibilantly from their scabbards. Gwalchmai upended the table and leapt to the right, drawing his gladius. Caradoc moved left, his sword extended.

'Six against two,' said Gwalchmai, grinning. 'Typical of the Brigantes!'

'The object of battle is to win,' said Scarface, his eyes gleaming, his colour deepening. Caradoc's left hand dropped to his belt, coming up with a heavy dagger. Just as the Brigantes tensed for the attack Caradoc's arm flashed forward and the dagger entered Scarface's throat below the chin strap of his bronze helm. With a gurgling cry he sank to the floor as Caradoc and Gwalchmai charged into the mass, hacking and cleaving.

Victorinus cursed, drew his gladius from within his robe and leapt to join them, plunging his blade deep into the back of a stocky warrior. The tavern was filled with the discordant sounds of battle – iron on iron, iron on flesh. Within seconds the fight was over. Victorinus despatched two of the men, as did Gwalchmai. Caradoc finished his own opponent and then sank to the floor. Victorinus knelt beside him, staring in anguish at the sword that jutted from the Belgae's belly.

'I think he's finished me,' said Caradoc, gritting his teeth against the pain.

'I am afraid that he has,' Victorinus agreed gently.

'You'd better leave me here. I have much to consider.'

Victorinus nodded. 'You were a fine companion,' he said.

'You too – for a Roman!'

Gwalchmai joined them. 'Is there anything I can do?'

'You could look after my woman, Gwal. She's pregnant again. You could . . .' His eyes lost their sparkle and breath rattled from his throat.

Gwalchmai swore. 'You think they guessed who we were?' he asked.

'Perhaps,' replied Victorinus, 'but it is more likely to have been the normal British penchant for tribal disharmony. Come, we had better be on our way.'

'How far is it to the Wall of Hadrian?'

'Too far – unless the Gods smile.'

Cael chuckled at his brother's discomfort as they walked across the cobbled courtyard to the carles' quarters. 'You should not have mentioned the Sword,' said the taller man.

'Go ahead – enjoy yourself, Cael. But I know what I saw. When he threw that blade out over the ice, a hand came up out of the water and drew it down.'

'Yes, brother. Was it a man's hand?'

'Your mockery does not upset me. Two other men saw the hand, even if you did not.'

'I was too busy putting the finishing blow to the Roman's neck,' snapped Cael.

'A blow, I notice, that came from behind. Even without his sword you did not have the courage to cut him from the front.'

'You speak of courage?' sneered Cael, pausing before the oak doors of the carles' quarters. 'Where were you? You did not land a blow.'

'I considered eighteen to one good enough odds even for you, Cael.'

'You miserable sheep! Bleat all you want. I did not hear your voice raised in argument when Father's plan was made known.'

'The deed was ignobly done. There is no credit in such a murder. And, by all the Gods beyond, he died well. Even you must admit that.'

'He had a choice then, you think? Even a cornered rat will fight for its life.'

Cael finished the conversation by turning away from his brother and pushing ahead into the dimly lit quarters seeking Alantric. Moret turned back across the courtyard and returned to his apartments, where his young wife Alhyffa waited. She was dark-haired

33

and sloe-eyed and Moret's passion for her grew daily. He had not wanted to wed the Saxon girl and had argued long into the night with his father. But in the end, as he had known he would, he gave in and the betrothal was secretly agreed. He had travelled by ship to meet his bride, all the way round the coast to the lands they were now calling the South Saxon.

Her father had met him in an inlet near Anderida forest and he had been taken to the Long Hall to see his bride. His heart had been heavy until the moment she entered the Hall . . . then it all but stopped. How could a barbarous animal like Hengist produce such an offspring? As she approached he bowed low, breaking all precedent. If she was surprised, she did not show it. He stopped her as she was about to kneel.

'You will never need to kneel before me,' he whispered.

And he had been true to his word — a fact that had surprised Alhyffa, especially after her father's disparaging comments concerning the treacherous family.

'Have no fear,' he had told her. 'Within a few seasons I shall be at Deicester Keep with an army and then we'll find a good husband for you.'

Yet now Alhyffa was not sure that she wanted her father riding north to take her back. Her husband was not a powerful man, nor yet a weak one, but he was gentle and loving and he aroused in her a feeling not unlike love. As he entered the room she watched his expression move from his perennial look of sadness to an almost juvenile joy. He swept her into his arms and swung her high into the air.

She draped her arms over his broad shoulders and kissed him lightly.

'I have missed you,' he said.

'You liar! You have not been gone an hour.'

'It's true, I swear it.'

'How went it with your father?'

He shrugged and released her, his face once more sad and wistful. 'I have no use for his lust for power. And my brother is as bad — if not worse. You know, Aurelius Maximus was not a bad High King.'

34

'My father spoke of him always with respect.'

'And yet your father connived in his murder?'

She pulled him to the window bench and sat beside him in the sunshine. 'The High King would have connived in the murder of Hengist, yet I do not doubt that he also respected my father. There has never been a king with clean hands, Moret. You are altogether too sensitive.' He grinned and looked so terribly young that she took his face in her hands and kissed his fair cheeks, running her fingers through his long blond hair. 'You have given me happiness. I pray to Odin that you receive a proper reward for it.'

'You are reward enough for any man.'

'You say that now, young prince, but what when my beauty fades?'

'Ask me that in twenty years. Or thirty. Or forty. Or a hundred!'

Her face became serious. 'Do not wish for the passing of time, Moret, my love. Who knows what the future holds for any of us?'

'Whisht! Do not look sad. The future is all gold, I promise you.'

Alhyffa pulled his head in to her breast and stroked his hair, while her sky-blue eyes stared out towards the south. She saw three horsemen riding and each was holding aloft a severed head. They came closer – riding across the sky towards the window where she sat – and the sky darkened, lightning flashing behind them. She could not see their faces, nor would she look at the heads they carried; she closed her mind's eye against them and heard the bitter laughter as they rode on: Odin's messengers, the Stormcrows, taunting her with premonitions of disaster.

She had never loved her father and thus never cared about his victories or his setbacks. But now she was torn. Moret's family was linked with Hengist and therefore she should wish him success. Yet once successful, her father would turn on Eldared and destroy him and all his get. Eldared with all his cunning could not fail to see this, therefore he must be planning the same tactic. And then what would be the future for Hengist's daughter?

'Do not think of tomorrow, Moret. Enjoy the Now, for it is all any of us ever have.'

35

4

Thuro awoke in a narrow room with log walls and a single window looking out over the mountains. The room was icy-cold and the young prince burrowed under the blankets, hugging them to his sleep-warm body. He could not remember coming to bed, only the seemingly endless journey to Culain's log cabin nestling in a wood of pine. At one point Thuro's legs had given way beneath him, and Culain had lifted him effortlessly and carried him like a babe across his chest. Thuro remembered being dumped in a wide leather chair as the warrior tindered a fire in the stone hearth, and he could recall staring into the growing flames. But somewhere about that time he must have passed out.

He looked out across the room and saw his clothes laid on a narrow chair. Glancing below the covers he saw that he was naked. He hoped fervently that Laitha had not been present when he was undressed.

The door opened and Culain entered. His long dark hair was tied at the nape of his neck, and he was wearing a high-necked shirt of thick wool and dark leather leggings over mountain boots of cured sheepskin.

'Time to be up, prince! And doing!'

He walked to the bed and dragged back the covers. 'Dress yourself and join me in the other room.'

'Good morning to you,' Thuro told his departing back, but Culain did not respond. The prince climbed from the bed and into his green woollen leggings and shirt of cream-coloured wool, edged with braid. Then he pulled on his boots and returned to sit on the bed. The events of the previous day washed over him like icy water. His father was dead, his own life in peril. He was hundreds of miles from friends and home, at the mercy of a

36

grim-faced stranger he did not know. 'I could do with your help now, Maedhlyn,' he whispered.

Taking a deep breath and offering a prayer to the Earth Goddess, he joined Culain in the main room. The warrior was stacking logs in the hearth when he entered and did not look up.

'Outside you will find an axe and a hatchet. Chop twenty logs no bigger than you see here. Do it now, boy.'

'Why should I chop logs for you?' asked Thuro, disliking the man's tone.

'Because you slept in my bed and I don't doubt you'll want to eat my food. Or is payment above you, prince?'

'I will chop your logs and then I will leave you,' said Thuro. 'I like nothing about your manners.'

Culain laughed. 'You are welcome to leave, but I will be interested to know in which snowdrift you are planning to die. You are weaker than any boy I have ever known. I doubt you have the strength to walk down the mountain, and you certainly do not have the wit to know which direction to take.'

'Why should my fate concern you?'

'I'll answer that question when I'm ready,' said Culain, rising to his feet and moving to tower over the youngster. Thuro stood his ground and answered the firm gaze with uplifted chin, giving not an inch.

Culain smiled. 'Well, boy, you may have no strength in your arms but your spirit is not lacking, thank the Source. Now chop the logs and we'll discuss your departure over breakfast.'

Thuro felt he had won a small victory, but he was not sure what the prize might be or whether the win was worth a lick of salt. He left the cabin and located the wood-store some eighty feet away, near a stand of trees.

He found the axe embedded in a log and wrestled it clear. Then he lifted the log to stand upon a thick ring of pine and hefted the axe over his head. His first swing saw the axe-head miss the log, burying itself in the snow-covered ground. He wrenched it clear, steadied his feet and tried once more. This time the head glanced from the log, tearing the axe from Thuro's slender fingers; he retrieved it. On the third swing the axe hit into the log, stopping halfway through and trapping the head. After several minutes he worked it loose, then he stood and thought about the action necessary to complete the task. He planted his feet wider apart, with his right leg slightly ahead, swung the axe – and split the log. He continued work for some time, until his breathing became ragged, and his face was white with exhaustion. He counted the logs. Eleven . . . and Culain had asked for twenty! More slowly now, he continued the chore. His hands hurt him and he put down the axe to check the skin; four large blisters decorated his palm. He glanced towards the cabin but there was no sign of Culain. Once more he counted the logs: eighteen. He took the axe in his injured hand and set to work until twenty had been split, leaving forty solid chunks.

Returning to the cabin he found Culain sitting in the wide leather chair, his feet raised on a small table. The warrior looked up as he entered.

'I thought you'd fallen asleep out there, prince.'

'I did not fall asleep, and I dislike the tone in your voice when you use my title – you make it sound like a dog's name. My name is Thuro; if you are uncomfortable around royalty, you may use that.'

'May I indeed' What a singular honour! Where is the wood?'

'It is all chopped.'

'But it needs to be in here to be of any use, boy.'

Swallowing his anger, Thuro returned to the wood-store and hefted three chunks which he carried with ease back to the cabin, up the three steps and in to the hearth. He repeated this maneouvre eight times, before his arms burned like fire and his feet dragged in the snow. Culain merely sat, offering no assistance. Twice more Thuro stumbled back bearing wood, then he staggered and fell to the cabin floor. Culain leaned from his chair and tapped the boy on the back.

'Seven more chunks, I think, young Thuro?'

The prince rolled to his knees, anger giving him strength as he staggered out into the snow and this time hefted four pieces which he carried slowly back. His right hand was hot and sticky and as he

38

dumped the wood in the hearth he noticed blood was leaking from the torn blisters. He returned to the wood-store and with a supreme effort carried the last of the chunks back to the cabin.

'Never leave an axe naked to the air,' said Culain. 'Always embed it in wood; it protects the edge.'

Thuro nodded, but lacked the strength for a retort. Once more in the open, he took the axe and plunged the head into a log.

'Anything else?' he called. 'Or is it part of the game that I return first?'

'Come and eat,' called Culain.

The two broke fast with cold meat and cheese, and Thuro wolfed his small portion swiftly. This was followed by a dark ale, so bitter that the prince choked. Culain said nothing, but Thuro finished the foul brew to pre-empt any sneer.

'How do you feel?' asked Culain.

'I am fine.'

'Would you like me to tend to your hand?'

Thuro was about to refuse when he saw that this was what the other man expected. He recalled the advice of Ptolemy, as reported by Plutarch: 'As long as you react, your enemy holds your destiny in the palm of his hand. When you force him to react, you hold his neck in yours.' Thuro smiled. 'That would be kind.'

Culain's eyebrows rose. 'Hold out your hand.' Thuro did so and the warrior tipped salt from the shaker directly on to the wound. It stung like needles of fire. 'That should suffice,' said Culain. 'Now I would like you to do me a service.'

'I owe you nothing. I have paid for my breakfast.'

'Indeed you have, but I would like you to carry a message to Laitha. I don't suppose you would want to leave without wishing her goodbye?'

'Very well. Where is she?'

'She and I built a cabin, higher in the peaks. She likes the solitude. Go to her and tell her I would appreciate her company this evening.'

'Is that all?'

'Yes.'

39

'Then I shall bid you farewell, Culain lach Feragh – whatever that title may mean – and thank you for your awesome hospitality.'

'I think you should delay your departure – at least until you know where to find Laitha.'

'Then be so kind as to tell me.'

Culain gave him simple directions and Thuro left without another word. The morning was bright and chill without a trace of breeze, and he wandered through the bleak winter landscape for over an hour before coming to the path Culain had indicated, marked by a fallen tree. He turned to the right and continued the climb, stopping often to rest. It was almost dusk when the exhausted prince came to Laitha's small cabin. She helped him inside and he sat slumped before a log-fire for several minutes, gathering his breath.

'I thought I would die out there,' he said at last.

She sat beside him. 'Climb out of those wet clothes and get warm.'

'It is not fitting,' he replied, hoping she would offer an argument. She did not.

'I'll fetch you something to eat. Some bread and cheese, perhaps?'

'That would be wonderful. I haven't been this hungry since . . . I can't remember.'

'It's a long haul to my home. Why did you come?' She offered him some dark bread and a round of white cheese.

'Culain asked me to give you a message. He said he wanted your company this evening.'

'How strange.'

'The man is strange, and quite the most discourteous individual I have ever met.'

'Well, I think it best you gather your strength and feed a little warmth into your body before we head back.'

'I shall not be going back. I have said my farewells,' Thuro told her.

'You must go back. It is the only way off the mountain and it will be well after dark before we reach his cabin. You'll have to spend at least one more night there.'

'Can I not stay here? With you?'

'As you said, Prince Thuro, that would not be fitting.'

'He knew that,' said Thuro. 'He knew I would be trapped here. What evil game is he playing?'

'I think you presume too much,' she snapped. 'You are speaking of a friend of mine – the greatest friend anyone could ever have. Perhaps Culain does not like spoiled young princelings. But he saved your life, as he saved mine ten years ago – at no small risk to himself. Did he ask you for payment for that, Thuro?'

Instinctively he reached out and touched her hand. She withdrew it as if stung. 'I am sorry,' he said. 'I did not mean to offend you. North of the Wall, you are now the only friend I have. But even you said it was strange that he asked me to come here. Why was that?'

'It does not matter. We should be going.'

'But it *does* matter, Laitha. Let me hazard a guess. You were surprised because you were going to him anyway. Is that not true?'

'Perhaps. Or perhaps he forgot.'

'He does not strike me as a forgetful man. He knew I would be forced back to his cabin.'

'Ask him when you see him,' she countered, donning a heavy sheepskin jerkin and opening the door of the cabin. Outside, a heavy snowfall was in progress and the wind was picking up alarmingly. With a curse Thuro had last heard from a soldier, she slammed the door. 'We cannot leave now,' she said. 'You'll have to stay the night.' Thuro's mood brightened considerably.

Just then the door opened and Culain stepped inside, pausing to brush a dusting of snow from his shoulders.

'Not a good night for travelling, prince,' he said. 'Still, one or two chores in the morning and you'll soon pay for your keep.'

Victorinus and Gwalchmai had been riding for four days, and for the last two they had been without food. The Roman was more concerned about the state of their supplies than the possibility of capture, for the horses needed grain and without horses they had no chance of leaving the land of the Brigantes.

'What I would not give for a good bow,' said Gwalchmai, as they spotted several deer on the flanks of a low hill.

Victorinus did not respond. He was tired and the growth of beard on his square chin made him irritable. A man who liked to be clean, the smell of his own stale sweat also galled him as he scratched at his face, cursing the lack of a razor.

'You are beginning to look human,' said Gwalchmai. 'Another few months and I'll braid the beard for you – then you can walk in respectable company.'

Victorinus grinned and some of his ill-humour evaporated. 'We have no coin left, Gwal, but somehow we must find food for the horses.'

'I suggest we aim for the high ground,' said Gwalchmai, 'and try to spot a village or settlement. We can trade some of Caradoc's gear; his sword should fetch a good price.' Victorinus nodded, but he did not like the idea. The saddest fact about the British tribes was that they were incapable of mixing together without bloodshed. The thought of Gwalchmai riding in to any Brigante or Trinovante settlement filled him with apprehension.

They camped that night in a glade nestling in the bowl of the hills and out of the wind. It snowed heavily, but the two men and their mounts were snug within the shelter of a heavily laden pine and the fire kept their blood from freezing.

The following morning they located a small settlement consisting of some twelve huts and rode warily in. Gwalchmai seemed unconcerned and Victorinus marvelled anew at the British optimism which pervaded the tribes. They had a total inability to learn from past mistakes, and greeted each new day as an opportunity to replay the errors of the past twenty-four hours.

'Try not to insult anyone,' urged Victorinus.

'Have no fear, Roman. Today is a good day.'

They were met by the village head man, an elderly warrior with braided white hair and a blue tattoo on his forehead in the shape of a spider's web.

'Greetings, Father,' said Gwalchmai, as a small crowd gathered behind the head man.

'I am no father to you, South Rat,' answered the man, grinning and showing only one tooth at the top of his jaw.

'Do not be too sure, Father. You look like a man who spread his seed wide as a youngster, and my mother was a woman who attracted such men.'

The crowd chuckled and the old man stepped forward, his blue eyes bright. 'Now you mention it, there is a certain family resemblance. I take it you've brought a gift for your old father?'

'Indeed I have,' said Gwalchmai, stepping down from the saddle and presenting the old man with Caradoc's best knife, an oval-bladed weapon with a hilt of carved bone.

'From across the Water,' said the old man, hefting the weapon. 'Good iron – and a fine edge.'

'It is pleasant to be home,' said Gwalchmai. 'Can we rest the night and feed our horses?'

'But of course, my son.' The old man called forward two young-sters and they led the horses back towards a paddock east of the settlement. 'Join me in my hut.'

The hut was sparsely furnished, but it was a welcome respite from the wind. There was a cot bed and several rugs, and an iron brazier was burning coal. An elderly woman bowed as they entered and fetched bowls of dark ale and some bread and cheese. The three men sat by the brazier and the ancient identi-fied himself as Golaric, once the champion of the old King Cascioc.

'A fine king – good with sword or lance. He was murdered by his brother and that cursed Roman, Aurelius.' Golaric's bright eyes switched to Victorinus. 'It is not often that an Order Taker bothers to visit my small village.'

'I am not an Order Taker,' owned Victorinus.

'I know that. My teeth may be gone, but my mind is unaffected. You are Victorinus, the Centurion. And you, my wayward son, are Gwalchmai the Cantii, the Hound of the King. Word travels with exceptional speed.'

'We are hunted men, Father,' said Gwalchmai.

'Indeed you are. Is it true that bastard Roman is dead?'

43

'Yes,' said Victorinus, 'and I'll not hear that term used of him – alive or dead.'

'Short-tempered, is he not?' asked Golaric, seeing Victorinus' hand straying towards his gladius.

'You know these Romans, Father. No control,' said Gwalchmai. 'Why are you so open with your knowledge?'

'It pleases me to be so.'

Gwalchmai smiled. 'I know something of Brigante history. Cascioc was Eldared's elder brother; he was slain in his bed. There was almost a civil war amongst the tribes of the old Caledonian Confederacy. What part did you play in that, Father?'

'As I said, I was the King's Champion. I had a good arm in those days and I should have gone to Eldared and cut his throat, but I did not. The deed was done and I was sworn on Blood Oath to defend the king with my life. But Eldared was now the king so I left his service. And now he offers good gold to kill the men who are a danger to him. I am not interested in his gold; I am interested only in his downfall.'

'I cannot promise that,' said Victorinus. 'All I can say is that he will succeed if we do not reach Eboracum. Eldared bragged of having around fifteen thousand men at his call. Lucius Aquila has only four thousand at Eboracum. Taken by surprise, he would be routed.'

'I do not care whether a Roman survives at Eboracum, but I understand the point you are making. Your horses will be fed and watered tonight, but tomorrow you will leave. I will give you food to carry – not much, for we are a poor village. But be warned, there are hunting parties south and east of you. You must move west and then south.'

'We will be careful, Father,' said Gwalchmai.

'And you can stop calling me "Father". I never slept with a Cantii woman in my life – they were all bearded.'

Gwalchmai chuckled. 'He's right,' he told Victorinus. 'It's one reason I joined the king's army.'

'There's something else for you to think of,' said Golaric. 'The huntsmen seem unconcerned about your capture; they say that Mist Magic is being used to track you. If that is true, I pity you.'

44

The colour drained from Gwalchmai's face. 'What does he mean?' asked Victorinus.

'Death,' whispered Gwalchmai.

Throughout the long day the two men rode together and Victorinus grew steadily more uncomfortable with the silence. The land was open, the wind bitterly cold, but it was Gwalchmai's frightened eyes that dominated the Roman's thinking. He had known Gwalchmai for four years, since arriving at Camulodunum as a raw eighteen-year-old fresh from Rome. In that time he had come to hold the man in high regard for his eternal optimism and his reckless bravery, but now he rode like a man possessed – his eyes unseeing, his manner echoing his defeat. They camped in the lee of a rockface and Victorinus prepared a fire.

'What is wrong with you, man?' he asked, as Gwalchmai sat passively staring into the flames.

'It is well for you that you do not understand,' said Gwalchmai.

'I understand fear when I see it.'

'It is worse than fear; it is the foreknowledge of death. I must ready myself for the journey.'

At a loss for a response, Victorinus laughed in his face. 'Is this Gwalchmai I see before me? Is this the King's Hound? More like a rabbit in the torchlight, waiting for the arrow to strike. What is the matter with you, man?'

'You do not understand,' repeated Gwalchmai. 'It is in the bones of this land . . . in the Gods of Wood and Lake. This land was once the home of the Gods, and they still walk here within the Mist. Do not mock me, Roman, for I know whereof I speak. I have seen scaled dragons in the air. I have seen the Atrol walk. I have heard the hissing of dead men's breath. There is no escaping it; if the old gods walk our trail, there is nowhere to hide.'

'You talk like an old woman. What I can see, I can cut. What I can cut, I can kill. There is no more to be said. Gods, indeed! Look around you. Where are the Atrols? Where are the dragons? Where are the dead that walk?'

'You will see, Victorinus. Before they take you, you will see.'

45

A cloud obscured the moon and an owl swooped over the camp-site. 'There is your dragon, Gwalchmai. Out hunting mice!'

'My father angered an Enchanter once,' said Gwalchmai softly, 'and he summoned a witch woman. They found my father on a hillside – or rather, they found the bottom half of him. The top had been ripped away and I saw the fang marks on his back.'

'Perhaps you are right,' offered Victorinus, 'and perhaps demons do walk. But if they do, a man must face them. Fear is the killer here, Gwal.' A distant wolf howled, the sound echoing eerily through the glade. Victorinus shivered and cursed inwardly. He wrapped his blanket round his shoulders and stoked up the fire, adding fresh branches to the blaze.

'I'll keep watch for a couple of hours,' he said. 'You get some sleep.'

Obediently Gwalchmai wrapped himself in his blankets and lay down by the fire while Victorinus drew his gladius and sat with his back to a tree. The night wore on and the cold grew. The Roman added more fuel to the fire until the last broken branch was all but finished, then he pushed himself to his feet and stretched his back, moving off into the darkness to gather more dead wood. He put down his gladius and had stooped to lift a long windfall branch when a low, whispering sound alerted him. Still on edge following the conversation with Gwalchmai, he dropped the wood, swept up his sword and dived to the right. Something touched the skin of his back and he rolled, gladius sweeping up into the darkness that threatened to overwhelm him. The blade struck something solid and a bestial scream followed. Victorinus rolled once more as a dark shadow loomed over him, then with a battlecry he leapt to meet his assailant. His sword plunged home, then a blow to the side of the head sent him hurtling back into the campsite to skid across the glowing coals of the fire. The clouds parted, the moon shining her silver light upon the scene. Victorinus came to his feet – and froze . . . Before him was a creature some nine feet tall, covered in long brown hair. Its eyes were red, shining like fresh-spilled blood, and its fangs were the length of daggers and wickedly curved. The creature's arms were disproportionately long, hanging almost to the ground, and from the end of each of its four fingers grew gleaming serrated talons.

A grey mist swirled around Victorinus' legs, rising even as he noticed it. The creature advanced. The Roman swiftly wiped his sword hand free of sweat and gripped the leather hilt of his gladius. It was the wrong weapon for this beast; he needed a spear.

'Come forward and die!' he called. 'Have a taste of Roman iron!'

The creature stopped – and spoke. Victorinus was so surprised that he almost dropped his sword.

'You cannot fight destiny, Victorinus,' it said, its voice sibilant. 'This is the day of your passing. Cease your struggle. Rest and know peace. Rest and know joy. Rest . . .' The voice was hypnotic and as the beast advanced Victorinus blinked and tried to rouse himself from the lethargy it induced in him. The mist rose about his shoulders, billowing like woodsmoke.

'No!' he said, backing away.

Suddenly an unearthly scream pierced the silence. The mist parted and Victorinus saw Gwalchmai behind the beast, raising his bloody sword for a second strike. The Roman raced forward to plunge his blade into the hairy throat. The talons lashed at him, ripping the front of his robes and scoring the skin. Gwalchmai struck once more from behind and the creature fell. The mist thickened – then vanished.

The beast was gone.

Victorinus staggered back to the campsite, gathering together the hot coals with his sword-blade and blowing flames to life. Gwalchmai joined him but they said nothing until the fire was once more lit.

'Forgive me,' said the Roman. 'I mocked in ignorance.'

'There is nothing to forgive. You were right – a man must fight for life, even when he believes all is lost. You taught me a lesson today, Roman. I will not forget it.'

This is obviously a day for lessons. What was that thing?'

'An Atrol – and a small one. We were lucky, Victorinus. By now they will know they have failed and the next demon will not die as easily.'

'Maybe not – but it *will* die.'

Gwalchmai grinned and slapped him on the shoulder. I believe you.'

'One of us ought to,' said the Roman.

'I think we should leave this place,' offered Gwalchmai. 'Now they have the scent, they will be close behind us.'

As if to emphasise his words, a dreadful howling came from the north. It was answered from the east and west.

'Wolves?' asked Victorinus, dreading the answer.

'Atrols. Let us ride.'

5

Thuro stared at the unsmiling Culain and for the first time in his young life felt hatred swell inside him. His father was dead, his own life in ruins and now he was at the mercy of this strange mountain man. He stood up from the floor before the fire.

'I'll work for my keep tonight,' he said, 'despite your trickery. But then I leave.'

'I fear not, young prince,' said Culain, stripping off his leather jerkin and moving to stand before the fire. 'The lower valleys will be cut off by morning and the snow will be drifting over ten feet deep. I am afraid we are forced to endure your company for at least two months.'

'You are a liar!'

'Rarely is that true,' replied Culain softly, kneeling to extend his hands to the flames. 'And certainly not on this occasion. Still, look on the summer side, Thuro. You do not have to see much of me – a few simple chores and you can keep Laitha company. Added to this, you may not be able to leave but neither can your enemies come upon you. By spring you will be able to make the journey home a far less dangerous one. You may even learn something.'

'You have nothing to teach me. I need to acquire none of your ways.'

Culain shrugged. 'As you will. I am tired. I am not as young as once I was. May I rest my old bones upon your cot, Gian?'

'Of course,' said Laitha. Thuro saw the look in her eyes and wished he could inspire such a reaction. Her love for Culain was a radiant thing and Thuro was amazed that he had not realised it before. He felt like an interloper, an intruder, and his heart sank. Why should the forest girl not love this man of action – tall and oak-strong, mature and powerful? Thuro turned away from the love in her eyes and wandered to the far window. It was shut tight against the weather and he made a point of examining the wood, noting the neatness with which it fitted the frame. Not a breath of draught troubled him. When he turned back Culain had gone into the back room, Laitha with him. Thuro returned to the fire. He could hear them speaking in low tones, but could distinguish no words.

Laitha returned a few minutes later and lit two candles. 'He is sleeping,' she said.

'Forgive me, Laitha. I had not wished to intrude.'

Her large brown eyes focused on him, her look quizzical. 'In what way intrude?'

He swallowed hard, aware that he walked a dangerous path. 'On you and Culain. You seem happy together and probably did not need . . . more company. I will be gone as soon as I am able.'

She nodded. 'You were wrong, Thuro. There is much you can learn here – if you use your time well. Culain is a good man, the best I have known. There is no malice in him – whatever you may think. But there is always a reason for his actions that has little to do with selfishness.'

'I do not know him as well as you,' said Thuro in his best neutral tones.

'Indeed you do not. But you might, if only you would start thinking instead of reacting.'

'I do not understand your meaning. Thinking is perhaps the one strength I have. In all my life, my mind has never let me down as have my legs and lungs.'

She smiled and reached out to touch his shoulder and he felt an almost electric thrill in his blood. 'Then think, Thuro. Why is he here?'

'How can I answer that?'

'By examining the evidence before you and reaching a conclusion. Think on it as a riddle.'

Here was a situation in which Thuro felt comfortable. Even the word riddle made him feel more at home, remembering his evenings with Maedhlyn in the oak-panelled study. His mind switched effortlessly to a new path. Culain had asked him to visit

50

Laitha, bringing a message, but then had come himself, thus negating the need for Thuro's journey. Why? He thought of the long arduous climb to this lonely cabin, and realised that the mountain man must have set out soon after he had. He looked up and found Laitha staring at him intently. He smiled, but her face remained fixed.

'Have you come upon the answer?' she asked.

'Perhaps. He was watching out for me – in case I collapsed in the snow.'

Now it was her turn to smile and he watched the tension flow from her shoulders. 'Do you still see him as an ogre?'

'The fact remains that there was no necessity for me to come here at all.'

'Think about that too,' she said, rising smoothly and moving to a long chest by the far wall. She removed two blankets and passed them to him. 'Sleep here before the fire. I will see you in the morning.'

'Where will you sleep?' he asked.

'Alongside Culain.'

'Oh. Yes, of course.'

'Yes, of course,' she repeated, the hint of fire in her eyes. He coloured deeply and looked away.

'I did not mean to offend. Truly.'

'Your words are not as offensive as the look in your eye.'

He nodded and spread his hands. 'I am jealous. Forgive me.'

'Why should I forgive you? What is your crime? You see and you do not see. You make judgements on the flimsiest evidence. Do not be misled, Thuro, as to your strengths. True, your body is not as strong as your mind. But what does that tell us? Your body is so weak that you have mistakenly inflated the true power of your intellect. Your mind is undisciplined and your arrogance unacceptable. Good night to you.'

He sat for a long time watching the fire burn, adding logs and thinking on what she had said. He should have known that Culain had followed him from the moment the tall warrior entered the cabin – just as he should have known why he had been told to

51

come here. True, it was to trap him in the mountains for the remainder of the winter, but there was no gain in it for Culain; only for Thuro, safe now from his enemies. He lay on the floor with the blanket over his shoulders, feeling foolish and young and far out of his depth. Laitha first, and then Culain, had saved his life. He had repaid them with arrogance and lack of gratitude.

He awoke early, having slept dreamlessly. The fire was down to grey ash, with an occasional glowing ember. He carefully shifted the ash, allowing air to circulate, and added the last of the logs. Then he rose and left the cabin. Outside the snow had stopped and the air was fresh and bitterly cold. He located the wood-store and took up a long-handled axe. His first stroke sliced a thick log and he felt pride roar through him. He grinned and drew in a deep, searing breath. The blisters on his hand had dried, but the skin was still sore. He ignored the growing discomfort and continued to chop the wood until twenty logs had been rendered to forty-six chunks. Then he gathered them and sat down on the chopping ring, sweat dripping from his face. He no longer felt cold, he felt alive. His arms and shoulders burned with the raw physical effort, and he waited a little while until his breathing returned to normal. Then he took up three chunks and carried them back to the hearth. Just like the day before, he began to feel light-headed after several trips, so he slowed his action and rested often. In this way he completed his task without collapse, and felt a ridiculous sense of achievement when the hearth was full. He returned to the wood-store and hammered the axeblade into a log. His hand was bleeding again and he sat staring at the congealing blood, as proud of it as of a battle scar.

A brightly coloured bird fluttered down to sit on a branch above his head. Its breast was reddish brown, while its head was black, as if a little cap was perched there. On its back the feathers were grey, like a tiny cape, and the ends of its wings and tail were black with a white stripe – like the symbol of a Pilus Primus, a first centurion.

Thuro had seen birds like this before in Eboracum wood, but had never stopped to examine their beauty. It gave a soft, piping whistle and then vanished off into the woods.

52

'It was a Pyrrhula, a bullfinch,' said Culain and Thuro jumped. The man's approach had been as silent as the arrival of dawn. 'There are many beautiful birds in the high country. Look there!' Thuro followed his pointing finger and saw the most comical sight. It was a small orange bird with a white beard and black moustache, looking for all the world like a tiny sorcerer. That is a Panurus Biarmicus, a bearded tit,' said Culain. 'There are very few left now.'

'It looks like a friend of mine. I wish he could see it.'

'You speak of Maedhlyn – and he has already seen it.'

'You know Maedhlyn?'

'I have known Maedhlyn since the world was young. We grew up in the city of Balacris, before Atlantis sank. And you asked about my title – Culain lach Feragh: Culain the Immortal.' He smiled. 'But not any longer. Now I am Culain the man and the happier for it. I greet every new grey hair as a gift.'

'You are from the Land of Mist?'

'Maedhlyn and I, and several others, created the Land. It was not easy, and even now I am not sure it was worthwhile. What do you think?'

'How can I answer that? I have never been there. Is it wondrous?'

'Wondrous dull, boy! Can you imagine immortality? What is there that is new in the world to pique your interest? What ambitions can you foster that are not instantly achievable? What joy is there in an endless sequence of shifting seasons? Far better to be mortal and grow old with the world around you.'

'There is love, surely?' said Thuro.

'There is always love. But after a hundred years, or a thousand, the flames of passion are little more than a glow in the ash of a long-dead fire.'

'Is Laitha immortal?'

'No, she is not of the Mist. Are you taken with her, Thuro? Or are you bored, stuck in these woods?'

'I am not bored. And yes, she is beautiful.'

'That is not what I asked.'

'Then I cannot answer. But I would not presume to approach your lady – even were she to receive me.'

Culain's grey eyes sparkled and a wide grin crossed his features. 'Well said! However, she is not my lady. She is my ward.'

'But she sleeps with you!'

'Sleeps, yes. Was life so sheltered for you in Eboracum? What can Maedhlyn have been thinking of?'

'And yet she loves you,' said Thuro. 'You cannot deny it.'

'I would hope that she does, for I have been a father to her – as best I could.'

For the first time in his short relationship with the Mist Warrior, Thuro felt strangely superior. For he knew that Laitha loved Culain as a man; he could see it in her eyes and the tilt of her head. Yet Culain could not see it; this made him truly mortal and Thuro warmed to him.

'How old are you?' he asked, switching the subject.

'The answer would dazzle you, and I shall not give it. But I will say that I have watched this island and its people for over seven hundred years. I was even the king once.'

'Of which tribe?'

'Of all the tribes. Have you not heard of Cunobelin?'

'The Trinovante king? Yes. That was you?'

'For over forty years I ruled. I was a legend, they tell me. I helped build Camulodunum. Seutonius wrote of me that I was the Brittanorum Rex – the king of all Britain – the greatest of the Belgic kings. Ah, but I had an ego in those days and I did like so to be flattered!'

'Some of the tribes believe that you will return when the land is threatened. It is taught around the camp-fires. I thought it a wonderful fable, but it could be true. You could come back; you could be king again.'

Culain saw the brightness of hope in the boy's eyes. 'I am not the king any longer, Thuro. And I have no wish to rule. But you can.'

Thuro shook his head. 'I am not like my father.'

'No, there is a great deal of your mother in you.'

'Did you know her?'

'Yes, I was there the day Maedhlyn brought your father home. Alaida gave up everything for him, including life. It is not a subject it pleases me to speak of, but you have a right. Alaida was my daughter, the only child I have fathered in my long life. She was nineteen when she left the Feragh, twenty when she died. Twenty! I could have killed Maedhlyn then. I nearly did. But he was so penitent I realised it was a greater punishment to leave him be.'

'Then you are my grandfather?' asked Thuro, savouring the feel of the word and seeing for the first time that Culain's eyes of woodsmoke grey were the image of his own.

'Yes,' said Culain.

'Why did you never come to see me? Did you hate me for killing my mother?'

'I think that I did, Thuro. Great age does not always ensure great wisdom – as Maedhlyn knows! I could have saved Alaida, but I refused to allow her to take a Stone from the Feragh.'

'Are the stones magical there?'

'Not all of them, but there is a special Stone we call the Sipstrassi, and it is the source of all magic. What a man can dream he can create. The most imaginative of men become Enhancers; they liven an otherwise tedious existence with their living dreams.'

'Maedhlyn is one of these,' said Thuro, 'I have seen him conjure winged horses no longer than my fingers, and whole armies to battle on my father's desk-top. He showed me Marathon and Thermopylae, Platea and Phillipi. I saw the great Julius fought to a standstill in Britain by Caswallon. I listened to Antony's funeral oration.'

'Yes, I too have seen these things,' said Culain, 'but I was speaking of Alaida.'

'I am sorry,' said Thuro, instantly contrite.

'Do not be. Boys and magic make for excitement. She had her own Stone but I would not allow her to take it from the Feragh. I thought, somehow, that when she needed me she would call. I knew I would hear her wherever I was. But she did not call. She chose to die. Such was her pride.'

'And you blame yourself for her death?'

'Who else would I blame? But that is in the past and you are the present. What am I to do with you?'

55

'Help me get back to Eboracum?'

'Not as you are, Thuro. You are only half a man. We must make you strong; you will not survive a day as the weakling prince.'

'Will you use Stone magic to make me strong?'

'No. Earth magic,' said Culain. 'We will look inside you and see what we can find.'

'I am not cut out to be a warrior.'

'You are my grandson and the son of Aurelius and Alaida. I think you will find that blood runs true. We already know you can swing an axe. What other surprises do you hold in store?'

Thuro shrugged. 'I do not want to disappoint you, as I disappointed my father.'

'Lesson one, Thuro: from now on you have no one to disappoint but yourself. But you must agree to abide by what I say and obey every word I utter. Will you do this?'

'I will.'

'Then prepare to die,' said Culain. And there was no humour in his eyes.

Thuro stiffened as Culain stood and pulled a gladius from a sheath behind his belt. The blade was eighteen inches long and double edged, the hilt of leather. He reversed the weapon and handed it to Thuro. It felt blade-heavy and uncomfortable in his hand.

'Before I can teach you to live, you must learn to die – how it feels to be vanquished,' said Culain. 'Move on to open ground and wait.' Thuro did as he was bid and Culain produced a small golden stone from his pocket, closing his fist around it. The air thickened before Thuro, solidifying into a Roman warrior with bronze breastplate and leather helm. He seemed young, but his eyes were old. The warrior dropped into a fighting crouch with blade extended and Thuro backed away, uncertain.

The warrior advanced, locking Thuro's gaze. The blade lunged. Instinctively Thuro parried, but his opponent's gladius rolled over his own and plunged into the boy's chest. The pain was sickening and all strength fled from the prince. His knees buckled and he fell with a scream as the Roman dragged free his blade.

56

Moments later Thuro rose out of darkness to feel the snow on his face. He pushed himself to his knees and felt for the wound. There was none. Culain's strong hand pulled him to his feet and Thuro's head spun. Culain sat him on the chopping ring.

'The man you fought was a Roman legionary who served under Agricola. He was seventeen and went on to become a fine gladiator. You met him early in his career. Did you learn anything?'

'I learnt I am no swordsman,' admitted Thuro ruefully.

'I want you to use your brain and stop thinking with your feelings. You knew nothing of Plutarch before Maedhlyn taught you. There are no born swordsmen; it is an acquired skill, like any other. All it requires is good reflexes, allied to courage. You have both. Believe it! Now follow me, there is something I want you to see.'

Thuro offered the gladius to Culain, who waved it away. 'Carry it with you always. Get used to the feel and the weight. Keep it sharp.'

The Mist Warrior walked out past the cabin and down the slope towards the valley below. Thuro followed, his belly aching for food. The return trip to Culain's cabin was made in less than an hour and the prince was frozen when they arrived. The cabin was cold and there was no wood in the hearth.

'I shall prepare breakfast,' said Culain. 'You . . .'

'I know. Chop some logs.'

Culain smiled and left the boy by the wood-store. Thuro took up the axe in his sore hands and began his work. He managed only six logs and carried the chunks into the hearth. Culain did not berate him and gave him a wooden bowl filled with hot oats, sweetened with honey. The meal was heavenly.

Culain cleared away the dishes and returned with a wide bowl brimming with clear water. He placed it before Thuro and waited for the ripples to settle.

'Look into the water, Thuro.' As the prince leaned forward, Culain lifted a golden stone over it and closed his eyes.

At first Thuro could see only his reflection and the wooden beams above his head. But then the water misted and he found himself staring down from a great height to the shores of a frozen lake. A group of riders was gathered there. The scene swelled, as if Thuro were swooping down towards them, and he recognised his father. A burning pain began in his chest, tightening his throat, and tears blurred his vision. He blinked them back. By the lake a man stepped from behind a rock, a long-bow bent. The arrow flashed into his father's back and his horse reared as his weight fell across its neck, but he held on. The other riders swarmed forward and the king drew his sword and cut the first man from the saddle. A second arrow took his horse in the throat and the beast fell. The king leapt clear and ran to the edge of the lake, turning with his back to the ice. The riders – seventeen of them – dismounted. Thuro saw Eldared at the rear with one of his sons. The group rushed forward and the king, blood staining his beard, stepped in to meet them with his double-handed sword hacking and cleaving. The killers fell back in dismay. Five were now down, two others retired from the fray with deep wounds to arm and shoulder. The king stumbled and bent double, blood frothing from his mouth. Thuro wanted to look away, but his eyes were locked to the scene. An assassin ran in to plunge a dagger to the king's side; the dying monarch's blade sliced up and over, all but beheading the man. Then the king turned and staggered on to the ice and, with the last of his strength, hurled the sword far out over the lake. The assassins swarmed around the fallen king and Thuro saw Cael deliver the death blow. And in that dreadful moment the prince watched as something akin to triumph flared in Aurelius' eyes. The sword hung in the air, hilt down, just above a spot at the centre of the lake where the ice had broken. A slender hand reached up from below the water and drew the sword down.

The scene fragmented and blurred and Thuro's own astonished face appeared on the surface of the water in the bowl. He leaned back and saw Culain watching him intently.

'What you saw was the death of a man,' said Culain softly, respectfully, as if conveying the greatest compliment. 'It was meet that you should see it.'

'I am glad that I did. Did you see his eyes at the end? Did I misread them, or was there joy there?'

'I wondered that, and only time will supply an answer. Did you see the sword?'

'Yes, what did it mean?'

'Simply that Eldared does not have it. And without it he cannot become High King. It is the Sword of Cunobelin. My sword!'

'Of course. My father took it from the stone at Camulodunum; he was the first to be able to draw it.'

Culain chuckled. 'There was little skill in that. Aurelius had Maedhlyn to guide him, and it was Maedhlyn who devised the Stone ploy in the first place. The reason no one could draw the sword was that it was always a heartbeat ahead in time. Draw it? No man could touch it. It was part of the legend of Cunobelin, a legend Maedhlyn and I established four hundred years ago.'

'For what reason?' asked Thuro.

'Vanity. In those days, as I have told you. I had a great ego. And it was fun, Thuro, to be a king. Maedhlyn helped me to age gracefully. I still had the strength of a twenty-five-year-old, within a body that looked wonderfully wrinkled. But then I grew bored and Maedhlyn staged my death – but not before I had dramatically planted my sword in the boulder and created the legend of my return. Who knew then, but that I might want to? Unfortunately events did not fare too well after my departure. A young man named Caractacus decided to anger the Romans and they took the island by force. By then I was elsewhere. Maedhlyn and I crossed the Mist to another age. He had fallen in love with the Greek culture and became a travelling philosopher. But he couldn't resist meddling and he trained a young boy and made him an emperor – conquered most of the world.'

'What did you do?'

'I came home and did what I could for the Britons. I felt somewhat responsible for their plight. But I did not take up arms until the death of Prasutagas. After he died, the Romans flogged his wife Boudicca and raped his daughters. I raised the Iceni under Boudicca's banner and we harried the invincible Roman army all the way to Londinium, which we burnt to the ground. But the tribes never learnt discipline and we were smashed at Atherstone by that wily fox Paullinus. I took Boudicca and her daughters back to the Feragh and they lived there in some contentment for many years.'

'And did you fight again?' asked Thuro.

'Another day, Thuro. How do you feel?'

'Weary.'

'Good.' Culain removed his own fur-lined jerkin and handed it to the boy. 'This should keep you warm. I want you to return to Laitha's cabin, restore yourself in her good grace and then return here.'

'Could I not rest for a while?'

'Go now,' said Culain. 'And if you can, when you come in sight of her cabin, run. I want some strength built into those spindly legs!'

6

Prasamaccus was proud of his reputation as the finest hunter of the Three Valleys. He had worked hard on his bowmanship, but knew that it was his patience that set him apart from the rest. No matter the weather, burning heat or searing cold, he could sit silently for hours waiting for the right moment to let fly. No stringy meat for Prasamaccus, for his quarry dropped dead instantly, shot through the heart. No deer he killed had run for a mile with its lungs bubbling and its juices swelling the muscles to jaw-breaking toughness.

His bow was a gift from his clan leader Moret, son of Eldared. It was a Roman weapon of dark horn, and he treasured it. His arrows were straight as shafts of sunlight and he trimmed each goose-feather with careful cuts. In a tourney last Astarte Day, he had brought a gasp from the crowd when he sliced to the bull through the shaft of his last hit. It was a fluke and yet highlighted his awesome eye.

Now, as he sat hidden in the bushes of the hillside, he needed all his patience. The deer were slowly but steadily making their way towards him. He had been hidden here for two hours and his blood felt like ice even through the sheepskin cloak gathered about his slender frame. He was not a tall man, and his face was thin and angular, blue eyes set close together. His chin was pointed, emphasised by a straggly blond beard. Crouched as he now was, it was impossible to spot the deformity that set him apart from his fellows, which has deprived this finest of hunters from taking a bride.

The deer was almost within killing range and Prasamaccus chose a fat doe as his target. With infinite lack of speed he drew a long shaft from his doeskin quiver and notched it to the bowstring.

Just then the lead stag's head came up and the small herd scattered. Prasamaccus sighed and stood. He limped forward, his

61

twisted leg causing him to hobble in a sadly comical manner. When he was a toddler he had fallen in the path of a galloping horse that smashed his left leg to shards. Now it was some eight inches shorter than the right, the foot mangled and pointing inward. He waited as the riders galloped towards him. There were two men and their horses were lathered; they ignored him and thundered past. As a hunter himself, he knew they were being pursued and glanced back along the trail. Three giant beasts were loping across the snow and Prasamaccus blinked. Bears? No bear could move that fast. His eyes widened. Lifting his hand to his mouth he let out a piercing whistle and a bay mare came galloping from the trees. He pulled himself into the saddle and slapped her rump. Unused to such treatment from a normally gentle master, the mare broke into a run. Prasamaccus steered her after the riders, swiftly overtaking their tired mounts.

'Veer left!' he shouted. 'There is a ring of stones and a high hollow altar.'

Without checking to see if they followed him, he urged the mare up the snow-covered hill and over the crest, where black stones ringed the crown of the hill like broken teeth. He clambered from the saddle and limped to the centre where a huge altar stone was set atop a crumbling structure some eight feet high. Prasamaccus clawed his way to the top, swung his quiver to the front and notched an arrow to his bow.

The two riders, their mounts almost dead from exhaustion, reached the circle scant seconds before the beasts. Prasamaccus drew back the bow-string and let fly. The shaft sped to the first beast as it towered over a running tribesman with a braided blond beard. The arrow took the beast in its right eye and it fell back with a piercing scream that was almost human. The two men scrambled up alongside Prasamaccus, drawing their swords.

A mist sprang up around the circle, swirling between the stones and rising to stand like a grey wall beyond the monoliths. The two remaining Atrols faded back out of sight and the three men were left at the centre in ghostly silence.

'What are those creatures?' asked Prasamaccus.

'Atrols,' answered Gwalchmai.

'I thought they must be, but I expected them to be bigger,' said the bowman. Victorinus smiled grimly. The mist around the stones was now impenetrable, but it had not pervaded the centre. Victorinus glanced up. There was no sky, only a thick grey cloud hovering at the height of the stones.

'Why are they not attacking?' asked the Roman. Gwalchmai shrugged. From beyond the stones came a sibilant, whispering voice.

'Come forth, Gwalchmai. Come forth! Your father is here.' A figure appeared at the edge of the mist, a bearded man with a blue tattoo on both cheeks. 'Come to me, my son!' Gwalchmai half-rose, but Victorinus grabbed his arm. Gwalchmai's eyes were glazed; Victorinus struck him savagely across the cheek, but the Briton did not react. Then the voice came again.

'Victorinus . . . your mother waits.' And a slender white-robed woman stood alongside the man.

An anguished groan broke from Victorinus' lips and he released his hold on Gwalchmai, who scrambled down the altar. Prasamaccus, understanding none of this, pushed himself to his feet and sent an arrow into the head of Gwalchmai's father. In an instant all was changed. The image of the man disappeared to be replaced by the monstrous figure of an Atrol, tearing at the shaft in its cheek. Gwalchmai stopped, the spell broken. The image of Victorinus' mother faded back into the mist.

'Well done, bowman!' said Victorinus. 'Get back here, Gwal!'

As the tribesman turned to obey the mist cleared, and there at the edge of the stones were a dozen huge wolves standing almost as tall as ponies.

'Mother of Mithras!' exclaimed Prasamaccus.

Gwalchmai sprinted for the stones as the wolves raced into the circle. He leapt, reaching for Victorinus' outstretched hand. The Roman grabbed him and hauled him up, just ahead of the lead wolf whose jaws snapped shut bare inches from Gwalchmai's trailing leg.

Prasamaccus shot the beast in the throat and it fell back. A second wolf leapt to the altar, scrabbling for purchase, but Victorinus kicked it savagely and it pitched to the ground. The wolves were all around them now, snarling and snapping. The three men backed to the centre of the altar. Prasamaccus sent two shafts into the milling beasts, but the rest ignored their wounded comrades. With only three shafts left, Prasamaccus refrained from loosing any more arrows.

'I don't like to sound pessimistic,' said Gwalchmai, 'but I'd appreciate any Roman suggestions at this point.'

A wolf jumped and cleared the rock screen around the men. Gwalchmai's sword rammed home alongside Prasamaccus' arrow.

Suddenly the ground below began to tremble and the stones shifted. Gwalchmai almost fell, but recovered his balance in time to see Victorinus slip from the shelter. The tribesman hurled himself across the altar, seizing the Roman's robe and dragging him to safety. The wolves also cowered back as the tremor continued. Lightning flashed within the circle and a huge wolf reared up, his flesh transparent, his awesome bone structure revealed. As the lightning passed the beast fell to earth and the stink of charred flesh filled the circle. Once more lightning seared into the wolves and three died. The rest fled beyond the stones into the relative sanctuary of the mist.

A man appeared from within a glow of golden light beside the altar. He was tall and portly, a long black moustache flowing on to a short-cropped white beard. He wore a simple robe of purple velvet.

'I would suggest you join me,' he said, 'for I fear I have almost used up my magic'

Victorinus leapt from the altar, followed by Gwalchmai. 'Hurry now, the Gate is closing.' But Prasamaccus, with his ruined leg, could not move at speed and the golden globe began to shrink. Gwalchmai followed the wizard through, but Victorinus ran back to aid the bowman. Breathing heavily, Prasamaccus hurled himself through the light. Victorinus hesitated. The glow was no bigger than a window, and shrinking fast as the wolves poured into the circle. A hand reached through the golden light, hauling the Roman clear. There was a sensation like ice searing hot flesh and

Victorinus opened his eyes to see Gwalchmai still holding him by the robe . . . only now they were standing in Caerlyn wood, overlooking Eboracum.

'Your timing is impeccable, Lord Maedhlyn,' said Victorinus.

'Long practice,' said the Enchanter. 'You must make your report to Aquila, though he already knows that Aurelius is dead.'

'How?' asked Gwalchmai. 'Did someone else escape?'

'He knows because I told him,' snapped Maedhlyn. 'That's why I am an Enchanter and not a cheesemaker, you ignorant moron.'

Gwalchmai's anger flared. 'If you are such an Enchanter, then why is the king dead? Why did your powers not save him?'

'I'll not bandy words with you, mortal,' hissed Maedhlyn, looming over the tribesman. 'The king is dead because he did not listen, but the boy is alive because I led him clear. Where were you, King's Hound?'

Gwalchmai's jaw dropped. 'Thuro?'

'Is alive, no thanks to you. Now begone to the barracks.' Gwalchmai stumbled away and Victorinus approached the Enchanter.

'I am grateful, my lord, for your aid. But you were wrong to berate Gwalchmai. I led him from Deicester; we believed the boy dead.'

Maedhlyn waved his hand as if swatting a fly. 'Wrong, right! What does it matter? The clod made me angry; he was lucky I didn't turn him into a tree.'

'If you had, my lord,' said Victorinus, with a hard smile, 'I'd have slit your throat.' He bowed and followed Gwalchmai towards the barracks.

'And what is your part in this?' Maedhlyn asked Prasamaccus.

'I was hunting deer. This has not been a good day for me.'

Prasamaccus hobbled into the barrack square, having lost sight of the swifter men. Some children gathered to mock him, but he was used to this and ignored them. The buildings here were grand, but even Prasamaccus could tell where the old Roman constructions

65

had been repaired or renovated; the craftsmanship was less skilled than the older work.

The roads and alleyways were narrow and Prasamaccus passed through the barracks square and on to the Street of Merchants, pausing to stare into open-fronted shops and examine cloth, or pottery, and even weapons in a large corner building. A fat man wearing a leather apron approached him as he examined a curved hunting-bow.

'A fine weapon,' said the man, smiling broadly. 'But not as fine as the one you are carrying. Are you looking to trade?'

'No.'

'I have bows that could outdistance yours by fifty paces. Good strong yew, well seasoned.'

'Vamera is not for sale,' said Prasamaccus, 'though I could use some shafts.'

'Five denarii each.'

Prasamaccus nodded. It had been two years since he had seen money coin, and even then it had not been his. He smiled at the man and left the shop. The day was bright, the snow absent from the town, though still to be seen decorating the surrounding hills. Prasamaccus thought of his predicament. He was a hunter without a horse, and with only two arrows, in a land that was not his own. He had no coin and no hope of support. And he was hungry. He sighed, and wondered which of the Gods he had angered now. All his life people had told him the Gods did not like him. The injury to his leg was proof of that, they said. The only girl he had ever loved had died of the Red Plague. Not that Prasamaccus had ever told her of his love but even so, as soon as his affection materialised within him, she had been struck down. He turned his pale blue eyes to the heavens. He felt no anger at the Gods. How could he? It was not for him to question their likes and dislikes. But he felt it would be pleasant at least to know which of them held him in such low esteem.

'What's wrong with your leg?' asked a small, fair-haired boy of around six years.

'A dragon breathed on it,' said Prasamaccus.

66

'Did it hurt?'

'Oh yes. It still does when the weather turns wet.'

'Did you kill the dragon?'

'With a single shaft from my magic bow.'

'Are they not covered with golden scales?'

'You know a great deal about dragons.'

'My father has killed hundreds. He says you can only strike them behind their long ears; there is a soft spot there that leads to the brain.'

'Exactly right,' said Prasamaccus. 'That's how I killed mine.'

'With your magic bow.'

'Yes. Would you like to touch it?' The boy's eyes sparkled and his small hand reached out to stroke the black, glossy frame.

'Will the magic rub off?'

'Of course. The next time you see a dragon, Vamera will appear in your hand with a golden arrow.'

Without a goodbye the boy raced off shouting his father's name, desperate to tell him of his adventure. Prasamaccus felt better. He hobbled back into the barrack square and followed the smell of cooking meat to a wide building of golden sandstone. Inside was a mess hall with rows of bench tables and at the far end a huge hearth where a bull was spitted. Prasamaccus, ignoring the stares as he passed, moved slowly to the line of men waiting for food and picked up a large wooden platter. The line moved on, each man receiving two thick slabs of meat and a large spoonful of sprouts and carrots. Prasamaccus reached the server, a short man who was sweating profusely. The man watched him for a moment, offering no meat.

'What are you doing here, cripple?'

'I am waiting to eat.'

'This is the Auxiliaries' dining-hall. You are no soldier.'

'The Lord Maedhlyn said I could eat here,' lied Prasamaccus smoothly. 'But if you wish, I will go to him *and* say you refused. What is your name?'

The man dumped two slabs of meat on his plate. 'Next!' he said. 'Move along now.'

67

Prasamaccus looked for a nearby empty table. It was important not to sit too closely to other men, for all who saw him knew he was despised by the Gods and none would want that luck rubbing off. He found a table near the window and sat down; taking his thin-bladed hunting-knife from its sheath, he sliced the meat and ate it slowly. It tasted fine, but the fat content was high. He belched and leaned back, content for the first time since the incident with the Atrols. Food was now no longer a problem. The magic name of Maedhlyn cast a powerful spell, it seemed.

A stocky, powerfully built man with a square-cut beard sat opposite him. Prasamaccus looked up into a pair of dark brown eyes. 'I understand the Lord Enchanter told you to eat here,' said the man.

'Yes.'

'I wonder why,' the man went on, his suspicion evident.

'I have just returned from the north with Gwalchmai and . . . the other fellow.'

'You were with the king?'

'No. I met Gwalchmai and came with them.'

'Where is he now?'

'Making a report.' Prasamaccus could not remember the name of the clan leader, used by Maedhlyn.

'What news from the north?' asked the man. 'Is it true the king is dead?'

Prasamaccus remembered the savage joy in his own Brigante village on hearing the news. 'Yes,' he answered. 'I am afraid that it is.'

'You do not seem too concerned.'

Prasamaccus leaned forward. 'I did not know the man. Gwalchmai feels his loss keenly.'

'He would,' said the man, relaxing. 'He was the King's Hound. How was the deed done?'

'I do not know all the facts. You must ask Gwalchmai and . . .'

'Who?'

'I am bad with names a tall man, dark-haired, curved nose.'

'Victorinus?'

68

'That was it,' said Prasamaccus, remembering the sibilant calls of the Atrols.

'What happened to the others?'

'What others?'

'The king's retainers?'

'I do not know. Gwalchmai will answer all your questions.'

'I am sure that he will, my Brigante friend, and until he arrives you must consider yourself my guest.' The man stood and called two soldiers over. 'Take this man into custody.'

Prasamaccus sighed. The Gods were surely laughing today.

The two soldiers walked Prasamaccus across the square, keeping out of arm's reach of the cripple. One carried his bow and quiver, the other had taken possession of his hunting-knife. They led him to a small room with a barred door and no window. Inside was a narrow pallet bed. He listened as the bar dropped into place and then lay down on the bed. There was a single blanket and he covered himself. Food had been taken care of and now they had given him a bed. He closed his eyes and fell asleep almost instantly.

His dreams were good ones. He had killed a Mist demon – he, 'Prasamaccus the Cripple'. In his dreams his leg was restored to health and beautiful maidens attended him.

He was not happy to be awakened.

'My friend, please accept my sincere apologies,' said Victorinus as Prasamaccus sat up, rubbing his eyes. 'I had to make my report, and I forgot all about you.'

'They fed me and gave me a place to sleep.'

'Yes, I see that. But I want you to be a guest in my home.'

Prasamaccus swung his legs from the bed. 'Can I have my bow back?'

Victorinus chuckled. 'You can have your bow, as many arrows as you can carry and a fine horse from my stable. Your own choice.'

Prasamaccus nodded sagely. Perhaps he was still dreaming after all.

7

For three weeks now Thuro had followed the instructions of Culain. He had run over mountain trails, chopped and sawed, carried and worked, and been 'killed' on countless occasions by a succession of swordsmen conjured by the Mist Warrior. His greatest moment had been when he finally beat the young Roman. He had noticed during their three previous bouts that his opponent was thick-waisted and unbending, so he had advanced, dropped to his knees and thrust his gladius up into the man's groin. The soldier had vanished instantly. Culain had been well pleased, but had added a cautionary note.

'You won, and should enjoy your triumph. But the move was dangerous. Had he anticipated it, he would have had an easy kill with a neck thrust.'

'But he did not.'

'True. But tell me, what is the principle of sword-fighting?'

'To kill your opponent.'

'No. It is *not* to be killed *by* your opponent. It is rare that a good swordsman leaves an opening. Sometimes it is necessary, especially if you find your enemy is more skilled, but such risks are generally to be avoided.'

After that Culain had conjured a Macedonian warrior from the army of Alexander. This man, grim-eyed and dark-bearded, had caused Thuro great problems. The boy had tried the winning cut he had used against the Roman, only to feel the hideous sensation of a ghostly sword entering his neck. Shamefaced, he had avoided Culain's eye but the Mist Warrior did not chide him.

'Some people always need to learn lessons the painful way,' was all he said.

One morning Laitha came to watch him, but his limbs would not operate smoothly and he tripped over his apparently enlarged feet. Culain shook his head and sent the laughing Laitha away.

Thuro finally despatched the Macedonian with a move Culain taught him. He blocked the man's sweeping cut from the left, swung on his heel to ram his elbow into the man's face and finished him with a murderous slice to the neck.

'Tell me, do they feel pain?'

'They?'

'The soldiers you conjure.'

'They do not exist, Thuro. They are not ghosts, they are men I knew. I create them from my memories. Illusions if you like.'

'They are very good swordsmen.'

'They were bad swordsmen – that's why they are useful now. But soon you will be ready to tackle adequate warriors.'

When he was not working Culain would walk him through the woods, pointing out animal tracks and identifying them. Soon Thuro could spot the spoor of the red fox with its five-pointed pads or the cloven hooves of a trotting fallow deer, light and delicate on the trail. Some animals left the most bewildering evidence of their passing; one such they found by a frozen stream, four closely-set imprints in a tight square. Two feet further on there were another four . . . and so on.

'It is a bounding otter,' said Culain. 'It kicks off with its powerful hind legs and comes down on its front paws. The rear paws then land just behind the front and the beast takes off for another bound, leaving four tracks close together. Obviously it was frightened.'

At other times Thuro would walk with Laitha, whose interest was trees and flowers, herbs and fungi. In her cabin she had sketches, richly coloured, of all kinds of plants. Thuro was fascinated.

'Do you like mushrooms?' asked Laitha, one day in early spring.

'Yes, fried in butter.'

'Does this look tasty?' She showed him a beautifully sketched picture of four capped fungi growing from the bole of a tree. They were the colour of summer sunshine.

'Yes, they look delicious.'

'Then you would be wise to remember what they look like. They are Sulphur Tufts and a meal of these would leave you in great

71

pain and probably kill you. What of this one?' It was a foul-looking object in cadaver grey.

'Edible?'

'Yes, and very nutritious. It also tastes pleasant.'

'What is the most dangerous?' he asked.

'You should be interested in the most nutritious, but since you ask it is probably this,' she answered, producing a drawing of a delicate white and yellow-green fungi. 'It is usually found near oak.' she said, 'and is called Death Cap; I leave it to you to guess why.'

'Do you never get lonely up in the mountains?'

'Why should I?' she replied, putting down her drawings. 'I have Culain as my friend, and the animals and birds and trees to study and draw.'

'But do you not miss people, crowds, fairs, banquets?'

'I have never been among crowds – or to a banquet. The thought does not thrill me. Are you unhappy here, Thuro?'

He gazed into her gold-flecked eyes. 'No, I am not lonely – not with you, anyway.' He was aware that his tone was too intense and he flushed deep red. She touched his hand.

'I am something you can never have,' she told him. He nodded and tried to smile.

'You love Culain.'

'Yes. All my life.'

'And yet you cannot have him, as I can never have you.'

She shook her head. 'That has yet to be decided. He still sees me as the child he raised. It will take time for him to realise I am a woman.'

Thuro closed his mouth, stopping the obvious comment from being voiced. If Culain could not see it now, he would never see it. Added to which, here was a man who had known life since the dawn of history. How many women had he known? How many had he wed? What beauties had lain beside him through the centuries?

'How did he find you?' asked Thuro, seeking to move from the painful subject.

'My parents were Trinovante and they had a village some sixty miles south. One day there was a raid by Brigantes. I cannot

72

remember much of it, for I was only five, but I can still see the burning thatch and hear the screams of the dying. I ran up into the hills and two horsemen pursued me. Then Culain was there with his silver lance; he slew the riders and carried me high into the mountains. Later we returned, but everyone was dead. So he kept me with him; he raised me and he taught me all I know.'

'It is hardly a surprise that you love him. I wish you success . . . and happiness.'

Every morning Culain would put Thuro through two hours of heavy exercise: running, lifting rocks, or making him hang by his arms from the branch of a tree and raise his weight until his chin touched the branch. At first Thuro could only raise himself three times before his arms would tremble and refuse the burden. But now, as spring painted her dazzling colours on the mountainside, he could manage thirty. He could run for an hour with no sign of fatigue, and he had despatched twelve of the ghostly opponents Culain created. The last had proved difficult; he was a Persian from the army of Xerxes and he fought with dagger and sabre. Four times he defeated Thuro before the youth won through. He did it by leaving a fractional opening twice, and covering late; the third time he lured the Persian into a lunge, side-stepped and cut his gladius into his opponent's neck. Culain had clapped him on the back and said nothing. Thuro was sweating hard, for the fight had lasted more than ten minutes.

'Now I think,' said Culain, 'that you are ready for the reasonable swordsmen.'

A movement to Thuro's left and a ghostly sword cut into his shoulder, numbing his left arm. He threw himself from the log on which he sat and rolled to his feet. The man before him was a blond giant over six feet tall, wearing a bronze helm adorned with a bull's horns. He held a longsword and was wearing a chainmail vest.

Thuro blocked the man's sudden charge, but his opponent's shoulder crashed into him, sending him sprawling to the grass. Thuro rolled as the longsword flashed for his head. With his enemy off-balance, he regained his feet and launched a blistering attack, but his arm was weary and he was beaten back. Three times he

73

almost found a way through, but his opponent – with his longer sword and greater reach – fended him off. Sweat dripped into the youth's eyes and his sword-arm burned. The warrior lunged, Thuro parried, swung on his heel and hammered his elbow into the man's face. The warrior staggered back and Thuro, still moving round, plunged his sword into the man's chest. As his enemy disappeared the young prince fell to his knees, his breath coming in great gasps. After several minutes his angry eyes locked on Culain.

'That was unfair!'

'Life is unfair. Do you think your enemies will sit back and wait until you are fresh? Learn to marshal your strength. Were I to produce another warrior now, you would not last five heartbeats.'

'There is a limit to every man's strength,' observed Thuro.

'Indeed there is – a good point to remember. One day, perhaps, you will lead an army into battle. You will be filled with the urge to draw your sword and fight alongside your men. You will think it heroic but your enemy will rejoice, for it is folly. As the long day wears on, all enemy eyes will be upon you and your weakening body. All their attacks will be aimed at you. So always bear that in mind, young prince. There is a limit to every man's strength.'

'And yet do the men you lead not need to know you will fight alongside them? Will it not raise their morale?' asked Thuro.

'Of course.'

'Then what is the answer to the riddle? Do I fight, or not fight?'

'Only you can decide that. But use your head. At some time in every battle, there is a moment when it can turn. Weaker men blame it on the Gods, but it has more to do with the hearts of the warriors. You must learn to read these moments, that is when you enter the fray, to the bitter dismay of your enemies.'

'How is such a moment recognised?'

'Most men recognise it only in hindsight. The truly great general sees it in an instant. But I cannot teach you that, Thuro. That is a skill you either have or do not have.'

'Do you have it?'

'I thought that I did, but when Paullinus lured me to attack him at Atherstone my talent deserted me. He sensed the moment and attacked, and my brave Britons collapsed around me. We outnumbered him twenty to one. An unpleasant man, Paullinus, but a wily general.'

Often, when not with either Culain or Laitha, Thuro would wander the hillsides, enjoying the freshness of spring in the mountains. Everywhere was colour: white-petalled wood anemone tinged with purple, golden celandine, mauve violets, snow-white wood sorrel and the tall, glorious purple orchid with its black-spotted leaves and petals shaped like winged helms.

Early one morning, with his chores completed, Thuro wandered alone in the valley below Culain's cabin. His shoulders had widened and he could no longer squeeze into the clothes he had worn a mere two months ago. Now he wore a simple buckskin tunic and woollen leggings over sheepskin boots.

He sat by a stream, watching the fish glide below the water until he heard a horse moving along the path. Then he stood and saw a single rider. The man spotted him and dismounted. He was tall and slender, with shoulder-length red hair and green eyes, and he wore a long-sword at his waist. He walked to Thuro and stood with hands on hips.

'Well, it has been a long chase,' he said, 'and you are much changed.' He smiled. His face was open and handsome and Thuro could detect no malice there.

'My name is Alantric,' said the newcomer, 'I am the King's Champion.' He sat down on a flat rock, tugged free a length of grass and placed it between his teeth. 'Sadly, boy, I have been instructed to find your body and bring your head to the king.' The man sighed. 'I do not like killing children.'

'Then return and say you could not find me.'

'I would like to . . . truly. But I am a man of my word. It is unfortunate that I serve a king whose character is less than saintly. Do you know how to use that sword, boy?'

'That you will find out,' said Thuro, his heart-rate increasing as fear wormed into his heart.

'I will fight you left-handed. It seems more fair.'

'I wish for no advantage,' snapped Thuro, regretting it as he spoke.

'Well said! You are your father's son after all. When you meet him, tell him I had no part in his killing.'

'Tell him yourself,' said Thuro.

Alantric stood and drew his longsword and Thuro's gladius flashed into the air. Alantric moved out on to open ground, then spun and lunged. Thuro side-stepped and blocked, rolling his gladius over the blade and slicing a thin cut on Alantric's forearm. 'Well done!' said the champion, stepping back, his green eyes blazing. 'You've been taught well.' He advanced once more, with care. Thuro noted the liquid grace of his enemy's style, the perfect balance and the patience he showed. Culain would have been impressed by this man. Thuro attacked not at all, merely blocking his opponent at every turn while studying his technique.

Alantric attacked, his sword flashing and cutting, and the discordant clash of iron on iron echoed in the woods. Suddenly the Brigante faked a cut, twisted his wrist and lunged. Caught by surprise Thuro parried hastily, feeling the razor-sharp blade slide across his right bicep. Blood began to seep through his shirt. A second attack saw Alantric score a similar wound at the top of Thuro's shoulder, close to the throat. The youth moved back and Alantric sprang forward. This time Thuro read the attack, swayed and lanced his gladius into Alantric's side. But the Brigante was fast and he leapt back before the blade had penetrated but an inch.

'You have been taught well,' he said again. He raised his sword to his lips in salute, then attacked once more. Thuro, desperate now, resorted to the move Culain had taught him. He blocked a thrust and spun on his heel, his elbow flashing back – into empty air! Off-balance, the young prince fell to the grass. He rolled swiftly, but felt Alantric's sword resting on his neck.

'A clever move, Prince Thuro, but you tensed before you tried it and I read your intent in your eyes.'

'At least I . . .' In the moment of speaking Thuro kicked Alantric's legs from under him and rolled to his feet. The Briton sat up and smiled.

'You are full of surprises,' he said as he stood and sheathed his sword. 'I think that I could kill you, but the truth is I do not wish to. You are worth ten of Eldared. It seems I must break my word.'

'Not at all,' said Thuro, sheathing his gladius. 'You were sent to look for my corpse. It is true to say that you did not find it.'

Alantric nodded. 'I could serve you, Prince Thuro . . . should you ever be a king.'

'I will remember that,' Thuro told him, 'as I will remember your gallantry.' Alantric bowed and walked to his horse.

'Remember, Prince Thuro, never let your enemy read your eyes. Do not think of an attack – just do it!'

Thuro returned the bow and watched as the warrior mounted and rode from sight.

Prasamaccus followed Victorinus to the Alia stables where the young Roman ordered a chestnut gelding with three white fetlocks to be saddled for the Brigante. Having not genuinely believed he would be allowed to pick his own mount, Prasamaccus was therefore not disappointed with the beast. Victorinus mounted a black stallion of some seventeen hands and the two rode west along the wide Roman road outside Caerlyn. They skirted Eboracum and continued west for an hour until they came to the fortress town of Calcaria.

'My villa is beyond the next hill,' said Victorinus. 'We can rest there and bathe.'

Prasamaccus smiled dutifully and wondered what, under the sun, was a villa. Still, the sun was shining, his leg felt almost at ease and he was not yet hungry again. All in all, the Gods must be sleeping. A villa, it turned out, was a Roman name for a palace. White walls covered with vines, a garden, terrace steps and pretty maidens running to take the reins of their horses. Gorgeous young creatures – all with teeth.

He fought to look dignified, copying the solemn expression on Victorinus' swarthy face. Unfortunately he could not slide from the saddle with the Roman's grace, but even so he climbed down sedately and made every effort to keep his limp to the minimum. It surprised him not at all when no one laughed. Who would laugh at the guest of so important a chieftain? They moved inside and Prasamaccus looked around for evidence of a fire, but there was none. The mosaic floor depicted a hunting scene in glorious reds and blues, golds and greens. Beyond this was an arch, and here the two men were helped from their clothes and offered goblets of warmed wine. It seemed bland compared with the Water of Life distilled in the north, but even so Prasamaccus could feel its heat slipping through his veins.

Yet another room contained a deep pool and Prasamaccus gingerly followed the Roman into the warm water. Below the surface there were seats of stone and the Brigante leaned his head against the edge of the bath and closed his eyes. This, he thought, was the closest to paradise he had ever known. After some twenty minutes the Roman climbed from the water and Prasamaccus dutifully followed. They sat together on a long marble bench, saying nothing. Two young girls, one as black as night, came from the archway bearing bowls of oil. If the bath had been paradise, there was little left to describe the sensation that followed as the oil was softly rubbed into their skin and then scraped away with rounded knives of bone.

'Would you feel better for a massage?' asked Victorinus, as the girls moved away.

'Of course,' said Prasamaccus, wondering if one ate it or swam in it.

Victorinus led them through to a side-room where two tables were placed next to each other. The Roman stretched his lean, naked frame out on the first and Prasamaccus took the second. Two more girls entered and began to rub yet more oil into their bodies, but this they did not scrape off. Instead they kneaded the muscles of the upper back, stroking away knots of tension of which Prasamaccus was previously unaware. Slowly their hands moved down, and the men's shoulders were covered with warm white cloths. The Brigante sensed the girl's uncertainty as she reached his ruined leg. Her fingers floated over the skin like moths' wings and then she began, with skilful strokes, to ease the deep ache that was always with him. Her skill was beyond words and Prasamaccus felt himself slipping towards the sleep of the blessed. Finally the girls stepped back and two male servants approached with togas of white. Dressed in one of these Prasamaccus felt faintly ridiculous and not a little overdressed. Yet another in an apparently interminable series of rooms followed. Here two divans were set alongside a table laden with fruit, cold meats and pastries. Prasamaccus waited while the Roman settled himself on a divan, leaning on his elbow, then the Brigante once more copied the pose.

'You are obviously a man of some breeding,' said Victorinus. 'I hope you will feel at home within my house.'

'Of course.'

'Your bravery in aiding us will not go unrewarded, though I can imagine your distress at being taken from your home and family must be great.'

Prasamaccus spread his hands and hoped his expression conveyed the right emotions – whatever they might be.

'As you no doubt know, there will be a war between the tribes that follow Eldared and our own forces. We will of course win, but the war will hamper our battles in the south against the Saxon and Jute. What I am saying is that it will be difficult to assist you in getting home. But you are welcome to stay.'

'Here in your villa?' asked Prasamaccus.

'Yes – though I don't doubt you would rather risk the perils of the road north. If that is the case, as I said, you must pick your own horse from the stable and I will assist you with supplies and coin.'

'Does Gwalchmai live here?'

'No. He is a soldier and lives in the barracks at Caerlyn. He has a woman there, I believe.'

'Ah, a woman. Yes.'

'How foolish of me!' said Victorinus. 'Any of the slaves who take your fancy, you may feel free to bed. I would recommend the Nubian, who will guarantee a good night's sleep. And now I must leave you. I have a meeting to attend at the castle but I will be back at around midnight. My man, Grephon, will show you to your room.'

79

Prasamaccus watched the Roman leave and then wolfed into the food. He was not hungry, but he had found it never paid to waste the opportunity to eat.

The servant Grephon approached silently, then cleared his throat. He watched as the Briton gorged himself, but kept his face carefully void of expression. If his master had chosen to bring this savage to the villa there was obviously good reason for it. At the very least the man must be a prince among the northern tribes and therefore, despite his obvious barbarism, would be treated as if he were a senator. Grephon was a life servant to the Quirina family, having served Victorinus' illustrious father for seven years in Rome; he ran the household with iron efficiency. He was a short man, stocky and bald – despite being only twenty-five – with round unblinking eyes, dark as sable. Originally he had come from Thrace, a boy slave brought into the Quirina household as a stable-boy.

His swift mind had brought him to the attention of Marcus Lintus, who had taken him into the household as a playmate for his son, Victorinus. As the years passed, Grephon's reputation grew. He was undeniably loyal, close-mouthed and with an eye for organisation. By the age of nineteen he was organising the household. When Marcus Lintus died four years ago, young Victorinus had asked Grephon to accompany him to Britain. He had not wished to come and could have refused, for he had become a freedman on the death of Marcus. But the Quirina family were rich and Grephon's future was assured with them, so with a heavy heart he had made the long journey through Gaul and across the sea to Dubris and up through the cursed countryside to the villa at Calcaria. Here he had staffed it and run it to perfection while Victorinus followed the High King as Primus Pilus, the first centurion to Aurelius' rag-bag auxiliaries. Grephon could not understand why a high-born Roman could concern himself with such a rabble.

He cleared his throat once more and this time the savage noticed him. Grephon bowed.

'Is there anything you desire, sir?' The man belched loudly.

'A woman?'

'Yes, sir. Do you have a choice in mind?' The Briton's pale blue eyes fixed on Grephon.

'No. You choose.'

'Very well, sir. Let me show you to your room and I will send someone up to you.'

Grephon moved slowly, aware of the guest's disability, and led him up a short stairway to a narrow corridor and an oak door. Beyond it was a wide bed, surrounded by velvet curtains. It was warm, though there was no fire. Prasamaccus sat down on the bed as Grephon bowed and departed. Damned if he would send the Nubian to such as this, he decided. He walked briskly to the kitchen and summoned the German slave girl, Helga. She was short, with hair like flax and pale blue eyes devoid of passion. Her voice was guttural as she struggled with the language, and though she was good enough at heavy work none had so far seen fit to bed her. She was certainly not good enough to catch Victorinus' eye.

He explained her duties and was rewarded by a look close to fear in her eyes. She bowed her head and walked slowly towards the inner house. Grephon poured himself a goblet of fine wine and sipped it slowly, eyes closed, picturing the vineyards beyond the Tiber.

Helga climbed the stairs with a heavy heart. She had known this day would come and had dreaded it. Ever since being captured and raped by men of the Fourth Legion in her native homeland, she had lived with the secret fear of being abused once more. She had almost come to feel safe within this household, for the men were happily indifferent to her. Now she was being used to humour a crippled savage, a man whose deformity would have ensured his death in her own tribe.

She opened the door to the bedroom to see the British prince kneeling by a hot air vent and peering into the dark interior. He looked up and smiled but she did not respond. She walked to the bed and unfastened her simple green dress, a colour that did not match her eyes.

The Briton limped to the bed and sat down.

'What is your name?'

'Helga.'

He nodded. 'I am Prasamaccus.' He gently touched the soft skin of her face, then stood and struggled to free himself from the toga. Once naked, he slipped under the covers and invited her to join him. She did so and lay back across his arm. They stayed motionless for several minutes and then Prasamaccus, feeling her warmth against his body, drifted to sleep.

Helga gently raised herself on one elbow, looking down into his face. It was slender and fine-boned, lacking cruelty. She could still feel the soft touch of his hand on her cheek. She had no idea what to do now. She had been told to make him happy, so that he could rest well. Now that he was resting, she should return to the kitchens. Yet if she did, they would question why she had returned so quickly; they would think he had sent her away and perhaps punish her. She settled down beside him and closed her eyes.

At dawn she awoke to feel a soft hand touching her body. She did not open her eyes and her heart began to hammer within her. The hand slid, so slowly, across her shoulder and down to cup her heavy breast. The thumb circled the nipple, then the touch moved on, up and over the curve of her hip. She opened her eyes and saw the Briton staring at her body, his face lost in a kind of wonderment. He saw that she was awake and flushed deep red, pulling the covers back over her. Then he lay down and moved his body more closely alongside her, softly kissing her brow, then her cheek and finally her lips. Almost without thinking she reached up and curled her arm over his shoulder. He groaned . . . and she knew. In that instant she knew it all, as if she held Prasamaccus' soul under her eyes.

For the first time in her life Helga knew the meaning of power. She could choose; to give, or not to give. The man beside her would accept her choice. Her mind flew back to the brutality of her captors, men she would like to have killed. But they were men unlike this one.

This man left her free to choose, not even understanding that he did so. She looked into his eyes once more and saw that they were

82

wet with tears. Leaning forward she kissed each eye, then drew him to her.

And in giving freely, she received a greater gift.

Her memories of lust and cruelty dissolved and returned to the past devoid of the power ever to haunt her again.

For several days Victorinus rose early and returned late, seeing little of his house guest who spent most of the time locked in his room with the kitchen-maid. The Roman had weightier problems on his mind. The Fifth Legion was stationed at Calcaria, auxiliary militia who were allowed home in spring to see to their farms and their families. Now, with Eldared and his Selgovae and Novantae allies ready to invade, and the Saxon King Hengist preparing to ravage the south, there was no way these auxiliaries could be allowed to disband for two months. Tension was running high among the men, many of whom had not seen their wives since the previous September, and Victorinus feared a mutiny.

Aquila had asked him to help build morale by offering coin and salt to the men, but this had not been enough and desertions were increasing daily. The choices were limited. If they allowed the men home, Eboracum and the surrounding countryside would be defended by only one regular legion – five thousand men. Ranged against them would be a possible thirty thousand. Alternatively, they could recall a legion from the south, but the Gods knew how badly the general Ambrosius needed men around Dubris and Londinium.

The third choice was to recruit and train a new militia, but this would be the same as sending children out against wolves. The Brigante and their vassal tribes were renowned warriors.

Victorinus dismissed the Nubian slave, Oretia, and climbed from his bed. He dressed and made his way to the central room, where he found Prasamaccus sitting by the far window staring out over the moonlit southern hills.

'Good evening,' said Victorinus. 'How are you faring?'

'Well, thank you. You seem tired?'

'There is much to do. Does Helga please you?'

'Yes, very much.'

Victorinus poured himself a goblet of watered wine. It was almost midnight and his eyes ached for the sleep he knew would evade him. It annoyed him that the Briton was still here after six days. He had only invited him so as to offset the rough treatment he had received in being gaoled, otherwise he would have placed him in the barracks with Gwalchmai. Now it looked as if he had a permanent house guest. The small fortress town was alive with rumours concerning the Brigante – all had him marked as a prince at the very least. Grephon had purchased some new clothes for him and these only added to the image: the softest cream wool edged with braid, leather troos decorated with silver discs, and fine riding-boots of softest doeskin.

'What is your problem?' asked Prasamaccus.

'Would that there were only one.'

'There is always one larger than the others,' said the Brigante.

Victorinus shrugged and explained – though he knew not why – the problems with the militia men. Prasamaccus sat silently as the Roman outlined the choices.

'How much of this coin is available for the men?' he asked.

'It is not a great sum – perhaps a month's extra pay.'

'If you allow some of the men home, the amount for each man left would grow, yes?'

'Of course.'

'Then make known the total amount on offer and tell the men they can go home. But explain that the coin will be distributed amongst those who choose to remain.'

'What will that serve? What if only one man remains? He would be as rich as Crassus.'

'Exactly,' agreed Prasamaccus, though he had no idea who Crassus was.

'I do not follow you.'

'No, that is because you are rich. Most men dream of riches. Myself, I have always wanted two horses. But the men who want to go home will now have to wonder how much they lose by doing so. What if – as you say – only one is left? Or ten?'

84

'How many do you think will remain?'

'More than half – if they are anything like the Brigantes I have known.'

'It would entail great risk to do as you suggest, but I feel it is wise counsel. We will attempt it. Where did you learn such guile?'

'It is the Earth Mother's gift to lonely men,' answered Prasamaccus.

His advice was proved right when 3,000 men chose to stay, earning an extra two months' pay per man. It eased Victorinus' burden and earned him plaudits from Aquila.

Three days later an unexpected guest arrived at the villa. It was Maedhlyn – hot, dusty and irritable from his ride. An hour later, refreshed by a hot bath and several goblets of warmed wine, he sat talking for some time with Victorinus. Then they summoned Prasamaccus. When the Brigante saw the portly Enchanter his heart sank. He sat quietly, refusing the wine Victorinus offered.

Maedhlyn sat opposite him, fixing him with his hawk-like eyes.

'We have a problem, Prasamaccus, one which we think you will be able to solve. There is a young man trapped in Brigante territory far to the north of the Antonine Wall in the Caledones mountains. He is important to us and we want him brought home. Now, we cannot send our own men, for they do not know the land. But you do, and could travel there without suspicion.'

Prasamaccus said nothing, but now he reached for the wine and took a deep draught. The Gods give, the Gods take away. But this time they had gone too far, they had allowed him to taste a joy he had previously believed to be fable.

'Now,' said Maedhlyn persuasively, 'I can magic you to a circle of stones near Pinnata Castra, some three days' ride from Deicester Castle. All you will need to do is locate the boy, Thuro, and return him to the circle exactly six days later. I will be there – and I will return every night at midnight thereafter in case you are delayed. What do you say?'

'I have no wish to return north,' said Prasamaccus softly. Maedhlyn swallowed hard and glanced at Victorinus as the Roman sat beside the Brigante.

'You would be doing us a great service, and would be well rewarded,' Victorinus told him.

'I will need a copper bracelet edged with gold, a small house, also enough coin to purchase a horse and supply a woman with food and clothing for a year. Added to this, I want the slave Helga freed to live in this house.' As he had been speaking, the colour left his face and he feared he had set the price at an awesome level.

'Is that all?' asked Victorinus and Prasamaccus nodded. 'Then it is agreed. As soon as you return, we will arrange it.'

'No,' said the Brigante sternly. 'It will be arranged tomorrow. I am not a foolish man and know I may not survive this quest. The land of the Caledones is wild and strangers are not welcome. Also the boy, Thuro, is the son of the Roman king. Eldared will wish him dead. It is not meet that you should ask me to undertake your duties, but since you have then you must pay . . . and pay now.'

'We agree,' said Maedhlyn swiftly. 'When do you wish the marriage to take place?'

'Tomorrow.'

'As a Druid of long standing I shall officiate,' declared Maedhlyn. 'There is an oak tree back along the trail and we shall travel there in time for the birth of the new sun. You had best tell your lady.'

Prasamaccus stood and bowed and, with as much dignity as allowed a limping man, returned to his room.

'What was that about marriage?' asked Victorinus.

'The bracelet is for her. It marks the Ring of Eternity and the neverending circle of life that springs from the union of love. Touching!'

8

Alantric knew his life would be forfeit should anyone find out about his meeting with the prince, so the only person he told was his wife Frycca, as she stitched the wound in his arm. Frycca loved him dearly and would do nothing to harm him, but she was proud of his gallantry and spoke of it to her sister, Marphia, swearing her to the strictest secrecy. Marphia told her husband, Briccys, who only told his dearest friend on the understanding that the secret was to remain locked within him.

Within two days of his return Alantric was dragged from his hut by three of Eldared's carles. Realising at once that he was doomed, he turned and shouted back to Frycca: 'Your loose tongue has killed me, woman!'

He did not struggle as they pulled him towards the horses, but walked with head down, totally relaxed. The guards relaxed with him and he tore his right arm free and smote the nearest man on the ear. As the guard staggered, Alantric pulled free the man's sword and plunged the blade into the heart of the second soldier. The third stepped back, dragging his own blade into the air and Alantric leapt for the nearest horse, but the beast shied. Now a dozen more guards came running and the King's champion backed away to the picket fence, a wild smile on his features.

'Come then, brothers,' he called. 'Learn a lesson that will last all your lives!'

Two men rushed in. Alantric blocked a blow, sent a backhand cut to the first man's throat and grunted as the second attacker's sword slid into his side. Twisting, he trapped the blade against his ribs and skewered the swordsman.

'Alive! Take him alive!' screamed Cael from the battlements above.

'Come down and do it yourself, whoreson!' shouted Alantric as the guards came in a rush. Alantric's blade wove a web of death and in the mêlée that followed a sword entered his back, tearing open his lungs. He sank to the ground and was hauled into the castle; he died just as Cael ran into the portcullis entrance.

'You stupid fools!' bellowed Cael. 'I'll see you flogged. Get his wife!' But Frycca, in her anguish, had cut her own throat with her husband's hunting-knife and lay in a pool of blood by the hearth.

Eldared's torturer worked long into the night on the others who had shared the secret, emerging with only one indisputable fact. The boy prince was indeed alive, and hiding in an unknown area of the Caledones mountains.

Eldared summoned Cael to him. 'You will go to Goroien and tell her I need the Soul Stealers. We have six people below whose blood should please her, and as many whelps as she needs. But I want the boy!'

Cael said nothing. Of all the dark legends of the mist, the Soul Stealers alone made him shiver. He bowed and left the brooding king to sit alone, staring into the hills of the south.

Thuro awoke still feeling the pain of the wound that had killed him, a lightning-fast roll and thrust from the Greek's short-sword. Culain helped him to his feet.

'You did well, better than I could have hoped. Give me another month and there will not be a swordsman to rival you in all of Britain.'

'But I lost,' said Thuro, recalling with a shiver the ice-cold eyes of his young opponent.

'Of course you lost. That was Achilles, the finest warrior of his generation, a demon with sword or lance. A magnificent fighter.'

'What happened to him?'

'He died. All men die.'

'I had already surmised that,' said Thuro. 'I meant how.'

'I killed him,' said Culain. 'I had another name then; I was Aeneas, and Achilles killed a friend of mine during the war against Troy. Not only that but he dragged the body round and round the city behind his chariot. He humiliated a man of great courage, and brought pain to the father.'

88

'I have heard of Troy. It was taken by a wooden horse with men hidden inside.'

'Do not be misled by Homer, for he was jesting. "Wooden Horse" is slang for a useless object, or for something pretending to be what it is not. It was a man who went to the Trojans pretending to betray his masters, the Greeks. The king, Priam, believed the man. I did not. I left the city with those who would follow me and fought my way to the coast. Later we heard that the man, Odysseus, had opened a side gate to allow Greek soldiers to enter the city.'

'Why did the king believe him?'

'Priam was a romantic who saw the best in everyone. That is how he allowed the war to begin, by seeing the best in Helen. The face that launched a thousand ships was merely a scheming woman with dyed yellow hair. The Trojan War was begun by her husband Menelaus and planned by Helen. She seduced Priam's son, Paris, into taking her to his city. Menelaus then sought the aid of the other Greek kings to get her back.'

'But why go to so much trouble over one woman?'

'They did not do it for a woman, or for honour. Troy controlled the trade routes and levied great taxes on ships bound for Greece. It was – as are all wars – brought for profit.'

'I think I prefer Homer,' said Thuro.

'Read Homer for enjoyment, young prince, but do not confuse it with life.'

'What has made you so gloomy today?' asked Thuro. 'Are you ailing?'

Culain's eyes blazed briefly, and he walked away towards his cabin. Thuro did not follow at first, but noticed the Mist Warrior glance back over his shoulder. The prince grinned, sheathed his gladius and followed to find Culain sitting at the table nursing a goblet of strong spirit.

'It's Gian,' said Culain. 'I have caused her distress; it is not something I intended, but she rather surprised me.'

'She told you she loved you?'

'Do not be too clever, Thuro,' snapped Culain. He waved his hand, as if to wipe away the angry words. 'Yes, you are right. I was

89

a fool not to see it. But she is wrong; she has known no other man and has lifted me to the skies. I should have taken her to a settlement long since.'

'What did you tell her?'

'I told her I saw her as my daughter, and could not love her more than that.'

'Why?'

'What sort of a question is why? Why what?'

'Why could you not take her to wife?'

'There was my second mistake, for she asked the same question. I have already given my heart; there can be no one else for me while my lady lives.' Culain smiled. 'But she will not have me because I choose to be mortal, and I cannot love her while she remains a goddess.'

'And this you told to Laitha?'

'Yes.'

'It was not wise,' said Thuro. 'I think you should have lied. I am not versed in the ways of women, but I think Laitha would forgive you anything except being in love with someone else.'

'I can do many things, Thuro, but I cannot turn back the hours of my life. I would not wish pain on Gian, but it is done. Go to her; help her to understand.'

'Not an easy task, and the more difficult for me because I do love her, and would take her to wife tomorrow.'

'I know that – so does she. So you are the one who should go to her.'

Thuro stood, but Culain waved him to his chair once more. 'Before you go, there is something I want you to see and a gift I wish you to have.' He fetched a bowl of water and placed it before the prince. 'Look deeply into the water, and understand.' Culain took a golden stone from his pocket and held it over the bowl until the water misted. Then he left the cabin, pulling shut the door behind him.

Thuro gazed down to find himself staring into a candle-lit room, where several men stood silently around a wide bed in which lay a slender child with white-blond hair. A man Thuro recognised as Maedhlyn leaned over and placed his hand on the child's head.

90

'His spirit is not here,' came Maedhlyn's voice, whispering inside Thuro's mind. 'He is in the Void; he will not return.'

'Where is this Void?' came another voice that brought a pang of deep sadness to the boy. It was Aurelius, his father.

'It is a place between Heaven and Hell. No man can fetch him back.'

'I can,' said the king.

'No, sire. It is a place of Mist Demons and darkness. You will be lost, even as the boy is lost.'

'He is my son. Use your magic to send me there. I command it!'

Maedhlyn sighed. 'Take the boy into your arms and wait.'

The water misted once more and Thuro saw the child wandering in a daze on a dark mountainside, his eyes blank and unseeing. Around him stalked black wolves with red eyes and slavering jaws. As they crept towards the child, a shining figure appeared bearing a terrible sword. He smote the wolves and they fled. Then he swept the child into his arms and knelt with him by a black stream where no flowers grew. The child awoke then and cuddled into the chest of the man, who ruffled his hair and told him all was well. Three terrible beasts approached from a sudden mist, but the king's sword shone like fire.

'Back!' he said. 'Or die. The choice is yours.'

The beasts looked at him, gauging his strength, then returned to the mist.

'I will take you home, Thuro,' said the king. 'You will be well again.' His father kissed him then.

Thuro's tears splashed to the bowl, disturbing the scene, but just as it faded a dark shadow flitted across his vision.

Culain entered silently. 'Gian said you regretted having no memory of the scene. I hope it was a gift worth having.'

Thuro cleared his throat and wiped his eyes. 'I am more in your debt now than ever. He came into Hell to find me.'

'For all his faults he was a man of courage. By all the laws of Mystery he should have died there with you, but such men are made to challenge the immutability of such laws. Be proud, Thuro.'

'One more question, Culain. What kind of man has a grey face and opal eyes?'

'Where did you see such a man?'

'Just as the vision faded, I saw a man in black running forward with a sword raised. His face was grey and his eyes clouded, like a blind man – only he was not blind.'

'And you felt he was looking at you?'

'Yes. There was no time to feel fear; it was gone in an instant.'

'Fear is what you should feel, for the man was a Soul Stealer, a drinker of blood. They exist in the Void and none know their origins. It was a source of great interest in the Feragh. Some contend they are the souls of the evil slain, others that they come from a race similar to our own. Whatever the truth they are dangerous, for their speed is like nothing human and their strength is prodigious. They feed on blood and nothing else, and cannot stand strong sunlight; it causes their skin to blister and peel, and eventually can kill them.'

'Why would I see one?'

'Why indeed? But remember you were looking into the Void, and that is their home.'

'Can they be slain?'

'Only with silver, but few men can stand against them even then. They move like shadows and strike before a warrior can parry. Their knives and swords do not cut, they merely numb. Then a man feels their long hollow teeth in his throat, drawing his life-blood. Give me your gladius.'

Thuro offered the weapon hilt first. Culain ran his golden stone along both edges of the blade, then returned it. The prince examined it, but could see no change.

'Let us hope you never do,' said Culain.

Thuro found Laitha in the upper mountains, sitting on a flat rock and sketching a purple butterburr. Her eyes were red-rimmed and the sketch was not of her usual high quality.

'May I join you?'

She nodded and placed her parchment and charcoal stick to her left. She was wearing only a light green woollen tunic and her fingers and arms were blue with cold. He removed his own sheep-skin jerkin and draped it over her shoulders.

'He told you then,' she said, not looking at him.

'Yes. It is cold here – let us go back to your cabin and light a fire.'

'You must think me very foolish.'

'Of course I do not. You are one of the brightest people I have ever met. The only foolishness is Culain's. Now let's go back.' She smiled wanly and climbed from the rock. The sun was sinking in fire and a bitter wind was whispering through the rocks.

Back at the cabin, with the fire roaring in the hearth, she sat before the flames hugging her knees. He sat opposite her, nursing a goblet of watered wine from a cask in the back room.

'He loves someone else,' she said.

'He has loved her since before you were born – and he is not a fickle man. You would not love him yourself if he were.'

'Did he ask you to speak for him?'

'No,' lied Thuro. 'He merely told me how distressed he was to cause you pain.'

'It was my own fault. I should have waited a year; it was not so long. I am still lean like a boy; I will be more womanly next year. Perhaps by then he will realise his own true feelings.'

'And perhaps not,' warned Thuro softly.

'She is not here – whoever she is. I am here. He will come to me one day.'

'You are already beautiful, Laitha, but I think you underestimate him. What is a year to a man who has tasted eternity? He will never love you in the way you desire. Your passion will hurt you both.'

Her eyes came up and the look hit him like a blow. 'You think I don't know why you are saying this? You want me yourself. I can see it in your moon-dog eyes. Well, you won't have me. Ever! If I can't have Culain, I will have no man.'

'Fifteen is a little young to make such a decision.'

'Thank you for that advice, Uncle.'

'Now you are being foolish, Laitha. I am not your enemy and you gain nothing by hurting me. Yes, I love you. Does that make me a villain? Have I ever pressed my suit upon you?'

She stared into the flames for several minutes, then smiled and reached out to touch his hand. 'I am sorry, Thuro. Truly. I am so hurt inside I just want to strike out.'

'I have something to thank you for,' he said. 'You told Culain about me wanting to recall the day my father held me, and he used his magic Stone to bring it to pass.' He went on to explain about the vision, and how Culain had touched his sword.

'Let me see,' she asked.

'There is nothing to see.' He drew the gladius and the blade shone like a mirror.

'He has turned it to silver,' said Laitha.

A dark shadow flitted by the window and Thuro hurled himself across the room just as the door began to open. His shoulder slammed into the wood and the door closed with a crash. Thuro fumbled for the bar, dropping it into place.

'What is happening?' cried Laitha and Thuro swung round. The window was shuttered and barred against the cold. The door to the back room opened and a dark shadow swept across the hearth. Laitha, half rising, slumped to the floor as a grey blade touched her flesh. Thuro dived to his left, rolled and rose. With preternatural speed the shadow closed on him and his blade flashed up instinctively, slicing through the dark, billowing cloak. There was an unearthly cry, and Thuro saw a corpse-grey face and opal eyes just before the creature vanished in smoke. A stench filled the room that caused Thuro to retch. Dropping to his knees, he crawled to Laitha; her eyes were open, but she was unmoving. He ran into the back room just as a second shadow darkened the window; his sword snaked out and the apparition fled back into the night. He slammed the shutters and barred them.

Returning to Laitha, he stared into her eyes. She blinked. 'If you can hear me, blink twice.' She did so. 'Now blink once for yes, twice for no. Is there any movement at all in your limbs?' Twice she blinked.

A crash came at the window and a sword-blade shattered the wood. Thuro, his own gladius burning with blue fire, ran to the window and waited. A second crash came from the back room, then another unearthly cry rose from outside the cabin and Thuro risked a glance through the shattered window.

Culain was standing alone in the clearing, his silver lance in his hands. Three figures moved towards him with blistering speed. He dropped to his knees, the lance flashing and lunging. Two cloaked assassins fell. Thuro tore open the cabin door and rushed into the night as four others closed on Culain.

'No, Thuro!' bellowed Culain, but it was too late for a Soul Stealer flew at the prince. Thuro blocked a thrust and sliced his silver blade across his enemy's throat and the creature vanished. Two others were on their way. Culain attacked the two facing him, blocking and cutting, despatching one with a thrust to the belly. The second advanced, but Culain pressed a stud in the lance and a sharp silver blade flashed through the air and into the Soul Stealer's chest.

Thuro managed to kill the first of the assassins, but the second sank a cold knife between his ribs. All strength fled from him and his legs gave way. He fell on his back and saw the grey face looming above him, huge hollow teeth descending towards his throat.

Culain ran forward three paces, then threw the heavy lance. It sliced into the creature's back, plunging through to jut from its chest. It vanished, and the lance fell to the ground beside Thuro.

Culain lifted the paralysed prince and carried him into the cabin where Laitha was beginning to stir. 'Get the fire built up and lock the door,' he said.

He moved to her bow and emptied her quiver. There were twenty arrows. He touched his Sipstrassi Stone to the head of each but nothing happened. Culain lifted Thuro's gladius; once more it was iron.

'What were they?' asked Laitha, rubbing limbs that ached with cold.

'Void killers. We are no longer safe here. Come here!' As she approached he lifted her hand. A copper bracelet graced her left wrist and he touched the Stone to it. 'If ever it shines silver, you know what it will mean?'

She nodded. 'I am sorry, Culain. Will you forgive me?'

95

'There is nothing to forgive, Gian Avur. I should have told you about my lady, but I have not seen her for more than forty years.'

'What is her name?'

'Her name is an old one, meaning Light into Life. She is called Goroien.'

Culain sat up through the night, but the Soul Stealers did not return. Thuro awoke in the morning, his head seemingly full of wool, his movements slow and clumsy. Culain took him outside and the crisp air drove the drowsiness from him.

'They will come again,' said Culain. 'There is no end to them. They did not expect you to be armed with silver.'

'I cannot stand against them, they are too fast.'

'I have spoken to you, Thuro, of Elearimas, the Emptying. It is something you will need to master. Skill is not enough, speed is insufficient; you must free your instinct, empty your mind.'

'I have tried, Culain. I cannot master it.'

'It took me thirty years, Thuro. Do not expect to excel in a matter of hours.' The sun was shining with golden brilliance and the events of the night seemed of another age. Laitha was still sleeping. The Mist Warrior looked gaunt and jaded, the silver at his temples shining like snow on the distant mountain peaks. Dark rings circled his eyes. 'Eldared has recruited an ally from the Feragh,' he said. 'No one else could open the Void. I thank the Source that you saw the vision, but who knows what will come next? Atrols, serpents, dragons, demons. The perils of the Mist are infinite. I blame myself, for I first used the floating gateways.'

'In what way?' asked Thuro.

'When I led Boudicca's Iceni against the Romans there was an elite Legion, the Ninth. They marched south from Eboracum to catch us and trap us between themselves and Paullinus. But I sent the Mist and they marched onto it and out of history.'

'The legendary Ninth,' whispered Thuro. 'No one has ever known of their fate.'

'Nor will any man. Even I. They died out of sight of their friends, their families and even their land.'

'Five thousand men,' said Thuro. 'That is power indeed.'

'I would not do such a thing again . . . but someone has.'

'Who has the power?'

'Maedhlyn. Myself. Maybe a dozen others. But that presupposes the lack of intellect and imagination in any of a hundred thousand worlds within worlds that make up the Mist. Perhaps someone has travelled a new road.'

'What can I do? I cannot just remain here until they find me, and it puts both you and Laitha in peril.'

'You must find your father's sword and your own destiny.'

'Find . . .? It was taken by a ghostly hand below the surface of the lake. I cannot travel there.'

'Would that it were truly so simple. But the sword is not in the lake – I have searched there. No, it is in the Mist and we must travel there to find it.'

'You said there were thousands of worlds within the Mist. How will we know where to search?'

'You are joined to the sword. We will take a random path and see where it leads us.'

'You will forgive me for saying that it does not sound very hopeful.'

Culain chuckled. 'I will be with you, Thuro. Though, yes, it will be like searching for one pebble in a rockslide. But better than waiting here for the demons to strike, yes?'

'When do we leave?'

'Tomorrow. I must prepare the path.'

'And we must spend one more night waiting for the Soul Stealers?'

'Yes, but we have an advantage now. We know they are coming.'

'A slim advantage indeed.'

'Perhaps as slender as the difference between life and death.'

9

I would not do such a thing again . . . but everyone . . .
Who has the power?

Maedhlyn, Maximus, Alaric, others. But that presupposes the task of training and preparation to any of . . . no clear thread would widen, could thus make up the Mist, for thus sequence but

Prasamaccus was grateful for the tears Helga shed so publicly as he mounted the huge black stallion, chosen this morning from Victorinus' stable. No warrior should leave on a dangerous hunt without such a display from a loving wife. He had been lucky, for Maedhlyn had been forced to wait five weeks after his magic disclosed to him that the passes into the Caledones mountains were all blocked by heavy snow. Prasamaccus had used the time well, getting to know Helga and she him. Happily they both liked what they found. The house on the outskirts of Calcaria had been bought by Grephon at a fraction of its value, the owner being terrified of the coming war. At the back of the small white building was a ramshackle paddock, and two fields that could be given over to crops.

Now Prasamaccus leaned over his saddle. 'Hush woman!' he said. 'This is not seemly.' But Helga's tears would not cease and it was with a happy heart that Prasamaccus rode alongside the Enchanter towards the remnants of the stone circle above Eboracum.

For his part Maedhlyn was less than happy with the choice of messenger-escort he was sending to Thuro. The slender blond cripple was obviously a man of wit, but hardly a warrior. And could he be trusted?

The Brigante cared nothing for the doubts he saw in Maedhlyn's sullen expression. The Caledones were, in fact, sparsely peopled, and the Vacomagi that did dwell in the foothills were renowned as a friendly tribe. With luck his mission would require no more than a six-day round journey and a swift return to his white palace. He glanced nervously at the sky; he had kept his face blank, but the gods had a way of reading men's eyes.

Only two broken teeth remained of the circle and Prasamaccus stood now where he had appeared six weeks before, overlooking the fortress city.

'You understand? Six days,' said Maedhlyn.

'Yes. I'll notch a stick,' replied Prasamaccus.

'Do not be flippant. You will appear above Pinnata Castra. In the mountains you will meet a man named Culain; he is tall, with eyes the colour of storm-clouds. Do not anger him. He will take you to the prince.'

'Storm eyes. Yes, I'm ready.'

With a muttered curse Maedhlyn produced a yellow-gold Stone and waved it over his head. A golden glow filled the circle. 'Ride west,' said the Enchanter and Prasamaccus mounted and headed the stallion forward. It shied, and came down running, directly at the largest stone. Prasamaccus closed his eyes. A smell like oil burning on cloth smote his nostrils, and his ears ached. He opened his eyes as the horse charged out of the circle where he had killed the Atrol. He pulled Vamera from his saddle pouch and strung her swiftly. Then, with an angry oath he hung the bow on his pommel.

'Stupid wizard,' he said. 'This is the wrong circle. I am days from the Caledones.'

Throughout the day Culain worked to assemble a circle of slender golden wire in the clearing below his cabin. He looped the wire around four birch trees, then marked the earth within the circle in a series of pentangles highlighted with chalk. At the centre of the circle he constructed a perfect square, measuring the distances with great care from the angles of the square to the furthest points of the pentangles.

At noon he stopped and Thuro brought him a goblet of wine, which he refused.

'This needs a clear head, Thuro.'

'What are you doing?'

'I am recreating the base layout of a minor Circle – creating a gateway, if you like. But if I am more than a hair's breadth out in my calculations, we will end up in a world or a time we do not desire.'

'Where is Laitha?'

'She is watching the valley for sign of Eldared's hunters.'

'Can I fetch you some food?'

'No. I must finish the circle and lay on the lines of magic. It will work only once; we will not be able to return here.'

'I will watch with Laitha.'

'No,' said Culain sharply, 'you are necessary here. This whole circle is geared to you and your Harmony. It is our only hope of finding the sword.'

Towards dusk Laitha came running into the clearing.

'There is a single rider moving up the valley,' she said. 'Shall I kill him?'

Culain looked bone-weary. 'No. No needless slaying. I am almost ready. Thuro, go with Laitha and see the man. Gian, stay hidden and if the rider has hostile intent, shoot him down.'

'I thought you needed me,' said Thuro.

'The work is nearly done, the destination set. We will leave at dawn.'

'Would it not be safer to leave now?' asked Laitha.

'The sun is almost gone, and we need its energies. No, we must survive one more night in the mountains.'

Thuro and Laitha set off to intercept the rider, moving swiftly down the forest trails. As Thuro ran behind the lithe girl he found his mind straying from concern at the horseman to appreciation of the supple, liquid grace of Laitha's movements.

Thuro spotted the rider moving carefully up the mountain trail and squatted down with Laitha behind a thick bush. The man rode a tall black stallion of almost seventeen hands and was dressed in a cream woollen tunic edged with braid and black troos decorated with small silver discs; he carried a dark bow of horn. He was in his early twenties, with fair hair and a straggly blond beard.

Thuro stepped out on to the path as Laitha notched an arrow to her bow.

'Welcome, stranger,' said Thuro.

The man reined in. 'Prince Thuro?'

'Yes.'

'I have been sent to find you.'

'Then step down from your mount and draw your sword.'

100

Laitha had no intention of allowing Thuro to fight and loosed her shaft. At that moment an owl fluttered from a nearby branch and the stallion shied. Laitha's arrow took the horse in the throat and it fell, throwing the rider into the bushes beside the trail. Thuro was furious. He ran forward and helped the man to his feet, noticing for the first time that the rider was a cripple. Laitha stood with a second arrow notched.

'Damn you!' yelled Thuro. 'Get out of my sight!' He moved to the horse which was writhing on the ground, and opened its jugular with his hunting-knife. 'I am sorry,' he told the man. 'It was none of my doing.'

'It was a fine horse – best I ever owned. I hope you have others?'

'No.'

The man sighed. 'The Gods give, the Gods take away.'

'Where is your sword?' asked Thuro.

'For what should I need a sword?'

'To fight me, of course. Or were you intending to use your bow?'

'Maedhlyn sent me to fetch you home. My name is Prasamaccus; I have been staying with Victorinus.'

Thuro!' called Laitha. 'Look!'

Further down the trail some dozen riders were following the tracks left by Prasamaccus.

'Your friends have arrived,' said the prince.

'No friends of mine. What I told you was true.'

'Then you had better follow me,' said Thuro. 'Here, let me carry your bow.'

Prasamaccus handed him the weapon and the trio set off, keeping away from the path. The sun was sinking now and the three faded from sight in the gathering gloom. They moved on for more than a quarter of an hour, forced to walk slowly to allow the limping Prasamaccus to keep up.

They reached the cabin as the moon cleared the clouds and Culain ran forward to meet them.

'Who is he?'

'He says Maedhlyn sent him,' answered Thuro, 'but Eldared's hunters are only minutes behind us.' Culain cursed.

101

A gasp came from Laitha and the three men swung towards her. She was holding up her arm and staring at the bracelet on her wrist; it had begun to glow faintly.

'The Soul Stealers,' whispered Thuro.

'Would it be possible to have my bow back?' asked Prasamaccus.

Culain drew a silver knife and held it gently to the Brigante's throat, then he took the Sipstrassi Stone from his pocket and touched it to the man's temple. 'Tell me why Maedhlyn sent you?'

'He said to bring the prince to the Circle of Stones near Pinnata Castra. Then he would spirit us both home.'

The knife returned to Culain's sheath. 'Give him his bow, and let me have the arrows.' The Mist Warrior touched his stone to each of the twenty arrow-heads and handed the quiver to Prasamaccus.

He notched an arrow to the string. The head shone with a white-blue light. 'Very pretty,' he said. A dark shadow sped from the trees and before Laitha could react Prasamaccus had drawn and loosed. The shaft took the assassin in the chest; the dark cloak billowed and fell to the ground, the Brigante's arrow beside it.

'Into the circle!' yelled Culain. More dark shapes moved into sight. Prasamaccus and Laitha both loosed shafts while Culain ran forward, sweeping up his lance from the ground beside the golden wire. 'Move to the central square,' said Culain. As Thuro, Laitha and Prasamaccus clambered over the wire, the Mist Warrior swung in time to block the thrust of a grey blade, cutting the lance-head through the assassin's neck. More of the shadows converged towards the circle. Culain leapt the wire, but a cold knife cut into his shoulder. As his limbs lost their power, he shouted one word. A golden light filled the circle, forcing the shadow killers back. Bright as noonday, the glare was blinding. When it faded the circle was empty, the golden wire gone, the earth smouldering.

Culain awoke in a broken circle of stones on the side of a high hill overlooking a deserted Roman fortress. He sat up and breathed deeply until the unearthly drowsiness left his limbs. The fortress below had partially collapsed, and several huts nearby had been constructed partly of stone from the ruined building. Culain glanced at the sky; a single moon hung there. The sky was clear and he examined the stars. He was still in Britain. He cursed loudly.

A glow began to his left and he swept up his lance and waited. Maedhlyn appeared.

'Oh, it's you,' said the Enchanter. 'Where is the boy?'

'Gone seeking his father's sword.'

'Alone?'

'No, he has a girl and a cripple with him.'

'Wonderful,' said Maedhlyn.

Culain pushed himself to his feet. 'It is better than him being dead.'

'Marginally,' agreed Maedhlyn. 'What happened?'

'Soul Stealers came upon us. I sent Thuro and the others through a gateway.'

'Which one?'

'I made it.'

'Made? Oh Culain, that was foolhardy indeed.'

'Worse than you know. I had to send them at night.'

'Better and better.' Maedhlyn sniffed loudly and cleared his throat. 'You look older,' he said. 'Do you need a Stone?'

'I have one, and I look older because I choose to. It is time to die, Maedhlyn. I have lived too long.'

'Die?' whispered Maedhlyn, his eyes widening. 'What nonsense is this? We are immortal.'

'Only because we choose to be. I choose not to be.'

'What does Athena say about this?'

'Her name is Goroien. We left that Greek nonsense behind centuries ago – and I have not seen her in forty years.'

'It is cold here. Let us return to my palace; we'll talk there.'

Culain followed him within the glow and the two walked down the long hill to Eboracum and the converted villa Maedhlyn owned near the southern wall. Inside a fire burned brightly in an ornate stone hearth. The Enchanter had always heartily disliked Roman central heating, claiming it made his head thick and disturbed his concentration.

'You used not to think it nonsense,' said the Enchanter, as they sat together drinking mulled wine by the fire. 'You made a wonderful Ares, a fine god of war. And we did help the Greeks after a fashion; we gave them philosophy and algebra.'

'You always were a capricious meddler, Maedhlyn. How do you maintain your appetite for it?'

'People are wonderful creatures,' said the Enchanter. 'So inventive. I never tire of them and their gloriously petty wars.'

'Have I mentioned before that I dislike you intensely?'

'Once or twice, Culain, now I come to recall – though I cannot understand why. You know I would have given my life to save Alaida . . .'

'Do not speak of her!'

Maedhlyn settled back in his deep leather chair. 'Getting old does not suit you,' he said. Culain chuckled, but there was little humour in the sound.

'Getting old? I *am* old – as old as time. We should have died with the waves that destroyed Balacris.'

'But we did not, thank the Source! Why did you leave Goroien?'

'She could not understand my decision to become mortal.'

'That's understandable. If you remember, she fell in love with the hero Gilgamesh and watched him age; some problem with his blood that the Stone could not overcome. But I can see how she would not want to watch such an event again.'

'I liked him,' said Culain.

'Even though he took Goroien from you? You are a strange man.'

'It was a passing fancy, and it is truly ancient history. What are your plans now, my Lord Enhancer? Now that someone else is playing your game?'

'Enchanter, if you please. And I am unconcerned. Whoever it is can never play as well as I. You should know that, Culain; you have witnessed my genius through the ages. Did I not inspire the building of Troy? Did I not take Alexander to the brink of domination? To name but two small achievements. You think Eldared's petty sorcerer can oppose me?'

'As always, your arrogance is a joy to behold. You seem to forget how it has humbled you in the past. Troy fell, despite your attempts to save it. Alexander took a fever and died. And as for Caligula . . . what on earth did you see in that boy?'

'He was bright as a button – much maligned. But I take your point. So who do you think is behind Eldared?'

'I have no idea. Pendarric has the power, but he tired of mortals long ago. Brigamartis, perhaps.'

'She took to playing the Gods' game with the Norse, but she's gone now. I haven't heard of her in a century or more. What of Goroien?'

'She would never use the Soul Stealers.'

'I think you forget how ruthless she could be.'

'Not at all. But not for someone else – not a petty king like Eldared. He couldn't pay enough. However, that is your problem now, Enchanter. I want nothing more to do with it.'

'You surprise me. If Eldared has the power to summon the Soul Stealers and open a gate on your mountain, then he has the power to send assassins after the boy wherever he is. I take it you left nothing belonging to the prince on the mountain?'

Culain closed his eyes. 'I left his old clothes in a chest.'

'Then they can find him. Unless you stop them.'

'What are you suggesting?'

'Find the power behind Eldared and slay it. Or slay the king.'

'And what will you be doing while I am scouring the countryside?'

'I will use this,' said the Enchanter, lifting a yellowed leather-covered wedge of parchment. 'It is the most valuable possession Thuro had. The works of Plutarch. Much of his Harmony remains in it. I shall follow him through the Mist.'

Prasamaccus gazed around him. The landscape had changed; it was more rugged and open, the mountains stretching out into the distance beyond an immediate wooded valley. And it was bright . . . he looked up, and his heart sank. Two moons hung in the sky, one huge and silver-purple, the other small and white. The Brigante feared he knew what such phenomena might mean, and it was not good news. There was no sign of the warrior with the storm-cloud eyes.

'Where is Culain?' screamed Laitha.

'He did not manage to reach the central square,' said Thuro softly. His eyes met those of Prasamaccus, who understood the unspoken thought. Culain had fallen among the Soul Stealers; both had seen it. Laitha began to search beyond the circle of white stones, calling Culain's name. Thuro sat down alongside Prasamaccus.

'I did not think anything could kill him,' said Thuro. 'He was an amazing man.'

'I regret not having known him,' said Prasamaccus, with as much sincerity as he could muster. 'Tell me, how do we get home?'

'I have no idea.'

'Strange, I thought you were going to say that. Do you know where we are?'

'I am afraid not.'

'I should have been a fortune-teller. I am beginning to know the answers to these questions before you speak. One last question. Does that second moon mean what I think it means?'

'I am afraid so.'

Prasamaccus sighed and opened his pouch, producing a small seed cake. Thuro smiled; he was beginning to like the crippled archer.

'How did you meet Victorinus?'

Prasamaccus swallowed the last of the seed cake. 'I was out hunting . . .' He told Thuro the tale of seeing the Atrols and fleeing to a stone circle, and of the journey with Maedhlyn back to Eboracum. He did not mention Helga; the thought of never seeing her again was too painful. Meanwhile Laitha wandered back into the circle and sat down, saying nothing. Prasamaccus offered her his last seed cake, but she refused.

'It's your fault, cripple,' she snapped. 'If we had not had to wait for you, we could have escaped with Culain.'

Prasamaccus merely nodded. It did not pay to argue with women.

'Nonsense!' stormed Thuro. 'If you had not killed the poor man's horse, we would have arrived the sooner.'

'You are saying it is my fault he is dead?'

'You are the one who introduced the question of fault, not I. Now if you cannot be civil, hold your tongue!'

'How dare you? You are not my kinsman, nor my prince. I owe you nothing.'

'If I might . . .' began Prasamaccus.

'Be quiet!' snarled Thuro. 'I may not be your prince, but you are my responsibility. It is what Culain would have wanted. '

'How would you know what he wanted? You are a boy; he was a man.' She stood and stalked off into the darkness.

'Arguing with women offers no reward,' said Prasamaccus softly. 'They are always right; I saw that in my village. You'll only have to apologise to her.'

'For what?'

'For pointing out that she was wrong. What are your plans, prince?'

Thuro sat back. 'Are you not angry with her for accusing you?'

'Why should I be? She was right; I slowed you down.'

'But . . .'

'I know, she killed my horse. But how far can we take this back? Had I not been riding into the mountains you would not have been delayed at all. Had you not been missing, I would not have been riding. Is it your fault? Arguing about it will not light us a fire, or find food.'

'You are very philosophical.'

'Of course,' agreed Prasamaccus, wondering what it meant. He stood and limped out beyond the circle, seeking twigs for a fire, but there were none. 'I think we should camp in those woods until morning,' he said.

'I'll fetch Laitha.'

'I'll do it,' said Prasamaccus swiftly, limping out to where she sat.

The trio found a sheltered hollow and lit a camp-fire against a fallen trunk. Without blankets or food they sat silently, each lost in thought. Laitha grappled with grief and ill-understood anger.

107

Thuro wondered what plan Culain might have conceived following their arrival. Would he have known this land? And if he had not, what would he have done? Set off north? South? Prasamaccus lay down beside the fire and thought of Helga. Five weeks of bliss. He hoped she would not have to wait for him too long.

When Thuro awoke Prasamaccus had already started a fire and four clay spheres were sitting in the flames. The prince stretched his cramped muscles. Laitha still slept.

'You are up early,' said Thuro, glancing at the dawn sky.

'Best to catch pigeons while they sleep. Are you hungry?'

'Ravenous.' Prasamaccus hooked a ball from the fire with a short stick, then cracked a rock to it. The clay split cleanly, taking all feathers from the bird. The meat was dark and similar to beef and Thuro devoured it swiftly, sucking clean the fragile bones.

'I found a high hill,' said Prasamaccus, 'and from there studied the land. I could see no sign of building, but there is some evidence of tilled fields to the west.'

He rolled another ball from the fire and split it; then he moved to where Laitha lay and gently pushed her shoulder. She awoke and he smiled at her. 'There is breakfast cooking. Come eat.' She did so in silence, careful to avoid even looking at Thuro.

'Why did Storm-eyes send you here?' asked the Brigante.

'To find my father's sword, the Sword of Cunobelin. But I do not know where to look, and I am not even sure that this is the world we were meant to enter. Culain said we needed the power of the sun, and we certainly left without that.'

Prasamaccus cracked another clay sphere and sat back quietly. He had Vamera and therefore a constant supply of food. When they found people, he could trade skins and meat and perhaps buy a horse eventually. He would not starve, but what of his wards? What skills could the young prince bring to bear on this new world, where he was not even a prince? The girl was not a concern, for she was young and pretty and her hips looked good for childbirth. She would not go hungry. Suddenly an unpleasant thought struck him. This was another world. Supposing it was the world of the Atrols, or other demons? He remembered the tilled fields and was partially relieved. Demons tilling fields were somehow less demonic.

'We will go west,' said Thuro, 'and find the owners of the field.'

Prasamaccus was relieved that Thuro had decided to be the leader; he was much more content to follow and advise and that way little blame could attach should matters go awry. The trio set off through the woods, following obvious game trails and coming across the spoor of deer and goat. The tracks were somewhat larger than Prasamaccus had known, but not so large that they gave cause for concern. By mid-morning they spotted the first deer. It was almost six feet high at the shoulders, which were humped, and it had a flap of skin hanging on its throat. Its antlers were sharp, flat and many-pointed.

'It would need a fine strike to kill that beast,' said Prasamaccus. He said no more, for his ruined leg was beginning to ache from the long walk. Thuro noticed his limp growing more pronounced and suggested a halt.

'We have only come about three miles,' protested Laitha.

'And I am tired,' snapped Thuro, sitting down against a tree. The Brigante sank gratefully to the grass. The boy would make a fine leader if he lived long enough, he thought.

After a short rest it was Prasamaccus who suggested they move on, smiling his thanks to Thuro, and towards late afternoon they emerged from the wood into a rolling land of gentle hills and dales. The distant mountains reared white and blue against the horizon, and in their shadow – some two miles further west – was a walled stockade around a small village. Cattle and goats could be seen grazing on a hillside.

Thuro gazed long at the village, wondering at the wisdom of walking in. Yet what choice did he have? They could not spend their lives hiding in the woods. The path widened and they followed it until they heard the sound of horsemen. Thuro stood in the centre of the road; Prasamaccus moved to the left, Laitha to the right.

There were four men in the party, all heavily armoured and wearing high plumed helms of shining brass. The leader halted his mount and spoke in a language Thuro had never heard. The prince swallowed hard, for this was a consideration that had not occurred to him. Whatever it was that the man said, he repeated it – this time more forcefully. Instinctively Thuro's hand curved around the hilt of his gladius.

'I asked what you were doing here,' said the rider.

'We are travellers,' answered Thuro, 'seeking rest for the night.'

'There is an inn yonder. Tell me, have you seen a young woman, heavily pregnant?'

'No, we have just come from the woods. Is she lost?'

'She is a runaway.' The warrior turned to his men, lifted his arm and the four horsemen thundered by. Thuro took a deep, calming breath. Prasamaccus limped towards him and spoke. The words were unintelligible, a seemingly rhythmless series of random sounds.

'What are you talking about?' asked the prince. Prasamaccus looked startled and swung towards Laitha, whose words were equally strange, though almost musical. Thuro clapped his hands and they both turned towards him. He slowly pulled clear his gladius, offering the hilt to Prasamaccus; the Brigante reached out and touched it. 'Now do you understand me?'

'Yes. How do you come by this magic?'

Laitha interrupted them with an incomprehensible question.

'Might be best to leave her like that,' said Prasamaccus. Laitha was becoming angry and she shook her fist at Thuro. As she did so, the copper bracelet on her arm slid down over her tunic sleeve and touched the skin of her wrist.

'Thuro, you miserable whoreson? Do not leave me like this.'

'I will not,' said Thuro. Her eyes closed in relief, then they flared open.

'What happened to us?'

'Culain touched my sword and your bracelet with his magic Stone. I suspect we are now speaking whatever language is common to this world.'

'What did the riders want?' asked Laitha, dismissing the previous problem from her thoughts.

'They were seeking a runaway woman – heavily pregnant.'

'She is hiding in those rocks,' Prasamaccus told them. 'I saw her just as we heard the soldiers.'

'Then let us leave her be,' declared Thuro. 'We want no trouble.'

'She is hurt,' said Prasamaccus. 'I think she's been whipped.'

'No! We have problems enough.'

Prasamaccus nodded, but Laitha walked away from the path and up the short climb to the rocks. There she found a young girl, no older than herself. The girl's eyes widened in terror and she bit her lip, her slender hand moving protectively across her swollen stomach.

'I shall not hurt you,' said Laitha, kneeling beside her. The girl's shoulders were bleeding and it was obvious a whip had been laid there with considerable force. 'Why are you hunted?'

The girl touched her belly. 'I am one of the Seven,' she said, as if that answered the question.

'How can we help you?'

'Take me to Mareen-sa.'

'Where is that?' The girl seemed surprised, but she pointed up into the hills where a shallow wood opened beyond a group of marble boulders. 'Come, then,' said Laitha, holding out her hand. The girl rose, and with Laitha's support began the climb.

Below them Prasamaccus sighed and Thuro fought to control his anger.

'Easier to tame a wild pony than a wild woman,' muttered the Brigante. 'Said to be worth the effort, though.'

Thuro felt the anger seep from him in the face of the man's mildness.

'Does nothing disturb you, my friend?'

'Of course,' said Prasamaccus, hobbling off in the wake of the woman.

Thuro followed, his eyes sweeping the hills for sign of the horsemen.

10

The vanguard of the Brigante army – some seven thousand fighting men – crossed the Wall of Hadrian at Cilurnum, moving on in a ragged line to the fortress town of Corstopitum. The force was led by Cael and spearheaded by seven hundred riders of the Novontae, skilled horsemen and ferocious swordsmen.

Corstopitum was a small town of fewer than four hundred people, and the council leaders sent messages of support to Eldared, promising supplies of food to the army on its arrival. They also ordered the withdrawal of the British garrison and the hundred soldiers marched to Vindomara twelve miles south-east. The town leaders in this larger settlement had studied the omens and followed the example of their northern neighbours. Once more, the garrison was expelled.

Eldared was winning the war even before the first battle lines had been drawn.

Now, kneeling behind a screen of bushes in the woods above Corstopitum, Victorinus studied the camp below. The Brigantes had pitched their tents in three fields outside the city, the Novontae riders further to the west beside a swift-flowing stream.

Gwalchmai moved silently alongside the swarthy Roman. 'At least two thousand more than we expected, and the main force still to come,' said the Cantii.

'Eldared is hoping his show of force will cow Aquila.'

'That is not unreasonable. The cities do not relish a war.'

Behind the two men waited a full cohort of Alia, four hundred and eighty hand-picked fighting men, trained for battle as either foot soldiers or *cohors equitana*, mounted warriors. Victorinus moved back from the bushes and summoned the troop commanders to him. As with the old Roman army the cavalry was split into turma – or troops – of thirty-two men each, with sixteen turmae to a cohort.

The commanders gathered around Victorinus in a tight circle as he outlined the night's plan of action. Each commander was given a specific target and the various counter-options open to him depending on the fortunes of the battle. Within such a ferocious skirmish the best-laid plans could come to nothing and Victorinus knew there would be no opportunity for tactical changes once the fight began. Each turma would accomplish its own task and then withdraw. Under no circumstances would one group go to the aid of another.

For more than an hour they discussed the options, then Victorinus walked among the soldiers checking weapons and horses and talking to the men. He wore, as did they, a leather-ringed breastplate and wooden helm covered with lacquered cow-hide, with scimitar shaped ear-guards tied under the chin. His thighs were protected by a leather kilt, split into five sections above copper-reinforced boots which had replaced the more traditional greaves. The men were nervous, yet anxious to inflict punishment on the proud Brigantes.

At one hour after midnight, with the Brigante camp silent, three hundred horsemen thundered down the hill. Four turmae rode to the Brigante supply wagons, overturning them and putting them to the torch. Another troop galloped to the Novontae picket line, killing the guards and driving the horses up and into the hills. Brigante warriors streamed from their tents, but a hundred veteran lancers led by Gwalchmai hammered into them, driving them back. Behind the lancers two turmae galloped around the tents, hurling flaming brands to the canvas. The camp was in an uproar.

High above Corstopitum, Victorinus watched with concern as the flames grew and the pandemonium increased.

'Now, Gwalchmai! Now!' whispered the Roman. But still the battle raged, and the Brigante leaders began to restore order. As Victorinus verged on the edge of rage, he saw Gwalchmai's lancers wheel into the 'flying arrow' formation and charge. The wedge, with Gwalchmai at the point of the arrow, sundered the gathering Brigante, and the other turmae galloped in behind the wings of the lancers as they broke clear into the fields. Several horses went down, but the main force escaped into the hills. In their wake Victorinus viewed with pleasure the burning wagons and tents and the scores of Brigante bodies that littered the fields.

The days of blood had begun . . .

Bitterness was so much part of Korrin Rogeur's life that he was hard pressed to remember a time when different emotions had fuelled his spirit. He stood now on the outskirts of the forest of Mareen-sa, watching the small group make its way down the hill towards the trees. He recognised Erulda and was pleased at her escape – though not for her sake, but for the chagrin it would cause the Magistrate. In Korrin Rogeur's world, the only moments of pleasure came when his enemies were discomfited.

He was a tall man, wand-slim, and wearing hunting garb of browns and dark greens which allowed him to merge with the forest. By his side was a longsword, and across his back a longbow of yew and a quiver of black-feathered arrows. His eyes were dark and a permanent scowl had etched deep lines into his brow and cheeks, making him seem older than his twenty-four years.

As the group grew closer he studied the woman helping Erulda. She was young, tall and lithe, long-legged and proud as a colt. Behind her came a fair-haired young man, and behind him a cripple.

Korrin scanned the skyline for sign of soldiers lying in wait, aware that the arrival of Erulda could herald a trap. He signalled the men hiding in the bushes then moved out on to open ground. Erulda saw him first and waved; he ignored her.

'And where do you think you are going, Pretty?' he asked Laitha.

Laitha said nothing. Her upbringing with Culain had lacked some of the finer points of communication. She drew her hunting-knife and stepped forward.

'My, my,' said Korrin, 'a ferocious colt! Do you plan to stick me with your pin?'

'State your business, Ugly, and be done with it,' she told him.

Korrin ignored her and turned to Thuro. 'Your women fight for you, do they? How pleasant.'

Thuro advanced to stand before the taller woodsman. 'Firstly, she is not my woman. Secondly, I do not like your tone. That may seem a small matter, especially as you have five men in the bushes even now, with shafts aimed. However, believe me when I tell you I can kill you before they can aid you.'

Korrin grinned and walked beyond Thuro to where Prasamaccus had seated himself on the grass. 'Your turn to offer me violence, I believe?'

'This is a foolish and foolhardy game,' said the Brigante, rubbing at his aching leg. 'There are soldiers hunting this girl, who could come riding over the rise at any moment. I take it from her reaction when she saw you that you are a friend, so why not act like one?'

'I like you, cripple. You are the first of your group to make sense. Follow me.'

'No,' said Thuro softly. 'We are looking for no trouble with the soldiers. You have the girl; we will leave.'

Korrin lifted his arm and five men stepped from the trees, arrows notched to taut bowstrings. 'I fear not,' he said. 'I must insist you join us for a midday meal. It is the least I can offer.'

Thuro shrugged, pulled Prasamaccus to his feet and followed the woodsman into the forest. Erulda ran forward to walk beside Korrin, linking her arm in his.

The pace was too swift for Prasamaccus, despite the fist that kept prodding his back, and on a slippery patch where the path rose he fell. As Thuro leaned to assist him, a dark-bearded woodsman kicked Prasamaccus in the back, hurling him to the ground once more. Thuro hit the man backhanded across the face, spinning him to the grass. A second man leapt forward, but Thuro spun and hammered his elbow into his attacker's throat. Prasamaccus scrambled to his feet as the others swarmed in to tackle the prince.

'Stop!' bellowed Korrin and the men froze. 'What is going on?'

'He struck me,' stormed the first woodsman, pointing at Thuro.

'You are a troublesome boy,' said Korrin.

'Ceorl kicked the cripple,' said another man. 'He got what he asked for.'

Ceorl swore and rounded on the speaker, but Korrin stepped between them.

'You fight when I tell you, never before. And you will not strike a brother, Ceorl. *Ever*. All we have is our bond, one to the other. Break it and I'll kill you.' He swung on Thuro. 'I will say this once: You are at present a guest, albeit a reluctant one. So curb your temper, lest you truly wish to be treated like an enemy.'

'There is a difference between the two?'

'Yes. We kill our enemies. Bear that in mind.'

They walked on at a reduced pace, and Prasamaccus was pleased to note the absence of the fist in his back. Still his leg was raging by the time they reached the campsite, a honeycomb of caves in a rocky outcrop. He, Thuro and Laitha were left to sit in the open under the eyes of four guards while Korrin and Erulda vanished into a wide cave-mouth.

'You must learn not to be so hot-headed,' said Prasamaccus. 'You could have been killed.'

'You are right, my friend, but it was a reaction. How is your leg?'

'It hardly troubles me at all.'

'She did not even thank me,' said Laitha suddenly. Thuro took a deep breath, but Prasamaccus tapped his arm sharply.

'It was a fine gesture nonetheless,' said the Brigante.

Laitha dipped her head. 'I am sorry I said what I did, Prasamaccus. You did not cause Culain's death. Will you forgive me?'

'I rarely recall words said in anger or grief. There is nothing to forgive. What we must decide is how to deal with our current situation. We appear to be sitting at the heart of a war.'

'Surely not,' said Laitha. 'This is just an outlaw band.'

'No,' put in Thuro, 'the girl was some kind of hostage. And if these men were truly outlaws, they would have searched us for coin. They appear to be a brotherhood.'

'And a small one,' said the Brigante, 'which probably makes them the losing side.'

'Why does that affect us?' asked Laitha. 'We mean them no harm.'

116

'What we may intend is not the point,' said Thuro. 'This looks to be a more or less permanent camp and now we know how to find it. If the soldiers question us, we could betray the brotherhood.'

'So? What are you suggesting?'

'Simply that we will either be slain out of hand or offered a place among them. The latter is more likely since we were not killed back in the hills.'

Prasamaccus merely nodded.

'So what should we do?' asked Laitha.

'We join them – and escape when we can.'

Korrin emerged from the cave and summoned Thuro. 'Leave your sword and knife with your friends, and follow me.' The prince did as he was bid and walked behind the woodsman deep into the torchlit maze of caves, arriving at last at a wide doorway cut into the sandstone. Korrin halted. 'Go inside,' he said softly. From within the entrance came a deep, throaty growl and Thuro froze.

'What is in there?'

'Life or death.'

The prince stepped into the shadow-haunted interior. Only one flickering candle lit the room beyond and Thuro waited as his eyes grew accustomed to the dark. In the corner sat a hunched figure, seemingly immense in the shadows. The prince approached and the figure turned and rose, towering over him. The head was grotesque, bulging-eyed and savagely marked, while the face was a mixture of man and bear. Saliva dripped from the jaws and though the figure was robed in white like a man, the huge paws that extended from the sleeves were clawed and bestial.

'Welcome to Mareen-sa,' said the creature, its voice deep and rolling, its words slurred almost beyond recognition. 'Tell me of yourself.'

'I am Thuro. A traveller.'

'A servant of whom?'

'I am no man's servant.'

'Each man is a servant. From where have you travelled?'

'I have walked the Mist. My world is far away.'

117

'The Mist!' whispered the creature, moving closer, its claws resting on Thuro's shoulder close to his throat. 'Then you serve the Witch Queen?'

'I have not heard of her. I am a stranger here.'

'You know, do you not, that I am ready to slay you.'

'So I understand,' replied Thuro.

'I do not wish to. I am not as you see me, boy. Once I was tall and fair, like my brother Korrin. But it does not pay to fall into the clutches of Astarte. Worse it is to love her, as I loved her. For then she does not kill you. No matter . . . go away, I am tired.'

'Do we live or die?'

'You live . . . today. Tomorrow? We will talk again tomorrow.'

The prince backed from the chamber as the hunched figure settled down in the corner. Korrin was waiting.

'How did you enjoy your meeting?' asked the woodsman. Thuro looked deeply into his eyes, sensing the pain hidden there.

'Can we talk somewhere?' The man shrugged and walked back towards the light. In a side chamber containing a cot and two chairs Korrin sat down, beckoning Thuro to join him.

'What would you like to talk about?'

'This may seem hard to believe, but I and my companions know nothing of your lands or your troubles. Who is Astarte?'

'Hard to believe? No. Impossible. You cannot travel anywhere on the face of this world without knowing Astarte.'

'Even so, bear with me. Who is she?'

'I have no time for games,' said Korrin, rising.

'This is not a game. My name is Thuro and I have travelled the Mist. Your land, your world, is new to me.'

'You are a sorcerer? I find that hard to take. Or are you really hundreds of years old and only pretending to be a beardless boy?'

'I came here – was sent here – by a man of magic. He did it to enable us to escape being murdered. That is the simple truth – question my friends. Now, who is Astarte?'

Korrin returned to his seat. 'I do not believe you, Thuro, but you gain nothing by hearing me speak of her, so I will tell you. She is the Dark Queen of Pinrae. She rules from ocean to ocean, and if sailors can be believed she controls lands even beyond the waters. And she is evil beyond any dream of man. Her foulness is such that if you truly have not heard of her you will not believe her depravity. The girl you helped was one of the Seven. Her fate was to be taken to Perdita, the castle of iron, and there to see her babe devoured by the Witch Queen. Think on that! Seven babes every season!'

'Eaten?' said Thuro.

'Devoured, I said, by the Bloodstone.'

'But why?'

'How can you ask a sane man why? Why does she destroy rather than heal? Why did she take a man like Pallin and turn him into the beast that he is becoming? You know why she did that? Because he loved her. Now do you understand evil? Every day that good man becomes more of a beast. One day he will turn on us and rend and slay, and we will have to kill him. Such is the legacy of the Witch Queen, may the Ghosts disembowel her!'

'I take it she has an army?'

'Ten thousand strong, though she has disbanded twice that number following her conquests of the Six Nations. But she has other weapons – dread beasts she can summon to rip a man to bloody ribbons. Have you heard enough?'

'How is it that you survive against such a foe?'

'How indeed? If she killed us now, how would we suffer? Allowing us to live and watch Pallin go mad, that is wondrously venomous. When we have been forced to kill him and our hearts are broken, then they will come.'

'She sounds vile indeed,' said Thuro. 'Now I understand what you meant about the bond of brotherhood. But tell me, why do the people stand for such evil? Why do they not rise up in their thousands?'

Korrin leaned back, fixing his dark eyes on Thuro as if seeing him for the first time. 'Why should they? I did not – until my wife's name was drawn from the list. Until they dragged her screaming from our home, carrying a babe I would never see. Life is not unpleasant in Pinrae. There is enough food and work and there are no enemies any longer across the borders. Now the only danger is

119

to pregnant women – and only twenty-eight of those a year from a nation of who knows how many thousand? No, why should a man seek to overthrow such a benign ruler? Unless his wife and child are slain . . . unless his brother is turned into a foul monster, doomed to be killed by his own kin.'

'How long has Astarte ruled Pinrae?'

Korrin shrugged. 'That is a matter for historians. She has always been Queen. And yet to look at her . . . My brother journeyed to the castle of iron to plead for Ishtura, my wife. The Queen took him to her bosom and he fell for her golden beauty. What a price he paid to bed her!'

'Why do you not flee the land?' asked the prince.

'To where? Across the oceans? Who knows what evil dwells there? No, I shall stay and attempt all in my power to destroy her, and all who serve her. What a burning there will be on that glad day!'

Thuro rose. 'Oil never killed a fire,' he said softly. 'I think I will return to my friends.'

'The fire I shall light will never be put out,' said Korrin, his eyes gleaming in the torchlight. 'I have the names on a scroll of life. And when she is dead others will be named, and they can follow her screaming into darkness.'

'The names of people who did not fight her?'

'Exactly.'

'Names like yours – before they took your wife?'

'You do not understand. How could you?'

'I hope I never do,' said Thuro, walking out into the corridor and on into the warmth of the afternoon sun.

Thuro and the others were not called to see the man-beast Pallin during the next four days, and Korrin Rogeur all but ignored them. Prasamaccus was infuriated at the lack of skill shown by the brotherhood's hunters, who returned empty-handed at dusk each day, complaining that the deer were too fast, too canny, or that their bows were not strong enough, their shafts not straight enough. On the fourth day they brought back a doe whose meat was so tough as to be indigestible. Prasamaccus sought out Korrin as the woods-man was setting off to scout in the north.

'What is it, cripple' I have little time.'

'And little food . . . and even less skill.'

'Make your meaning plain.'

'You do not have a huntsman in your tiny army who could hit a barn wall from the inside – and I am tired of chewing on roots or meat unfit for a hunter. Let me take my bow and bring some fresh meat to the caves.'

'Alone?'

'No. Give me someone who has a little patience and will do as he is told.'

'You are arrogant, Prasamaccus,' said Korrin, using the Brigante's name for the first time.

'Not arrogant, merely tired of being surrounded by incompetents.'

Korrin's eyebrows rose. 'Very well. Do you have anyone in mind?'

'The quiet one who spoke out against Ceorl.'

'Hogun is a good choice. I'll tell him to kill you if you so much as appear to be trying to escape.'

'Tell him what you wish – but tell him now!'

Thuro watched as the two men left the clearing, Prasamaccus limping behind the taller Hogun. Korrin Rogeur approached him. 'Can he use that bow?'

'Time will tell,' said Thuro. Korrin shook his head and departed with four other men. Laitha sat beside the prince.

'They brought in three other pregnant women last night,' she told him. 'I heard them talking. It seems Korrin raided a convoy they were with: four soldiers killed and several others wounded.

Thuro nodded. 'It is his only chance to hurt Astarte – rob her of her sacrifices. But he is doomed, poor man, just like his brother.'

'While he lives, there is hope – so Culain used to say.'

Thuro nodded. 'There is truth in that, I suppose. But there are not more than fifty men here – against an army of ten thousand. They cannot win. And have you noticed the lack of organisation?

It is not just that they lack skill as huntsmen, but they do nothing but sit and wait for Pallin to go mad. There are not enough scouts out to adequately protect the camp; they have no meetings to discuss strategy; they do not even practise with their weapons. A more disorganised band of rebels I have never heard of; they wear defeat like a cloak.'

'Perhaps they were just waiting for a prince with your battle experience,' snapped Laitha.

'Perhaps they were!' Thuro pushed himself to his feet and approached the nearest guard, a hulking youngster armed with a longbow. 'What is your name?' asked Thuro.

'Rhiall.'

'Tell me, Rhiall, if I were to walk from this camp what would you do?'

'I would kill you. Would you expect me to wave?' This brought a chuckle from the other three guards who had gathered around.

'I do not think you could kill me with that bow – not were I ten feet tall, six feet wide and riding a giant tortoise.' The other men grinned at Rhiall's discomfort. 'What is there for the rest of you to smile about? You!' hissed Thuro, pointing at a lean man with a dark beard and green eyes. 'Your bow is not even strung. Were I to run yonder into the trees you would be useless.'

'It doesn't pay to be insulting boy,' said the huntsman.

'Wrong,' Thuro told him. 'It does not pay to insult *men*. What are you, runaway servants? Clerics? Bakers? There is not a warrior amongst you.'

'That does it!' said the lean man. 'It is time someone taught you a lesson in manners, boy.' Thuro stepped back, allowing the man to draw his longsword, then the prince's gladius snaked into the sunlight.

'You are right about lessons, forester.' The prince leapt lithely back as the huntsman raised his sword and charged, slashing the weapon in a vicious arc towards Thuro's left side. The prince blocked the sweep with ease, pivoted on his heel and hammered the man from his feet. The huntsman's sword flew through the air to clatter against the trunk of a nearby tree. 'Lesson One,' said Thuro. 'Rage is no brother to skill.'

122

A second man came forward, more carefully. Thuro engaged him and their blades whispered together. He was more skilful than his comrade, but he had not been trained by Culain lach Feragh. Thuro stepped forward, rolled his sword over his opponent's blade, then flicked his wrist. The huntsman's sword followed that of his comrade and the man backed away, but Thuro sheathed his gladius. 'Laitha, come over here!'

Scowling, the forest girl obeyed. Thuro turned to the guards. 'I will not lower myself to best you with the bow, but I'll wager my sword against your bows that even this woman can outshoot you.'

'I'll take that wager,' said the lean man.

'I'll not play your games,' stormed Laitha. Thuro swung on her, lashing his open hand across her face; she staggered back, shocked and hurt.

'This time you will do exactly as I say,' snapped Thuro, his eyes blazing. 'I have had enough of your childish outbursts. We are here because of your stupidity. Act your age, woman! And think of Culain!'

At the mention off his name Laitha's anger flowed from her and she walked to the nearest man. 'Name a target,' she whispered.

'The tree yonder,' said Rhiall.

'I said a target, not a monument of nature!'

'Then you name one.'

'Very well.' Leaning forward, she deftly scooped Rhiall's dark cap from his head and walked to the tree he had indicated. There she drew her hunting-knife and plunged it through the hat, pinning it to the trunk. Then she paced out thirty steps and waited for the men to join her.

Rhiall strung his bow and notched an arrow. 'That was a good hat,' he grumbled as he pulled back the string, aimed and loosed. The shaft glanced from the trunk and vanished into the forest. The second man's shot missed the hat by a foot; the third man clipped the rim, bringing applause from the others. Lastly the lean huntsman took aim; his shaft hit the handle of Laitha's knife and failed to pierce the target.

'Shoot again,' said Laitha. He did so and scored a full hit in the crown of the hat. Laitha took Rhiall's bow and paced off another ten steps. She turned, drew back the string, froze, released her breath and loosed. The shaft slammed through the crown of the hat alongside the lean man's arrow.

He sniffed loudly and walked to her mark, then took aim and released the string. The arrow creased the rim. Laitha moved back another ten paces and pierced the hat again. Then she approached Thuro, dropped the bow at his feet and leaned in close.

'Touch me again,' she whispered, 'and I'll kill you.' Turning her back, she returned to her place near the circle of rocks. The lean huntsman stepped forward.

'My name is Baldric. Perhaps you would teach me the move that disarmed me?'

'Gladly,' said Thuro. 'And if you wish to live beyond the spring you should practise your skills. One day soon the soldiers will come.'

'It's not the soldiers we fear,' said Baldric, 'It's the Vores.'

'Vores? I have not heard the name.'

'Great cats. They can crush an ox-skull in their jaws. Astarte uses them for sport – hunting the likes of us. Once they are loosed in the forest, we are truly lost.'

'If the beast is mortal, it can be slain. If one can be slain, ten can die – or a hundred. What you need is to plan for the moment the Vores are loosed.'

'How can you plan to fight a creature that runs faster than a horse and kills with either paw or fang? There used to be Vore hunts when I was a boy: twenty men with bows, another ten on horseback with long lances. And still men would die in the hunt. And here we are talking of twenty Vores, or thirty. And we have no hunting horses and no lances.'

'You are a pitiful bunch, to be sure. The Vores eat meat?'

'Of course.'

'Then set traps. Dig pits, with sharpened stakes at the foot. A man is never beaten until the last drop of his blood drips from the wound. And if you haven't the heart to fight, then leave the forest. But do not dither in the shadows.'

'What is your interest?' asked the hulking Rhiall. 'You are not one of us.'

'Happily true. But I am here and you need me.'

'How so?' asked Baldric.

'To teach you to win. Savour the word. *Win*.'

A terrifying roar came from the cave-mouth and the men swung towards it. There, stark against the rock face, was a towering bear with no semblance of humanity. It saw the men gathered around Thuro, dropped on all fours . . .

. . . and charged.

The beast which had been Pallin moved at ferocious speed, hammering into the group before they could run. Rhiall, the slowest to move, was hurled ten feet in the air to land unconscious by a tall rock. The others were thrown to the ground, where they scrambled to their feet to sprint for the relative safety of the trees. Thuro dived to his left, rolling on his shoulder and rising as the beast reared up on its hind legs, its great talons raking the air. The prince drew his gladius and backed away. The bear advanced, dropped to all fours and charged again. This time Thuro leapt high, coming down on the beast's back with sword raised; but he could not plunge it into the creature's neck, knowing what it once had been. The bear began to thrash around, seeking to dislodge the young warrior. In his efforts to hold on Thuro dropped his sword; it fell to the beast's back and a blinding white light blazed from the blade. The bear dropped without a sound and Thuro jumped clear of the falling body. The bestial features softened and the young Briton watched as the fur shrank back to reveal the half-human face he recalled from the first meeting deep in the caves. He retrieved his sword, noting the heat emanating from the blade – and the answer came to him.

'Laitha!' he shouted. 'Come quickly!' She ran to him and gazed in horror at Pallin's deformed features.

'Kill it quickly before it recovers.'

'Give me your bracelet. Now!' Swiftly she pulled the copper band clear and Thuro took it and held it to the twisted face. Once more light blazed and Pallin's features softened still further.

'What about the arrows?' whispered Laitha. 'Culain touched those also.'

Thuro nodded and she raced across the clearing to fetch her quiver. One by one Thuro touched the arrow-heads to the stricken half-beast – and each time more of the man emerged. At last the magic was exhausted and Pallin's face was clearly more human than before, but the taloned paws remained and the huge sloping, fur-covered shoulders. His eyes opened.

'Why am I not dead?' he asked, his anguish terrible to hear.

The guards ran forward and knelt before him.

'This young man restored you, Lord,' said Baldric. 'He touched you with his magic sword. Your face . . .' Baldric swept off his brass helm and held it before Pallin's eyes. The man-monster gazed at his distorted reflection, then turned his sad blue eyes on Thuro.

'You have only delayed the inevitable, but I thank you.'

'My friend Prasamaccus has another twenty arrows that were touched by magic. When he returns I will bring them to you.'

'No! Against Astarte we have no magic. Keep them safe. I am doomed, though your aid should grant me another month of life as a man.' He looked down at his terrible hands. 'As a man? Sweet gods of earth and water! What kind of man am I?'

'A good man, I think,' said Thuro. 'Have faith. What magic can do, magic can undo. Are there no Enchanters in this world?'

'You mean the Dream Shapers?' answered the man Baldric.

'If they work magic, yes.'

'There used to be one in the Etrusces – mountains west of here.'

'Do you know where in the mountains he lived?'

'Yes; I could take you.'

'No!' said Pallin. 'I want no one to risk danger for me.'

'You think there is less danger in these woods?' asked Thuro. 'How long before the Vores or the soldiers rip your brotherhood to pieces, or drag your people before Astarte to suffer your fate?'

'You do not understand: this is all a game to the Witch Queen,' said Pallin. 'She told me she could see my every movement, and would watch me slain by my brethren. Even now she has heard your plans and therefore has negated it. The Dark Lady watches us at this moment.'

The guards eased back from the stricken monster, glancing fearfully at the sky. Thuro himself felt a cold shiver on his back, but he forced a laugh and stood.

'Do you think she is the only power in the world?' he scoffed. 'If she is so invincible, why are you not dead? Can you hear me, Witch Queen? Why is he not dead? Come Baldric, lead me to the Dream Shaper.'

Two hundred miles away the silvered mirror shimmered as Astarte passed an ivory hand before it.

'You interest me, sweet boy. Come to me. Come to Goroien!'

11

At sunset Prasamaccus limped into the camp as Thuro and Baldric were preparing for their journey. Behind him came the red-faced Hogun, staggering under the weight of the deer the crippled Brigante had killed two hours before. Prasamaccus sank to the ground beside Laitha.

'What is going on?'

'The noble prince has decided to take on the Witch Queen,' she answered. 'He is heading off to some mountain range to find a wizard.'

'Why are you angry? He has obviously earned their confidence.'

'He is a boy,' she said dismissively.

Tired as he was, Prasamaccus rose and limped to the group where Thuro outlined the events of the day. The Brigante said nothing, but he sensed the growing excitement among the men. The man-beast Pallin had returned to the caves.

'How will you find the Dream Shaper?' asked Thuro.

As Baldric was about to answer Prasamaccus interrupted sharply: 'A word with you, young prince?'

Thuro followed the Brigante to a sturdy oak. 'You obviously disbelieve that the Witch Queen overlooks us, but that is an assumption and therefore unwise. Let the man lead us, but do not discuss the exact location.'

'She cannot be everywhere, she is not a goddess.'

'We do not know that. But she must have known the length of her spell on Pallin and she could have been watching for his death. Give me your sword.'

Thuro did so and Prasamaccus took three arrows from his quiver and ran them down the blade. 'I do not know if the magic can be transferred in this way, but I see no reason why not.' He returned the sword to the prince. 'Now let us find this Enchanter.'

'No, my friend. Pallin says that you and Laitha must remain. They will not allow all of us to leave the forest. Look after her and I will see you soon.'

Prasamaccus sighed and shook his head, but he said nothing and watched silently as the two men walked away into the shadows of the trees. Helga seemed so far away. The camp women gathered around the deer, quartering it expertly, and the Brigante lay down beside Laitha, covering himself with a borrowed blanket.

'He did not even say goodbye,' said Laitha.

Prasamaccus closed his eyes and slept.

Two hours later he was awakened by the point of a boot nudging his side. He sat up to see Korrin Rogeur squatting down beside him.

'If your friend does not return, I will cut your throat.'

'You woke me to tell me what I already know?'

Korrin sat down and rubbed at tired eyes. 'Thank you for the deer,' he said, as if the words were torn from him under duress, 'and I am grateful that your friend helped my brother.'

'Was your scouting mission successful?'

'Yes and no. There is an army camped now at the northern border – a thousand men. At first we thought they would enter the forest, but then they were ordered to dismount and return to their camp. It would seem this was around the time that the boy used his magic on Pallin.'

'Then he saved not only your brother, but your people as well,' said Prasamaccus.

'That is how it seems,' admitted Korrin. 'We are doomed here, and it galls me. When I was a child my father told me wonderful stories of heroes who could overcome impossible odds. But that is not life is it? There are thirty-four fighting men here. *Thirty-four*. Not exactly an army.'

'Look at it from Astarte's point of view,' said the Brigante. 'You are important enough to merit the attention of one-tenth of her army. She must fear you, for some reason.'

'We have nothing she should fear.'

129

'You have a flame here, Korrin. Admittedly it is a small flame, but I once saw an entire forest consumed from the glowing coals of a carelessly lit camp-fire. That is what she fears: that your flame will grow.'

'I am tired, Prasamaccus. I will see you in the morning.'

'Come hunting with me.'

'Perhaps.' Korrin stood and moved away towards the caves.

'You are a wise man,' said Laitha, pushing back her blanket and joining Prasamaccus. He smiled.

'I wish that were true. But were it the case I would be back in the Land Between Walls, or in Calcaria with my wife.'

'You are married? You have not mentioned her.'

'Memory is sometimes painful and I try not to think of her. Wherever she is now, she is not seeing the same stars as I. Good night, Laitha.'

'Good night, Prasamaccus.' For a few minutes there was silence, then Laitha whispered, 'I am glad you are here.'

He smiled, but did not answer. This was not a time for conversation . . . not when Helga was waiting within his dreams.

Thuro and Baldric walked through most of the night in a forest lit by the bright light of two moons – a silvered, almost enchanted woodland that Thuro found bordering on the beautiful. They slept for two hours and at dawn were at the western edge of the forest, facing the open valleys before the white-blue mountains.

'Now the danger begins,' said Baldric. 'May the Ghosts preserve us!'

The two men strode out into the open. Baldric strung his bow and walked with an arrow ready. Thuro scanned the skyline, but there was no sign of soldiers. Small huts and larger houses dotted the land and there were cattle grazing on the hillsides.

'Who are these Ghosts you pray to?' he asked Baldric.

'The Army of the Dead,' answered the lean huntsman.

At noon they stopped at a farmhouse and Baldric was offered a loaf of dark bread. The inhabitants, a young man and woman, seemed fearful and all too anxious for the travellers to move on.

Baldric thanked them for the food and they vanished within the house.

'You knew them?' asked the prince.

'My sister and her husband.'

'They were not very friendly.'

'To speak to me is death since the warrant went out.'

'What was your crime?'

'I killed a soldier who came for my neighbour's wife. She was one of the Winter Seven.'

'What happened to the woman?'

'Her husband handed her over two hours later and named me as the killer. I ran and joined Korrin.'

'I would have thought there would be more rebels?'

'There were,' said the huntsman. 'An army of two thousand rose in the north, but they were taken and crucified on the trees of Calip-tha-sa. Astarte wove a spell about them so that even when the crows had torn the flesh from their bones they were still alive. Their screams came from the forest for more than two years before she relented and released their souls. Now there are not many rebels.'

The two travellers came to the foothills of the Etrusces by mid-afternoon of the following day. The mountains reared above them, gaunt giants against the gathering storm-clouds. 'There is a cabin,' said Baldric, 'about a mile ahead, in a narrow valley. We will stay the night there.'

The building was deserted, the windows hanging open and their leather hinges rotted. But the night was not cold and the two men sat before a fire, saying little. Baldric seemed an insular, introverted man.

Towards midnight the storm broke above the mountains, rain lashing the sides of the cabin and driven through the open windows by a shrieking wind. Thuro wedged the broken windows into place and watched as lightning speared the sky. He was tired and hungry, and his mind drifted to thoughts of Culain. He had not realised how fond he had grown of the Mist Warrior. That he had died at the hands of the Soul Stealers was more than a travesty. At least

131

Aurelius had had the small satisfaction of taking some of his killers with him on the dark road. At the thought of his father, Thuro's mood mellowed to the point of melancholy. He could remember only four long conversations with the king; all of them had concerned his studies. But they never spoke as father and son . . .

A shadow moved across the clearing before the cabin and Thuro jerked upright, blinking rapidly to clear his vision; he could see nothing. He drew his sword; the blade was shining like dull silver.

The door exploded inwards, but Thuro was already moving. The shadow swept towards him even as Baldric awoke, reaching for his bow. Thuro's mind emptied as his gladius blocked a grey blade and slashed through the dark cape and up into the corpse-grey face. The demon vanished in an instant, cape fluttering to the floor. Thuro ran to Baldric, touching his sword to the man's arrow-head. They waited, but nothing moved in the storm. Thuro glanced down at his sword. Was it still silver, or iron grey? He could not tell, and a tense hour followed. Taking a risk he moved to the door, lifting it back into place and wedging it shut.

Baldric's face was white, his eyes fearful. 'What was that thing?'

'A creature from the Void. It is dead.'

'From its face it was dead before it came in. How did you match it? I have never seen anything as swift.'

'I used a trick taught me by a master. It is called Eleari-mas – the Emptying.' Thuro gave a silent prayer of thanks to the departed Culain and allowed his body to relax. He thrust the gladius into the wooden floor. 'If the blade glows silver, it means they have returned,' he told the huntsman.

'You are more than you seem, boy. A goodly deal more.'

'I think I have passed from youth to manhood in but a few days. Do not call me boy. My name is . . .'He stopped and smiled. 'I carry a boy's name still. My naming was due to have been conducted at Camulodunum in the summer, but I shall not be there. No matter. I need no druid nor Enchanter to tell me that I am a man.' He dragged the sword from the wood and held it aloft. 'Thuro is now the memory the man carries, a memory of youth and lesser days. This sword is mine. It is the sword of Uther Pendragon, the man.'

Baldric stood and offered his hand. Uther took it in the warrior's grip, wrist to wrist. 'More than a man,' said Baldric. 'You are a brother.'

Gwalchmai sat with head bowed, the bandage on his arm dripping blood to the grass. His turma had been cut to pieces in a raid three miles from the merchant town of Longovicium. Twenty-seven men were dead or captured; the remaining four sat with Gwalchmai in a small wood thinking of their comrades: men who awoke to a bright sun and this afternoon stared sightlessly at a darkening sky.

Summer had arrived in northern Britain, but it had brought no joy to the beleaguered army of Lucius Aquila. The Brigantes, under Eldared and Cael, had conquered Corstopitum, Vindomara, Longovicium, Voreda and Brocavum. Now they besieged the fortress city of Cataractonium, pinning down six cohorts of fighting men from the Fifth Legion. News from the south was scarcely better; Ambrosius had been forced to retreat against Hengist and the Saxon king had taken Durobrivae in the south-east.

A Jute named Cerdic had raided the southwest and sacked the town of Lindinis, destroying two cohorts of auxiliaries. No one talked of victory now, for the British army was running short of men, and hope, and the early victory at Corstopitum no longer boosted morale. Rather it was the reverse, for it had raised expectations which had not been realised.

Gwalchmai sat, watching the blood on his arm thicken and dry. He made a fist and felt the pain in his bicep. It would heal – given time. But how much time did he have?

'If the king were still alive . . .' muttered a short, balding warrior named Casmaris, not needing to finish the sentence.

'He is not,' snapped Gwalchmai, torn between agreement with the unspoken sentiment and loyalty to Aquila. 'What is the point of this endless hankering for things past? *If* the king were alive. *If* Eldared could have been trusted, *If* we had ten more legions.'

'Well, I am tired of running and holding,' said Casmaris. 'Why can we not bring up the Fourth and take them on in one bloody battle?'

'All or nothing?' queried Gwalchmai.

'And why not? Nothing is what we will have anyway. This is the slow death we are suffering.'

Gwalchmai turned away; he could not argue. He was a Cantii tribesman, a Briton by birth and temperament, and he did not understand the endless strategies. His desire was simple: meet your enemy head on and fight until someone lost. But Aquila was a Roman of infinite patience, who would not risk an empire on one throw of the dice. Deep inside him, Gwalchmai could feel that they were both wrong. Perhaps there was a time for patience, but there was also a time for raw courage and a defiance of the odds.

He pushed himself to his feet. 'Time to ride,' he said.

'Time to die,' muttered Casmaris.

Uther awoke with his heart thumping erratically, fear making him roll and rise, groping for his sword. He had fallen asleep while on watch.

'Have no fear,' said Baldric, who was honing the blade of his hunting-knife as the dawn sunlight streamed through the open window. The storm had passed and the morning was bright and clear under a blue sky.

Uther smiled ruefully. Baldric offered him the last of the black bread, which the prince was forced to dampen with water from his companion's canteen before it became edible. They set off minutes later, heading higher into the timber-line of the mountains, following a narrow trail dotted with the spoor of mountain goats and big-horn sheep. At last, as the sun neared noon, they came to a high valley where a small granite-built house nestled in the hollow of a hill. The roof had been thatched, but was now black and ruined by fire.

The two men waited in the tree-line, scanning the countryside for signs of soldiers. Satisfied they were alone, they descended to the house, stopping at a huge oak. Crucified upon the trunk was the near skeleton of a man.

'This would be Andiacus,' said Baldric, 'and I do not think he can help us.' The leg bones were missing, obviously ripped away by wolves or wild dogs, and the skull had fallen to the earth by the tree-roots. Uther wandered to the house, which was well-built around a central room with a stone hearth. Everywhere was chaos – books and scrolls littering the floor, drawers pulled from chests, tables over-turned, rugs pulled up. The three back rooms were in similar condition. Uther righted a cane chair and sat, lost in thought.

'Time to be leaving,' said Baldric from the doorway.

'Not yet. Whoever did this was searching for the source of the Enchanter's power. They did not find it.'

'How can you say that? They have torn the place apart.'

'Exactly, Baldric. There is no evidence of an end to the search. It follows that either they found the source at the very last, or they did not find it. The latter is more probable.'

'If they did not find it, how can we?'

'We know where not to look. Help me clear the mess.'

'Why? No one lives here.'

'Trust me.' Together the two men righted all the furniture, then Uther sat down once more staring at the walls of the main room. After a while he stood and moved to the bedroom. The quantity of books and scrolls showed Andiacus to be a studious man. Some of the manuscripts were still tied and Uther studied them. They were carefully indexed.

'What are we looking for?' asked the huntsman.

'A Stone. A golden Stone, black-veined, possibly the size of a pebble.'

'You think he hid it before they killed him?'

'No. I think he hid it as a matter of course, probably every night. And he did not have it with him when they captured him, which could mean they took him in his sleep.'

'If he hid it, they would have found it.'

'No. If *you* hid it, they would have found it. We are talking of an Enchanter and a magic Stone. He hid it in plain sight, but he changed it. Now all we must do is think of what it might have been.'

Baldric sat down. 'I am hungry, I am tired, and I do not under-stand any of this. But last night a creature of darkness tried to kill us, and I would like to be gone from these mountains before nightfall.'

Uther nodded. He had been thinking of the Soul Stealer and wondering whether it had been sent by Eldared or Astarte, or was merely a random factor associated with neither. He pushed his fears from his mind and returned to the problem at hand. Maedhlyn had often told him not to waste his energies on matters beyond his knowledge.

The murdered Enchanter either hid the Stone or transformed it. Had it been hidden, the searchers would have found it. Therefore it was transformed. Uther rose from the bed. Any one of the scattered objects on the floor could be Sipstrassi. Think, Uther, he told himself. Use your mind. Why would the Enchanter disguise the Stone? To safeguard it, so that no one would steal it. Around the room were ornate goblets, gold-tipped quills, items of clothing, blankets, candle-holders, even a lantern. There were scrolls, books and charms of silver, bronze or gold. All would be worth something to a thief and therefore useless as a disguise for a magic Stone. Uther eliminated them from his thoughts, his eyes scanning the room – seeking an object that was functional and yet worthless. There was a desk by the window, the drawers ripped out and smashed. Beside it lay piles of scattered papers . . . and there in the corner, nestling against the wall, an oblong paperweight of ordinary granite.

Uther pushed himself from the bed and moved to the rock. It was heavy, and ideal for the purpose it served. He held it over the desktop and concentrated hard. After several seconds his hand grew warm and there appeared two platters of freshly roasted beef. The granite in his hand disappeared, to be replaced by a thumbnail-sized Sipstrassi Stone with thick black veins interweaving on the golden surface.

'You did it!' whispered Baldric. 'The Dream Shaper's magic.'

Uther smiled, holding his elation in check, savouring the feeling of triumph – the triumph of mind. 'Yes,' he said at last, 'but the power of the Stone is not great. As the magic is exhausted, these black veins swell. When the gold is used up, the power is gone.

136

Enjoy the meat. We cannot afford to waste any more enchantment; we must heal Pallin.'

The food was as close to divine as either man had tasted. Then gathering their weapons, Uther and Baldric left the house, the younger man carrying the Sipstrassi Stone in his hand. As they passed the skeleton the Stone grew warmer and Uther paused. A whisper like a breeze through dry leaves echoed inside his head and a single word formed.

'Peace.' It was a plea born of immense suffering. Uther remembered Baldric's word about the army of rebels who had been crucified and yet not allowed to die. Stooping he lifted the skull, touching the Stone to its temple. White light blazed and the voice inside Uther's head grew in power.

'I thank you, my friend. Take the Stone to Erin Plateau. Bring the Ghosts home.' The whisper faded and was gone, and the black threads on the Stone had swelled still further.

'Why did you do that?' asked Baldric.

'He was not dead,' answered Uther. 'Let us go.'

Maedhlyn hurled the black pebble to the tabletop where Culain swept it up. Neither man said anything as Maedhlyn poured a full goblet of pale golden spirit and drained it at a swallow. The Enchanter looked in a dreadful condition, his face sallow, the skin sagging beneath his beard. His eyes were bloodshot, his movements sluggish. For seven days he had tried to follow Thuro, but the Standing Stones above Eboracum merely drained the power from his Sipstrassi. The two men had travelled to another circle to the west, outside Cambodunum. The same mysterious circumstances applied. Maedhlyn worked for days on his calculations, snatching only an hour's sleep in mid-afternoons. Finally he attempted to travel back to Eboracum, but even that could not be achieved.

The companions had returned to the capital on horseback where Maedhlyn searched through his massive library, seeking inspiration and finding none.

'I am beaten,' he whispered, pouring another goblet of spirit.

137

'How can it be that the Standing Stones no longer operate?' asked Culain.

'What do you think I have been working on this past fortnight? The rising price of apples?'

'Be calm, Enhancer. I am not seeking answers, I am searching for inspiration. There is no reason for the Stones to fail. They are not machines, they merely resonate compatibly with Sipstrassi. Have you ever known a circle to fail?'

'No, not fail. And how can I be calm? The immutable laws of Mystery have been overturned. Magic no longer works.' Maedhlyn's eyes took on a fearful look. He sat bolt upright and fished in the pocket of his dark blue robe, producing a second Sipstrassi Stone. He held it over the table and a fresh jug of spirit materialised; he relaxed. 'I have used up the power of two Stones that should have lasted decades, but at least I can still make wine.'

'Have you ever been unable to travel?'

'Of course. No one can travel where they already are, you know that. Law number one. Each time scale sets up its own opposing forces. It pushes us on – makes us accept, in the main, linear time. At first I thought I could not follow Thuro because I was already there. No Circle would accept my journey on that score. Wherever he is, and in whatever time, then I am there also. But that is not the case. It would not affect a journey from Cambodunum to Eboracum in the same time scale. The Circles have failed and I do not understand why.'

Culain stretched out his lean frame on the leather-covered divan. 'I think it is time to contact Pendarric.'

'I wish I could offer an argument,' said Maedhlyn. 'He is so dour.'

'He is also considerably more wise than both of us, your arrogance notwithstanding.'

'Can we not wait until tomorrow?'

'No, Thuro is in danger somewhere. Do it, Maedhlyn!'

'Dour is not the word for Pendarric,' grumbled the Enchanter. Taking his Stone he held his fist over the table and whispered the words of Family, the Oath of Balacris. The air above the table crackled and Maedhlyn hastily withdrew the two jugs of spirit. A fresh breeze filled the room with the scent of roses and a window appeared on to a garden, wherein sat a powerful figure in a white toga. His beard was golden and freshly curled, his eyes a piercing blue. He turned, laying down a basket of perfect blooms.

'Well?' he said and Maedhlyn swallowed his anger. There was a wealth of meaning in that single word, and the Enchanter remembered his father using the same tone when young Maedhlyn had been found with the maidservant in the hay wagon. He pushed the humiliating memory from his thoughts.

'We seek your advice, Lord,' muttered Maedhlyn, afraid that the words would choke him. Pendarric chuckled.

'How that must pain you, Taliesan. Or should I call you Zeus? Or Aristotle? Or Loki?'

'Maedhlyn, Lord. The Circles have failed.' If Maedhlyn had expected Pendarric to be ruffled by the announcement, he was doomed to disappointment. The once-king of Atlantis merely nodded.

'Not failed, Maedhlyn. They are closed. Should they remain closed, then yes, they will fail. The resonance will alter.'

'How can this be? Who has closed them?'

'I have. Do you wish to dispute my right?'

'No, Lord,' said Maedhlyn hastily, 'but might I enquire the reason?'

'You may. I did not mind the more capricious of my people becoming gods to the savages – it amused them and did little real harm – but I will not tolerate the same lunacy we suffered before. And before you remind me, Maedhlyn, yes, it was my lunacy. But the world toppled. The tidal waves, the volcanoes and the earthquakes almost ripped the world asunder.'

'Why should it happen again?'

'One of our number has decided it is not enough to play at being a goddess; she has decided to *become* one. She has built a castle spanning four gateways and she is ready to unleash the Void upon all the worlds that are. So I have closed the pathways.'

139

Maedhlyn spotted a hesitation in Pendarric's comment and leapt on it: 'But not *all* of them?'

The king's face showed a momentary flash of annoyance. 'No. You were always swift, Taliesan. I cannot close her world . . . not yet. But then I did not believe any immortal would be foolish enough to repeat my error.'

Culain leaned forward. 'May I speak, Lord?'

'Of course, Culain. Are you standing by your decision to become mortal?'

'I am. When you say your error, you do not mean the Bloodstone?'

'I do.'

'And who is the traitor?' asked Culain, fearing the answer.

'Goroien.'

'Why would she do it? It is inconceivable.'

Pendarric smiled. You remember Gilgamesh, the mortal who could not accept Sipstrassi immortality? It seems he had a disease of the blood and he gave it to Goroien. She began to age, Culain. You, of all of us, know what that must have meant to her. She now drains the life force from pregnant women into her Bloodstone. It will not be enough; she will need more souls, and more again. In the end a nation's blood will not satisfy her, nor a world's. She is doomed and will doom us all.'

'I cannot accept it,' said Culain. 'Yes, she is ruthless. Are we not all ruthless? But I have seen her nurse a sick faun; help in childbirth.'

'But what you have not seen is the effect of the Bloodstones. They eat like cancers at the soul. I know, Culain. You were too young, but ask Maedhlyn what Pendarric was like when the Bloodstone ruled Atlantis. I ripped the hearts from my enemies. Once I had ten thousand rebels impaled. Only the end of the world saved me. Nothing will save Goroien.'

'My grandson is lost in the Mist. I must find him.'

'He is in Goroien's world, and she is seeking him.'

'Then let me go there. Let me aid him. She will hate him, for he is Alaida's son – and you know Goroien's feelings for Alaida.'

'Sadly, Culain, I know more than that. So does Maedhlyn. And, no the gates stay closed – unless, of course, you promise to destroy her.'

'I cannot!'

'She is not the woman you loved; there is nothing but evil left in her.'

'I have said no. Do you know me not at all, Pendarric?'

The king sat silent for a moment. 'Know you? Of course I know you. More, I like you, Culain. You have honour. If you should reconsider, journey to Skitis. One gateway remains. But you will have to slay her.'

Storm-clouds swirled in Culain's eyes and his face was white. 'You survived the Bloodstone, Pendarric, though many would have liked to slay you. Widows and orphans in their thousands would have sought your blood.'

The king nodded agreement. 'Yet I was not diseased, Culain. Goroien must die. Not for punishment – though some would argue she deserves it – but because her disease is destroying her. At the moment she sacrifices two hundred and eighty women a year from ten nations under her control. Two years ago she needed only seven women. Next year, by my calculations, she will need a thousand. What does that tell you?'

Culain's fist rammed to the table. 'Then why do you not hunt her? You were a warrior once. Or Brigamartis?'

'This would make you happy, Culain? Bring you contentment? No, Goroien is a part of you and you alone can come close to her. Her power is grown. If it is left to me to destroy her, I will have to shatter the world in which she dwells. Then thousands will die with her, for I will raise the oceans. Your choice, Culain. And now I must go.'

The window disappeared. Maedhlyn poured another goblet of spirit and passed it to Culain but the Mist Warrior ignored it.

'How much of this did you know?' he asked Maedhlyn. The Enchanter sipped his own drink, his green eyes hooded.

'Not as much as you think. And I would urge you to follow your own advice and be calm.' Their eyes met and Maedhlyn swallowed hard, aware that his life hung by a gossamer thread. 'I did not know of Goroien's illness, only that she had taken to playing goddess once more. That I swear.'

'But there is something else, Enhancer – something Pendarric is aware of. So out with it!'

'First you must promise not to kill me.'

'I'll kill you if you do not!' stormed Culain, rising from his chair.

'Sit down!' snapped Maedhlyn, his fear giving way to anger. 'What good does it do you to threaten me? Am I your enemy? Have I ever been your enemy? Think back, Culain. You and Goroien went your separate ways. You took Shaleat to wife and she gave you Alaida. But Shaleat died, bitten by a venomous snake. You knew – and do not deny it – that Goroien killed her. Or if you did not know, you at least suspected. That is why you allowed Aurelius to take Alaida from the Feragh. You thought that Goroien's hatred would be nullified if Alaida chose mortality. You did not even allow her a Stone.'

'I do not want to hear this!' shouted Culain, fear shining in his eyes.

'Goroien killed Alaida. She came to her in Aurelius' castle and gave her poison. The babe took it in and it changed Alaida's blood. When she gave birth, the bleeding would not stop.'

'No!' whispered Culain, but Maedhlyn was in full flow now.

'As for Thuro, he had no will to live and I used up a complete Stone to save him. But Goroien was always close through those early years, and I could not allow Thuro to grow strong. I gave him the weakness in his chest. I robbed him of his strength. Goroien saw the king's suffering and let the boy live. She was always a vindictive witch, only you were too blind to see it. At last she decided the time had come to wreak her full vengeance. She it was who went to Eldared, lifting him with dreams of glory. Not to kill the king, but Alaida's child – your grandson.

'You blamed me for Alaida's death. I said nothing. But when I left her on that fateful morning her pulse was strong, her body fit, her mind happy. She did not have the disease of kings at that time, Culain.'

142

The Mist Warrior lifted his goblet and drained the spirit, feeling its warmth cut through him. 'Have you ever loved anyone, Maedhlyn?'

'No,' replied the Enchanter, realising as he said it the regret he carried.

'You are right. I knew she killed Shaleat, yet I could not hate her for it. It was why I decided on mortality.' Culain laughed without humour. 'What a weak response for a warrior. I would die to punish Goroien.'

'It is ironic, Culain. You are dying when you do not have to, and she is dying when she does not wish to. What will you do?'

'What choice do I have? My grandson is lost in her world, along with another I love dearly. To save them I must kill the woman I have loved for two thousand years.'

'I will come with you to Skitis Island.'

'No, Maedhlyn. Stay here and aid the Roman, Aquila. Hold the land for Thuro.'

'We cannot hold. I was thinking of taking up my travels once more.'

'What is left for you?' asked Culain. 'You have enjoyed the glories of Assyria, Greece and Rome. Where will you go?'

'There are other worlds, Culain.'

'Give it a little time. We have both given a great deal to this insignificant island. I would rather Eldared did not inherit it — or the barbarian Hengist.'

Maedhlyn smiled wistfully. 'As you say, we have given a great deal. I will stay awhile. But I feel we are holding back the sea with a barrier of ice . . . and summer is coming.'

12

Prasamaccus sat with Korrin Rogeur behind a screen of bushes on the eastern hills of Mareen-sa, watching a herd of flat-antlered deer grazing three hundred paces away.

'How do we approach them?' asked Korrin.

'We do not. We wait for them to approach us.'

'And if they do not?'

'Then we go home hungry. Hunting is a question of patience. The tracks show the deer follow this trail to drink. We sit here and we let the hours flow over us. Your friend Hogun chose to sleep the time away, which is as good a way as any – so long as someone stays on watch.'

'You are a calm man, Prasamaccus. I envy you.'

'I am calm because I do not understand hate.'

'Has no one ever wronged you?'

'Of course. When I was a babe a drunken hunter rode his horse over me. All my life since I have known pain – the agony of a twisted limb, the hurt of being alone. Hatred would not have sustained me.'

The dark huntsman smiled. 'I cannot be like you, but being *with* you calms me. Why are you here in Pinrae?'

'I understand we are seeking a sword. Or rather that Thuro is seeking a sword. He is the son of a king – a great king by all accounts – who was murdered a few months ago.'

'From which land across the water do you come?'

Prasamaccus sat back and stretched his leg. 'It is a land of magic and mist. It is called Britain by the Romans, but in reality is many lands. My tribe is the Brigante, possibly the finest hunters of the world – certainly the most ferocious warriors.'

Korrin grinned broadly. 'Ferocious? They are not all like you then?'

Before Prasamaccus could reply the deer stampeded in a mad run towards the west. The Brigante pushed himself to his feet. 'Quickly,' he said. 'Follow me!' He limped towards an ancient oak and Korrin joined him.

'What are you doing?'

'Help me up.' Korrin linked his lands and levered the Brigante high enough to grab an overhanging branch and haul his body across it.

'Swiftly now, climb!' urged Prasamaccus. The Brigante moved aside and strung Vamera, notching a long shaft to the string. A terrible roar reverberated through the forest and Korrin leapt for the branch, pulling himself up just as the first Vore bounded into the clearing. Prasamaccus' arrow flashed into its throat, but its run continued unchecked.

A second shaft bounced from its skull as it sprang towards the hunters. Its claws scrabbled at the branch but Korrin kicked out, his boot smashing into the gaping jaws. The beast fell back and two others joined it, pacing round the tree. Prasamaccus sat very still, a third arrow ready, and stared at the great cats. They were each some eight feet long, with huge flat faces, oval yellow eyes and fangs as long as a man's fingers. The first beast sat down and worried at the arrow in its throat, snapping it with his paw. He then continued to prowl the tree. The beasts' backs were ridged with muscle and the Brigante could see no easy way to kill them.

'Shoot at them!' urged Korrin. At the sound of his voice the beasts began to roar and leap for the branch, but none could get a hold. Prasamaccus lifted his finger to his lips and mouthed a single word.

'Patience!'

He swung his quiver to the front and began to examine his arrows. Some were single-barbed, others double. Some had smooth heads for easy withdrawal; some were light, others heavy. Finally he chose a double-barbed shaft with a strongly weighted head. He notched it. It seemed to the Brigante that the only weak spot the Vore had was behind the front leg at the back of the ribs. If he could angle a shot correctly . . .

145

He waited for several minutes, occasionally drawing back the string, but hesitating. The watching Korrin grew ever more tense – but he held his tongue. A Vore paced away from the tree, presenting his back and Prasamaccus whistled softly. The beast stopped and turned. In that instant the arrow flashed through the air, slicing into the Vore's back and through to its heart. It slumped to the ground without a sound.

Selecting a fresh arrow, the Brigante waited. A second Vore approached the dead beast and began to push at the corpse with its snout, trying to raise it. Another arrow sang through the clearing and the Vore reared and fell to its back, its hind legs kicking. Then it was still. The third beast was confused; it approached its comrades and then backed away, smelling blood. It roared its anger to the skies.

A single bugle call echoed through the forest and the Vore turned towards the sound, then padded away swiftly. For some minutes the two men remained where they were, then Korrin made to climb down.

'Where are you going?'

'The beast is gone.'

'There may be others further west. Let us wait awhile.'

'Good advice, my friend. How did you know the Vores were loose?'

'The deer did not just run, they fled in panic. A man's smell would not do that, nor would a wolf. Since the wind was coming from behind and to the right of us, I reasoned the beasts must be close.'

'You are a canny man to have around, Prasamaccus. Perhaps our luck has changed.'

As if to evidence his words, a large Vore raced across the clearing before them, oblivious to their presence and leapt the corpses in a headlong rush towards the bugle call.

'You think it is safe now?' asked Korrin.

'A few more minutes.' Prasamaccus could feel sadness riding him. Korrin had not yet stopped to consider the full meaning of the attack, and the Brigante hesitated to voice his fears. If four Vores

146

had been loosed, why not all of them? And if that were the case, what had befallen the brotherhood at the caves? 'I think it is safe now,' he said at last.

Korrin sprang to the ground and waited to aid the slower Prasamaccus.

'I owe you my life. I shall not forget it.'

He began to walk back towards the camp, but Prasamaccus' slender hand fell on his shoulder. 'A moment, Korrin.' The taller man swung towards him, his face paling as he saw the look of concern in Prasamaccus' eyes. Then realisation struck.

'No!' he screamed and tore himself from the Brigante's grip to race away through the trees. Prasamaccus notched an arrow and followed at his own halting pace. He did not hurry, having no wish to arrive too soon. When at last he did come in sight of the caves, his worst fears were realised. Bodies scattered the clearing and in his path was a leg dripping blood to the grass. It was a scene of carnage. In the cave-mouth knelt Korrin alongside the giant body of his brother. Prasamaccus approached. The man-beast lay beside the bodies of three Vores and his talons were red with their blood. Beyond Korrin, cowering in the darkness, were three children and Laitha. Part of his burden lifted as he saw that she was safe. Korrin was weeping openly, holding a bloodstained paw in his lap. The man-beast's eyes opened.

Prasamaccus touched Korrin's shoulder. 'He lives,' he whispered.

'Korrin?'

'I am here.'

'I stopped them, Korrin. The Witch Queen did me a service after all. She gave me the strength to stop her own hunting cats.' He took a deep shuddering breath and Prasamaccus watched as his lifeblood continued to flow from the dreadful wounds.

'Four of the Seven are safe within the caves. Some of the men ran into the forest; I do not know if they survived. Get them away from here, Korrin.'

'I will, brother. Rest. Be at peace.' The body shimmered as if in a heat haze, then shrank to that of a normal man, slender and fine-

147

boned, the face handsome and gentle. 'Oh, sweet Gods,' whispered Korrin.

'Very touching,' came a woman's voice and Prasamaccus and Korrin turned. Sitting on a nearby rock was a golden-haired woman in a dress of spun silver that looped over one ivory-skinned shoulder.

Korrin lunged to his feet, dragging his sword clear. He ran at the woman, who lifted a hand and waved her fingers as if casually swatting a fly. Korrin flew from his feet to land against the rocks ten feet away.

'I said I would watch him die . . . and I have. Bring my women to the camp in the north. Perhaps then I will allow the rest of you to live.'

Prasamaccus laid down his bow, feeling her eyes upon him.

'Why do you not attempt to kill me?' she asked.

'To what purpose, lady? You are not here.'

'How perceptive of you.'

'It takes no great perception to see that you cast no shadow.'

'You are disrespectful,' she chided. 'Come to me.' Her hand pointed and Prasamaccus felt a pull at his chest, hauling him to his feet. He stumbled on his bad leg and heard her soft lilting, mocking laughter. 'A cripple? How delicious! I was going to play a game with you, little man – make you suffer as Pallin suffered. But I see there is no need. Fate has perhaps dealt with you more unkindly than I could. And yet, you should suffer some pain for your insolent glances.' Her eyes shone.

Prasamaccus was still holding the arrow he had notched earlier and as her hand came up once more he raised the arrow-head before him. A blaze of white light came from her fingers, touched the arrow and returned to smite her in the chest. She screamed and stood . . . and in that moment Prasamaccus saw the golden hair show silver at the temples. Her hand shot to her aging face and panic replaced the malevolent smile. She disappeared in an instant.

Korrin stumbled to the Brigante's side. 'What did you do?'

Prasamaccus looked down at the arrow; the shaft was black and useless, the head a misshapen lump of metal. He hurled it aside.

'We must get the women from here before the soldiers come, as surely they will. Is there another hiding place in the forest?'

'Where can we hide from her?'

'One step at a time, Korrin. Is there a place?'

'Perhaps.'

'Then let us gather what is useful and go.' As he spoke, five men emerged from the trees. Prasamaccus recognised the tall Hogun and the hulking Rhiall.

'So,' said the Brigante, 'the brotherhood still lives.'

Laitha strode from the cave to the body of a dead warrior and unbuckled the man's sword-belt. Swinging it round her lean hips she drew the blade, hefting it for weight. The hilt was long and tightly covered with dark leather, and she could grip it double-handed for the cut or sweep. Yet the blade was not so long or heavy that she was unable to use it one-handed. She found a suitable whetstone and began to hone the edge. Prasamaccus joined her.

'I am sorry you had to suffer such an ordeal.'

'I did not suffer; Pallin kept the Vores from me. But the screams of the dying . . .'

'I know.'

'That woman radiated evil – and yet she was so lovely.'

'There is no mystery in that, Laitha. Pallin was a good man, yet sight of him would cause sleepless nights. All that is good is not always handsome.'

'I do not like to admit this, but she frightened me. All the way down to my bones. Before we left Culain I saw a Soul Stealer from the Void. Its face was the grey of death, yet it inspired less fear in me than the Witch Queen. How was it that you were able to speak so to her?'

'I do not follow you.'

'There was no fear in your voice.'

'It was in my heart, but all I saw was an evil woman. All she could do was kill me. Is that so terrible? In fifty years no one will remember my name. I will be merely the dust of history. If I am

149

lucky, I will grow old and rot. If not, I will die young. Whatever, I will still die.'

'I never want to die – or grow old. I want to live for ever,' said Laitha. 'Just as Culain had the chance to do. I want to see the world in a hundred years, or a thousand. I never want the sun to shine without it shining on me.'

'I can see how that would be . . . pleasant,' said the Brigante, 'but for myself I think I would rather not be immortal. If you are ready, we should be on our way.'

Laitha looked deeply into his sad blue eyes, not understanding his melancholy mood. She smiled, rose smoothly and pulled him to his feet. 'Your wife is a lucky woman.'

'In what way?'

'She has found a gentle man who is not weak. And yes, I am ready.'

The small group, joined by four other survivors, numbered nineteen people as they headed high into the hills at the centre of Mareen-sa. There were four pregnant women, three children and, counting Laitha, twelve warriors.

Due to the advanced stage of one of the pregnancies the pace was slow, and it was dusk when Korrin led them up a long hill to a circle of black stones each some thirty feet high. The circle was more than a hundred yards in diameter and several – now deserted – buildings had been constructed around the eight-foot altar. Korrin dragged open a rotted door and pushed his way into the largest building. Prasamaccus followed him. Inside was one vast room over eighty feet long. Ancient dust-covered tables were set at right-angles to the walls, with bench seats alongside.

Korrin made his way to a large hearth, where a fire had been neatly laid. A huge cobweb stretched from the logs to the chimney-breast. Korrin ignored it and sparked the tinder. Flames rose hungrily at the centre of the dead wood, and a warm red light bathed the central hall.

'What is this place?' asked Prasamaccus.

'The Eagle sect once dwelt here – seventy men who sought to commune with the Ghosts.'

'What happened to them?'

'Astarte had them slain. Now no one comes here.'

'I cannot bring myself to blame them,' said the Brigante, listening to the wind howling across the hilltop. One of the women began to moan and sank to the floor. It was Erulda.

'The babe is due,' said Hogun. 'We'd best leave her to the women.' Korrin led the men outside to a smaller building where a dozen rotted cot-beds lined the walls. A rats' nest had been built against the far wall and the room stank of vermin. Once more a fire had been laid and Korrin ignited it.

Prasamaccus tested several beds, then gingerly laid himself down. There was no conversation and the Brigante found himself thinking of Thuro, and wondering if the Vores had killed him. He awoke an hour before dawn, half-convinced he had heard the sound of drums and marching feet. He stretched and sat up. Korrin and the other men were still sleeping around the dying fire. He swung his legs from the cot and stood, suppressing a groan as the weight came down on his twisted limb. Taking up his bow and quiver, he stepped out into the predawn light. The door of the main building opened and Laitha moved into sight. She smiled a greeting, then ran across to him. 'I have been waiting for you for a full hour.'

'Did you hear the drums?'

'No. What drums?'

'I must have been dreaming. Come, we'll find some meat.' The two of them, both armed with bows, set off down the hill.

On this day Prasamaccus could do no wrong. He killed two deer and Laitha slew a big-horn sheep. Unable to carry the meat home, they quartered the beasts, hanging the carcases from three high tree branches.

With Prasamaccus carrying the succulent loin section of the deer, Laitha stopped to gather several pounds of mushrooms which she carried inside her tunic blouse; the two hunters were greeted with smiles on their return. After a fine breakfast Korrin sent Hogun, Rhiall and a man called Logay to scout for the soldiers, while Prasamaccus told them where he had hidden the rest of the meat. Somehow the terrifying events of yesterday seemed less

151

hideous in the wake of Erulda delivering a fine baby son. His lusty cries were greeted with smiles among the women, and Prasamaccus marvelled anew at the ability of man to cope with terror. Even Korrin seemed less tense.

There was a stream at the bottom of the hill, near a basin of clay. The three remaining women spent the day creating pitchers and firing them in a kiln built some thirty feet from the stream. It made little smoke. Prasamaccus watched them work and thought of Helga back in Calcaria. Had the war reached her? How was she faring? Did she miss his presence as much as he missed hers, or had she even now found a fit husband with two good legs? He would not blame her if she had. She had given him a gift beyond price, and had he believed in benevolent Gods he would have prayed for her happiness.

He glanced down at his leather leggings. They were filthy and torn and several of the silver discs had come loose. His fine woolen tunic was grimy and the gold braid at the cuffs was frayed. He hobbled to the stream and removed his tunic, dipping it in the cool water and cleaning it against a rock. On impulse he stripped his troos and sat in the water, splashing it to his pale chest. The women nearby giggled and waved; he bowed gravely and continued to wash. Laitha wandered down the hill and one of the women approached her, offering her something Prasamaccus could not make out. The forest girl smiled her thanks and removed her boots, wading out to where Prasamaccus sat.

'What did she want?'

'She had a gift for the hunter,' answered Laitha, showing him a small phial stoppered with wax. 'It is a cleansing oil for the hair.' So saying she tugged him backwards, submerging him. He came up spluttering and she broke the wax seal, pouring half the contents over his head. Tucking the phial into her belt, she began to massage his hair, which was an experience to rival the ministrations of Victorinus' slaves. She spoiled it by ducking him again when she was done. He sat up to hear the chuckling of the working women and the rich, rolling laughter of the men who sat at the top of the hill.

152

The good humour lasted until Hogun and the others returned at dusk. Prasamaccus knew something was wrong, for they had not bothered to gather the meat. He limped across to Korrin and the dark huntsman looked up from his seat.

'The soldiers are coming,' he said simply.

The small amphitheatre was bare of spectators, bar the queen who sat at the centre on a fur-covered divan. Below her on the sand stood four warriors, their swords raised in salute. She leaned forward.

'You are each the finest gladiators of your lands. None of you has tasted defeat, and all have killed more than a score of opponents. Today you have the opportunity of carrying from Perdita your own weight in gems and gold. Does that excite you?' As she spoke her right hand caressed the skin of her throat and neck, enjoying the smooth silky feel of young flesh. Her blue eyes raked the warriors: strong men, lean and wolf-like, their eyes confident as they looked upon one another, each feeling he was destined to be the victor. Goroien smiled.

'Do not seek to gauge the men around you. Today you fight as a team, against the champion of my choosing. Kill him and all the rewards you have been promised will be yours.'

'We are all to fight one man, lady?' asked a tall warrior with a jet-black beard.

'Just one,' she whispered, her voice growing hoarse with excitement. 'Behold!'

The men turned. At the far end of the arena stood a tall figure, a black helm covering his face. His shoulders were wide, his hips lean and supple. He wore a cut-away mailshirt and a loincloth and carried a shortsword and a dagger.

'Behold,' said the queen once more. 'This is the queen's champion, the greatest warrior of this or any age. He too has never known defeat. Tackle him singly, or all at once.'

The four men looked at one another. The riches were there, so why take risks? They advanced on the tall helmed warrior, forming a half-circle. As they approached he moved with dazzling swiftness,

153

seeming to dance through them. But in his wake two men fell, disembowelled. The others circled warily. He dived forward, rolling on his shoulder, the dagger slicing the air to plunge home in Black-beard's throat. Continuing his roll he came alongside the last man, blocked his lunge and sent a dazzling riposte through his enemy's jugular. He walked forward and bowed to the queen.

'Always the best,' she said, the colour high on her cheeks. She held out her hand and he rose through the air to stand before her. She stood and ran her hands over his shoulders and down his glistening flanks.

'Do you love me?' she whispered.

'I love you. I have always loved you.' The voice was soft and distant.

'You do not hate me for bringing you back?'

'Not if you do as you promised, Goroien.' His hand circled her back, pulling her to him. 'Then I will love you until the stars die.'

'Why must you think of him?'

'I must be the Lord of Battle. I have nothing else. I never had. I am faster now – more deadly. And still he haunts me. Until I kill him I will never be that which I desire.'

'But he is no longer a match for you. He has chosen mortality and grows older. He is not what he was.'

'He must die, Goroien. You promised him to me.'

'What is the point? He could not have beaten you at his best. What will you prove by slaying a middle-aged man.'

'I will know that I am what I always was, that I am a warrior.' His hands roved her body: 'I will know that I am still a man.'

'You are, my love. The greatest warrior who ever lived.'

'You will bring him to me then?'

'I will. Truly I will.'

Slowly he removed the helm. She did not look at his eyes . . . could not. Ever since the day she had brought him back from the grave, they had defeated her.

Glazed as they had been in death, the eyes of Gilgamesh remained to torment her.

★   ★   ★

154

Uther and Baldric entered the forest of Mareen-sa just after dawn following a perilous journey from the Etrusces mountains. Three times they had hidden from soldiers, and once had been pursued by four mounted warriors, escaping by wading through a narrow stream and climbing an almost sheer rock face. They were tired now, but Uther's spirits were high with the thought that they were almost home. He would lift the spell from the man-beast Pallin, and then continue his search for his father's sword.

He was mildly ashamed of himself as he contemplated the jubilant scenes when Pallin was restored, the cheers and the congratulations, and his modest reactions to their compliments on his heroism. He pictured Laitha, seeing the admiration in her eyes and her acceptance of his manhood. He grew almost dizzy with the fantasy and wrenched his thoughts back to the narrow trail they were following. As he did so, his eyes lit on a massive track beside the path. He stopped and stared; it was the pad of a giant cat.

Baldric, walking ahead, swung and saw the prince kneeling by the wayside. He strolled back, froze as he saw the print and pulled an arrow from his quiver.

'The Vores are loose,' he whispered, his eyes scanning the trail.

Uther stood, his grey eyes narrowed in concentration. There was a stream nearby and the prince walked to it and began to dig a narrow channel in the bank.

'What are you doing?' asked Baldric but Uther ignored him. He widened the channel into a circle and watched as the water slowly filled it. When it was still, he lay full-length and stared into it, raising the Sipstrassi Stone above the water, whispering the words of power Culain had used. The surface shimmered and he saw the caves and the bodies. Two foxes were tugging at the flesh of a severed leg. He stood.

'They have attacked the camp. Many are dead, but there is no sign of Korrin, Prasamaccus or Laitha.'

'You think they have been taken?'

'I do not know, Baldric. Where else could they be?'

The man shrugged. 'We are lost.' He sat down and buried his face in his hands. Uther saw a shadow flash across the ground and

155

glanced up to see a huge eagle circling high overhead. The prince gripped the Stone and focused on the bird. His head swam and his mind merged. The forest was far below him and he could see as he never had before: a rabbit in the long grass, a fawn hidden in the undergrowth. And soldiers moving towards a high hill, on which stood a circle of jutting black stones. There were some three hundred fighting men on foot, but walking ahead of them was a line of Vores, held in check by forty dark-garbed woodsmen. Uther returned to his body, stumbled and almost fell.

Taking a deep breath to steady himself he began to run, ignoring the slumped Baldric. Up over the narrow trail and down into a muddy glen he slipped and slithered.

A huge stag bounded into his path. He lifted the Stone and the creature froze. Swiftly Uther clambered to its back; the deer turned and ran towards the hill. Several times Uther was almost dislodged, but his legs gripped firmly on the barrel of the creature's body. It leapt into the open and raced up the flanks of the hill, swerving to stand before the Vores. Behind him Uther had seen Prasamaccus, Laitha and several others waiting with arrows ready. Ahead of him the soldiers came into view, darkeyed men in helms of bronze, black cloaks billowing.

The stag stood statue-still.

'Withdraw or die!' called Uther. After the initial shock of seeing a blond youth riding a wild deer, there had been silence among the soldiers. Now laughter greeted his words. A command rang out and the dark-garbed woodsmen released the chains on the forty Vores. They leapt forward, their roars washing over Uther like thunder. He lifted the Stone, his grey eyes cold as Arctic ice.

The Vores stopped their charge and turned, raging down into the massed ranks of the soldiers. Claws raked flesh, fangs closed on skull and bone. Horses reared and whinnied in terror as the mighty beasts ripped into the startled fighting men. Within seconds the savage carnage gave way to a mass panic and the soldiers fled in all directions as the Vores continued their destruction. Uther turned the stag and slowly rode up the hill. At the top he slid from the creature's back, patting its neck. The deer bounded away.

From the forest the awful screams of the dying filled the air. Korrin approached Uther.

'Are you a God?'

Uther glanced down at the Stone. It was no longer gold with black threads, but black with golden threads. There was little magic left.

'No, Korrin, I am not a God. I am just a man who arrived too late. Yesterday I could have saved Pallin and the others.'

'It is good to see you, Thuro,' said Prasamaccus.

'Not Thuro, my friend. The child is dead. The man walks. I am Uther Pendragon, son of Aurelius. And I am the king, by right and by destiny.'

Prasamaccus said nothing, but he bowed low. The other men, still shocked after their escape, followed suit. Uther accepted the honour without comment and walked away to sit alone on a broken rock overlooking the stream, where Prasamaccus joined him.

'May I sit with you, lord?' he asked, with no hint of sarcasm.

'Do not think me arrogant, Prasamaccus. I am not. But I have killed the Undead and flown on the wings of an eagle. I have ridden the forest prince and destroyed an army. I know who I am. More, I know *what* I am.'

'And what are you, Prince Uther?'

Uther turned and smiled softly. 'I am a young man, barely of age, who needs wise counsel from trusted friends. But I am also the King of all Britain, and I will reclaim my father's throne. No force of this world, or any other, will deter me.'

'It is said,' offered Prasamaccus, 'that blood runs true. I have seen the reverse at times – the sons of brave fathers becoming cowards. But in your case, Prince Uther, I think it is true. You have the blood of a great king in your veins, and also the spirit of the warrior Culain. I think I will follow you, though never blindly. And I will offer you counsel whenever you ask for it. Do I need to kneel?'

Uther chuckled. 'My first command to you is that you never kneel in my presence. My second is that you must always tell me when you feel that arrogance is surfacing in my nature. I have studied well, Prasamaccus, and I know that power has many counterpoints. My father had a tendency to believe himself right at all times, merely because he was the king. He dismissed from his service a warrior-friend who had grown up alongside him. The man disagreed with him on a matter of strategy and my father had him branded disloyal. Yet Aurelius was not a bad man. I have studied the lives of the great, and all become afflicted with pride. You are my champion against such excesses.'

'A heavy burden,' said Prasamaccus, 'but a burden for another day. Today you are not a king; you are a hunted man in the forest of another world. I take it from the manner of your arrival that you found the Dream Shaper?'

'I did. He was dead, but I have the source of his magic'

'Is it strong enough to get us back home?'

'I do not think so. It is almost gone.'

'Then what do you plan?'

'The spirit of the Dream Shaper came to me, and told me to bring the Ghosts home. Baldric says the Ghosts are an army of the dead. I will try to raise them against the queen.'

The Brigante shivered. 'You will raise the dead?'

'I will if I can find Erin Plateau.'

Prasamaccus sighed. 'Well, that should not prove too arduous. You are sitting on Erin Plateau – and that is the sort of luck I have come to expect.'

'I have little choice, Prasamaccus. I have no intention of dying here – not with my father's murderers tearing at the heart of my kingdom. If I could, I would summon the Demon King himself.'

The Brigante nodded and rose, 'I will leave you to your plans,' he said sadly.

Two hours later Laitha sat shrouded in misery at the edge of the hill beneath the light of the two moons. Since Thuro's return he had not spoken to her or acknowledged her existence. At first she had been angry enough to ignore this, but as the day passed her fury had melted, leaving her feeling lonely and rejected. He was the one link she had to the wonderful world of her childhood. He had known Culain, and knew of her love for him. With him she should have been able to share her grief and, perhaps, exorcize it. Now he

158

was lost to her, as much as she was lost to Culain and the Caledones mountains.

And he had struck her! Before all those men. In retrospect she had been shrewish, but it had been only to bolster her confidence. Her life with Culain had taught her self-sufficiency, but she had always had the Mist Warrior close when real fear pervaded their world. She had felt Thuro was a true friend and had grown to love him in those early weeks, when his gentle nature had shown itself. His lack of skill with weapons made her feel protective. As he had grown in stature under Culain's tutelage, she had grown jealous of the time he spent with her man. All nonsense now.

A chill wind blew and she hugged her shoulders, wishing she had brought out a blanket but not desiring to return inside to fetch one. She wondered if the pain of Culain's passing would ever leave her. Something warm draped her shoulders and she looked up to see Prasamaccus standing by her. He had brought a blanket warmed by the fire. She gathered it around her, then burst into tears. He sat beside her, pulling her to him, saying nothing.

'I feel so alone,' she said at last.

'You are not alone,' he whispered. 'I am here. Uther is here.'

'He despises me.'

'I think that he does not.'

'Uther!' she hissed. 'Who does he think he is? A new name every day perhaps?'

'Oh, Laitha! You cannot see, can you? The boy has flown. You have told me of the weakly child he was when you found him, but that is not him any more. Look at his strength when he stood alone against the Vores. He could not be sure he had the strength or the power to turn those cats, yet he did it. That was the work of a man. He says the power is almost gone and many men would flee. But not Uther. Other men would use the remaining magic to find the sword. Not Uther. He seeks to aid the people he has befriended. Do not judge him by yesterday's memories.'

'He does not speak to me.'

'All paths run in two directions.'

'He once said he loved me.'

159

'Then he loves you still, for he is not a fickle man.'

'I cannot go to him. Why should I? Why should a man alone be allowed the virtue of pride?'

'I am not sure it is a virtue. However, I am here to be a friend. And friends are sometimes helpless between lovers.'

'We are not lovers. I loved Culain . . .'

'Who is dead. But no matter – lovers or friends, there is really very little difference that I can see. You do not need me to tell you how perilous is our situation. None of us can expect to survive long against the Witch Queen. Tomorrow she may return with a thousand men – ten thousand. Then we will be dead and your misery will seem even less important. Go to Uther and apologise . . .'

'I will not. I have nothing to apologise for.'

'Listen to me. Go to him and apologise. He will then tell you what you want to hear. Trust me . . . even if it means lying.'

'And if he laughs in my face?'

'You have lived too long in the forest, Laitha; you do not understand the world. Men like to think they control it but this is nonsense. Women rule, as they always have. They tell a man he is god-like. The man believes them and is in their thrall. For without them to tell him, he becomes merely a man. Go to him.'

She shook her head, but stood. 'I will take your advice, friend. But in future call me Gian. It is special to me, it is the language of the Feragh: Gian Avur, fawn of the forest.' Then she smiled and wandered to the main building. She opened the door and stepped inside. Uther was sitting with the other men, and they were listening intently to his words. He looked up and saw her. Conversation ceased as he rose smoothly and came to her, stepping out into the night. Prasamaccus was nowhere to be seen.

'You wanted me?' he asked, his chin held high, his tone haughty.

'I wanted to congratulate you, and . . . and to apologise.'

He relaxed and his face softened, breaking into the self-conscious grin she remembered from their first day.

'You have nothing to apologise for. It has been hard for me to become a man. Culain taught me to fight and Maedhlyn, to think.

160

Bringing the two together was left to me. But you have suffered greatly and I have been of little help. Forgive me?' He opened his arms and she stepped into his embrace.

In the background, crouched behind the rocks, Prasamaccus sighed and hoped they would not stand too long in the cold. His leg was aching and he yearned for sleep.

Uther returned to the building, gathered his blankets and took Laitha to the west of the hilltop, where a great stone had fallen – making a windbreak. He gathered wood for a small fire and spread the blankets on the ground. All this was done in silence, amid a growing tension of their bodies that did not affect the communion of their eyes. With the fire glowing they sat together and did not notice the limping Prasamaccus returning to his bed.

Uther dipped his head and kissed Laitha's hair, pulling her more closely to him. She lifted her face. He smelt the musky perfume of her skin and brushed his lips against her cheek. His head swam and a dreamlike sensation swept over him. He, the night and Laitha were one. He could almost hear the whispering memories of the giant stones, feel the pulsing distance of the stars. She lay back, her arms curling around his shoulders, drawing him to her. His hand moved slowly down the curve of her back, feeling the flesh beneath her tunic. He was torn between the urge to tear her clothes from her, and yet to savour this moment of moments. He kissed her and groaned. She tugged gently away from him and removed her tunic and leggings. He watched as her skin emerged from the clothing; it gleamed and glistened in the firelight. Stripping himself naked, he hesitated to pull her to him, his eyes drinking in her beauty. His hands were trembling as he reached for her. Laitha's body melted against him and everywhere she touched him seemed to burn. She pushed herself under him, but he resisted. Her eyes opened wide in surprise, but he smiled softly.

'Not swiftly,' he whispered. 'Never swiftly!'

She understood. His head lowered to kiss her once more, his hand moving over her skin as gentle and warm as morning sunlight – touching, stroking, exploring. Finally, his head pounding, he rose

161

above her. Her legs snaked over his hips and he entered her. Thoughts and emotions raged and swirled inside his mind, and he was surprised to find regret swimming amidst the joy. This was a moment he had dreamed of, yet now could never come again. He opened his eyes, looking down on her face, desperate to remember every precious second.

Her eyes opened and she smiled. Reaching up she cupped his face, pulling him closer, kissing him with surprising tenderness. Passion swallowed his regret and he passed into ecstasy.

For Laitha the sensation was different. She too had dreamed of the day she would surrender her virginity to the man she loved. And in a way she had. For Uther was all that was left of Culain and she could see the Mist Warrior in Uther's storm-cloud eyes. And Prasamaccus was right. The weakly youth in the forest had gone for ever, replaced by this powerful, confident young man. She knew she could grow to love him, but never with the wild, wonderful passion she had felt for Culain. As she thought of him, her mind blended her memories with the slow, rhythmic contact at the centre of her being and she felt it was the Lance Lord moving so powerfully above her. Her body convulsed in a searing sea of pleasure that bordered on pain. And in her ecstasy she whispered his name.

Uther heard it, and knew he had lost her in the moment of gaining her . . .

13

Baldric returned to Erin Plateau early the following morning. When the Vores had turned on the soldiers the lean huntsman had swiftly scaled a tree and watched as the carnage continued. The beasts had killed scores of men and horses, driving the army from the forest. Baldric had followed them for some distance and now reported that Mareen-sa was free of threat. Korrin sent out scouts to watch for the enemy's return, glancing at Uther for approval. Uther nodded.

'The enemy will return,' said the prince, 'but we must make the delay work for us.' Uther summoned Prasamaccus, sending him and Hogun to hunt for fresh meat. Laitha went with them to gather mushrooms, herbs and other edible roots. Rhiall and Ceorl were sent to the city of Callia to see what effect the news of the soldiers' defeat would have.

Finally Uther called Korrin to him and the two men walked to the edge of the stone circle, looking out over the vast forest and the sweeping hills of Mareen-sa.

'Tell me about the Ghosts,' said Uther. The woodsman shrugged.

'I have only seen them once – and that from a distance.'

'Then tell me the legend.'

'Is it wise to raise an army of the dead?'

'Is it wise for nineteen people to rebel against a Witch Queen?' responded Uther.

'I take your point. Well, the legend says that the Ghosts were soldiers of an ancient king, and when he died they marched into the underworld to fetch him back. But they became lost and now march for ever through the wilderness of the Void.'

'How many are there?'

'I have no idea. When I saw them I only took one swift glance, and that was over my shoulder while running.'

'Where did you see them?'

'Here,' said Korrin, 'on Erin.'

'Then why have we not seen them?'

'It is the moons – but then you would not know that. On certain nights of the year the light of Apricus, the large moon, cannot be seen. Only Sennicus shines. On those nights the Ghosts walk and the circle is shrouded in mist.'

'How soon before Sennicus shines alone?'

Korrin shrugged. 'I am sorry, Uther, I do not know. It happens about four times a year, sometimes six. Rhiall would know. His father studied the stars and he must have learned something. When he gets back I will ask him.'

Uther spent the day exploring the woodland around the hill, seeking out hiding places and trails the rebels might be forced to take when the soldiers returned. His frustration was great as he walked, for all the warriors whose lives had been researched by Plutarch had one thing in common. They each, at some time in their lives, ruled armies. There was little Uther could achieve with ten woodsmen, a crippled hunter and a forest girl skilled with the bow. And even should he be able to raise a force from amongst the population, how long would it take to train them? How much time would Astarte allow?

He shared the concern of both Prasamaccus and Korrin about using an army of corpses. Yet an army was an army. Without it they were lost.

Hungry and tired, he sat down by a shallow stream and allowed his thoughts to return to the subject he had forced from his mind. At the height of his passion, Laitha had whispered the name of Culain and this caused a terrible split in his emotions. He had worshipped Culain and was now jealous of him – even as he loved Laitha and was now angry with her. His mind told him it was not her fault that she still loved Culain, but his heart and his pride could not accept second place.

'Greetings,' said a voice and Uther leapt to his feet, sword in hand. A young woman sat close by, dressed in a simple tunic of shining white cloth. Her hair was gold, her eyes blue.

'I am sorry,' he said. 'You startled me.'

'Then it is I who am sorry. You seem lost in thought.'

She was quite the most beautiful woman Uther had ever seen. She rose and walked to stand beside him, reaching out to touch his arm. As she looked into his eyes, he saw a strange look come into hers.

'Is something wrong, lady?'

'Not at all,' she said swiftly. 'Sit with me for a while.' The songs of the forest birds faded into what was almost a melody of soft-stringed lyres. The sun bathed them both, and all the colours of the forest shone with ethereal beauty. He sat.

'You remind me of someone I once knew,' she said, her face close to his, the perfume of her breath sweet and arousing.

'I hope it was someone you liked?'

'Indeed I did. Your eyes, like his, are the colours of the Mist.'

'Who are you?' he whispered, his voice husky.

'I am a dream, perhaps. Or a wood nymph. Or a lover?' Her lips brushed his face and she lifted his hand, pressing it to her breast.

'Who are you?' he repeated. 'Tell me.'

'I am Athena.'

'The Greek goddess?' She drew back from him then, surprised.

'How is it that you know of me? This world is far from Greece.'

'I am far from home, lady.'

'Are you of the Mist?'

'No. What other names have you?'

'You know of the Feragh, I see. I am also called Goroien.'

Now it was Uther's turn to show surprise. 'You are Culain's lady; he spoke of you often.'

She moved subtly away from him. 'And what did he say?'

'He said that he had loved you since the dawn of history. I hope you will forgive me for saying that I can see why?'

She acknowledged his compliment with a slight smile. 'His love was not so great as you think. He left me and chose to become mortal. How would you explain that?'

'I cannot, lady. But I knew Culain and he thought of you always.'

'You say "knew" and "thought". Have you lost touch with him?'

Uther licked his lips, suddenly nervous. 'He is dead, lady. I am sorry.'

'Dead? How?'

'My enemies destroyed him: Soul Stealers from the void.'

'You saw him die?'

'No, but I saw him fall – just before the Circle brought us to Pinrae.'

'And who are you?' she asked, smiling sweetly, her left hand on his back. As she spoke the nails of the hidden hand grew long and silver and hovered over his heart.

'I am Uther.' The talons vanished.

'I do not know the name,' she said, rising and moving to the centre of the clearing.

'Will you help us?' he asked.

'With what?'

'This world is ruled by a Witch Queen and I seek to overthrow her.'

Goroien laughed and shook her head. 'Foolish boy! Sweet, foolish boy. I *am* the Witch Queen. This is my world.'

Uther rose. 'I cannot believe that!'

'Believe it, Prince Uther,' said Prasamaccus, stepping from the shadow of the trees.

'Ah, the cripple,' said Goroien, 'with the magic arrows.'

'Shall I kill her?' asked the Brigante, a shaft aimed at her heart. Goroien turned to Uther, her eyebrows raised.

'No!'

'A wise choice, sweet boy, for now I will let you both live . . . for a little while. Tell me, how long has your name been Uther?'

'Not long, lady.'

'I thought not. You are the boy Thuro, the son of Alaida. Know this, Uther. I slew your mother; I planned your father's death; and I sent the Soul Stealers into the Caledones mountains.'

'Why?'

'Because it pleased me.' She turned on Prasamaccus. 'Loose your arrow, fool!'

166

'No!' shouted Uther, but the Brigante had already released the string. The shaft flashed in the sunlight, only to be caught in a slender hand and snapped in two.

'You said sweet words to me, Uther. I will not kill you today. Leave this place, hide in the world of Pinrae. I shall not seek you. But in four days I will send an army into this forest, with orders to kill all they find. Do not be here.' She raised her hand in a cutting motion and the air beside her parted like a curtain. Beyond her, in a room adorned with shields, swords and weapons of war, Uther saw a tall man wearing a dark helm. And then they were both gone.

'She came to kill you,' said Prasamaccus.

'But she did not.'

'She is capricious. Let us fetch Laitha and leave this place.'

'I must wait for the one moon.'

'You asked me to be a wise counsellor . . .'

'This is not a time for wisdom,' snapped Uther. 'This is a time for courage.'

Under a bright moon a lone figure scaled the outer wall of Deicester Castle, strong fingers finding the tiniest cracks and crevices. Culain moved slowly and with great care. His horse and lance had been hidden in the woods two miles away, and his only weapon was a long hunting-knife in a scabbard at the back of his belt.

The climb would not have been difficult in daylight, for the castle was over two hundred years old and the outer walls were pitted and scarred. But at night he was forced to test every hand- and toe-hold. He reached the battlements just after midnight and was not surprised to find no sentries. For who did Eldared fear in the Caledones? What army could penetrate this far into his territory? He swung his body over the wall and crouched in the moon shadows below the parapet. He wore dark leggings of dyed wool and a close-fitting leather shirt as soft as cloth. He stayed motionless, listening to the sounds of the night. In the barracks below and to the right were only a dozen soldiers. He had counted them from his hiding place during the day; now he could hear some of them playing at dice. To his left the gate sentry was asleep, his feet planted on a chair, a blanket round his shoulders. Culain moved silently to the stairwell. The steps were wooden and he moved down them keeping close to the wall, away from the centre of the slats where the movement and therefore the noise would be greatest. Earlier he had noted the flickering lights at the highest western window of the keep, the rest of the upper living quarters dark and silent.

He crossed the courtyard at a run, halting before the door beside the locked gates of the keep. It was open. Once inside he waited until his eyes grew accustomed to the darkness within, then found the stairs and climbed to the upper levels. A dog growled close by and Culain opened the pouch at his side and pulled clear a fresh-cut slice of rabbit meat. He walked boldly into the corridor. The dog, a grey war-hound, rose threateningly, its lips drawn back to reveal long fangs. Culain crouched down and offered his hand. The dog, smelling the meat, padded forward to snatch it from Culain's fingers. He patted the hound's wide head and moved on.

At the furthest door he stopped. A light still showed faintly in the cracks around the frame. He drew his hunting-knife and stepped inside. A candle was guttering by the bedside and in the broad bed lay a man and a woman. Both were young – the woman no more than sixteen, the man a few years older. They were asleep in each other's arms like children, and Culain felt a pang of regret. The woman's face was oval and yet strong even in sleep. The man was fair-haired and fine-boned. Culain touched the cold knife-blade to the man's throat. His eyes flared open and he jerked, cutting the skin alongside his jugular.

'Do not hurt her!' he pleaded. Culain was touched, despite himself, for the man's first thought had been for the woman beside him. He gestured Moret to rise and, gathering the candle, led him through the bedroom into a side chamber, pushing shut the door behind him.

'What do you want?'

'I want to know how you contacted the Witch Queen.'

Moret moved to stand beside a high window overlooking the Caledones mountains. 'Why do you wish to see her?'

'That is my concern, boy. Answer me and you may live.'

'No,' said Moret softly. 'I need to know.'

Culain hesitated, considering killing the man and questioning the woman. But then if she knew nothing his mission would be ruined, for Cael and Eldared were away at war.

'I plan to destroy her,' he said at last.

Moret smiled. 'Go from here to the Lake of Earn. You know it?' Culain nodded. 'There is a circle of stones and a small hut. Before the hut is a tiny cairn of rounded rocks. Build a fire there when the wind is to the north. The smoke enters the hut and Goroien comes forth.'

'Have you seen her?'

'No, my brother travels there.'

Culain returned his knife to his scabbard. 'It is against my better judgement to allow you to live, but I shall. Do not make me regret the decision, for I am not an enemy you would desire.'

'No man who seeks to destroy Goroien could be an enemy of mine,' answered Moret. Culain backed to the door and was gone within seconds. Moret stood for a while by the window, then returned to his bed. Outside the door, Culain heard the bed creak and returned his knife once more to its scabbard.

Rhiall and Ceorl returned from Callia in high spirits. Behind them was a convoy of three wagons, sixty-eight men and twelve women, two of them pregnant. The huge youth bounded up the hill, grabbing Korrin's arm.

'The soldiers ransacked the town. They took twenty pregnant women and burnt the shrine to Berec. Two council leaders were hanged. The place is in an uproar.'

'What are they all doing here?' asked Korrin, staring down at the crowd forming a half-circle below the hill.

'They've come to see Berec reborn. The story is spreading like a grass fire that Berec has returned to earth, riding a forest stag and ready to overthrow the Witch Queen.'

'And you let them believe it?'

Rhiall's face took on a sullen look. 'Who is to say it is not true? He did ride a stag, just like Berec, and his magic vanquished the soldiers.'

'What is in the wagons?'

Rhiall's good humour returned. 'Food, Korrin. Flour, salt, dried fruit, oats, wine, honey. And there are blankets, clothes, weapons.'

Uther approached and stared down at the gathering, which grew hushed and silent. The sun was behind him and he appeared to the crowd to be bathed in golden light. Many in the group fell to their knees.

Rhiall and Korrin joined him. 'How many fighting men?' asked Uther.

'Sixty-eight.'

Uther grinned and laid his hand on Rhiall's shoulder. 'That is a good omen. In my land the men fight in Centuries of eighty warriors each. With our own people and these we now have a Century.'

Korrin grinned. 'Your arithmetic is not as strong as your magic. Surely a century is one hundred?'

'True, but with cooks, quartermasters and camp followers the fighting strength is eighty. Our army is formed by such units. Six Centuries equal four hundred and eighty men, or one Cohort, and ten Cohorts make a Legion. It is a small beginning, but a promising one. Korrin, go down among them and find out who the leaders are. Get the men in groups of ten. Add one of your own men to each group, two to the last. Find the groups work to make them feel part of the brotherhood – and weed out the weak in heart, for they will need to fight within four days.'

'One small problem, Uther,' said Korrin. 'They think you are a god. When they find out you are a man we could lose them all.'

'Tell me about the god – everything you can remember.'

'You will play the part then?' asked Rhiall.

'I will not risk losing sixty-eight fighting men. And it is not necessary for me to lie, or to use any deceit. If they believe it, let them continue. In four days we will either have an army or be dead on this forest floor.'

'Does that not depend,' put in Korrin, 'on when Sennicus shines alone?'

'Yes.' Both men turned to Rhiall. 'When will such an event happen again?' asked Uther.

'In about a month,' said the youngster. Uther said nothing, his face without expression. Korrin cursed softly.

'Get the men in groups,' said the prince, walking away to the edge of the stone circle, holding the bitter edge of his anger in check. In four days a terrible enemy would descend on the forest. His one hope was the army of the dead, and they could not be seen for a month. He needed to think, to plan, yet how could he devise a strategy with such limited forces at his disposal? All his life he had studied war and the making of war, seen the plans of generals from Xerxes to Alexander, Ptolemy to Caesar, Paullinus to Aurelius. But never had they been in such a position as his. The unfairness of his situation struck him like a coward's blow. But then why should life be fair, he reasoned? A man could do only his best with the favours the Gods bestowed.

Prasamaccus joined him, sensing his unease.

'Are the Gods being kind?' asked the Brigante.

'Perhaps,' replied Uther, remembering that he had not yet learned of the life of Berec.

'The burden of responsibility is not light.'

Uther smiled. 'It would be lighter if I had Victorinus and several legions behind me. Where is Laitha?'

'She is helping unload the wagons. Is all well between you?'

Uther closed his mouth, cutting off an angry retort, then looked into the Brigante's cool understanding eyes.

'I love her, and she is now mine.'

'But?'

'How do you know there is a but?'

Prasamaccus shrugged. 'Is there not?'

'Where did you learn so much of life?'

'On a hillside between the walls. What is wrong?'

'She loved Culain and it chains her still. I could not compete with him in life – nor in death, it seems.'

Prasamaccus sat silently for a moment, marshalling his thoughts. 'It must be exceptionally hard for her. All her life she has lived with this hero, worshipping him as a father, loving him as a brother, needing him as a friend. It is not difficult to see how she came to believe she wanted him as a lover. And you are right, Prince Uther, you cannot compete. But in time Culain will fade.'

'I know it is arrogance,' said Uther, 'but I do not want a woman who sees me as the shadow of someone else. *I* made love to her and it was beautiful . . . and then she whispered Culain's name. She lay beneath me and in her mind I was not there.'

There was nothing for the Brigante to say and he had the wisdom to know it. Laitha was a foolish undisciplined child. It would not have mattered if she had screamed his name inside her mind, but to speak it at such a time showed a stupidity beyond comparison. It was with some surprise that Prasamaccus realised he was angry with her; it was not an emotion he usually carried. He sat in silence with the prince for some time and then, when Uther was lost in thought, he rose and limped back to where Korrin waited with a group of strangers.

'These are the leaders of the Callia men,' said the woodsman. 'Is . . . the God ready to receive them?'

'No, he is communing with the spirits,' answered Prasamaccus. Some of the men backed away. The Brigante ignored them and wandered away to the long hall.

Uther the man stared out over the forest, while Thuro the boy sat inside his skull. Only a few short months ago the boy had been weeping in his room, frightened of the dark and the noises of the night. Now he was acting the man, but the torments of adolescence were still with him. As summer was beginning outside Eboracum, the boy Thuro had wandered into the woods and played a game where he was a hero, slaying demons and dragons. Now, with the summer here once more, he sat on a lonely hill and all the demons were real. Only there was no Maedhlyn. No Aurelius with his invincible legions. No Culain lach Feragh. Only the pretend man, Uther. 'I am the king, by right and by destiny.' Oh how the words haunted him now in his despair!

A frightened child sat among the stones of another world, playing a game of death. His melancholy deepened and he realised he would give his left arm if Maedhlyn or Culain could appear at this moment. More, he would offer ten years of his life. But the wind blew over the hilltop and he was alone. He turned and gazed on the group waiting silently some thirty paces away. Young men, old men, standing patiently, waiting for the 'God' to acknowledge them and their fealty. Turning his face from them, he thought of Culain and smiled. Culain really had been a God: Ares, the God of War to the Greeks, who became Mars for the Romans. Immortal Culain!

Well, thought Uther, if my grandfather was a God, then why not me? If the fates have decided I shall die in this deadly game, then let me play it to the full.

Without looking back he raised his hand, beckoning the group forward. There were twelve of them and they shuffled hesitantly to stand before him. He spread his arms, gesturing at the ground and they sat obediently.

'Speak!' he said and Korrin introduced each of the men, though Uther made no effort to remember their names. At the end he leaned forward and looked deeply into each man's eyes. All looked away the moment his gaze locked on theirs. 'You!' said Uther, gazing directly at the oldest man, grey-bearded and lean as a hunting wolf. 'Who am I?'

'It is said you are the God, Berec.'

'And what do you say?'

The man reddened. 'Lord, what I said last night was said in ignorance.' He swallowed hard, 'I merely voiced the doubts we all carried.'

Uther smiled. 'And rightly so,' he said. 'I have not come to guarantee victory, only to teach you how to fight. The Gods give, the Gods take away. All that is of worth is what a man earns with his sweat, with his courage and with his life. Know this: you may not win. I shall not rise to the sky and destroy the Witch with spears of fire. I am here because Korrin called me. I shall leave when I please. Do you have the heart to fight alone?'

The bearded man's head rose, his eyes proud. 'I do. It has taken me time to know it, but I know it now.'

'Then you have learned something greater than a God-gift. Leave me – all but Korrin.'

The men almost scrambled from his presence, some backing away, others bowing low. Uther ignored them all and when they were out of earshot Korrin moved forward.

'How did you know what that man said?' he asked.

'What do you think of them?' The woodsman shrugged.

'You picked the right man to speak to. He is Maggrig, the armourer. Once he was the most feared swordsman in Pinrae. If he stands, they all will. Do you wish me to tell you of Berec?'

'No.'

'Are you well, Uther? Your eyes are distant.'

'I am well, Korrin,' answered the prince, forcing a smile, 'but I need to think.' The green-eyed huntsman nodded his understanding.

'I shall have food brought to you.'

After he had gone Uther ran his mind back over the meeting. It was no mystery how he had focused on Maggrig; the man's stance showed him to be a warrior and he was the first to come forward, the others crowding around him. It had been a pleasant surprise when Maggrig had misinterpreted Uther's question. But then, as Maedhlyn always said, the prince had a swift mind.

Somehow the meeting left Uther feeling less melancholy. Was it so easy to be a God?

The answer would come within four days.

And it would be written in blood.

14

Culain lach Feragh sat before the cairn of stones watching the smoke from his small fire wafting in through the shattered windows of the derelict house. The Mist Warrior laid his silver lance by his side and pulled on two leather gauntlets edged with silver. His long hair was bound at the nape of the neck and over his shoulders he wore a silver-ringed protector, expertly sewn to a short cape of soft leather. A thick silver-inlaid belt was buckled to his waist and his legs were protected by thigh-length boots, reinforced by silver strips to the fronts and sides. A flickering blue light began inside the dwelling and Culain rose smoothly, placing a silver-winged helm upon his head, tying the scimitar-shaped ear-guards under his chin.

A slender figure came forward through the smoke which billowed and died, the fire quenched in an instant. As he saw her, his mouth went dry and he longed to step forward and pull her into his arms. She in turn stopped in her tracks as she recognised him, her hand flying to her mouth.

'You are alive!' she whispered.

'Thus far, lady.' She was wearing a simple dress of silver thread, her golden hair held in place by a black band at the brow.

'Tell me that you have come back to be with me.'

'I cannot.'

'Then why do you summon me?' she snapped, her blue eyes bright with anger.

'Pendarric says there is naught but evil in you and he asked me to destroy you. But I cannot until I am convinced he is right.'

'He was always an old woman. He had the world and he lost it. Now it is the turn of others. He is finished, Culain. Come with me; I have a world to myself. Soon it will be four worlds. I have power undreamt of since the fall of Atlantis.'

175

'And yet you are dying,' he said, the words cutting him like knife wounds.

'Who says that I am?' she hissed. 'Look at me! Am I any different? Is there a single sign of age or decay?'

'Not on the surface, Goroien. But how many have died . . . how many will die to keep you so?'

She moved towards him and the music began in his mind. The air was still and all the world was silent. Her arms came up around his neck and he smelt the perfume of her skin, felt the warmth of her touch. Reaching up he pulled her arms clear of him, pushing her away.

'What will you prove?' he asked. 'That I love you still? I do. That I want you? That too. But I will never have you. You killed Shaleat, you killed Alaida – and now you will destroy a world.'

'What are these savages to you, with their ten-second lives. There will always be more to replace those who die. They are unimportant, Culain. They always were, only you were too obsessed to see it. What does it matter now that Troy fell, or your friend Hector was slain by Achilles? What does it matter that the Romans conquered Britain? Life moves on. These people are as shadows to you and me. They exist to serve their betters.'

'I am one of them now, Goroien,' he said. 'My ten-second life is a joy. I never understood winter before, or truly felt the joy of spring. Come with me. Live out a life unto death, and we will see together what comes after.'

'Never!' she screamed. 'I will never die. You speak of pleasure. I see your decaying face and it makes me want to vomit: lines by your eyes, and I don't doubt that under that helm the silver is spreading like a cancer through your hair. In human terms what are you now, thirty? Forty? Soon you will begin to wither. Your teeth will rot. Young men will push you aside and mock you. And then you will fall and the worms will eat your eyes. How could you do this?'

'All things die, my love. Even worlds.'

'Do not speak to me of love, you never loved me. Only one man ever loved me and I have brought him back from the grave. That is what power is, Culain. Gilgamesh is with me once more.'

176

He stepped back from the glare of triumph in her eyes. 'That is not possible!'

'I kept his body throughout the centuries, surrounded by the glow of five Stones. I worked and I studied. And one day I succeeded. Go away and die somewhere, Culain, and I shall find your body and bring it back. Then you will be mine.'

'I am coming to Skitis, Goroien,' he said softly. 'I shall destroy your power.'

She laughed then, a rich mocking laughter that caused the colour to flood his cheeks. '*You* are coming? Once that would have put terror into my heart, but not now. A middle-aged man, soft and decaying, is coming to challenge Gilgamesh? You have no idea how often he speaks of you, dreams of killing you. You think to stand against him? I will show you how your arrogance has betrayed you. You always liked the Shade games – play this one.' She gestured with her right hand and the air shimmered. Before Culain stood a tall warrior with golden hair and bright blue-green eyes. He carried a curved sword and a dagger. 'Here is Gilgamesh as he was.' The warrior leapt forward and Culain swept up the lance, twisted the handle and pulled clear the hidden sword. He was just in time to block a savage cut. Then another . . . and another. Culain fought with all the skill of the centuries, but Goroien was right; his aging body was no longer equipped to tackle the whirlwind that was Gilgamesh, the Lord of Battle. Culain, growing desperate, took a risk, spinning on his heel in the move he had taught Thuro. His opponent leapt to the left, avoiding Culain's raised elbow, and a cold sword slid beneath the Mist Warrior's ribs.

He crumpled, hitting the hard clay ground on his face and dislodging the silver helm. He fought to stay conscious, but his mind fell into darkness. When he awoke Goroien was still there, sitting by the cairn of stones.

'Go away, Culain,' she said. 'What you fought was Gilgamesh as he was. Now he is stronger and faster; he would kill you within seconds. Either that or use this.' She dropped a yellow pebble on the ground before him; it was pure Sipstrassi, with virtually no sign of black veins. 'Become immortal again. Become what you were . . . what you should be. Then you have a chance.'

He pushed himself to his feet. 'It is not usual to give your enemy a chance at life, lady.'

'How could you be my enemy? I have loved you since before the Fall. I will love you on the day the universe ends in fire.'

'We will never be lovers again, lady,' he said. 'I will see you on Skitis Island.'

She stood. 'You fool! You will not see me. You will see your death coming towards you in every stride Gilgamesh takes.'

She walked into the derelict house without a backward glance and Culain slumped to the ground, tears in his eyes. It had taken all his strength to tell her their love was ended. He stared down at the Sipstrassi Stone and lifted it. She was right, he was in no condition to face Gilgamesh. Her voice drifted back to him, as if from a great distance.

'Your grandson is a handsome boy. I think I will take him. Do you remember my time as Circe?' Her laughter echoed into silence.

Culain sat with head bowed. After the Trojan war Goroien had wreaked her vengeance on the Greeks, causing the bloody deaths of Agammemnon the warlord and Menelaus the Spartan king. But by far the most hideous of her vengeful acts was the shipwreck of Odysseus. For Goroien, as Circe the witch, turned some of the survivors into swine, tricking the others into cooking and eating them.

He picked up his sword and brushed the dirt from the blade.

Walking to his horse, he touched the Sipstrassi Stone to its temple and stepped back. The beast's body collapsed, then swelled and stretched, its smooth flanks growing silver-edged scales of deep rust-red. Its head shimmered, its eyes becoming slanted like a great cat's, its snout stretching, fangs erupting from a cavernous mouth. Huge wings unfolded from its ribs and its hoofs erupted into taloned claws. Its long neck arched back and a terrible cry filled the air. Culain looked down at the black pebble in his hand and tossed it to the ground. Sliding his sword back into the haft of his lance, he climbed to the saddle on the dragon's back, whispering the word of command. The beast rose on its powerful legs, the wings spreading wide, then it soared into the night air heading north-west to Skitis.

On the third night a fearsome storm broke over Erin Plateau, shafts of lightning spearing the sky. Uther remained where he had stayed for three days now, sitting at the edge of the circle. Prasamaccus and Korrin gathered food and blankets for the prince and stepped out into the driving rain. At that moment lightning streaked the sky and both men saw Uther stand and raise his arms over his head, his blond hair billowing in the shrieking wind. Then he vanished. Korrin ran to the stones, Prasamaccus hobbling behind, but there was no sign of the prince.

The storm broke, the rain easing to a fine drizzle. Korrin sank to a rock.

'It is over,' he said, bitterness returning to his voice for the first time since the Vores turned on the soldiers. Korrin began to curse and swear and the Brigante moved away from him; he too felt demoralised and beaten, and he sat on the fallen stone overlooking the forest.

'What will we tell them?' said Korrin. The Brigante gathered his cloak tightly around his slender frame. His leg ached, as it always did when the weather turned damp, and his heart told him he would never see Helga again. He could offer Korrin no advice. Just then the two moons appeared from behind the breaking clouds and a third man joined them.

'Where is Berec?' asked Maggrig but neither man answered. 'So, we are alone, as he said we might be.' He scratched his greying beard and sat beside Korrin. 'We've set some snares and dug a few pits, which should slow them a little. And there are some five good ambush points.'

Korrin glanced up, surprised. The news of Berec's departure seemed to affect Maggrig not at all. 'We should hit them first at the Elm Hollow. The horsemen will not be able to charge up the rise and we'll have some hundred feet of killing ground. Even our archers should be unable to miss at that distance. We could down perhaps a hundred men.'

'You are talking of eighty men against an army,' said Korrin. 'Are you mad?'

'Eighty men is all we had yesterday. Gods, man, no one lives for ever.'

'Except the Witch Queen,' said Korrin, adding a savage curse.

'Take some advice from an old warrior: tell no one Berec has gone for good. Just say he has . . . who knows? . . . journeyed back to his castle in the clouds. In the meantime, let us hit them hard.'

'Good advice,' said Prasamaccus. 'We do not know how many soldiers are coming, and the forest is immense. We should be able to lead them a merry chase.'

Below, in the tiny village of tents that had sprung up by the stream, a young woman wandered out into the forest to be alone for a while. As she entered the darkness she caught sight of the moonlight reflecting from metal in the distance. She climbed a stout oak and peered to the west.

Moving silently through the trees came the army of Goroien.

For more than thirty hours Uther had been awake and worrying at the problem of the Void, searching every angle, exploring all the facts at his disposal. His reasoning and his training told him that he had overlooked a salient point, but try as he could there seemed no way to home in on it.

And then, just as the storm broke, the answer sailed effortlessly into his mind. Just because the Ghost Army could not be *seen* did not necessarily mean they were not *there*.

It was so simple. The freezing rain was forgotten. Prasamaccus had told him that he had dreamt of drums and marching feet on his first night on Erin Plateau, and Uther should have leapt on that thought like a striking falcon.

All that was left now was to enter the Void – the home of Atrols and Soul Stealers. Yes, he thought, that is all. Do not stop to think, Uther, he told himself. Just do it! He stood, raised his arms above his head, gripped the Stone tightly and wished for the Void.

His head spun and he fell. Around him the Mist swirled. Pushing himself to his knees, he drew his gladius. The Sipstrassi Stone was almost black. He risked touching his sword-blade; it shone with a white light and in the Mist he could see dark shadows and grey, cold faces. A long time ago, Thuro the child had wandered here in a fever dream and Aurelius had brought him back. The fear of that time returned to haunt him, and as his fear grew the shadow-shapes moved closer. Uther the man stood and steadied himself, lifting his sword high above his head. The light shone from the blade, pushing back both the Mist and the shadows within it.

As the Mist rolled away Uther saw the desolate landscape of the Void, a place of ash-grey hills and long-dead trees beneath a slate-dark sky. He shivered. It was no place for a man to die. Far off to his right, he caught the faint sound of drums. Holding his sword high like a lantern, he walked towards the sound. The shadows followed him and he could hear whispering voices calling his name. The prince ignored them. He climbed a low hill and stopped in wonder. There, in a dusty valley, was a defensive enclosure made up of mounds of grey earth thrown up from a huge square ditch. Sharpened stakes had been set into the banks. Within the enclosure were scores of tents and at the centre of the square stood a staff bearing a golden eagle, its wings spread. Uther stood for several minutes staring at the camp, unable to accept the vision before his eyes. Yet all the clues had been before him. Korrin had spoken of the Eagle sect who had tried to commune with the Ghosts. The soldiers marched to the drum in perfect order.

And Culain had talked of his greatest regret, when he had consigned an army to the Mist.

Uther stood on the lonely hilltop and gazed in wonder at the Eagle of the Ninth Legion.

The prince walked slowly down the hill to stand before the wide opening to the enclosure. Two legionaries stepped into his path – their eyes tired, their spears sharp. He was commanded to halt. The language was recognisable, but lacked the later British additions. He thought back to his training under Maedhlyn and Decianus, and answered them in their own archaic tongue.

'Who is your Legate?'

The legionaries glanced at one another and the taller man stepped forward.

'Are you Roman?'

'I am.'

'Are we close to home?' The voice quavered.

'I am here to bring you home. Who is your Legate?'

'Severinus Albinus. Wait here.' The soldier raced away and Uther stood, still holding the shining sword. Ten men returned some minutes later and the prince was ushered into the enclosure, an honour guard of five legionaries on either side of him. Men rushed from their tents to see the stranger, their faces ashen, their eyes dull. The guard halted before a wide tent. Uther surrendered his weapons to the centurion at the entrance and ducked inside. A young man of maybe twenty-five, dressed in polished bronze breastplate, was seated on a low stool.

'Your name?' he asked.

'You are Severinus Albinus?' responded Uther, aware that the success of his mission depended on maintaining the initiative.

'I am.'

'The Legate of Legio IX?'

'No. Our Legate is Petillius Cerialis; he did not accompany us. Who are you?' Uther sensed the young man, like all the men he had seen, was on the edge of desperation.

'I am Uther.'

'Where is this place?' asked Severinus, rising. 'We have marched here for months. No food. No water. Yet no thirst, nor hunger. There are creatures within the accursed Mist who drink blood. There are beasts the like of which I have never dreamt of. Are we all dead?'

'I can return you to Eboracum,' said Uther, 'but first there is much you should know.' He walked past the young soldier and seated himself on a divan at the back of the tent. Severinus Albinus joined him. 'Firstly, you marched from Eboracum to aid Paullinus against the Iceni uprising. You entered the Mist – a world of the dead.'

'I know all this,' said Severinus. 'How do we get home?'

Uther raised his hand. 'Gently. Listen to every word. Paullinus defeated Boudicca more than four hundred years ago.'

'Then we are dead. Sweet Jupiter, I cannot march any longer!'

'You are not dead, believe me. What I am attempting to tell you is that the world you knew is dead. The Roman Empire is fading. Britain no longer boasts a single Roman legion.'

'I have a wife . . . a daughter.'

'No,' said Uther sadly. 'They have been dead for four centuries. I can take you to Eboracum. The world is much changed, but the sun still shines and the grapes make wine, and the streams flow clear and the water is good to drink.'

'Who rules in Britain now?' asked Severinus.

'The land is at war. The Brigantes have risen and the Saxons and Jutes have invaded. The Romano-Britons led by Aquila, a pure-blood Roman of noble family, are fighting for their lives. There was a king named Aurelius, but he was murdered. I am his son. And I have journeyed beyond the borders of death to bring you home.'

'To fight for you?'

'To fight for me,' said Uther, 'and for yourselves.'

'And you will take us to Eboracum?'

'Not immediately,' said Uther, and told the Roman of the war in Pinrae and the rule of the Witch Queen. Severinus listened in silence.

'There was a time,' he said, when Uther fell silent, 'that I would have mocked your tale. But not here, in this ashen wilderness. You want us to fight for you, Uther? I would sell my soul for one day in the sunshine. No, for a single hour. Just take us away from here.'

Fear had brought Uther to the edge of panic. With the four thousand six hundred men of the Ninth Legion marching behind him, he returned to the hill he had first encountered upon entering the Void. Now, after an hour, still he could not open the pathway between the worlds. He had willed himself back, the Stone had glowed and for a moment only he had seen the giant stones of Erin, misty shadows shimmering just out of reach. He heard Severinus Albinus behind him and waved the man back, fighting

183

for calm. He glanced at the Stone; only the thinnest thread of gold remained.

He knew now for certain that the power of the Stone was insufficient to open a gateway large enough to allow the Legion through. He was not even sure whether he himself could return, and his agile mind once more began the long slow examination of all the possibilities.

At last he decided on one supreme effort. He closed his eyes and pictured himself back in Pinrae, but all the while holding the image of the Ninth Legion in his mind. Behind him, Severinus saw Uther grow less tangible, almost wraith-like, but then he was back as before. The prince stared down at the black pebble in his hand and could not find the courage to turn and face the expectant soldiers.

Beyond the Void the army of Goroien had circled the base of the hill, waiting for the order to attack. Maggrig and Korrin had placed archers all around the stones, but there was no way they could repel the armoured soldiers. At best they would wound a score or so, and it seemed to Korrin that more than two thousand men were assembled below.

'Why do they not attack?' he asked the lean wolf-like Maggrig.

'They are afraid of Berec's magic. But they will come soon.'

Twenty paces to their left, kneeling behind a fallen stone, Laitha waited with an arrow notched, her eyes fixed on a tall warrior with a purple plume to his helm. She had already decided he would be her target, for no other reason than that she disliked the arrogant way he strode amongst the men below, issuing orders. It made her feel somehow better to know that the strutting peacock would die before she did.

A hand touched her shoulder and she turned to see a tall broad-shouldered man with a golden beard. She could not remember having seen him before.

'Follow me,' he said, his manner showing he was obviously used to being obeyed. He did not look back as Laitha followed him to the centre of the plateau.

'Who are you?' she asked.

'Hold fast to your questions and climb the altar.' She moved up on the broken central stones, clambering over the scarred and pitted runes worked into the surfaces.

The bearded man spoke just as she reached the highest point and stood precariously on the top stone, some six feet from the ground.

'Now lift your hand above your head.'

'For what purpose?'

'You feel there is time for debate? Obey me.'

Biting back her anger, she raised her right arm. 'Higher!' he said. As she did so her fingers touched something cold and clinging and she withdrew her hand instinctively. 'It is only water,' he assured her. 'Push high and open your fingers. Grasp what is there and draw it down.'

Suddenly a great cry went up, a battle roar that chilled the blood, and the soldiers of Goroien swept up the hill. Arrows sang down to meet them, some glancing from armoured breastplates or helms, others wedging in the flesh of bare legs and arms.

'Reach up!' ordered the tall stranger. 'Swiftly, if you value your life.'

Laitha pushed her hand through the invisible barrier of water and opened her fingers. She felt the cold touch of metal and the yielding warmth of leather. Grasping the object tightly, she drew it down. In her hand was a great sword with an upswept hilt of burnished gold and a silver blade, double-edged, engraved with runes she could not recognise.

'Follow me,' said the man, running towards the rocks where Uther had last been seen. Halting, he pulled Laitha forward. 'When I finish speaking, smite the air before you.' The words which followed meant nothing to Laitha, but the air around him hissed and crackled as if a storm was due. 'Now!' he shouted. The sword slashed forward and a great wind blew up. Lightning flashed towards the sky and the Mist billowed from where she struck. Laitha was hurled backwards to the ground.

Uther leapt from the Mist, glancing around him. At the far end of the plateau the rebels began to stream back and the prince could see the plumed helms of Goroien's soldiers. Just then, Severinus

185

Albinus stepped into the sunshine with the Ninth Legion following him. Some of the men fell to their knees as the sunshine touched them, others began to weep in their joy and relief. Severinus, though young, was a seasoned campaigner and he took in the situation in an instant.

'Alba formation!' he yelled and Roman discipline was restored. Legionaries bearing their embossed rectangular bronze shields drew their swords and formed a fighting line, pushing forward and spreading out to allow the spearmen through. As the rebels ran back, the line opened before them.

Goroien's soldiers had an opportunity then to rush the line, but they did not. They were mostly men of Pinrae and they knew the legend of the Ghost Army. They stood transfixed as the Legion formed a square and advanced with shields locked, long spears protruding. The soldiers of Pinrae were not cowards – they would face, and had faced, overwhelming odds – but they had already seen the coming of the God, Berec. Now more and more spirits of the dead were issuing from the Mist, and this they could not bear. Slowly they backed away, returning to the base of the hill. The Legion halted at the circle of stones, awaiting orders.

In the safety of the square Uther helped Laitha to her feet. 'How did you do that? I thought I was fin . . .' He stumbled to a halt as he saw the great sword lying on the ground at Laitha's feet. He dropped to his knees, his hand curling round the hilt. 'My father's sword!' he whispered. 'The Sword of Cunobelin.' He rose. 'How?'

Laitha swung around, seeking the man with the golden beard, but he was nowhere in sight. She explained swiftly as Severinus Albinus approached.

'What are your orders, Prince Uther? Shall we attack?'

Uther shook his head and, carrying the longsword, strode to the edge of the square. The legionaries stepped aside and he walked down the hill, halting some thirty feet from the enemy line. A bowman notched an arrow.

'Draw the string and I'll turn your eyes to maggot balls,' said the prince. The man dropped both bow and arrow instantly.

'Let your leader step forward!'

A short, stocky middle-aged man in a silver breastplate walked from the line. He licked his lips as he came but held his shoulders back, pride preventing him from a display of fear.

'You know who I am,' said Uther, 'and you can see that the Ghosts have come home. I gauge you are now outnumbered two to one, and I can see that your men are in no condition for battle.'

'I cannot surrender,' said the man.

'I see that, but neither would the queen desire you to throw away the lives of your men needlessly. Take your army from Mareen-sa and report to Astarte.'

The man nodded. 'What you say is logical. Might I ask why you are sparing us?'

'I am not here to see the men of Pinrae slaughter one another. I am here to destroy the Witch Queen. Do not misjudge my mercy. If we meet again on the field of battle, I will crush you and any who stand in my path.'

The man bowed stiffly. 'My name is Agarin Pinder, and if I am ordered to stand in your path I will do so.'

'I would expect no less from a man of duty. Go now!'

Uther swung on his heel and returned to the plateau, calling Severinus to him. The young Roman followed him into the long building.

'Gods, I am hungry,' said Severinus, 'and what a wonderful feeling it is!' On the table was a flagon of wine and Uther poured two goblets, passing one to the Roman.

'We must leave the forest and march on Callia, a town nearby,' said Uther. 'There are insufficient supplies here to feed a legion.'

Severinus nodded. 'You chose not to fight. Why?'

'The Roman army was once the finest the world had seen. The discipline was second to none, and many a battle was turned on that. But your men were not ready, not after the creeping horror of the Void. They need time to feel the sunlight on their faces; then they will be truly Legio IX.'

'You are a careful commander, Prince Uther. I like that.'

'Speaking of care, I want you to take your men from the plateau and prepare your defensive enclosure below; there is a stream there.

Do not allow your men to mix with the people of Pinrae. You have been part of their legends for hundreds of years and on certain nights they even watch you march. It is a trick of the Mist. But the important point is this: they believe you are of Pinrae, and part of their history. As such we will gain support from the country. Let no one suspect you are from another world.'

'I understand. How is it that these people speak Latin?'

'They do not, but I'll explain that at another time. Send out a scouting troop to follow Goroien's soldiers from the forest. I will try to arrange some food for your men.' Severinus drew himself upright and saluted and Uther acknowledged the gesture with a smile.

As Severinus left the room, Korrin and Prasamaccus entered.

Korrin almost ran forward, his green eyes ablaze with excitement. 'You did it!' he shouted, his fist punching the air.

'It is pleasant to be back,' said Uther. 'Where is the man with the golden beard?'

'I do not know who you mean,' answered Korrin.

Uther waved his hand. 'It does not matter. Tomorrow we march on Callia and I want your best men, trusted men, to precede us. The Ghost Army of Pinrae is returning to free the land and the word must be spread. With luck, the town will open its gates without a battle.'

'I'll send Maggrig and Hogun. Gods, man, to think I almost killed you!'

Uther reached out and gripped Korrin's shoulder. 'It is good to see you smile. Now leave me with Prasamaccus.' The huntsman grinned, stepped back and bowed deeply.

'Are you still set on leaving Pinrae?'

'I am – but not until Goroien is finished.'

'Then that will suffice.'

After he had gone, Prasamaccus accepted a goblet of wine and leaned in close, studying Uther's face. 'You are tired, my prince. You should rest.'

'Look,' said Uther, lifting the sword. 'The blade of Cunobelin, the Sword of Power, and I do not know how it came to Laitha.

188

Or why. I was trapped in the Void, Prasamaccus, and trying to find a way to tell almost five thousand men that I had raised their hopes for nothing. And just then, like a ghost, I saw Laitha raise a sword and cut the Mist as if it were the skin of a beast.'

Prasamaccus opened his mouth to phrase a question but stopped, his jaw hanging. Uther turned to follow the direction of his gaze. Sitting by a new fire was the golden-bearded man, holding tanned hands towards the blaze.

'Leave us,' Uther told the Brigante. Prasamaccus needed no second invitation and hobbled from the room as Uther approached the stranger.

'I owe you my life,' he said.

'You owe me nothing,' replied the man, smiling. 'It is pleasant to meet a young man who holds duty so dear. It is not a common trait.'

'Who are you?'

'I am the king lost to history, a prince of the past. My name is Pendarric.'

Uther pulled up a chair and sat beside the man. 'Why are you here?'

'We share a common enemy, Uther: Goroien. But aiding you was merely a whim – at least, I think it was.'

'I do not understand you.'

'It is especially pleasant after so many centuries to find that I can still be surprised. Did Laitha tell you how she came by the sword?'

'She said she drew it through the air, and her hand was wet as if dipped in a river.'

'You are a bright man, Uther. Tell me where she found the sword.'

'How can I? I know of . . .' The prince stopped, his mouth suddenly dry. 'Hers was the hand in the lake the day my father died. And yet she was with me in the mountains. How is this possible?'

'A fine question, and one which I should like to answer. One day, if you are still alive when I reach a conclusion, I shall come to you. All I know for certain is that it was right that it should happen. What will you do now?'

189

'I shall try to bring her down.'

Pendarric nodded. 'You are much like your grandfather – the same earnestness, the same proud sense of honour. It is pleasing to me. I wish you well, Uther, now and in the future.'

'You are of the Feragh?'

'I am.'

'Can you tell me what is happening in my homeland?'

'Aquila is losing the war. He smashed one Brigante army at Virosidum, and Ambrosius has destroyed Cerdic. But the Saxon Hengist is moving north with seven thousand men, hoping to link with Eldared for a conclusive battle at Eboracum.'

'How soon will this happen?'

'It is not possible to say, Uther – any more than it is possible to predict your future. It may be that you will defeat Goroien and not be able to return home. It may be that you will return only to face defeat and death. I do not know. What I do know is that you are Rolynd and that counts for more than crowns.'

'Rolynd?'

'It is a state of being, a condition of harmony with the unknown universe. It is very rare – maybe only one man in ten thousand. In material terms it means you are lucky, but also that you earn your luck. Culain is Rolynd; he would be proud of you.'

'Culain is dead. The Soul Stealers killed him.'

'No, he is alive – but not for long. He also is riding to face Goroien – and there he will meet an enemy he cannot conquer. And now I must go.'

'Can you not stay and lead the war against the Witch Queen?'

Pendarric smiled. 'I could, Uther – but I am not Rolynd.'

He reached out as if to shake Uther by the hand, but instead dropped a Sipstrassi Stone into the Prince's palm.

'Use it wisely,' he said, and faded from sight.

15

Laitha found Uther sitting alone, lost in thought, staring into the flickering flames. She approached him silently and drew up a chair near him. 'Are you angry with me?' she asked, her voice soft and childlike. He shook his head, deciding it was better to lie than to face his pain. 'You have not spoken to me for days,' she whispered. 'Was it . . . was I . . . so disappointing?' He turned to her then and realised she did not know she had whispered Culain's name. He was filled with an urge to hurt her, to ram his bitterness home, but her eyes were innocent and he forced back his wrath.

'No,' he said, 'you did not disappoint me. I love you, Laitha. It is that simple.'

'And I love you,' she told him, the words tripping so easily from her tongue that his anger threatened to engulf him. She smiled and tilted her head, waiting for him to reach out and draw her to him. But he did not. He turned once more to the fire. A great sadness touched her then and she rose, hoping he would notice and bid her remain. He did not. She held back her tears until she was outside in the moonlight, then she ran to the edge of the stones and sat alone.

Inside the building Uther cursed softly. He had watched her leave, hoping this small punishment would hurt her, and found that it hurt him also. He had wanted to take her, to touch and stroke her skin; had needed to bury his head in her hair, allowing the perfume of her body to wash over him. And he had not told her that Culain was alive. Was that a punishment also – or a fear that she would turn from him? He wished he had never met her, for he sensed his heart would never be rid of her.

He stood and looked down at his ragged, torn clothing. Not much like a God, Uther – more like a penniless crofter. On impulse he took up the Stone and closed his eyes. Instantly he was clothed in the splendid armour of a First Legate, a red cloak draped over silver breastplate, a leather kilt decorated with silver strips, embossed silver greaves over soft leather riding-boots. The Stone still showed not a trace of black vein.

He moved out into the night and wandered down to the square ditch enclosure where the Legion had pitched their tents. The two legionary guards saluted him as he passed and he made his way towards the tent of Severinus Albinus. Everywhere huge fires were burning under the carcases of deer, elk and sheep, and songs were being sung around several of the blazes. Severinus rose and saluted as Uther entered his tent. The young Roman was a little unsteady on his feet and wine had stained the front of his toga. He grinned shamefacedly. 'I am sorry, Prince Uther. You find me not at my best.'

Uther shrugged. 'It must have been good to see the sunshine.'

'Good? I lost seventy men to the Void and many of them returned to stand outside the camp and call to their comrades. Only their faces were grey, their eyes red – it was worse than death. I will have nightmares about it for all my life. But now I am drunk, and it does not seem so terrible.'

'You have earned this night with your courage,' said Uther, 'but tomorrow the wax must stay firmly in place on the flagons. Tomorrow the war begins.'

'We shall be ready.'

Uther left the tent and returned to Erin, seeing Laitha sitting alone at the edge of the circle. He went to her, his anger gone.

'Do not sit here alone,' he said. 'Come join me.'

'Why are you treating me this way?'

He knelt beside her. 'You loved Culain. Let me ask you this: Had he taken you for his wife, would you have been happy?'

'Yes. Is that so terrible?'

'Not at all, lady. And if on your first night together he had whispered Goroien's name in your ear, would your happiness have continued?' She looked into his smoke-grey eyes – Culain's eyes – and saw the pain.

'Did I do that . . . to you?'

192

'You did.'

'I am so sorry.'

'As am I, Laitha.'

'Will you forgive me?'

'What is there to forgive? You did not lie. Do I forgive you for loving someone else? That is not a choice you made, it is merely a truth. There is no need for forgiveness. Can I forget it? I doubt it. Do I still want you, even though I know you will be thinking of another? Yes. And that shames me.'

'I would do anything,' she said, 'to take away the hurt.'

'You will become my wife?'

'Yes. Gladly.'

He took her hand. 'From this day forward we are joined and I will take no other wives.'

'From this day forward we are one,' she said.

'Come with me.' He led her to a small, still deserted hut behind the main building. Here he lifted his Stone and a bed appeared.

But the soaring passion of their first loving was not repeated, and both of them drifted to sleep nursing private sorrows.

The dragon circled Skitis Island twice before Culain directed it down to an outcrop of wooded hills some two miles from the black stone fortress Goroien had constructed. The edifice was huge, a great stone gateway below two towers, and a moat of fire – burning without smoke. Culain leapt from the dragon's back and spoke the words of power. The beast shrank back into the grey gelding it had been and Culain stripped the saddle from its back and slapped its rump. The horse cantered away over the hillside.

The Mist Warrior took up his belongings and walked the half-mile to the deserted cabin he had seen from the air. Once inside he laid a fire, then stripped his clothing and stepped naked into the dawn light. Taking a deep breath, he began to run. Within a short time his breathing became ragged, his face crimson. He pushed on, feeling the acids building in his limbs, aware of the pounding in his chest. At last he turned for home, every step a burning torture. Back at the cabin he stretched his aching legs, pushing his fingers deep into the muscles of his calves, probing the knots and strains. He bathed in an icy stream and dressed once more. Beyond the cabin was a rocky section of open ground. Here he lifted two fist-sized stones and stood with his arms hanging loosely by his sides. Taking a deep breath he raised his arms and lowered them, repeating the movement again and again. Sweat streamed from his brow, stinging his eyes, but he worked on until he had raised each rock-laden arm forty times. As dusk painted the sky he set off for another run, shorter this time, loosening the muscles of his legs. Finally he slept on the floor before the fire.

He was up at dawn to repeat the torture of the previous day, driving himself even harder, ignoring pain and discomfort, holding the one vision that could overcome his agony.

Gilgamesh, The Lord of Battle . . .

The most deadly fighting man Culain had ever seen.

As Uther had hoped the town of Callia opened its gates without a battle, the people streaming out to strew flowers at the feet of the marching Legion. A young girl, no more than twelve, ran to Uther and placed a garland of flowers over his head.

Agarin Pinder and the army of Goroien had vanished like morning mist. The legion camped outside the town and wagons bearing supplies rolled out to them. Uther met the town leaders, who assured him of their support. He found it distasteful that they flung themselves full-length on the ground before him, but made no effort to stop them. By the following day six hundred erstwhile soldiers of the Witch Queen had come to him swearing loyalty. Korrin had urged him to slay them all, but Uther accepted their oaths and they rode with him as the Legion set off on the ten-day march to Perdita, the castle of iron.

Prasamaccus was sent with Korrin to scout ahead. Each evening they returned, but no sign of opposition forces was found until the sixth day.

Tired and dust-covered, Prasamaccus gratefully accepted the goblet of watered wine and leaned back on the divan rubbing his aching left leg. Uther and Severinus sat silently, waiting for the Brigante to catch his breath.

'There are eight thousand footmen and two thousand horse. They should be here late tomorrow morning.'

'How was their discipline?' asked Severinus.

'They march in good order, and they are well-armed.' Severinus looked to Uther.

'Do they have scouts out?' asked the prince.

'Yes. I saw two men camped in the hills to the west watching the camp.'

'Order the men to take up a defensive position on the highest hills,' Uther told Severinus. 'Throw up a rampart wall and set stakes.'

'But, Prince Uther . . .'

'Do it now, Severinus. It is almost dusk. I want the men working on the ramparts within the next hour.' The Roman's face darkened but he stood, saluted and hurried from the tent.

'The Romans do not like fighting from behind walls,' commented Prasamaccus.

'No more do I. I know you are tired, my friend, but locate the scouts and come to me when they have gone. Do not let them know you are there.'

For two hours the men of the Ninth Legion constructed a six-foot wall of turf around the crown of a rounded hill. They worked in silence under the watchful eye of Severinus Albinus. An hour after dusk, Prasamaccus returned to Uther's tent.

'They have gone,' he said.

Uther nodded. 'Fetch Severinus to me.'

Dawn found Agarin Pinder and his foot-soldiers twenty-two miles from the newly built fortress. He sent his mounted troops to engage the defenders and hold them in position until the infantry could follow. Then he allowed rations to be given to each man – a small loaf of black bread and a round of cheese. When they had broken their fast, they set off in columns of three on the long march to battle. He did not push them hard, for he wanted them fresh for the onslaught; nor did he allow the pace to slacken, for he knew that fighting men did not relish a long wait. It was a fine line, but Agarin Pinder was a careful man and a conscientious soldier. His troops were the best trained of the six nations and also the best fed and best-armed. The three, he knew, were inseparable.

At last he came in sight of the fortified hill. Already his mounted troops had circled the base, just out of arrow range. Agarin dismounted. It was nearing noon and he ordered tents to be set up and cooking fires lit. He broke the columns and rode forward with his aide to check the enemy fortifications. As the tents were unrolled and the soldiers milled about the new camp, the Ninth Legion marched in two phalanxes from the woods on either side. They marched without drums and halted, allowing their five hundred archers to send a deadly rain of shafts into the camp. Hearing the screams of the dying, Agarin swung his horse and watched in disbelief as his highly trained troops milled in confusion. The Legion, in close formation, advanced into the centre of the camp, leaving two ranks of archers on the hills on either side.

Agarin cursed and hammered his heels into his horse's side, hoping to break through the red-cloaked enemy and rally his men. His horse reared and fell, an arrow in its throat. The general pitched over its neck, scrambled to his feet and drew his sword. Turning to his aide, he ordered the man from the saddle. As he was dismounting, two arrows appeared in his chest. The stallion reared as the dying man's weight fell to its back and galloped away. The thunder of hooves from behind caused Agarin to spin on his heel as Uther and twenty men in the armour of Pinrae rode from the trees. The prince dismounted, drawing a longsword.

'I told you once. Now you must learn,' said Uther. Agarin ran forward swinging his blade, but Uther blocked the blow, sending a vicious return cut through his enemy's throat. Agarin fell to his knees, his fingers seeking to stem the red rush of life-blood. He pitched to his face on the grass.

In the camp all was chaos, slaughter and panic. With no time to prepare, the men of Goroien's army either fought in small shield circles that were slowly and ruthlessly cut to pieces, or ran back towards the east in frantic attempts to regroup. Some two thousand men managed to break from the camp under the command of three senior officers. They ran the deadly gauntlet of shafts from the bowmen on the hillsides and tried to form a fighting square, but then four hundred cavalry thundered from the woods with lances levelled. The square broke as panic blossomed and the soldiers fled, pursued and slain by the lancers.

They received no help from their own cavalry who, seeing Agarin Pinder slain, rode south at speed. Within the hour the battle was over. Three thousand survivors threw away their weapons and pleaded for mercy.

The stench of death was everywhere, clinging and cloying, and Uther rode to the fortress hill where two hundred men of the Legion waited. They cheered as he rode in and he forced himself to acknowledge them with a smile. Korrin was ecstatic.

'What a day!' he said, as Uther slid from the saddle.

'Yes. Five thousand slain. What a day!'

'When will you kill the others?'

Uther blinked. 'What others?'

'Those who have surrendered,' said Korrin. 'They should all hang like the traitors they are.'

'They are not traitors, Korrin, they are soldiers – men like yourself. Strong men, courageous men. I'll have no part in slaughter.'

'They are the enemy! You cannot allow three thousand men – warriors – to go free. And we cannot feed and guard them.'

'You are a fool!' hissed Uther. 'If we kill them no one will ever surrender again. They will fight like trapped rats – and that will cost me men. When these survivors go back, they will carry the word of our victory. They will say – and rightly so – that we are superb fighting men. That will weaken the resolve of those still to come against us. We are not here, Korrin, to start a blood-bath, but to end the reign of the Witch Queen. And ask yourself this, my blood-hungry friend: when I leave this realm with my Legion, from where will you recruit your own army? It will be from among the very men you want me to slay. Now get away from me. I am tired of war and talk of war.'

Towards midnight, Severinus and two of his centurions entered Uther's tent. The prince looked up and rubbed his eyes. He had

197

been asleep, Laitha beside him, and for the first time in weeks his dreams had been untroubled.

'Your orders have been obeyed, Prince Uther,' said Severinus, his face set, his eyes accusing.

'What orders?'

'The prisoners are dead. The last of them tried to break free and I lost ten men. But now it is done.'

'Done! Three thousand men!' Uther rose to his feet, his eyes gleaming and advanced on Severinus. 'You killed them?'

'The man Korrin came to me with orders from you. We were to take the prisoners away in groups of a hundred and kill them out of earshot of the others. You did not give this order?'

Uther swung to the centurions. 'Find Korrin and bring him here. *Now!*'

The two men backed away hurriedly. Uther pushed past Severinus into the night, sucking in great gasps of air. He felt he was suffocating. Laitha, dressed in a simple white tunic, came out and placed her hand on his arm. 'Korrin has suffered greatly,' she said. Uther shook her hand loose.

Minutes later the two centurions returned with Korrin behind them, his arms pinned by two legionaries.

Uther moved back into the tent, returning with the sword of Cunobelin in his trembling hands.

'You wretch!' he told Korrin. 'You had to have your blood, did you not?'

'You were too tired to know what you were doing,' said Korrin. 'You didn't understand or you would have given the order yourself. Now release me. We have work to do – strategies to think of.'

'No, Korrin,' said Uther sadly. 'No more strategies for you. No more battles and no more murder. Today was the high point of your sad career. Today was the end. If you have a God, then make your prayer to him, for I am going to kill you.'

'Oh, no! Not before the Witch Queen is overthrown. Don't kill me, Uther. Let me see Astarte slain. It is my dream!'

'Your dreams are drowned in blood.'

'Uther, you cannot!' shouted Laitha.

The Sword of Cunobelin flashed up, entering Korrin's belly, sliding up under the ribcage and cutting through his heart. The body slumped in the arms of the legionaries.

'Take this carrion and leave it for the crows,' said Uther.

Back inside the tent Uther slammed the bloody sword into the hard-packed earth, leaving it quivering in the entrance. Laitha was sitting on the bed, her knees drawn up to her chest.

Severinus followed the prince inside.

'I am sorry,' he said. 'I should have queried an order of such magnitude.'

Uther shook his head. 'Roman discipline, Severinus. First, obey. Gods, I am tired. You had better send some men to the other Pinrae leaders, Maggrig, Hogun, Ceorl. Get them here.'

'You think there will be trouble?'

'If there is, kill them all as they leave my tent.' The soldier saluted and left. Uther moved to the sword jutting in the entrance, the blood staining the earth. He made as if to draw it clear, then stopped and returned to the divan beside the bed. Within minutes the rebel leaders were assembled outside and Severinus led them in. Maggrig's eyes were cool and distant, his emotions masked. The others, as always, avoided Uther's eyes.

'Korrin Rogeur is dead,' said Uther. 'That is his blood.'

'Why?' asked Maggrig.

'He disobeyed me and murdered three thousand men.'

'Our enemies, Lord Berec'

'Yes, our enemies. That is not the point at issue. I had other plans for them and Korrin knew that. His action was unforgivable. Now he has paid for it. You men have two choices. Either you serve me, or you leave. But if you serve me you obey me.'

'Will you replace the Witch Queen?' asked Maggrig softly.

'No. When she is overthrown I will leave Pinrae and return to my world. The Ghost Army will leave with me.'

'And we are free to leave if we choose.'

'Yes,' lied Uther.

'May I speak with the others?'

199

Uther nodded and the men filed out. There was silence in the tent until their return. Maggrig, as always, was the spokesman.

'We will stay, Lord Berec, but Korrin's friends wish him to be buried as befits a war leader.'

'Let them do as they please,' said the prince. 'In a few days we will reach Perdita. Strip the dead of weapons and arm your own men.' He waved them away, aware that the sullen expressions were still evident.

'You have lost their love, I think,' said Severinus.

'I want only their obedience. What were our losses today?'

'Two hundred and forty-one dead, eighty-six seriously wounded and another hundred or so with light cuts. The surgeons are dealing with them.'

'Your men fought well today.'

Severinus accepted the compliment with a bow. 'They are mostly Saxon and, as you know, they are fine warriors. They take to discipline well – almost as well as true-born Romans. And if I may return the compliment, your strategy was exemplary. Eight thousand enemy casualties for the loss of so few of our own men.'

'It was not new,' said Uther. 'It was used by Pompey and by the divine Julius. Antony executed a similar move at Phillippi. Darius the Great was renowned for taking his Immortals on lightning marches, and Alexander conquered most of the world with the same strategy. The principle is a simple one: always act, never react.'

Severinus grinned. 'Do you always *react* so defensively to compliments, Prince Uther?'

'Yes,' he admitted sheepishly. 'It is a guard against arrogance.'

After Severinus had left, Uther saw that Laitha had still not moved. She sat, hugging her knees and staring into the embers of the brazier fire. He sat beside her, but she pulled away from him.

'Speak to me,' he whispered. 'What is wrong?'

She swung on him then, her hazel eyes fierce in the candlelight. 'I do not know you,' she said. 'You killed that man so coldly.'

He said nothing for a moment. 'You think I enjoyed it?'

'I do not know, Uther. Did you?'

He licked his lips, allowing the question to sink into his subconscious.

'Well?' she asked. He turned his face towards her.

'In that moment – yes, I did. All my anger was in that blow.'

'Oh, Uther, what are you becoming?'

'How can I answer you?'

'But this war was being fought for Korrin. Now who is it for?'

'It is for me,' he admitted. 'I want to go home. I want to see Eboracum, and Camulodunum, and Durobrivae. I do not know what I am becoming. Maedhlyn used to say that a man is the sum total of all that happens to him. Some things strengthen, some things weaken. Korrin was like that. The death of his wife unhinged him and his heart was like a burning coal, desiring only vengeance. He once told me that if he won he would light fires under his enemies that would never go out. As for me, I am trying to be a man – a man like Aurelius, or Culain. I have no one to turn to, Laitha. No one to say, "You are wrong, Thuro. Try again." Killing Korrin may have been a mistake, but if I had done it earlier three thousand men would still be alive. And now – if we win – there will be no fires that never go out.'

'There was such gentleness in you when we were back in the Caledones,' she said, 'and you were a hunted prince, ill-suited to sword play. Now you are acting the general and committing murder.'

He shook his head. 'That is the sad part. I am not *acting* the general, I *am* the general. Sometimes I wish this was all a dream, and that I could wake in Camulodunum with my father still king. But he is dead and my land is being torn apart by wolves. For good or ill I am the man who can stop it. I understand strategy and I know men.'

'Culain would never have killed Korrin.'

'And such is the way of legends,' he mocked. 'No sooner the man dies than he becomes a wondrous figure. Culain was a warrior; that makes him a killer. Why do you think the Ninth Legion were in the Void? Culain sent them there. He told me about it back in the Caledones. It was a regret he carried, but he did it while fighting a war against the Romans four hundred years ago.'

201

'I do not believe you.'

'You are a foolish child,' he snapped, his patience gone.

'He was twice the man you are!'

Uther stood and took a deep breath. 'And you are a tenth of the woman you ought to be. Maybe that's why he rejected you.' She flew at him, her nails flashing towards his face, but he brushed aside her attack and hurled her facedown to the bed. Swiftly he straddled her back, pinning her. 'Now that is no way for a wife to behave.' She struggled for some minutes, then relaxed and he released her. She rolled to her back, her fist cracking against his chin, but he grabbed her arms and pinned her beneath him.

'I may not be right all the time,' he whispered, 'and I may have struck a bad bargain with you. But whatever I become I will always need you. And always love you.'

Outside, Prasamaccus heard the argument die away.

'I do not think they will want to see you now,' whispered a sentry.

'No,' agreed Prasamaccus, hobbling away into the darkness.

For two weeks Culain had toiled and struggled to regain lost strength and speed. He was now fitter and faster than he had been for years . . . and he knew it was not enough. Goroien had been right. In accepting mortality, Culain had lost the vital edge of youth. His doubts were many as he sat on the hard-packed ground before the cabin, watching the sun sink in fire.

Once, as Cunobelin the King, he had allowed his body to grow old and grey, but it had been a sham. Beneath the wrinkles his strength had remained.

For two days now he had exercised not at all, allowing his tired body to rest and replenish lost energy. Tomorrow he would walk to the Castle of Iron and seek a truth he felt he already knew.

He was glad now that he had used up the Stone in that wonderfully extravagant flight. The temptation to use its power on himself would today have proved irresistible. His thoughts turned to Gilgamesh, seeing the warrior as he had first known him, strong and proud, leading a hopeless fight against an invincible enemy.

202

Goroien had taken pity on him, which was unlike her, and helped him overthrow the tyrant king. Gilgamesh knew glory then and the adulation of a freed people. But it was not enough; there was a hunger in the Lord of Battle that no amount of victories could ease. Culain had never understood the demon that drove him. Three times Gilgamesh challenged Culain, and three times the Mist Warrior had refused to be drawn. Many in the Feragh had wondered at Culain's reasons. Few had realised the truth. Culain lach Feragh was afraid of the strange, dark quality within Gilgamesh that made him unbeatable.

Then came the day when news of his death had reached Culain. His heart had soared, for deep inside he had begun to believe the Lord of Battle would one day kill him. He recalled the day well – the sun clear in a cloudless sky, distant cornfields glowing gold and the high white turrets of Babylon cloaked in dark shadows. Brigamartis had brought the news, her face flushed with excitement. She had never liked Gilgamesh. Before his arrival she had been considered one of the finest sword duellists in the Feragh, but he had defeated her with ease in the Shade Games.

'There was something wrong with his blood,' said Brigamartis gleefully. 'It would not accept Sipstrassi power. He aged wonderfully; in the last two years even Goroien would not visit him. He had begun to drool, you know, and he was half-blind.'

Culain had waited five years before crossing the Mist. Goroien was as beautiful as ever, and acted as if her affair with Gilgamesh had never taken place. His name did not cross her lips for another three centuries.

Now the Lord of Battle had returned and Culain lach Feragh would truly taste the terrors of mortality. It was galling to live so long, only to face such bitterness. Thuro and Laitha were trapped in a world he could not reach, victims of a goddess he could never kill and menaced by a warrior he could not conquer.

He lifted his lance and drew the hidden sword. The edge was lethally sharp, the balance magnificent. He looked down at his reflection in the silver steel, gazing into his own eyes as if expecting to see answers there.

Had he ever truly known courage? How simple it had been for an immortal warrior to battle in the world of men. Almost all wounds could be healed, and he had on his side the knowledge and acquired skill of centuries. Even the great Achilles had been a child by comparison, the outcome of their duel never in doubt. Only his opponents had known courage. Culain smiled. His fear of Gilgamesh had made him run like a child in terror of the dark – and like all runners, he had hurtled headlong into greater fear. Had he killed Gilgamesh all those centuries ago Goroien would not now have taken into her body the dread disease that was killing her. From that he could reason that she might never have become the Witch Queen. So the terrors of this age came squarely to rest on Culain's shoulders.

He accepted the burden and sought the sanctuary of Eleari-mas, the Emptying. But his mind drifted into memory. He saw again the curiously beautiful end of the world. He was fifteen years old, standing in the courtyard of his father's house in Balacris. He saw the sun sink slowly into the west and then hurtle back into the sky. A great wind came up, and the palace of Pendarric began to glow. He heard someone scream and saw a woman pointing to the horizon. A colossal black wall was darkening the sky, growing ever larger. He had stared at it for some moments, thinking it a great storm. But soon the terror struck. It was a thundering thousand-foot wall of water, drowning the land. The golden glow from the palace spread over the city, reaching the outer sections just as the sea roared over them all. Culain had been rooted to the spot, desperate to draw the last second of life. As the sea struck him he screamed and fell, only to open his eyes and gaze at the sun in a blue sky. He stood, and found himself on a hillside with thousands of his fellow citizens. The horizon had altered; blue-tinged mountains and endless valleys stretched out before him.

It was the first day of the Feragh, the day Pendarric had rescued eight thousand men, women and children, turning Balacris into a giant gateway to another world. Atlantis was now gone, her glory soon to be forgotten.

Thus began the long immortal life of Culain lach Feragh, the Warrior of the Mist.

Unable to reach the heights of Eleari-mas, Culain opened his eyes and returned to the present. A thought struck him, easing the tension in his soul. Achilles and all the other mortals who died beneath Culain's blade must have felt as he did now. What hope was there for a mortal who stood against a god? Yet still they had taken swords in hand and opposed him, just as the mortal Culain would oppose the immortal, undead Gilgamesh. It was good that Culain's last earthly experience would be a new truth. At last he would know how they felt.

Later, as he sat in silent contemplation, Pendarric appeared, stepping into the cabin as if coming merely from another room.

Culain smiled and rose, and the two men gripped hands. A table appeared, then two divans, the table bearing flagons of wine and two crystal goblets.

'It is a fine night here,' said Pendarric. 'I have always loved the smell of lavender.'

Culain poured a goblet of wine and stretched himself on the divan. The king looked much as he always did, his golden beard freshly curled, his body powerful, his eyes ever watchful and masked against intrusion to his thoughts.

'Why did you come?''

Pendarric shrugged and filled his own goblet. 'I came to talk to an old friend on the night before he takes a long journey.'

Culain nodded. 'How is Thuro?'

'He is now Uther Pendragon and he leads an army. I thought you would like to know how he found it.'

Culain sat up. 'And?'

'He journeyed into the Void and brought back the Ninth Legion.'

'No?'

'And he has your sword, though I still do not know how.'

'Tell me . . . all of it.'

And Pendarric did so, until he reached the point of calling Laitha to the central altar. 'I still do not understand why I asked her to do it. It was like a voice in my mind. I was as surprised as she when she produced the sword – doubly so when the ramifications are considered. She reached back into the past, to a time and a place in which she already existed. As we both know, that is not possible. It is a wondrous riddle.'

'You should speak to Maedhlyn,' said Culain.

'I would, but I do not like the man. There is an emptiness in him; he does not know how to love. And I am not sure I want the riddle solved. One of the problems with being immortal is that there are few questions which escape answers over so many centuries. Let this be one of them.'

'Can Thuro . . . Uther . . . defeat Goroien?'

Pendarric shrugged. 'I cannot say. She has great power. But at this moment I am more concerned with Culain.' He stretched his hand over the table and opened his fingers. A golden Sipstrassi Stone tumbled to the wood.

'I cannot take it,' said Culain. 'But believe me, I want to.'

'Can you win without it?'

'Perhaps. I am not without skill.'

'I never liked Gilgamesh, and it seemed to me that his inability to accept Sipstrassi power was a judgement far above mine. But it has to be said that he was a towering warrior . . . truly Rolynd.'

'As am I.'

'As are you,' agreed Pendarric. 'But he, I think, has no soul. There is nothing of greatness in Gilgamesh – there never was. I think for him the world was grey. When Goroien brought him back she doomed herself, for the Bloodstone enhanced his disease, giving it the strength to infect her.'

'I still love her,' admitted Culain. 'I could not hurt her.'

'I know.' The king poured more wine, his eyes moving from Culain. There is something else – and I am not sure, even now, whether it will aid or condemn you.' Pendarric's voice trembled and Culain felt a strange tension seep into his body. The king licked his lips and sipped his wine. 'Goroien does not know that I am in possession of this . . . secret.' He lapsed into a silence Culain did not disturb. 'I am sorry, my friend,' said Pendarric. This is harder for me than I can say.'

'Then do not tell me,' said Culain. 'After tomorrow it will not matter.'

Pendarric shook his head. 'When I told you of Laitha and the sword, that was not all. Something . . . someone . . . bade me tell you the whole of the truth. So let it be done. You remember the days in Assyria when Goroien contracted a fever that brought her to the edge of madness?'

'Of course. She almost died.'

'She believed she hated you, and she left you.'

'Not for long!'

Pendarric smiled. 'No, a mere two decades. When she returned, was all as it should have been?'

'After a while. The disease took almost a century to leave her.'

'Did it ever truly leave? Did her ruthlessness not grow? Was the gentleness in her soul not vanished for ever?'

'Yes, perhaps. What are you saying?'

Pendarric took a deep breath. 'When she left you she was pregnant.'

'I do not want to hear this!' screamed Culain, leaping to his feet. 'Leave me!'

'Gilgamesh is your son and her lover.'

All the strength and anger flowed from Culain's body and he staggered; at once Pendarric was beside him, helping him to the divan.

'Why? Why did she not tell me?'

'How can I answer that? Goroien is insane.'

'And Gilgamesh?'

'He knows – it is why he hates you, why he has always desired your death. Whatever madness infected Goroien was carried on into him. When he could not accept immortality, he blamed you.'

'Why did you tell me?'

'Had you accepted the Sipstrassi Stone, I would not have spoken.'

'You think this knowledge will make me stronger?'

'No,' admitted Pendarric, 'but it might help to explain why you were so loth to fight him.'

'I was afraid of him.'

'That too. But the call of blood was touching your subconscious. I have seen you both fight and I know that the Culain of old could

207

defeat Gilgamesh. You were always the best; he knew that. It only added to his hatred.'

'How did you find out?'

'During the last years of his life, Goroien would not see him. I went to him two days before he died. He was senile then, and calling for his mother. It is not a pleasant memory.'

'I could have raised him without hate.'

'I do not think so.'

'Leave me, Pendarric. I have much to consider. Tomorrow I must try to kill my son.'

16

The ten cohorts of Legio IX arrived at the plain before Perdita, the Castle of Iron, five days after the battle in which Agarin Pinder's army was crushed. Uther ordered a halt and the twenty wagons bearing supplies and equipment were drawn into a hastily dug defensive enclosure. The rebel army now numbered more than six thousand men and Maggrig had been placed in command of the Pinrae warriors.

With Prasamaccus, Maggrig and Severinus, Uther walked to the edge of the trees overlooking the fortress, a cold dread settling on him as he gazed on the black castle rearing from the mist-shrouded plain. It seemed to the prince to resemble a colossal demonic head, with a cavernous mouth of a gateway. No troops were assembled to defend it, and the plain sat silent and beckoning.

'When do we advance?' asked Maggrig.

'Why has no further attempt been made to stop us?' countered Uther.

'Why count the teeth of the gifted horse?' said Prasamaccus. Maggrig and Severinus nodded agreement.

'We are not engaging an enemy force,' said Uther. 'We are fighting a war against a Witch Queen. No attempt has been made on my life; no other fighting force has been raised to oppose us. What does that suggest to you?'

'That she is beaten,' said Maggrig.

'No,' replied Uther. 'The opposite is the case. She used Agarin because his victory was the simple option, but she has other forces at her disposal.' He turned to Severinus. 'We have four hours before dusk. Leave a small force within the enclosure and march the Legion to where we stand.'

'And what of my men?' asked Maggrig.

'Wait for my order.'

209

'What do you plan?' asked Severinus.

Uther smiled. 'I plan to take the castle.'

On the high tower Goroien's eyes opened and she, too, smiled.

'Come to me, sweet boy,' she whispered. Beside her Gilgamesh stood, his dark armour gleaming in the sunlight.

'Well?' he asked.

'They are coming . . . as is Culain.'

'I would have liked the opportunity to kill the boy.'

'Be satisfied with the man.'

'Oh, I will be satisfied, mother.' Under the helm Gilgamesh grinned as he saw her shoulders stiffen and watched a crimson blush stain her porcelain features. She swung on him, forcing a smile.

'I wonder,' she said, her voice dripping venom, 'if it has occurred to you that after today you will have nothing to live for?'

'What do you mean?'

'All your life you have dreamed of killing Culain lach Feragh. What will you do tomorrow, Gilgamesh, my love? What will you do when there is no enemy to fight?'

'I will know peace,' he said simply. The answer shook her momentarily, for his voice had carried a note she had never heard from the Lord of Battle, a softness like the echoes of sorrow.

'You will never know peace,' she spat. 'You live for death!'

'Perhaps that is because I am dead,' he replied, the harsh edge returning.

'He is coming. You should prepare yourself.'

'Yes. I long to see his face and read his eyes in the moment I tell him who I am.'

'Why must you tell him?' she asked, suddenly fearful.

'What will it matter?' he responded. 'He will die anyway.' With that he turned and walked from the ramparts. Goroien watched him depart and felt again the curious arousal his movements inspired. So graceful, so strong – steel muscles beneath silk-soft skin. Once more she gazed at the line of trees in the distance, then she also returned to her rooms.

As she entered the inner sanctum, she stopped before a full-length mirror and closely examined her reflection. A hint of grey shone in the gold of her hair, and the finest of lines was visible beside her eyes. It was growing worse. She moved to the centre of the room, where a boulder-sized Bloodstone rested on a tree of gold. Around it were the dried-out husks of three pregnant women. Goroien touched the Stone, feeling its warmth spread into her. The corpses vanished and a shadow moved behind her.

'Come forth, Secargus!' she commanded and a hulking figure ambled into view. More than seven feet tall, he towered over the queen – his bestial face more wolf than man, his jaws slavering, his tongue lolling.

'Fetch five more.'

He reached out a taloned hand to touch her, his eyes pleading.

'Tonight,' she said. 'I will make you a man again, and you can share my bed. Would you like that?' The huge head nodded and a low growling moan escaped the twisted mouth. 'Now fetch five more.' He ambled away towards the dungeons where the women were kept and Goroien moved to the Stone; the black lines were thick in the red-gold. For some time she remained where she was, waiting for Secargus to bring the women to their timely deaths.

On the ramparts once more, Goroien waited patiently. The mist swirled on the plain, but her excitement grew as she waited for the inevitable moment of victory. With an hour to go before dusk, she saw the Legion march from the trees in battle order, ranks of five, spreading to form a long shield wall before their spearmen. On they came into the mist: five thousand men whose souls would feed her Bloodstone. Her hands were trembling as she watched them advance, their bronze shields gleaming like fire in the dying sunlight. She licked her lips and raised her arms, linking her mind with the dread Stone.

Suddenly the plain was engulfed in fire, white-hot and searing, the heat reaching even there on the battlements. Within the mist the soldiers burned, human torches that crumpled to the earth, their bodies blistering and burning like living candles. Black smoke obscured her vision and she returned to her rooms.

Culain would soon be arriving and she transformed her clothing into a tight-fitting tunic and leggings of forest green with a belt of spun gold. It had always been Culain's favourite.

Back at the edge of the woods, Uther collapsed. Prasamaccus and Severinus knelt beside him.

'It is exhaustion,' said Severinus. 'Fetch some wine!'

Maggrig stood close by, staring into the Mist where the vision of death had appeared. He was appalled, for he would willingly have led his own men across that plain and now would be lying scorched and dead on the blackened earth. Berec-Uther had halted the Legion within the woods, then knelt facing the plain.

Under the startled eyes of the rebel army Berec had lifted his hand, which glowed as if he held a ball of fire. Then a vision had appeared, of the Legion marching – a truly ghostly army. When the fire erupted and the heat washed over the watchers, Maggrig's stomach had heaved. The illusion had been so powerful he had almost smelt burning flesh.

Uther groaned. Severinus lifted him to a sitting position and held a goblet of wine to his lips. The prince drank deeply. Dark rings circled his eyes and his face was gaunt and grey.

'How did you know?' asked the Roman.

'I did not know. But she is too powerful not to have one more weapon.'

'This fell from your hand,' said Prasamaccus, offering Uther a black pebble with threads of gold. The prince took it.

'We will advance on the castle at midnight. Find me fifty men – the best swordsmen you have. The Legion will follow at dawn.'

'I will lead the raid,' said Severinus.

'No, it is my duty,' responded Uther.

'With respect, Prince, that is folly.'

'I know, Severinus, but I have no choice. I alone have a source of magic to use against her. It is weak now, but it is all we have. We do not know what terrors wait inside the castle – Void warriors, Atrols, Werebeasts? I have the Sword of Cunobelin, and I have the Stone Pendarric gave me. I must lead.'

'Let me go with you,' pleaded the Roman.

'Now *that* would be folly, but I am grateful for the offer. If all goes well, the Legion will follow at dawn and I shall greet you in the gateway. If not . . .' His eyes locked to Severinus' gaze. 'Make your own strategy – and a home for yourselves in Pinrae.'

'I'll pick your men myself. They will not let you down.'

Uther called Laitha to him and the two of them wandered away from the gathered men to a sheltered hollow near a huge oak.

Swiftly he told her of the attack he would be leading – explaining, as he had with Severinus, the reasons for his actions.

'I will come with you,' she said.

'I do not want you in danger.'

'You seem to forget that I also was trained by Culain lach Feragh. I can handle a sword as well as any man here – probably better than most.'

'It would destroy me if you were slain.'

'Think back, Uther, to the day we met. Who was it that slew the first of the assassins? It was I. This is hard for me, for I accept that as your wife I must obey you. But please let me live as I have been taught.'

He took her hand and drew her to him. 'You are free, Laitha. I will never own you, nor treat you as a servant or slave. And I would be proud if you were to walk beside me through the gate.'

The tension eased from her. 'Now I can truly love you,' she said, 'for now I know that you are a man. Not Culain, not his shadow, but a man in your own right.'

He grinned boyishly. 'This morning I washed in a stream and, as I looked down, I saw this child's face staring up at me. I have not yet needed to shave. And I thought how amusing Maedhlyn would find all this – his weakly student leading an army. But I am doing the best that I can.'

'For myself,' she admitted, 'I saw a tree this afternoon that seemed to grow into the clouds. I wanted to climb it and hide in the topmost branches. I used to pretend I had a castle in the clouds, where no one could find me. There is no shame in being young, Thuro.'

He chuckled, 'I thought I had put that name behind me, but I love to hear you say it. It reminds me of the Caledones when I did not know how to light a fire.'

Just short of midnight Severinus noisily approached the hollow, clearing his throat and treading on as many dry sticks as he could see. Uther came towards him, laughing, Laitha just behind.

'Is this Roman stealth I hear?' asked the prince.

'It is very dark,' answered the Roman with a grin.

'Are the men ready?'

The grin vanished. 'They are. I shall follow at dawn.'

Uther offered his hand, which Severinus took in the warrior's grip, wrist to wrist.

'I am your servant for life,' said the Roman.

'Be careful, Severinus, I shall hold you to that.'

'Make sure that you do.'

Culain lach Feragh stood before the gates of Perdita, the winds of Skitis Island shrieking over the rocks. He wore his black and silver winged helm and silver shoulder-guard, but no other armour protected him. His chest was covered merely by a shirt of doeskin, and upon his feet were moccasins of soft leather.

The black gate opened and a tall warrior stepped into the sunshine, his face covered by a dark helm. Behind him came Goroien and Culain's heart soared, for she wore the outfit he had first seen on the day they met. Goroien climbed to a high rock as Gilgamesh advanced to stand before Culain.

'Greetings, Father,' said Gilgamesh. 'I trust you are well.' The voice was muffled by the helm, but Culain could hear the suppressed excitement.

'Do not call me Father, Gilgamesh. It offends me.'

'The truth is sometimes painful.' Now there was disappointment in the voice. 'How did you find out?'

'You told Pendarric, but probably you do not remember. I understand you were senile at the time.'

'Happily you will not suffer the same fate,' hissed Gilgamesh. 'Today you die.'

'All things die. Do you object to me saying farewell to your mother?'

'I do. My lover has nothing to say to you.'

Suddenly Culain chuckled. 'Poor fool,' he said. 'Sad, tormented Gilgamesh! I pity you, boy. Was there ever a day in your life when you were truly happy?'

'Yes – when I bedded your wife!'

'A joy shared by half the civilised world,' said Culain, smiling.

'And there is today,' said Gilgamesh, drawing two short swords. 'Today my happiness is complete.'

Culain removed the winged helm and placed it at the ground by his feet.

'I am sorry for you, boy. You could have been a force for good in the world, but luck never favoured you, did it? Born to a mad goddess and diseased from the moment you first sucked milk. What chance did you have? Come then, Gilgamesh. Enjoy your happiness.' The lance slid in two, revealing the slanted sword. Culain laid the haft next to the helm and drew a hunting-knife from his belt. 'Come, this is your moment!'

Gilgamesh advanced smoothly and then leapt forward, his sword hissing through the air. Culain blocked the blow, and a second, and a third. The two men circled.

'Remove your helm, boy. Let me see your face.'

Gilgamesh did not answer but attacked once more – his swords whirling in a glittering web, but always blocked by the blades of Culain. On the rocks above, Goroien watched it all in a semi-daze. It seemed to her as if she viewed two dancers moving with impossible grace to the discordant music of clashing steel. Gilgamesh as always was beautiful, almost catlike in his movements, while Culain reminded her of a flame leaping and twisting in a fire. Goroien's heart was beating faster now as she tried to read the contest. Culain was stronger and faster than he had been when the shade of Gilgamesh had defeated him. And yet he was failing. Almost imperceptibly he was slowing. Gilgamesh, with the eye of the warrior born, saw the growing weakness in his opponent and launched a savage attack . . . but it was too early and Culain blocked

215

the blows and spun on his heel, his sword snaking out in a murderous riposte. Gilgamesh hurled himself backwards as the silver blade scored across his stomach, opening the top layers of skin.

'Never be hasty, boy,' said Culain. 'The best are never reckless.' No blood seeped from the wound. Gilgamesh tore his helm from his head, his golden hair catching the last of the sunlight and Culain saw him with new eyes. How could he ever have missed the resemblance to the mother? The Mist Warrior was growing tired – but not as weary as his body appeared. He was grateful now to Pendarric, for had he not known the truth he would be dead by now. He could not have fought so well while struggling to come to terms with the awful knowledge.

'Are you beginning to know fear, little man?' he asked. Gilgamesh mouthed a curse and came forward.

'I could never fear you,' he hissed, his dead grey eyes conveying no emotion.

Swords clashed and Culain's hunting-knife barely blocked a disembowelling thrust which had been superbly disguised. He leapt back, aware more than ever that he had to maintain his strategy, for there was more to a battle than mere skill with a blade.

'A nice move, but you must learn to disguise the thrust,' he said. 'Were you taught by a fishmonger?'

Gilgamesh screamed and attacked once more, his swords flashing with incredible speed. Culain blocked, twisted, moved – being forced back and back towards a jutting rock. He ducked under a whistling cut, hurled himself to the right, rolled on his shoulder and came back to his feet. A trickle of blood was running from a slashing cut in his side.

'That was better,' he said, 'but you were still open to a blow on the left.' It was a lie, but Culain said it with confidence.

'I never knew a man talk as much as you,' answered Gilgamesh. 'When you are dead, I'll rip the tongue from your head.'

'I should take the eyes,' advised Culain. 'Yours look as if the maggots still remain.'

'Damn you!' screamed Gilgamesh. His blades flashed for Culain's face and it was all the Mist Warrior could do to fend him off; there

216

was no opportunity for a counter-strike. Three blows forced their way through his defences only partially blocked – the first slashing a wide cut to his chest, the second piercing his side and the third plunging into his shoulder. Once more he escaped by hurling himself sideways and rolling to his feet.

'Where are your taunts now, Father? I cannot hear you.'

Culain steadied himself, his grey eyes focused on the lifeless orbs of his opponent. He knew now with a terrible certainty that he could not defeat Gilgamesh and live. He backed away, half-stumbling. Gilgamesh raced forward but Culain suddenly dived to the ground in a tumbler's roll, rising into Gilgamesh's path. The Lord of Battle's sword plunged home in Culain's chest, cleaving through the lungs, but his own sword sliced up into the enemy's belly to cut through the heart. Gilgamesh groaned, his head sagging to Culain's shoulder.

'I beat you!' he whispered, 'as I always knew I could.'

Culain dragged himself clear of the body, which slumped face-first to the ground. He stumbled, his lungs filling with blood and choking him. He fell to his knees and stared down at the hilt of the sword jutting from his chest. Blood rose in his throat, spraying from his mouth.

On the rock above, Goroien screamed. She leapt to the ground and ran to Culain's side, grabbing the sword-hilt and tearing it from his chest. As he sank to the ground she pulled a small Sipstrassi Stone from her tunic pocket, but as she placed it over the wound she froze, staring at her hands. They were wrinkled and stained with brown liver spots.

Yet it was impossible, for five thousand men had died to feed her Bloodstone. In that moment she knew her only chance for life was in the small Sipstrassi fragment held over Culain. She stared down at his face.

He tried to shake his head, willing her to live, then lapsed into the sleep of death.

Her hand descended, the power flowing into Culain, stopping the wound, healing the lungs, driving on and on, pushing back his mortality. His hair darkened, the skin of his face tightening. At last the Stone was black.

Culain awoke to see a white-haired skeletal figure lying crumpled at his side. He screamed his anguish to the skies and tried to lift her, but a whisper stopped him. The rheumy eyes had opened. He crouched low over her and heard the last words of Goroien, the Goddess Astarte, the Goddess Athena, the Goddess Freya.

'Remember me.'

The last flickering ember of life departed, the bones crumbling to white dust that the wind picked up and scattered on the rocky ground.

Uther, Prasamaccus and Laitha walked in silence, the fifty swordsmen of the Legion moving in a line with shields raised on either side of them. The black castle grew ever more large and sinister. No lights shone in the narrow windows and the gateway was darker than the night.

Prasamaccus walked with an arrow notched. Laitha kept close to Uther. Behind them came Maggrig and six Pinrae warriors; his eyes remained locked to Uther's back, for every time he looked at the castle his limbs trembled and his heart hammered. But where Berec walked, so too would Maggrig, and when the Witch Queen was dead the godling would follow. For Maggrig knew that the prince would never relinquish his hold on the people, and he was not prepared to allow another Enchanter to torment the land.

With each step the attackers grew more tense, waiting for the fire to reach out and engulf them, as it had the phantom Legion which Uther had conjured. Slowly they neared the castle, and at last Uther stepped on to the bridge before the gate towers. He drew the Sword of Cunobelin, glanced up at the seemingly deserted ramparts and advanced.

At once a bestial figure ran from the darkness, a terrible howl ripping the silence. More than seven feet tall, the giant wolf-beast roared towards the prince and in its taloned hands was an upswept axe. An arrow sang from Prasamaccus' bow, taking the creature in the throat, but its advance continued. Uther ran forward, leaping nimbly to his left as the axe descended. The Sword of Cunobelin swept up, shearing through the huge arm at the shoulder; the creature screamed and the sword sliced down into its neck with all the power Uther could exert with his double-handed grip. Before the eyes of the attackers the giant body shrank and Maggrig pushed forward to stare at the dead but now human face. 'Secargus,' he said. 'I served with him ten years ago. Fine man.'

At that moment a sound drifted to the tense warriors and men looked at one another in surprise. A baby's cry floated on the wind, echoing in the gateway.

'Take twenty men,' Uther told a centurion named Degas. 'Find out where it is coming from. The rest of you split into groups of five and search the castle.'

'We will come with you, Lord Berec,' said Maggrig, his hand on his sword. He did not meet Uther's gaze, for he was afraid his intent would be read in his eyes. Uther merely nodded and moved through the gateway. Inside was a maze of tunnels and stairwells and Uther climbed ever higher. The corridors were lit by lanterns, faintly aromatic and glowing with a blood-red light. Strangely embroidered rugs covered the walls, showing scenes of hunts and battles. Everywhere statues of athletes could be seen in various poses – throwing javelins, running, lifting, wrestling. All were of the finest white marble.

Near the topmost floor they came to the apartments of Goroien, where a massive bed almost filled a small room which had been created of silvered mirrors. Uther gazed around at a score of reflections. The sheets were of silk, the bed of carved ivory inlaid with gold.

'She certainly likes to look at herself,' commented Laitha. Prasamaccus said nothing. He felt uncomfortable and it had little to do with fear of Goroien. All she could do was kill him. Something else was in the air, and he did not like the way Maggrig kept so close to Uther and the other men of Pinrae also gathered round the prince. The group moved through to the far room, where a five-foot tree of gold supported a rounded black boulder veined with threads of dull red gold.

'The source of her power,' said Uther.

'Can we use it?' asked Maggrig.

Without answering Uther strode to the tree and raised the Sword of Cunobelin high over his head. With one stroke he smashed the stone to shards. At once the room shimmered – the hangings, the carpets and the furniture all disappearing. The group stood now in a bare, cold room, lit only by the moonlight streaming in silver columns through the tall narrow windows.

'She is gone,' said Uther.

'Where?' demanded Maggrig.

'I do not know. But the Stone is now useless. Rejoice, man. You have won!'

'Not yet,' said Maggrig softly.

'A moment of your time,' said Prasamaccus as the wolf-like Maggrig drew his knife. The warrior turned slowly, to find himself facing a bent bow with the shaft aimed at his throat.

The other Pinrae men spread out, drawing their weapons. Laitha stepped forward to stand beside the stunned Uther.

'Did Korrin truly mean so much to you?' asked the Brigante.

'Korrin?' answered Maggrig with a sneer. 'No, he was a head-strong fool. But you think I am foolish also? This is not the end of the terror, only the beginning of fresh evils. Your magic and your spells!' he hissed. 'No good ever came of such power. But we'll not let you live to take her place.'

'I have no wish to take her place,' said Uther. 'Believe me, Maggrig, the Pinrae is yours. I have my own land.'

'I might have believed you, but you've lied once. You told me we were free to serve you or leave, and yet the Legion archers were waiting in the shadows. We would all have been slain. No more lies, Berec. Die!'

As he spoke he hurled himself at Uther. The prince leapt back, his sword slashing up almost of its own volition. The blade took Maggrig in the side, cleaving up under his ribs and exiting in a bloody swathe. The other warriors charged and the first fell to Prasamaccus – an arrow through his temple – the second to Laitha.

'Halt!' bellowed Uther, his voice ringing with authority and the warriors froze. 'Maggrig was wrong! There is no betrayal! I speak not from fear, for I think you know we can slay you all. Now cease this madness.' For a moment he had them, but one man suddenly hurled a dagger and Uther swerved as the blade flashed by his ear. Laitha plunged her gladius into the chest of the nearest warrior and Prasamaccus shot yet another. The remaining pair rushed at Uther and he blocked one thrust, spinning on his heel to crash his elbow into the face of the second man. The Sword of Cunobelin cut through the man's neck, his head toppling to the floor. Laitha leapt forward, killing the last man with a dazzling riposte which ripped open his throat. In the silence that followed Uther backed away from the bodies, an awful sadness gripping him.

'I liked him,' he whispered, staring at the dead Maggrig. 'He was a good man. Why did he do it, Prasamaccus?'

The Brigante turned away with a shrug. Now was not the time to talk of the Circle of Life, and how a man's actions would always return to haunt him. Ever since, in his rage, Uther had killed Korrin, Prasamaccus had been waiting for the moment of Pinrae revenge. It was as inevitable as night following day.

'Why?' asked Uther again.

'This is a world of madness,' said Laitha. 'Put it from your mind.'

The trio left the room, slowly making their way to the courtyard. There Degas was waiting with more than forty pregnant women and one new mother. Some of the women were crying, but the tears were of relief. Two days ago there had been sixty women imprisoned in Perdita.

'This is a strange castle,' said Degas, a short powerfully built soldier. 'There are three more gates, but they lead nowhere: just blackness beyond them and a deadly cold. And a little while ago all the lanterns vanished, and the statues. Everything! All that is left is the building itself, and cracks have already started appearing near the battlements.' As he spoke the gate tower creaked and shifted.

'Let us leave,' said Uther. 'Are all the men here?'

'All the Romans, yes, but what of your guards?'

'They will not be coming. Let's get the women out.' A wall lurched behind them, giant stones shifting and groaning as the legionaries helped the women to their feet and out through the yawning gateway. Once on the plain, Degas stopped to look back.

221

'Mother of Mitra!' he said 'Look!'

The great Castle of Iron was turning to dust, huge clouds billowing in the pre-dawn breeze. From the woods the men of the Ninth Legion swarmed down, their cheers ringing in the night. Uther was swept from his feet and carried shoulder-high back to the camp. As the dawn sun rose over the plain, the castle had completely disappeared. All that was left was a great circle of black stones.

Uther left Severinus and the others and walked to the entrance of the enclosure, looking out at the silent camp of the Pinrae men. On impulse he strode from the safety of the legion encampment and walked alone to where the Pinrae leaders sat. Their eyes were sullen as he approached, and several men reached for their weapons. They were seated in a circle with the warriors behind them, as if in an arena. Uther smiled grimly.

'Tomorrow,' he said, 'I leave the Pinrae. And there is no joy, now, in our victory. Several days ago I had to kill a man I had thought was my friend. Tonight I killed another whom I respected and hoped would lead you when I had gone.' His eyes swept the faces around him. 'I came here to aid you; I have no desire to rule you. My own land is far from here. Korrin Rogeur died because he could not control the hatred in his heart; Maggrig died because he could not believe there was none in mine. Tonight you must choose a new leader – a king if you will. As for me, I shall return here no more.'

Not a word was spoken, but their hands were no longer on their sword-hilts. Uther looked at the men, recognising Baldric with whom he had travelled on the first quest of the Stone. In his eyes there was only a cold anger. Beside him sat Hogun, Ceorl and Rhiall. They made no move, but their hatred remained.

Uther wandered sadly back to the enclosure. Only a short time ago, as he had returned with Baldric, he had pictured their adulation. Now he felt he had learned a real lesson. During his short time in the Pinrae he had freed a people and risked his life, only to earn their undying enmity.

Here was a riddle for Maedhlyn to solve . . .

Prasamaccus met him at the entrance and the prince clapped him on the shoulder. 'Do you hate me also, my friend?'

'No. Neither do they. They fear you, Uther; they fear your power and your courage, but mostly they fear your anger.'

'I am not angry.'

'You were the night you killed Korrin. It was a bloody deed.'

'You think I was wrong?'

'He deserved to die, but you should have summoned the people of Pinrae to judge him. You killed him too coldly and had his body thrown in a field for the crows to peck at. Anger overruled your judgement. That's what Maggrig could not forgive.'

'But for you I would be dead now. I shall not forget it.'

Prasamaccus chuckled. 'You know what they say, Uther? That there are two absolutes with kings: the length of their anger and the shortness of their gratitude. Do not burden me with either.'

'Not even with friendship?'

Prasamaccus placed his hand on Uther's shoulder. It was a touching gesture which Uther sensed, rightly, would never be repeated.

'I think, my lord, that kings never have friends – only followers and enemies. The secret is to know which are which.'

The Brigante hobbled away into the night, leaving Uther more alone than he had ever been.

17

At dawn Uther walked alone to the circle of black stones upon which Perdita had been constructed. The dawn shadows were shrinking now, and a cool wind blew over the plain. At the centre altar sat the man Pendarric, his large frame wrapped in a heavy purple cloak, sheepskin-lined.

'You did well, Uther. Better than you know.'

The prince sat beside him. 'The people of Pinrae cannot wait to see my back. And if they see it for too long, they'll plunge knives in it.'

'Such is the path of the king,' said Pendarric. 'And I *know*. You will find – if you live long enough – some splendid contradictions. A man can be a robber all his life, and yet do one good deed and be remembered in song with great affection. But a king? He can spend his life in good works, yet perpetrate one evil deed and be remembered as a tyrant.'

'I do not understand.'

'You will, Uther. The rogue is looked down upon, the king looked up to. That is why the rogue can always be forgiven. But the king is more than a man; he is a symbol. And symbols are not allowed human frailties.'

'Are you seeking to dissuade me?'

'No, to enlighten you. Do you wish to go home?'

'Yes.'

'Even if I tell you the odds proclaim you will die there within the hour?'

'What do you mean?'

'Eldared and the Saxons have linked forces. As we speak, fewer than six thousand of your troops are surrounded by almost twenty-five thousand of the enemy. Even with the Ninth Legion, your chances of victory are remote.'

'Can you get me to the battlefield?'

'I can. But think of this, Uther. Britain will be a Saxon land. They are many, but you are few. You cannot prevail for ever. If you stay in the Pinrae, you can build an empire.'

'Like Goroien? No, Pendarric. I promised the Ninth Legion I would take them home and I keep my promises where I can.'

'Very well. There is one other fact you should know. Goroien is dead; she died saving Culain. No, do not ask me why, but the Lance Lord is now restored to youth. One day he will return to your life. Be wary, Uther.'

'Culain would never harm me,' answered Uther, feeling a sudden premonitory chill as he pictured Laitha. His eyes met Pendarric's and he knew the king understood. 'What will be, will be,' said Uther.

Victorinus slashed his sword across the face of a blond-bearded warrior, who fell only to be trampled by the surging, screaming tide of men behind him. An axe crashed against Victorinus' shield, numbing his arm. His gladius ripped upwards to plunge deep into the man's side. A sword cannoned from the Roman's helm and down to slice into the leather breastplate. A spear took the attacker in the chest and two legionaries pushed forward to lock their shields before Victorinus. He leapt back, allowing them room. Sweat dripped from his brow, stinging his eyes. He glanced left and right, but the line held. On the hill to the right Aquila was surrounded, his seven cohorts forming a shield wall against the Brigantes. Victorinus and his six cohorts were similarly confronted by eight thousand Saxon warriors led by Horsa, son of the legendary Hengist.

This was the battle which the Romans had sought to avoid. Ambrosius had harried the Saxon army throughout their long march north, but had then been trapped at Lindum, his two legions smashed in four days of bloody fighting. With the three cohorts still left to him – one thousand, four hundred and forty men – Ambrosius had fled to Eboracum. Now Aquila had no choice but to risk the kingdom on one desperate battle. But he had left it too late.

Eldared and Cael had pushed the Brigante army of fifteen thousand men to the west of Eboracum, linking with Horsa at Lagentium.

Aquila had made one last attempt to split the enemy, attacking the Brigante and Saxon camps with two separate forces, but the plan had failed miserably. Horsa had hidden two thousand men in the high woodlands and these hammered into Aquila's rearguard. The Romans had retreated in good order and linked forces on a range of hills a mile from the city; but now the Saxons had forced a wedge into the Roman line, which had buckled and regrouped as two fighting units. There was no hope of victory now and the six-thousand strong Romano-British army was being slowly cut to pieces by a force four times as powerful. Men fought merely to stay alive for a few more blessed hours, holding to impossible dreams of escape by night.

'Close up on the left!' yelled Victorinus, his voice straining to rise above the cacophonous clash of iron on bronze, as the Saxon axes and swords smashed at the shields and armour of the Roman soldiers.

The battle would have been over by now had it not been for the Roman gladius. The weapon was a short sword, eighteen inches from hilt to blade-tip; it had been designed for disciplined warfare, where men would be required to stand close together in a tight fighting unit. But the Saxon and the Brigante used swords up to three feet long and that meant they needed more space in which to swing the weapons. This caused problems for the attackers as they pressed against the shield wall, for the longswords became clumsy and unwieldy. Even so, sheer weight of numbers was forcing the wall to yield, inch by bloody inch.

Suddenly a section gave way and a dozen Saxon warriors, led by a tall man with a double-headed axe, raced into the centre. Victorinus dashed forward, knowing the rearguard would be following. He ducked under the swinging axe and buried his blade in the man's groin. A sword lanced for his face, his shield deflected it – and his attacker died with Gwalchmai's gladius in his heart.

The rearguard advanced in a half-circle, closing the gap and forcing the Saxons back into a tight mass where the longsword was useless. The legionaries pushed forward, their own blades plunging and cutting at the near helpless enemy. Within a few minutes the line was sealed once more and Gwalchmai, his rearguard reduced to forty men, rejoined Victorinus.

'It does not look good!' he said.

At the centre of the Roman square, the two hundred archers had long since exhausted their shafts and waited stoically with hands on the hilts of their hunting-knives. They had little armour and when the line broke they would be slaughtered like cattle. Some of them pushed close to the fighting line, dragging back the injured or dead and stripping them of armour and weapons.

Victorinus stared out over the sea of Saxon fighting men. Tall men they were, mostly blond or red-haired, and they fought with a savage ferocity he was forced to admire. Earlier in the battle some twenty Saxons had ripped their armour from their chests and attacked the line, fighting on with terrible wounds. These were the feared Baresarks, or naked warriors – called by the Britons, Berserkers. One man had fought on until he trod on his own entrails and slipped. Even then he had lashed out with his sword until he bled to death.

On the other hill Aquila calmly directed operations as if he was organising a triumphal march. He carried no sword and moved about behind the wall encouraging the men.

For two months now, Victorinus had experienced mixed feelings about the old patrician. He had been exasperated by his reluctance to take risks, but had always appreciated his courage and his caring for the welfare of the men under him. Under Aurelius he had been a careful and clever general, but without the charismatic monarch Aquila had been found wanting in the game of kings.

Three times the line buckled, and three times Gwalchmai led the rearguard into action to plug the gap. Victorinus gazed about him, sensing the day was almost done. The Saxons could sense it too; they fell back to regroup, then attacked with renewed frenzy. Victorinus wished the battle could fade away if only for a few seconds, so he could tell the men around him how proud he was to die alongside them. They were not truly Roman soldiers, merely auxiliaries hastily trained, but no Roman legionary could have bettered them on this day.

Suddenly thunder rolled across the sky, so loud that some of the Saxons screamed in terror, believing Donner the Storm God walked amongst them. Lightning speared up from a hill to the east and for a moment all fighting ceased. With the sun sinking behind him, Victorinus stared in disbelief as the sky over the distant eastern hill split apart like a great canvas to reveal a second sun blazing in the heavens. The field of battle was now lit like a scene from hell, double shadows and impossible brilliance blinding the warriors from both sides. Victorinus shielded his eyes and watched as a single figure appeared on the hill, holding aloft a great sword which shone like fire. Then warriors streamed out to stand alongside him, their shields ablaze.

And then the sky closed, the alien sun disappearing as if a curtain had been drawn across it. But the army remained. Victorinus blinked as he watched the new force close ranks with a precision that filled his heart with wonder. Only one army in the world could achieve such perfection . . .

The newcomers were Roman.

This thought had obviously struck the Saxon leader, who split his force in two, sending a screaming mass of warriors to engage the new enemy.

The shield wall opened and five hundred archers ran forward, the front line kneeling and the second rank standing. Volley after volley raked the Saxon line, which faltered halfway up the hill. A bugle sounded and the archers ran back behind the shield wall, which advanced slowly. The Saxons regrouped and charged. Ten-foot spears appeared between the shields. The first of the Saxon warriors tried to halt, but the mass behind pushed them on and the spears plunged home. From within the square the archers – with the angle of the hill to aid them – continued their murderous assault on the Saxon line and the Roman advance continued.

Back on the two hills, the Romano-British army fought with renewed vigour. No one knew, or cared, where this ally force had originated. All that mattered was that life and hope had been restored.

The Ninth Legion reached the bottom of the hill. The men left and right of the fighting square pulled back to create an arrow-shaped wedge at the centre which pushed on towards the Raven banner, where Horsa directed the Saxon force.

Inside the fighting wedge Uther longed to hurl himself forward, but good sense prevailed. As with the Saxons, the great Sword of Cunobelin would be useless at present. Yard by yard the Saxons fell back, unable to penetrate the wall of shields; they began to throw axes and knives over the wall. Severinus bellowed an order and the second rank of the square lifted their shields high, protecting the centre.

The early advance began to falter. Even with the addition of almost five thousand troops, the Britons were still outnumbered two to one.

On the western hill Aquila read the situation and signalled to Victorinus – raising his arm, bent at the elbow, and making a stabbing motion into the joint with his other hand. Victorinus tapped his breastplate, showing he understood; then he summoned Gwalchmai.

'We are going to attack,' he said and the Cantii grinned. This was the sort of madness a Briton could appreciate. Outnumbered and trapped, yet holding the high ground, they would throw away their only advantage and hack and slash their way into the enemy ranks. He turned and ran back to the waiting archers.

'Arm yourselves!' he yelled. 'We march!'

The archers moved forward, stripping breastplates from the dead, gathering swords and shields.

Gwalchmai ran along the line shouting instructions, then Victorinus pushed his way to the point at which the wedge would be formed. This was the moment of most extreme peril, for he would have to step in towards the enemy and the two men either side of him would turn their shields outwards to protect his flanks.

If either failed, he would be isolated in the midst of the Saxons. A sword lunged for him but he turned it on his shield and disembowelled the warrior. Gwalchmai's hand descended on his shoulder. 'Ready!' yelled the Cantii.

'Now!' bellowed Victorinus, stepping forward and slashing open the throat of a Saxon warrior. The line yielded at the angles of the square. Victorinus, swinging his sword in a frenzy, forced his way deeper into the enemy line. The man to the left of him went down, an axe embedded in his neck. Gwalchmai hurdled the body and took the dead soldier's place. Slowly the wedge began to force its way downhill.

At the same time Aquila ordered his square to attack. The Brigantes fell back in dismay as the wedge clove the centre of their line.

In the midst of the battle, Uther watched the British cohorts struggling to join him. The battle ground was condensing towards Horsa's Raven banner and the Red Dragon of Eldared. Uther moved back alongside Severinus.

'Order your archers to drop their shafts around the Dragon standard. That is where Eldared and his sons will be standing.' Severinus nodded, and within moments a deadly hail of barbed arrows began to flash from the sky.

Eldared saw his closest carle fall beside him, along with a score of warriors. Others ran forward to raise their shields over the king.

The battle had now reached a point of exquisite balance when the three Roman forces, heavily outnumbered, were still closing slowly on the enemy banners. If they could be held, or pushed back, Eldared would have the day. If they could not, he would be dead. It was a time for courage of the highest order.

At the Saxon centre Horsa, a blond giant in a raven-wing helm, bearing a longsword and rounded shield, gathered his carles and launched his own attack on the new enemy.

But Eldared had no wish to die; in his mind there would always be another day. With Cael beside him he fled the field, the Brigantes streaming after him. Horsa looked at his fleeing allies and shook his head; he had never liked Eldared. He glanced at the sky.

'Brothers in arms, brothers in Valhalla,' he said to the man beside him.

'Let the swords drink one last time,' replied the man.

The Saxons charged, almost cleaving through the wedge, but fury and courage were no match for discipline. The Roman line swung out like the horns of a bull, encircling the surging Saxons. Victorinus and Aquila linked forces behind them and the battle became a massacre.

Uther could contain himself no longer. Pushing his way to the front line, he snatched up a gladius and a shield and stepped into the fray, cutting a path towards the giant Saxon leader. Horsa saw the fighting figure of the silver breastplate and black-plumed helm and grinned. He too pushed his way forward, shouldering aside his own warriors. Behind him came the banner-bearer and a score of carles. The men to the left and right of Uther fell. The prince stabbed an attacker with his gladius, which became embedded in the warrior's side. Dropping his shield, he drew the Sword of Cunobelin and began to cleave his way forward with slashing double-handed strokes, moving ever ahead of the square.

Horsa leapt to meet him and their swords clashed. All around them the battle continued, until at last only Horsa and Uther still fought. The Saxon army had been destroyed utterly. Several Romans moved in, ready to kill the giant war-leader, but Uther waved them back.

Horsa grinned again as he saw the massed Roman ranks about him. His banner-bearer was dead, but in death he had plunged the banner staff into the ground and the Black Raven still fluttered above him.

He stepped back, lowering his sword for a moment.

'By the Gods,' he said to Uther, 'you are an enemy worth having.'

'I make a better friend,' responded Uther.

'You are offering me life?'

'Yes.'

'I cannot accept. My friends are waiting for me in Valhalla.' Horsa lifted his sword in salute. 'Come,' he said, 'join me on the Swan's Path to glory. We will walk together into Odin's hall of

231

heroes.' He leapt forward, his sword flashing in the dying light, but Uther blocked the blow, sending a reverse cut that half severed the giant's neck. Horsa fell, losing his grip on his sword. His hand scrabbled for it, his eyes desperate. Uther knew that many Saxons believed they could not enter Valhalla if they died without a sword in their hands. He dropped to his knees, pressing his own sword into the dying man's hand as Horsa's eyes closed for the last time.

The prince rose, retrieving the Sword of Cunobelin, and ordered Horsa's body to be draped in the Raven banner.

Lucius Aquila stepped forward, bowing low.

'Who are you, sir?' he asked.

The prince removed his helm. 'I am Uther Pendragon, High King of Britain.'

Epilogue

Uther returned in triumph to Camulodunum where he was crowned High King. The following spring he led the Ninth Legion into the Lands of the Wall, smashing the Brigante army in two battles at Vindolanda and Trimontium.

Eldared was captured and put to death, while Cael escaped by ship with two hundred retainers, sailing south to link with Hengist. Following news of the death of his son, Hengist had the Brigantes blood-eagled on the trees of Anderida, their ribs ripped open for the crows to devour.

Moret offered allegiance to Uther, who left him as the Brigante overlord.

Prasamaccus returned to the ruins of Calcaria and there found Helga, living once more with the servants of Victorinus. Their reunion was joyous. With the ten pounds of gold Uther had given him, Prasamaccus bought a large measure of land and set to breeding horses for the king's new *cohors equitana*.

Uther himself promoted Victorinus to head the Legions, barring the Ninth which the king kept for his own.

During the four bloody years which followed Uther harried the Saxons, Jutes and newly arrived Danes, building a reputation as a warrior king who would never know defeat. Laitha remained a proud yet dutiful wife, and rarely spoke of her days with Culain lach Feragh.

All that changed one summer's morning five years after the battle of Eboracum . . .

A lone rider came to the castle at Camulodunum. He was tall and dark-haired, with eyes the colour of storm-clouds. In his hands he carried a silver lance. He strode through the long hall, halting before the doors of oak and bronze.

A Thracian servant approached him. 'What is your business here?'

'I have come to see the king.'

'He is with his counsellors.'

'Go to him and tell him the Lance Lord is here. He will see me.'

Culain waited as the man timidly opened the door and slipped inside.

Uther and Laitha were sitting at an oval table around which also sat Victorinus, Gwalchmai, Severinus, Prasamaccus and Maedhlyn, the Lord Enchanter.

The servant bowed low. 'There is a man who wishes to see you, sire. He says his name is Lancelot.'

Acknowledgements

So much in the literary world depends on the skill of those who take the manuscript and edit it for publication. A writer can all too easily take the wrong direction, or lose the thread of the drama. A good editor will re-direct skilfully and enhance greatly the work that will then accrue credit to the author. Similarly a good copy-editor can, with an inserted word or two, or a clever deletion, polish a dull sentence to diamond brightness.

My thanks to my editor Liza Reeves for making it all seem so easy, to copy-editor Jean Maund for the fine-tuning and the elegant polishing, and to my agent Pamela Buckmaster for bringing us together.

Last Sword of Power

This novel is dedicated with great affection to the many people who have made my trips to Birmingham full of enchantment. To Rog Peyton, Dave Holmes and Rod Milner, of Andromeda, for the fun and the liquor, to Bernie Evans and the Brum Group, for the magic of Novacon, to Chris and Pauline Morgan, for the mysteries of the 'Chinese', and to the staff of the Royal Angus Hotel, for smiling in the face of sheer lunacy.

Prologue

Revelation stood with his back to the door, his broad hands resting on the stone sill of the narrow window, his eyes scanning the forests below as he watched a hunting hawk circling beneath the bunching clouds.

'It has begun, my lord,' said the elderly messenger, bowing to the tall man in the monk's robes of brown wool.

Revelation turned slowly, his smoke-grey eyes fastening on the man who looked away, unable to bear the intensity of the gaze.

'Tell it all,' said Revelation, slumping in an ivory-inlaid chair before his desk of oak and gazing absently at the parchment on which he had been working.

'May I sit, my lord?' asked the messenger softly and Revelation looked up and smiled.

'My dear Cotta, of course you may. Forgive my melancholy. I had hoped to spend the remaining days of my life here in Tingis. The African weather suits me, the people are friendly and, with the exception of Berber raids, the country is restful. And I have almost completed my book ... but then such ventures will always take second place to living history.'

Cotta sank gratefully into a high-backed chair, his bald head gleaming with sweat, his dark eyes showing his fatigue. He had come straight from the ship – eager to unburden himself of the bad news he carried, yet loth to load the weight on the man before him.

'There are many stories of how it began. All are contradictory, or else extravagantly embroidered. But, as you suspected, the Goths have a new leader of uncanny powers. His armies are certainly invincible and he is cutting a bloody path through the northern kingdoms. The Sicambrians and the Norse have yet to find him opposing them, but their turn will come.'

241

Revelation nodded. 'What of the sorcery?'

'The agents of the Bishop of Rome all testify that Wotan is a skilled nigromancer. He has sacrificed young girls, launching his new ships across their spread-eagled bodies. It is vile . . . all of it. And he claims to be a god!'

'How do the man's powers manifest themselves?' asked the Abbot.

'He is invincible in battle. No sword can touch him. But it is said he makes the dead walk – and more than walk. One survivor of the battle in Raetia swears that at the end of the day the dead Goths rose in the midst of the enemy, cutting and killing. Needless to add that the opposition crumbled. I have only the one man's word for this tale, but I think he was speaking the truth.'

'And what is the talk among the Goths?'

'They say that Wotan plans a great invasion of Britannia, where the magic is strongest. Wotan says the home of the Old Gods is Britannia, and the gateway to Valhalla is at Sorviodunum, near the Great Circle.'

'Indeed it is' whispered Revelation.

'What, my Lord Abbot?' asked Cotta, his eyes widening.

'I am sorry, Cotta, I was thinking aloud. The Great Circle has always been considered a place of magic by the Druids – and others before them. And Wotan is right, it is a gateway of sorts – and he must not be allowed to pass through it.'

'I cannot think there is a single army to oppose him – except the Blood King, and our reports say he is sorely beset by rebellion and invasion in his own land. Saxons, Jutes, Angles and even British tribes rise against him regularly. How would he fare against 20,000 Gothic warriors led by a sorcerer who cannot be bested?'

Revelation smiled broadly, his wood-smoke eyes twinkling with sudden humour. 'Uther can never be underestimated, my friend. He too has never known defeat . . . and he carries the Sword of Power, Cunobelin's blade.'

'But he is an old man now,' said Cotta. 'Twenty-five years of warfare must have taken their toll. And the Great Betrayal . . .'

'I know the history,' snapped Revelation. 'Pour us some wine, while I think.'

The Abbot watched as the older man filled two copper goblets with deep red wine, accepting one of them with a smile to offset the harshness of his last response.

'Is it true that Wotan's messengers seek out maidens with special talents?'

'Yes. Spirit-seers, healers, speakers in tongues . . . it is said he weds them all.'

'He kills them,' said Revelation. 'It is where his power lies.'

The Abbot rose and moved to the window, watching the sun sink in fire. Behind him Cotta lit four candles, then waited in silence for several minutes. At last he spoke. 'Might I ask, my lord, why you are so concerned about events across the world? There have always been wars. It is the curse of Man that he must kill his brothers and some argue that God himself made this the punishment for Eden.'

Revelation turned from the glory of the sunset and went back to his chair.

'All life, Cotta, is balanced. Light and dark, weak and strong, good and evil. The harmony of nature. In perpetual darkness all plants would die. In perpetual sunlight they would wither and burn. The balance is everything. Wotan must be opposed, lest he become a god – a dark and malicious god, a blood-drinker, a soul-stealer.'

'And you will oppose him, my lord?'

'I will oppose him'

'But you have no army. You are not a king, or a warlord.'

'You do not know what I am, old friend. Come, refill the goblets, and we will see what the Graal shows.'

Revelation moved to an oak chest and poured water from a clay jug into a shallow silver bowl, carrying it carefully to the desk. He waited until the ripples had died and then lifted a golden stone above the water, slowly circling it. The candle flames guttered and died without a hint of breeze and Cotta found himself leaning forward, staring into the now velvet-dark water of the bowl.

The first image that appeared was that of a young boy, red-haired and wild-eyed, thrusting at the air with a wooden sword. Nearby sat an older warrior, a leather cup strapped over the stump where his right hand should have been. Revelation watched them closely, then passed his hand over the surface. Now the watchers could see blue sky and a young girl in a pale green dress sitting beside a lake.

'Those are the mountains of Raetia,' whispered Cotta. The girl was slowly plaiting her dark hair into a single braid.

'She is blind,' said Revelation. 'See how her eyes face the sun unblinking?'

Suddenly the girl's face turned towards them. 'Good morning,' she said, the words forming without sound in both men's minds.

'Who are you?' asked Revelation softly.

'How strange,' she replied, 'your voice whispers like the morning breeze, and seems so far away.'

'I am far away, child. Who are you?'

'I am Anduine.'

'And where do you live?'

'In Cisastra with my father, Ongist. And you?'

'I am Revelation.'

'Are you a friend?'

'I am indeed.'

'I thought so. Who is that with you?'

'How do you know there is someone with me?'

'It is a gift I have, Master Revelation. Who is he?'

'He is Cotta, a monk of the White Christ. You will meet him soon; he also is a friend.'

'This I knew. I can feel his kindness.'

Once more Revelation moved his hand across the water. Now he saw a young man with long, raven-dark hair leading a fine herd of Sicambrian horses in the vales beyond Londinium. The man was handsome, a finely-boned face framed by a strong, clean shaven jaw. Revelation studied the rider intently.

This time the water shimmered of its own accord – a dark storm-cloud hurling silent spears of jagged lightning, streaming across a night sky. From within the cloud came a flying creature with leather wings and a long wedge-shaped head. Upon its back sat a yellow-bearded warrior; his hand rose and lightning flashed towards the watchers. Revelation's arm shot forward just as the water parted; white light speared up into his hand and the stench of burning flesh filled the room. The water steamed and bubbled, vanishing in a cloud of vapour. The silver bowl sagged and flowed down upon the table, a hissing black and silver stream that caused the wood to blaze. Cotta recoiled as he saw Revelation's blackened hand. The Abbot lifted the golden stone and touched it to the seared flesh. It healed instantly, but even the magic could not take away the memory of the pain and Revelation sagged back into his chair, his heart pounding and cold sweat on his face. He took a deep breath and stared at the smouldering wood. The flames died, the smoke disappearing as round them the candles flared into life.

'He knows of me, Cotta. But in attacking me I learned of him. He is not quite ready to plunge the world into darkness; he needs one more sacrifice.'

'For what?' whispered the old man.

'In the language of this world? He seeks to open the Gates of Hell.'

'Can he be stopped?'

Revelation shrugged. 'We will see, my friend. You must take ship for Raetia and find Anduine. From there take her to Britannia, to Noviomagus. I will meet you in three months. Once there you will find an inn in the southern quarter – called, I believe, the Sign of the Bull. Come every day at noon and wait one hour. I shall join you when I can.'

'The blind girl is the sacrifice?'

'Yes.'

'And what of the red-haired boy and the rider?'

'As yet I do not know. Friends or enemies . . . only time will tell. The boy looked familiar, but I cannot place him. He was wearing Saxon garb and I have never journeyed amongst the Saxons. As to the rider, I know him; his name is Ursus and he is of the House of Merovee. He has a brother, I think, and he yearns to be rich.'

'And the man upon the dragon?' asked Cotta softly.

'The Enemy from beyond the Mist.'

'And is he truly Wotan, the grey god?'

Revelation sipped his wine. 'Wotan? He has had many names. To some he was Odin the One-Eyed, to others Loki. In the East they called him Purgamesh, or Molech, or even Baal. Yes, Cotta, he is divine – immortal if you will. And where he walks, chaos follows.'

'You speak as if you know him.'

'I know him. I fought him once before.'

'What happened?'

'I killed him, Cotta,' answered the Abbot.

1

Grysstha watched as the boy twirled the wooden sword, lunging and thrusting at the air around him. 'Feet, boy, think about your feet!'

The old man hawked and spat on the grass, then scratched at the itching stump of his right wrist. 'A swordsman must learn balance. It is not enough to have a quick eye and a good arm – to fall is to die, boy.'

The youngster thrust the wooden blade into the ground and sat beside the old warrior. Sweat gleamed on his brow and his sky-blue eyes sparkled.

'But I am improving, yes?'

'Of course you are improving, Cormac. Only a fool could not.'

The boy pulled clear the weapon, brushing dirt from the whittled blade. 'Why is it so short? Why must I practise with a Roman blade?'

'Know your enemy. Never care about his weaknesses; you will find those if your mind has skill. Know his strengths. They conquered the world, boy, with just such swords. You know why?'

'No.'

Grysstha smiled. 'Gather me some sticks, Cormac. Gather me sticks you could break easily with finger and thumb.' As the boy grinned and moved off to the trees Grysstha watched him, allowing the pride to shine now that the boy could not see him closely.

Why were there so many fools in the world, he thought, as pride gave way to anger? How could they not see the potential in the lad? How could they hate him for a fault that was not his?

'Will these do?' asked Cormac, dropping twenty finger-thin sticks at Grysstha's feet.

'Take one and break it.'

'Easily done,' said Cormac, snapping a stick.

'Keep going, boy. Break them all.'

When the youngster had done so, Grysstha pulled a length of twine from his belt. 'Now gather ten of them and bind them together with this.'

'Like a beacon brand, you mean?'

'Exactly. Tie them tight.'

Cormac made a noose of the twine, gathered ten sticks and bound them tightly together. He offered the four-inch-thick brand to Grysstha but the old man shook his head.

'Break it,' he ordered.

'It is too thick.'

'Try.'

The boy strained at the brand, his face reddening, the muscles of his arms and shoulders writhing under his red woollen shirt.

'A few moments ago you snapped twenty of these sticks, but now you cannot break ten.'

'But they are bound together, Grysstha. Even Calder could not break them.'

'That is the secret the Romans carried in their short-swords. The Saxon fights with a long blade, swinging it wide. His comrades cannot fight close to him, for they might be struck by his slashing sword, so each man fights alone, though there are ten thousand in the fray. But the Roman, with his gladius – he locks shields with his comrades and his blade stabs like a viper bite. Their legions were like that brand, bound together.'

'And how did they fail, if they were so invincible?'

'An army is as good as its general, and the general is only a reflection of the emperor who appoints him. Rome has had her day. Maggots crawl in the body of Rome, worms writhe in the brain, rats gnaw at the sinews.'

The old man hawked and spat once more, his pale blue eyes gleaming.

'You fought them, did you not?' said Cormac. 'In Gallia and Italia?'

'I fought them. I watched their legions fold and run before the dripping blades of the Goths and the Saxons. I could have wept

248

then for the souls of the Romans that once were. Seven legions we crushed, until we found an enemy worth fighting: Afrianus and the Sixteenth. Ah, Cormac, what a day! Twenty thousand lusty warriors, drunk with victory, facing one legion of five thousand men. I stood on a hill and looked down upon them, their bronze shields gleaming. At the centre, on a pale stallion, Afrianus himself. Sixty years old and, unlike his fellows, bearded like a Saxon. We hurled ourselves upon them, but it was like water falling on a stone. Their line held. Then they advanced, and cut us apart. Less than two thousand of us escaped into the forests. What a man! I swear there was Saxon blood in him.'

'What happened to him?'

'The emperor recalled him to Rome and he was assassinated.' Grysstha chuckled. 'Worms in the brain, Cormac.'

'Why?' queried the boy. 'Why kill an able general?'

'Think on it, boy.'

'I can make no sense of it.'

'That is the mystery, Cormac. Do not seek for sense in the tale. Seek for the hearts of men. Now leave me to watch these goats swell their bellies and get back to your duties.'

The boy's face fell. 'I like to be here with you, Grysstha. I . . . I feel at peace here.'

'That is what friendship is, Cormac Daemonsson. Take strength from it, for the world does not understand the likes of you and me.'

'Why are you my friend, Grysstha?'

'Why does the eagle fly? Why is the sky blue? Go now. Be strong.'

Grysstha watched as the lad wandered disconsolately from the high meadow towards the huts below. Then the old warrior swung his gaze up to the horizon and the low, scudding clouds. His stump ached and he pulled the leather cap from his wrist, rubbing at the scarred skin. Reaching out, he tugged the wooden blade from the ground, remembering the days when his own sword had a name and a history and more, a future.

But that was before the day fifteen years ago when the Blood King clove the South Saxon, butchering and burning, tearing the

249

heart from the people and holding it above their heads in his mailed fist. He should have killed them all, but he did not. He made them swear an oath of allegiance, and loaned them coin to rebuild ruined farms and settlements.

Grysstha had come close to killing the Blood King in the last battle. He had hacked his way into the shield square, cleaving a path towards the flame-haired king, when a sword slashed down across his wrist, almost severing his hand. Then another weapon hammered into his helm and he fell dazed. He had struggled to rise, but his head was spinning. When at last he regained consciousness he opened his eyes to find himself gazing at the Blood King, who was kneeling beside him. Grysstha's fingers reached out for the man's throat – but there was no fingers, only a bloody bandage.

'You were a magnificent warrior,' said the Blood King. 'I salute you!'

'You cut off my hand!'

'It was hanging by a thread. It could not be saved.'

Grysstha forced himself to his feet, staggered, then gazed around him. Bodies littered the field and Saxon women were moving amongst the corpses seeking lost loved ones.

'Why did you save me?' snarled Grysstha, rounding on the King.

The man merely smiled and turned on his heel. Flanked by his Guards, he strode from the field to a crimson tent by a rippling stream.

'Why?' bellowed Grysstha, falling to his knees.

'I do not think he knows himself,' said a voice and Grysstha looked up.

Leaning on an ornate crutch carved from dark shining wood was a middle-aged Briton, with wispy grey-blond beard over a pointed chin. Grysstha saw that his left leg was twisted and deformed. The man offered the Saxon his hand but Grysstha ignored it and pushed himself to his feet.

'He sometimes relies on intuition,' said the man, gently, his pale eyes showing no sign of offence.

'You are of the Tribes?' said Grysstha.

'Brigante.'

250

'Then why follow the Roman?'

'Because the land is his, and he is the land. My name is Prasamaccus.'

'So I live because of the King's whim?'

'Yes. I was beside him when you charged the shield-wall; it was a reckless action.'

'I am a reckless man. What does he mean to do with us now? Sell us?'

'I think he means to leave you in peace.'

'Why would he do anything so foolish?'

Prasamaccus limped to a jutting boulder and sat. 'A horse kicked me,' he said, 'and my leg was not strong before that. How is your hand?'

'It burns like fire,' said Grysstha, sitting beside the tribesman, his eyes on the women still searching the field of battle as the crows circled, screeching in their hunger.

'He says that you also are of the land,' said Prasamaccus. 'He has reigned for ten years. He sees Saxons and Jutes and Angles and Goths being born in this Island of Mist. They are no longer invaders.'

'Does he think we came here to serve a Roman King?'

'He knows why you came – to plunder and kill and grow rich. But you stayed to farm. How do you feel about the land?'

'I was not born here, Prasamaccus.'

The Brigante smiled and held out his left hand. Grysstha looked down at it, and then took it in the warrior's grip, wrist to wrist.

'I think that is a good first use of your left hand.'

'It will also learn to use a sword. My name is Grysstha.'

'I have seen you before. You were at the great battle near Eboracum, the day the King came home.'

Grysstha nodded. 'You have a good eye and a better memory. It was the Day of the Two Suns. I have never seen the like since, nor would I wish to. We fought alongside the Brigante that day, and the coward-king Eldared. Were you with him?'

'No. I stood under the two suns with Uther and the Ninth Legion.'

251

'The day of the Blood King. Nothing has been right since then. Why can he not be beaten? How does he always know where to strike?'

'He is the land, and the land knows.'

Grysstha said nothing. He had not expected the man to betray the King's secret.

Of seven thousand Saxon warriors who had begun the battle, a mere eleven hundred remained. These Uther required to kneel and swear Blood Oath never to rise against him again. In return the land would be theirs, as before, but now by right and not by conquest. He also left them their own king, Wulfhere – son of Orsa, son of Hengist. It was a brave move. Grysstha knelt with the others in the dawn light before the King's tent, watching as Uther stood with the boy, Wulfhere.

The Saxons smiled, even in defeat, for they knew they knelt not before the conqueror but before their own sovereign lord.

The Blood King knew it too.

'You have my word that our friendship is as strong as this blade,' he said, hoisting the Sword of Cunobelin high into the air, where the dawn sun glistened like fire on the steel. 'But friendship has a price. This sword will accept no other swords in the hands of the Saxon.' An angry murmur rippled amongst the kneeling men. 'Be true to your word and this may change,' said the King, 'but if you are not true I shall return and not one man, not one woman, not one squalling babe will be left alive from Anderida to Venta. The choice is yours.'

Within two hours both the King and his army had departed and the stunned Saxons gathered in the Council of Wotan. Wulfhere was only twelve and could not vote, and Calder was appointed as steward to help him govern. The rest of the day was devoted to the election of men to the Council. Only two survived out of the original eighteen, but by dusk the positions were filled once more.

Two hours after dawn the Eighteen met and now the real business began. Some were for heading east and linking with Hengist's son, Drada, who was after all Wulfhere's uncle and blood-kin. Others were for waiting until another army could be gathered. Still more suggested sending for aid across the water, where the Merovingian wars were displacing fighting men.

Two events turned the day. At noon a wagon arrived bearing gifts of gold and silver from the King, to be distributed 'as the Council sees fit'. This gift alone meant that food could be bought for the savage winter ahead, and blankets and trade goods from the Merovingians in Gallia.

Second, the steward Calder made a speech that would live long in the minds, if not the hearts of his listeners.

'I fought the Blood King and my sword dripped red with the blood of his Guards. But why did we fight him? Ask yourselves that. I say it was because we felt he could be beaten, and there would be plunder from Venta, Londinium, Dubris and all the other merchant towns. But now we know. He cannot be beaten . . . not by us . . . perhaps not by Drada. You have seen the wagon – more coin than we could have taken in a campaign. I say we wait and judge his word: return to our farms, make repairs, gather harvests where we can.'

'Men without swords, Calder. How then shall we reach Valhalla?' shouted a tall warrior.

'I myself follow the White Christ,' said Calder, 'so I have no interest in Valhalla. But if it worries you, Snorri, then join Drada. Let any man who wishes to fight on do the same. We have been offered friendship – and surely there are worse things in the world to receive from a conqueror than a wagon of gold?'

'It is because he fears us,' said Snorri, lurching to his feet. 'I say we use his gold to buy men and arms and then march on Camulodunum.'

'You will perhaps take the barn with you on your campaign,' said Calder. Laughter followed his words, for it was well known that Snorri had hidden from the Romans under a blanket in the broad barn, only running clear when the enemy put it to the torch. He had been voted to the Council merely on the strength of his landholdings.

'I was cut off and it was that or die,' said Snorri. 'I'll take my gold and join Drada.'

'No one takes the gold,' said Calder. 'The gift is to the Council and we will vote on its use.'

At the last Snorri and four other landsmen, with more than two hundred men, joined Drada; the rest remained to build a new life as vassals of the Blood King.

For Grysstha the decision tasted of ashes. But he was Calder's carle and pledged to obey him, and the decisions of the great rarely concerned him.

That night, as he stood alone on High Hill, Calder came to him.

'You are troubled, my friend?' the steward asked.

'The Days of Blood will come again. I can feel it in the whisper of the wind. The crows know it too.'

'Wise birds, crows. The eyes of Odin.'

'I heard you told them you followed the White Christ?'

'You think the Blood King had no ears at our meeting? You think Snorri and his men will live to join Drada? Or that any of us would have been left alive had I not spoken as I did? No. Grysstha. I follow the old gods who understood the hearts of men.'

'And what of the treaty with Uther?'

'We will honour it for as long as it suits us, but one day you will be avenged for the loss of your sword-arm. I had a dream last night and I saw the Blood King standing alone on the top of a hill, his men all dead around him and his banner broken. I believe Odin sent that dream; it is a promise for the future.'

'It will be many years before we are as strong again.'

'I am a patient man, my friend.'

The Blood King slowly dismounted, handing the reins of his war-horse to a silent squire. All around him the bodies of the slain lay where they had fallen, under a lowering sky and a dark cloud of storm crows waiting to feast.

Uther removed his bronze helm, allowing the breeze to cool his face. He was tired now, more tired than he would allow any man to see.

'You are wounded, sire,' said Victorinus, approaching through the gloom, his dark eyes narrowed in concern at the sight of the blood seeping from the gash in the King's arm.

'It is nothing. How many men did we lose?'

'The stretcher-bearers are still out, sire, and the surgeon is too busy to count. I would say around eight hundred, but it might be less.'

'Or more?'

'We are harrying the enemy to the coast. Will you change your mind about not burning their ships?'

'No. Without ships they cannot retreat. It would cost near a legion to destroy their army utterly, and I do not have five thousand men to spare.'

'Let me bind your arm, sire.'

'Stop fussing over me, man! The wound is sealed – well, almost. Look at them,' said the King, pointing to the field between the stream and the lake and the hundreds of bodies lying twisted in death. 'They came for plunder. Now the crows will feast on their eyes. And will the survivors learn? Will they say, "Avoid the realm of the Blood King?" No, they will return in their thousands. What is it about this land that draws them?'

'I do not know, sire, but as long as they come we will kill them,' said Victorinus.

'Always loyal, my friend. Do you know what today is?'

'Of course, my lord. It is the Day of the King.'

Uther chuckled. 'The Day of the Two Suns. Had I known then that a quarter-century of war would follow . . .' He lapsed into silence.

Victorinus removed his plumed helm, allowing his white hair to flow free in the evening breeze. 'But you always conquer, my lord. You are a legend from Camulodunum to Rome, from Tingis to Bysantium: the Blood King who has never known defeat. Come, your tent is ready. I will pour you some wine.'

The King's tent had been pitched on the high ground overlooking the battlefield. Inside a brazier of coals was glowing beside the cot-bed. Uther's squire, Baldric, helped him out of his chainmail, his breastplate and his greaves, and the King sank gratefully to the cot.

'Today I feel my age,' he said.

'You should not fight where the battle is thickest. A chance arrow, a lucky blow . . .' Victorinus shrugged. 'We . . . Britain . . .

could not stand without you.' He passed the King a goblet of watered wine and Uther sat up and drank deeply.

'Baldric!'

'Yes, my lord.'

'Clean the Sword – and be careful now, for it is sharper than sin.'

Baldric smiled and lifted the great Sword of Cunobelin, carrying it from the tent. Victorinus waited until the lad had gone, then pulled up a canvas stool and sat beside the monarch.

'You are tired, Uther. Leave the Trinovante uprising to Gwalchmai and me. Now that the Goths have been crushed, the tribes will offer little resistance.'

'I will be fine after a night's sleep. You fuss over me like an old woman!'

Victorinus grinned and shook his head and the King lay back and closed his eyes. The older man sat unmoving, staring at the face of his monarch – the flaming red hair and the silver blond beard – and remembered the youth who crossed the borders of Hell to rescue his country. The hair was henna-dyed now and the eyes seemed older than time.

For twenty-five years this man had achieved the impossible, holding back the tide of barbarian invaders threatening to engulf the Land of Mist. Only Uther and the Sword of Power stood between the light of civilization and the darkness of the hordes. Victorinus was pure-blood Roman, but he had fought alongside Uther for a quarter of a century, putting down rebellions, crushing invading forces of Saxon, Norse, Goth and Dane. For how much longer could Uther's small army prevail?

For as long as the King lived. This was the great sadness, the bitter truth. Only Uther had the power, the strength, the personal magnetism. When he was gone the light would go out.

Gwalchmai entered the tent, but stood in silence as he saw the King sleeping. Victorinus rose and drew a blanket over the monarch; then, beckoning to the old Cantii warrior, he left the tent.

'He's soul-weary,' said Gwalchmai. 'Did you ask him?'

'Yes.'

'And?'

'What do you think, my friend?'

'If he dies, we are lost,' said Gwalchmai. He was a tall man, stern-eyed under bushy grey brows, and his long silver hair was braided after the fashion of his Cantii forebears. 'I fear for him. Ever since the Betrayal

'Hush, man!' hissed Victorinus, taking his comrade by the arm and leading him away into the night.

Inside the tent Uther's eyes opened. Throwing off the blanket, he poured himself some more wine and this time added no water.

The Great Betrayal. Still they spoke of it. But whose was the betrayal, he wondered? He drained the wine and refilled the goblet.

He could see them now, on that lonely cliff-top . . .

'Sweet Jesus!' he whispered. 'Forgive me.'

Cormac made his way through the scattered huts to the smithy where Kern was hammering the blade of a plough. The boy waited until the sweating smith dunked the hot metal into the trough and then approached him.

'You have work for me?' he asked. The bald thickset Kern wiped his hands on his leather apron.

'Not today.'

'I could fetch wood?'

'I said not today,' snapped the smith. 'Now begone!'

Cormac swallowed hard. 'I could clean the storeroom.'

Kern's hand flashed for the boy's head, but Cormac swayed aside causing the smith to stumble. 'I am sorry, master Kern,' he said, standing stockstill for the angry blow that smacked into his ear.

'Get out! And don't come back tomorrow.'

Cormac walked, stiff-backed, from the smithy and only out of sight of the building did he spit the blood from his mouth. He was hungry and he was alone. All around him he could see evidence of families – mothers and toddlers, young children playing with brothers and sisters, fathers teaching sons to ride.

The potter had no work for him either, nor the baker, nor the tanner. The widow, Althwynne, loaned him a hatchet and he chopped wood for most of the afternoon, for which she gave him some pie and a sour apple. But she did not allow him into her home, nor smile, nor speak more than a few words. In all of his fourteen years Cormac Daemonsson had seen the homes of none of the villagers. He had long grown used to people making the sign of the Protective Horn when he approached, and to the fact that only Grysstha would meet his eyes. But then Grysstha was different . . . He was a man, a true man who feared no evil. A man who could see a boy and not a demon's son. And Grysstha alone had talked to Cormac of the strange day almost fifteen years before when he and a group of hunters entered the Cave of Sol Invictus to find a great black hound lying alongside four squealing pups – and beside them a flame-haired babe still wet from birth. The hound attacked the hunters and was slain along with the pups, but no man among the saxons cared to kill the babe, for they knew he was sired by a demon and none wanted to earn the hatred of the pit-dwellers.

Grysstha had carried the child from the Cave and found a milk-nurse for him from among the captured British women. But after four months she had suddenly died and then no one would touch the child. Grysstha had taken him into his own hut and fed him with cow's milk through a needle pierced leather glove.

The babe had even been the subject of a Council meeting, where a vote was taken as to whether he lived or died. Only Calder's casting vote saved young Cormac – and that was given after a special plea from Grysstha.

For seven years the boy lived with the old warrior, but Grysstha's disability meant that he could not earn enough to feed them both and the child was forced to scavenge in the village for extra food.

At thirteen, Cormac realised that his association with the crippled warrior had caused Grysstha to become an outcast and he built his own hut away from the village. It was a meagre dwelling with no furniture save a cot-bed and Cormac spent little time there except in winter, when he shivered despite the fire and dreamed cold dreams.

That night, as always, Grysstha stopped at his hut and banged on the door-post. Cormac called him in, offering him a cup of water. The old man accepted graciously, sitting cross-legged on the hard-packed dirt floor.

258

'You need another shirt, Cormac, you have outgrown that. And those leggings will soon climb to your knees.'

'They will last the Summer.'

'We'll see. Did you eat today?'

'Althwynne gave me some pie — I chopped wood for her.'

'I heard Kern cracked your head?'

'Yes.'

'There was a time when I would have killed him for that. Now, if I struck him, I would only break my good hand.'

'It was nothing, Grysstha. How went your day?'

'The goats and I had a wonderful time. I told them of my campaigns and they told me of theirs. They became bored long before I did!'

'You are never tiresome,' said Cormac. 'You are a wonderful storyteller.'

'Tell me that when you've listened to another storyteller. It is easy to be the King when no one else lives in your land.'

'I heard a saga poet once. I sat outside Calder's Hall and listened to Patrisson sing of the Great Betrayal.'

'You must not mention that to anyone, Cormac. It is a forbidden song — and death to sing it.' The old man leaned back against the wall of the hut and smiled. 'But he sang it well, did he not?'

'Did the Blood King really have a grandfather who was a god?'

'All kings are sired by gods — or so they would have us believe. Of Uther I know not. I only know his wife was caught with her lover, that both fled and he hunted them. Whether he found them and cut them to pieces as the song says, or whether they escaped, I do not know. I spoke to Patrisson, and he did not know either. But he did say that the Queen ran off with the King's grandfather, which sounds like a merry mismatch.'

'Why has the King not taken another wife?'

'I'll ask him the next time he invites me to supper.'

'But he has no heir. Will there not be a war if he dies now?'

'There will be a war anyway, Cormac. The King has reigned for twenty-five years and has never known peace ... uprisings, invasions, betrayals. His wife was not the first to betray him. The Brigantes rose again sixteen years ago and Uther crushed them at Trimontium. Then the Ordovice swept east and Uther destroyed their army at Viriconium. Lastly the Jutes, two years ago. They had a treaty like ours and they broke it; Uther kept his promise and had every man, woman and child put to death.'

'Even children?' whispered Cormac.

'All of them. He is a hard, canny man. Few will rise against him now.'

'Would you like some more water?'

'No, I must be getting to my bed. There will be rain tomorrow – I can feel it in my stump – and I'll need my rest if I'm to sit shivering.'

'One question, Grysstha?'

'Ask it.'

'Was I really born to a dog?'

Grysstha swore. 'Who said that to you?'

'The tanner.'

'I have told you before that I found you in the cave beside the hound. That's all it means. Someone had left you there and the bitch tried to defend you, as she did her own pups. You had not been born more than two hours, but her pups were days old. Odin's Blood! We have men here with brains of pig-swill. Understand me, Cormac, you are no demon-child, I promise you that. I do not know why you were left in that cave, or by whom. But there were six dead men on the path by the cliff, and they were not killed by a demon.'

'Who were they?'

'Doughty warriors, judging by their scars. All killed by one man – one fearsome man. The hunters with me were convinced once they saw you that a pit-dweller was abroad, but that is because they were young and had never seen a true warrior in action. I tried to explain, but fear has a way of blinding the eyes. I believe the warrior was your father and he was wounded unto death. That's why you were left there.'

'And what of my mother?'

'I don't know, boy. But the gods know. One day perhaps they'll give you a sign. But until then you are Cormac the Man and you will walk with your back straight. For whoever your father was, he was a man. And you will prove true to him, if not to me.'

'I wish you were my father, Grysstha.'

'I wish it too. Good-night, boy.'

2

The King, flanked by Gwalchmai and Victorinus, walked out into the paddock field to view his new horses. The young man standing beside the crippled Prasamaccus stared intently at the legendary warrior.

'I thought he would be taller,' he whispered and Prasamaccus smiled.

'You thought to see a giant walking head and shoulders above other men. Oh, Ursus, you of all people ought to know the difference between men and myths.'

Ursus' pale grey eyes studied the King as he approached. The man was around forty years of age and he walked with the confident grace of the warrior who has never met his equal. His hair flowing to his mail-clad shoulders was auburn red, though his thick square-cut beard was more golden in colour and streaked with grey. The two men walking beside him were older, perhaps in their fifties. One was obviously Roman, hawk-nosed and steely-eyed, while the second wore his grey hair braided like a tribesman.

'A fine day,' said the King, ignoring the younger man and addressing himself to Prasamaccus.

'It is, my lord, and the horses you bought are as fine.'

'They are all here?'

'Thirty-five stallions and sixty mares. May I present Prince Ursus, of the House of Merovee?'

The young man bowed. 'It is an honour, my lord.'

The King gave a tired smile and moved past the young man. Taking Prasamaccus by the arm the two walked on into the field, stopping by a grey stallion of some seventeen hands.

'The Sicambrians know how to breed horses,' said Uther, running his hand over the beast's glistening flank.

'You look weary, Uther.'

'It reflects how I feel. The Trinovante are flexing their muscles once more, as are the Saxons in the Middle Land.'

'When do you ride?'

'Tomorrow, with four legions. I sent Patreus with the Eighth and the Fifth, but he was routed. Reports say we lost six hundred men.'

'Was Patreus amongst them?' Prasamaccus asked.

'If not, he'll wish he was,' snapped the King. 'He tried to charge a shield wall up a steep slope.'

'As you yourself did only four days ago against the Goths.'

'But I won!'

'You always do, my lord.'

Uther grinned, and for a moment there was a flash of the lonely youth Prasamaccus had first met a quarter of a century before. But then it was gone and the mask settled once more.

'Tell me of the Sicambrian,' said the King, staring across at the young dark-haired prince, clad all in black.

'He knows his horses.'

'That was not my meaning, and well you know it.'

'I cannot say, Uther. He seems . . . intelligent, knowledgeable.'

'You like him?'

'I rather think that I do. He reminds me of you – a long time ago.'

'Is that a good thing?'

'It is a compliment.'

'Have I changed so much?'

Prasamaccus said nothing. A lifetime ago Uther had dubbed him Kingsfriend, and asked always for his honest council. In those days the young prince had crossed the Mist in search of his father's sword, had fought demons and the Witch Queen, had brought an army of ghosts back to the world of flesh and had loved the mountain woman, Laitha.

The old Brigante shrugged. 'We all change, Uther. When my Helga died last year, I felt all beauty pass from the world.'

'A man is better off without love. It weakens him,' said the King, moving away to examine the horses. 'Within a few years we will have

263

a better, faster army. All of these mounts are at least two hands taller than our own horses, and they are bred for speed and stamina.'

'Ursus brought something else you might like to see,' said Prasamaccus. 'Come, it will interest you.' The King seemed doubtful, but he followed the limping Brigante back to the paddock gates. Here Ursus bowed once more and led the group to the rear of the herdsmen's living quarters. In the yard behind the buildings a wooden frame had been erected – curved wood attached to a straight spine, representing a horse's back. Over this Ursus draped a stiffened leather cover. A second section was tied to the front of the frame and the prince secured the hide, then returned to the waiting warriors.

'What in Hades is it?' asked Victorinus. Ursus lifted a short-bow and notched an arrow to the string.

With one smooth motion he let fly. The shaft struck the rear of the 'horse' and, failing to penetrate fully, flapped down to point at the ground.

'Give me the bow,' said Uther. Drawing back the string as far as the weapon could stand, he loosed the shaft. It cut through the leather and jutted from the hide.

'Now look, sire,' said Ursus, stepping forward to the 'horse'. Uther's arrow had penetrated a mere half-inch. 'It would prick a good horse, but it would not have disabled him.'

'What of the weight?' asked Victorinus.

'A Sicambrian horse could carry it and still work a full day as well as any British war-horse.'

Gwalchmai was unimpressed. The old Cantii warrior hawked and spat. 'It must cut down on the speed of the charge – and that is what carries us through the enemy. Armoured horses? Pah!'

'You would perhaps think of riding into battle without your own armour?' snapped the prince.

'You insolent puppy!' roared Gwalchmai.

'Enough!' ordered the King. 'Tell me, Ursus, what of the rains? Would they not soften your leather and add to the weight?'

'Yes, my lord. But each warrior should carry a quantity of oiled beeswax to be rubbed into the cover every day.'

264

'Now we must polish our horses as well as our weapons,' said Gwalchmai, with a mocking grin.

'Have ten of these . . . horse jerkins . . . made,' said Uther. 'Then we shall see.'

'Thank you, sire.'

'Do not thank me until I place an order. This is what you are seeking yes?'

'Yes, sire.'

'Did you devise the armour?'

'Yes, my lord, although my brother Balan overcame the problem of the rain.'

'And to him will go the profit for the wax I order?'

'Yes, my lord,' said Ursus, smiling.

'And where is he at present?'

'Trying to sell the idea in Rome. It will be difficult, for the emperor still sets great store by the marching legions even though his enemies are mounted.'

'Rome is finished,' said Uther. 'You should sell to the Goths or the Huns.'

'I would my lord, but the Huns do not buy – they take. And the Goths? Their treasury is smaller than my own.'

'And your own Merovingian army?'

'My King – long may he reign – is guided in matters military by the Mayor of the Palace. And he is not a visionary.'

'But then he is not assailed on all sides and from within,' said Uther. 'Do you fight as well as you talk?'

'Not quite.'

Uther grinned. 'I have changed my mind. Make thirty-two and Victorinus will put you in command of one Turma. You will join me at Petvaria and then I will see your horse armour as it needs to be seen – against a real enemy. If it is successful, you will be rich and, as I suspect you desire, all other fighting kings will follow Uther's lead.'

'Thank you, sire.'

'As I said, do not thank me yet. You have not heard my offer.'

With that the King turned and walked away. Prasamaccus draped his arm over Ursus' shoulder.

'I think the King likes you, young man. Do not disappoint him.'
'I would lose my order?'
'You would lose your life,' Prasamaccus told him.

Long after Grysstha had returned to his own hut in the shadow of the Long Hall Cormac, unable to sleep, wandered out into the cool of the night to sit below the stars and watch the bats circle the trees.

All was quiet and the boy was truly, splendidly, perfectly alone. Here in the glory of the hunter's moonlight there was no alienation, no sullen stares, no harsh words. The night breeze ruffled his hair as he gazed up at the cliffs above the woods and thought of his father, the nameless warrior who had fought so well. Grysstha said he had killed six men.

But why had he left the infant Cormac alone in the cave? And where was the woman who bore him? Who would leave a child? Was the man – so brave in battle – so cruel in life?

And what mother could leave her babe to die in a lonely cave?

As always there were no answers, but the questions chained Cormac to this hostile village. He could not leave and make a future for himself, not while the past was such a mystery.

When he was younger he had believed that his father would one day come to claim him, striding to the long Hall with a sword at his side, a burnished helm upon his brow. But no longer could the dreams of childhood sustain him. In four days he would be a man . . . and then what? Begging for work at the smithy, or the mill, or the bakery, or the slaughterhouse?

Back in his hut he slept fitfully beneath his threadbare blanket, rising before the dawn and taking his sling to the hills. Here he killed three rabbits, skinning them expertly with the small knife Grysstha had given him the year before. He lit a fire in a sheltered hollow and roasted the meat, enjoying the rare sensation of a full belly. But there was little goodness in rabbit meat and Grysstha had once told him a man could starve to death while feasting on such fare. Cormac licked his fingers and then wiped them on the long grass, remembering the Thunder Feast the previous Autumn where he had tasted beef at the open banquet, when King Wulfhere had visited his former steward, Calder. Cormac had been forced to stay back from the throng around the Saxon King, but had heard his speech. Meaningless platitudes mostly, coming from a weak man. He looked the part, with his mail-shirt of iron and his axe-bearing guards, but his face was soft and womanly and his eyes focused on a point above the crowd.

But the beef had been magnificent. Grysstha had brought him three cuts, succulent and rich with the blood of the bull.

'Once,' the old man said, between mouthfuls, 'we ate like this every day! When we were reavers, and our swords were feared. Calder once promised we would do so again. He said we would be revenged on the Blood King, but look at him now – fat and content beside the puppet king.'

'The King looks like a woman,' said Cormac.

'He lives like one,' snapped Grysstha. 'And to think his grand-father was Hengist! Would you like more meat?'

And they feasted that night like emperors.

Now Cormac doused his fire and wandered high into the hills, along the cliff-tops overlooking the calm sea. The breeze was strong here, and cool despite the morning sun, clear in a cloudless sky. Cormac stopped beneath a spreading oak and leapt to hang from a thick branch. One hundred times he hauled himself up to touch his chin to the wood, feeling the muscles in his arms and shoulders swell and burn. Then he dropped lightly to the ground, sweat gleaming on his face.

'How strong you are, Cormac,' said a mocking voice and he swung round to see Calder's daughter, Alftruda, sitting in the grass with a basket of berries beside her. Cormac blushed and said noth-ing. He should have walked away, but the sight of her sitting there cross-legged, her woollen skirt pulled up to reveal the milky white-ness of her legs . . . 'Are you so shy?' she asked.

'Your brothers will not be best pleased with you for speaking to me.'

'And you are frightened of them?'

Cormac considered the question. Calder's sons had tormented him for years, but mostly he could outrun them to his hiding places in the woods. Agwaine was the worst, for he enjoyed inflicting pain. Lennox and Barta were less overtly cruel, but they followed Agwaine's lead in everything. But was he frightened?

'Perhaps I am,' he said. 'But then such is the law that they are allowed to strike me, but it is death if I defend myself.'

'That's the price you pay for having a demon for a father. Cormac. Can you work magic?'

'No.'

'Not even a little, to please me?'

'Not even a little.'

'Would you like some berries?'

'No, thank you. I must be heading back; I have work to do.'

'Do I frighten you, Cormac Daemonsson?' He stopped in mid-turn, his throat tight.

'I am not . . . comfortable. No one speaks to me but I am used to that. I thank you for your courtesy.'

'Do you think I am pretty?'

'I think you are beautiful. Especially here, in the summer sunlight, with the breeze moving your hair. But I do not wish to cause you trouble.'

She rose smoothly and moved towards him and he backed away instinctively, but the oak barred his retreat. He felt her body press against his and his arms moved around her back, drawing her to him.

'Get away from my sister!' roared Agwaine and Alftruda leapt back with fear in her eyes.

'He cast a spell on me!' she shouted, running to Agwaine. The tall blond youth hurled her aside and drew a dagger from its sheath.

'You will die for this obscenity,' he hissed, advancing on Cormac.

Cormac's eyes flickered from the blade to Agwaine's angry face, reading the intent and seeing the blood-lust rising. He leapt to his right – to cannon into the huge figure of Lennox, whose brawny arms closed around him. Triumph blazed in Agwaine's eyes, but Cormac hammered his elbow into Lennox's belly and then up in a second strike, smashing the boy's nose. Lennox staggered back, almost blinded. Then Barta ran from the bushes, holding a thick branch above his head like a club. Cormac leapt feet first, his heel landing with sickening force against Barta's chin, and hurling him unconscious to the ground.

Cormac rolled to his feet, swinging to face Agwaine, his arm blocking the dagger blow aimed at his heart. His fist slammed against Agwaine's cheek, then his left foot powered into his enemy's groin. Agwaine screamed once and fell to his knees, dropping the dagger. Cormac swept it up, grabbed Agwaine's long blond hair and hauled back his head, exposing the throat.

'No!' screamed Alftruda. Cormac blinked and took a deep, calming breath. Then he stood and hurled the dagger far out over the cliff-top.

'You lying slut!' he said, advancing on Alftruda. She sank to her knees, her eyes wide and terror-filled.

'Don't hurt me!'

Suddenly he laughed. 'Hurt you? I would not *touch* you if my life depended on it. A few moments ago you were beautiful. Now you are ugly, and will always be so.'

Her hands fled to her face, her fingers touching the skin – questing, seeking her beauty. Cormac shook his head. 'I am not talking of a spell,' he whispered. 'I have no spells.'

Turning, he looked upon his enemies. Lennox was sitting by the oak with blood streaming from his smashed nose, Barta was still unconscious and Agwaine was gone.

There was no sense of triumph, no joy in the victory.

For in defeating these boys, Cormac had sentenced himself to death.

Agwaine returned to the village and reported Cormac's attack to his father Calder, who summoned the village elders, demanding justice. Only Grysstha spoke up for Cormac.

'You ask for justice. For years your sons have tormented Cormac and he has had no aid. But he has borne it like a man. Now, when set upon by three bullies, he defends himself and faces execution? Every man here who votes for such a course should be ashamed.'

'He assaulted my daughter,' said Calder. 'Or are you forgetting that?'

'If he did,' said Grysstha, rising, 'he followed in the tracks of every other able-bodied youth within a day's riding distance!'

'How dare you?' stormed Calder.

'Dare? Do not speak to me of dares, you fat-bellied pig! I have followed you for thirty years, living only on your promises. But now I see you for what you are – a weak, greedy, fawning boot-licker. A pig who sired three toads and a rutting strumpet!'

Calder hurled himself across the circle of men but Grysstha's fist thundered into his chin, throwing him to the dirt floor. Pandemonium followed, with some of the councillors grabbing Grysstha and other holding the enraged leader. In the silence that followed Calder fought to control his temper, signalling to the men on either side of him to let him go.

'You are no longer welcome here, old cripple,' he said. 'You will leave this village as a Nithing. I will send word to all villages in the South Saxon and you will be welcome nowhere. And if I see you after today I shall take my axe to your neck. Go! Find the dog-child and stay with him. I want you there to see him die.'

Grysstha shrugged off the arms holding him and stalked from the Hall. In his own hut he gathered his meagre belongings, pushed his hand-axe into his belt and marched from the village. Evrin the baker moved alongside him, pushing two black loaves into his arms.

'Walk with God,' Evrin whispered.

Grysstha nodded and marched on. He should have left a long time ago – and taken Cormac with him. But loyalty was stronger than iron rings and Grysstha was pledged to Calder by Blood-Oath. Now he had broken his word and was Nithing in the eyes of the law. No one would ever trust him again, and his life was worthless.

Yet even so joy began to blossom in the old warrior's heart. The heavy mind-numbing years as a goatherd were behind him now, as was his allegiance to Calder. Grysstha filled his lungs with clean, fresh air, and climbed the hills towards the Cave of Sol Invictus.

Cormac was waiting for him there, sitting on the altar stone, the bones of his past scattered at his feet.

'You heard?' said Cormac, making room for the old man to sit beside him on the flat stone. Grysstha tore off a chunk of dark bread and passed it to the boy.

'Word filtered through,' he said. Cormac glanced at the blanket-sack Grysstha had dumped by the old bones of the warhound.

'Are we leaving?'

'We are, boy. We should have done it years ago. We'll head for Dubris and get some work – enough to earn passage to Gallia. Then I'll show you my old campaign trails.'

'They attacked me, Grysstha. After Alftruda put her arms around me.'

The old warrior looked into the boy's sad blue eyes. 'One more lesson in life, Cormac: women always bring trouble. Mind you, judging from the way Agwaine was walking he will not be thinking about girls for some time to come. How did you defeat all three?'

'I don't know, I just did it.'

'That's your father's blood. We'll make something of you yet, lad!'

Cormac glanced around the cave. 'I have never been here before. I was always afraid. Now I wonder why. Just old bones.' He scuffed his feet in the loose dirt and saw a glint of light. Leaning forward he pressed his fingers into the dust, coming up with a gold chain on which hung a round stone like a golden nugget veined with slender black lines.

'Well, that's a good omen,' muttered Grysstha. 'We've only been free men for an hour and already you find treasure.'

'Could it have been my mother's?'

'All things are possible.'

Cormac looped the chain over his head, tucking the golden stone under his shirt. It felt warm against his chest.

'Are you in trouble too, Grysstha?'

The warrior grinned. 'I may have said a word or two too many, but they flew home like arrows!'

'Then they will be hunting us both?'

271

'Aye, come morning. We'll worry then. Now get some rest, boy.'

Cormac moved to the far wall and settled himself down on the dusty floor, his head resting on his arms. Grysstha stretched out on the altar and was asleep within minutes.

The boy lay listening to the warrior's deep heavy snoring, then drifted into a curious dream. It seemed he opened his eyes and sat up. By the altar lay a black warhound and five pups, and beyond her was a young woman with hair of spun gold. A man knelt beside her, cradling her head.

'I am sorry I brought you to this,' he said, stroking her hair. His face was strong, his hair dark and shining like raven's wings, his eyes the blue of a winter's sky.

She reached up and touched his cheek, smiling through her pain.

'I love you. I have always loved you . . .'

Outside a bugle call drifted through the morning air and the man cursed softly and stood, drawing his sword. 'They have found us!'

The woman moaned as her labour began and Cormac moved across to her, but she did not see him. He tried to touch her, but his hand passed through her body, as if it was smoke.

'Don't leave me!' she begged. The man's face showed his torment but the bugle sounded once more and he turned and vanished from sight. The woman cried out and Cormac was forced to watch impotently as she struggled to deliver her child. At last the babe came forth blood-covered and curiously still.

'Oh, no! Dear sweet Christ!' moaned the woman, lifting the child and slapping its tiny rump. There was not the flicker of movement. Laying the babe in her lap, she lifted a golden chain from around her neck, closing the child's tiny fingers around the stone at its centre. 'Live!' she whispered. 'Please live!'

But there was no movement . . . no sign of life.

From the sunlit world outside came the sound of blade upon blade, the cries of the wounded, the angry shouts of the combatants. Then there was silence, save for the birds singing in the forest trees. A shadow crossed the entrance and the tall man staggered

272

inside, blood pouring from a wound in his side and a second in his chest.

'The babe?' he whispered.

'He is dead,' said the woman.

Hearing something from beyond the cave, the man turned. 'There are more of them. I can see their spears catching the sun. Can you walk?' She struggled to stand but fell back and he moved to her side, sweeping her into his arms.

'He's alive!' shouted Cormac, tears in his eyes. '*I'm* alive! Don't leave me!'

He followed them out into the sunlight, watching the wounded man struggle to the top of the cliffs before sinking to his knees, the woman tumbling from his arms. A horseman galloped into sight and the warrior drew his sword, but the man hauled on the reins, waiting.

From the woods another man came limping into view, his left leg twisted and deformed. The tall warrior drew back his sword and hurled it into the trees, where it lanced into a thick ivy-covered trunk. Then he lifted the woman once more, turned and gazed at the sea foaming hundreds of feet below.

'No!' screamed the crippled man. The warrior looked towards the horseman who sat unmoving, his stern face set, his hands resting on the pommel of his saddle.

The warrior stepped from the cliff and vanished from sight, taking the woman with him.

Cormac watched as the cripple fell to earth with tears in his eyes, but the horseman merely turned his mount and rode away into the trees. Further down the trail Cormac could see the hunting party approaching the cave. He ran like the wind arriving to see the Stone in the child's hands glow like a burning candle and an aura of white light shine over the infant's skin. Then came the first lusty cry. The hunters entered and the black warhound leapt at them only to be cut down by knives and axes.

'Odin's Blood!' said one of the men. 'The bitch gave birth to a child.'

'Kill it!' cried another.

'You fools!' said Grysstha. 'You think the dog killed those Romans?'

Cormac could bear to watch no more and shut his eyes as Grysstha reached for the babe . . .

He opened them to see the dawn light creeping back from the cave-mouth and Grysstha still asleep upon the altar. Rising, he moved to the old man and shook him awake.

'It is dawn,' he said, 'and I saw my mother and father.'

'Give me time, boy,' muttered the old warrior. 'Let me get some air.' He stretched and sat up, rubbing at his eyes and groaning at the stiff, cold muscles of his neck. 'Pass me the water-sack.'

Cormac did so and Grysstha pulled the stopper and drank deeply. 'Now what is this about your mother?'

The boy told him of the dream, but Grysstha's eyes did not show great interest until he mentioned the crippled man.

'Tell me of his face.'

'Light hair, thin beard. Sad eyes.'

'And the horseman?'

'A warrior, tall and strong. A cold, hard man with red hair and beard, and wearing a helm of bronze banded by a circle of iron.'

'We'd best be going, Cormac,' said the old warrior suddenly.

'Was my dream true, do you think?'

'Who knows, boy? We'll talk later.'

Grysstha swung his blanket-sack to his shoulder and walked from the cave. There he stopped stock-still, dropping the sack.

'What is wrong?' asked Cormac, moving into the sunlight. Grysstha gestured him to silence and scanned the undergrowth beneath the trees.

Cormac could see nothing but suddenly a man rose from behind a thick bush with an arrow notched to his bow, the string drawn back. Cormac froze. Grysstha's arm hammered into the boy's chest, hurling him aside just as the archer loosed his shaft. The arrow sliced through Grysstha's jerkin, punching through to pierce his lungs. A second arrow followed. The old man shielded Cormac with his body as blood bubbled from his mouth.

'Run!' he hissed, toppling to the earth.

An arrow flashed by Cormac's face and he dived to the left as other shafts hissed by him, then rolled and came up running. A great shout went up from the hidden men in the undergrowth, and the sound of pounding feet caused Cormac to increase his speed as he hurdled a fallen tree and sprinted for the cliff tops. Arrows sailed over him and he dodged to left and right, cutting up through the forest path, seeking a hiding-place.

There were several hollow trees where he had previously hidden from Agwaine and his brothers. He was feeling more confident now as he increased the distance between himself and his pursuers.

But the baying of the warhounds brought fresh terror. The trees would offer no sanctuary now.

He emerged at the cliff-tops and swung, expecting to see the dark hurtling forms of Calder's twin hounds, fangs bared for his throat. But the trail was empty for the moment. He drew his slender skinning-knife, eyes scanning the trees.

A huge black hound bounded into sight. As it leapt Cormac dropped to his knees and rammed the blade into its belly, disembowelling it as the beast sailed above him. The stricken dog landed awkwardly, its paws entangling in its ribboned entrails. Cormac ignored it and ran back to the trees, forsaking the path and forcing his body through the thickest of the undergrowth.

Suddenly he stopped for there, embedded in the ivy-covered trunk of a spreading oak, was the sword of his dream. Sheathing his knife, he took hold of the ivory hilt and drew the blade clear. The sword was the length of a man's arm and not one spot of rust had touched the blade in the fifteen years it had been hidden here.

Cormac closed his eyes. 'Thank you, Father,' he whispered.

The hilt was long enough for the sword to be wielded double-handed and the boy swung the blade several times, feeling the balance.

Then he stepped out into the open as the second hound rounded the trail, hurtling at the slim figure before it. The blade lanced its neck, half severing the head. His eyes blazing with an anger he had

275

never experienced before, Cormac loped down the trail towards the following hunters.

Near a stand of elm the sound of their pursuit came to him and he stepped from the track, hiding himself behind a thick trunk. Four men ran into view – Agwaine in the lead, his brothers following, and, bringing up the rear, the blacksmith Kern, his bald head shining with sweat.

As they raced past Cormac's hiding place he took a deep breath, then leapt into the path to face the astonished Kern. The blacksmith was carrying a short double-headed axe but he had no time to use it, for Cormac's sword swept up, over and down to cleave the man's jugular. Kern staggered back, dropping his axe, his fingers scrabbling at the wound as he sought to stem the flooding life-blood.

Cormac ran back into the trees, following the other three. Agwaine and Lennox had disappeared from sight, but Barta was lumbering far behind them. Darting out behind him, Cormac tapped his shoulder and the blond youngster turned.

Cormac's blade slid through the youth's woollen jerkin and up into the belly, ripping through lungs and heart. Savagely he twisted the sword to secure its release, then dragged it clear. Barta died without a sound.

Moving like a wraith Cormac vanished into the shadow-haunted trees, seeking the last of the hunters.

On the cliff-top Agwaine had found the butchered hounds. Turning, he ran back to warn his brother that Cormac was now armed; then he and Lennox retreated back along the trail, finding the other bodies.

Together the survivors fled the woods. Cormac emerged from the trees to see them sprinting back into the valley.

At first he thought to chase them to the Great Hall itself, but common sense prevailed and, his anger ebbing, he returned to the Cave. Grysstha had propped himself against the western wall; his white beard was stained with his blood, his face pale and grey.

As Cormac knelt beside the old man, taking his hand, Grysstha's eyes opened.

'I can see the Valkyrie, Cormac,' he whispered, 'but they ignore me, for I have no sword.'

'Here,' said the boy, pushing the ivory hilt into the warrior's left hand.

'Do not . . . do not . . . tell anyone . . . about your birth.' Grysstha slid sideways to the ground, the sword slipping from his fingers.

For a while Cormac sat in silence with the body of his only friend. Then he stood and wandered into the sunlight, staring down at the village far below.

He wanted to scream his anger to the skies, but he did not. One of Grysstha's sayings sprang to his mind: Revenge is a better meal when served cold.

Sheathing the sword in his belt, he gathered Grysstha's possessions and set off for the east. At the top of the last rise he turned once more.

'I will return,' he said softly. 'And then you will see the Demon, I swear it!'

3

Prasamaccus stretched out his legs before the log-fire in the grate and sipped the honeyed wine. His daughter, Adriana, offered a goblet to Ursus who accepted it with a dazzling smile.

'Do not waste your charm,' said Prasamaccus. 'Adriana is betrothed to the herdsman's son, Gryll.'

'Are they in love?'

'Why ask me? Adriana is standing here.'

'Of course. My apologies, my lady.'

'You must forgive my father,' she said, her voice deep and husky. 'He forgets that the customs of his guests are rarely like his own. Are women still bought and sold by the Sicambrians?'

'That is somewhat harsh. Dowries are paid to prospective husbands – but then that is still the case in Uther's Britain, is it not? And a woman is servant to her husband. All religions agree on this.'

'My father told Gryll there would be no dowry. And we will be wed at the Midwinter Feast.'

'And are you in love?'

'Yes, very much.'

'But no dowry?'

'I think Father will relent. He has too much money already. And now, if you will excuse me I am very tired.'

Ursus stood and bowed as Adriana kissed Prasamaccus' bearded cheek and left the room.

'She is a good girl, but she must think I'm growing senile! She will slip out through the yard and meet Gryll by the stables. How is your wine?'

'A little sweet for my taste.'

Prasamaccus leaned forward, tossing a log to the fire. 'Honey aids the mind and clears the stomach. It also wards off evil spirits.'

Ursus chuckled. 'I thought that was bitter onions?'

'Those too,' agreed the Brigante. 'And mistletoe, and black dogs with white noses.'

'I think you have drunk a little too much wine, my friend.'

'It is a fault of mine on lonely evenings. You know, I was with the King before he *was* the King – when he was a hunted boy in the mountains and he crossed the Valley of Death to another world. I was young then. I watched him become a man; I watched him fall in love and I watched his great heart slowly die. He was always a man of iron will. But now that is all he has left: the iron. The heart is dead.'

'His wife, you mean?'

'The lovely Laitha. Gian Avur, Fawn of the Forest.'

'I understand the Song is forbidden here. I suppose it is understandable; a king cuckolded by a relative, betrayed by a friend.'

'There was more to it than that, Ursus. Far more. There always is. Culain lach Feragh was a warrior without peer, and a man of great honour. But his weakness was that he lived without love. Laitha was raised by him and she had loved him since a child, but they were doomed.'

'You speak as if man has no choices.'

'Sometimes he does not. Culain would have died before hurting Uther or Gian, but the King knew that his wife had always loved Culain and evil thoughts grew in him like a dry grass fire. He was always on some mission of war and he took to living with the army. He rarely spoke to Gian and appointed Culain as her champion. He forced them together, and finally they gave in to their desires.'

'How did he find out?'

'It was an open secret and the lovers grew careless. They would be seen touching hands, walking arm-in-arm in the gardens. And Culain often visited the Queen's apartments late in the night, emerging at dawn. One night the King's Guards burst into the Queen's bedchamber and Culain was there. They were dragged before the King, who sentenced them both to death. But Culain escaped three days later. He attacked the party taking the Queen to the scaffold and they got away.'

'But that is not the end of the story?'

279

'No. Would that it were.' Prasamaccus lapsed into silence, his head tipping back to rest on the high back of the chair. The goblet slipped from his fingers to the rug and Ursus scooped it up before the wine could stain the goatskin. Then the prince smiled and stood. There was a blanket draped across a stool by the bedroom door. He took it and covered Prasamaccus, then entered his own room.

Adriana smiled and pulled back the blankets. Slipping from his clothes he joined her, stroking the golden hair back from her face.

Her arm circled his neck, drawing him down.

Ursus washed in the barrel of cold water at the back of the lodge, enjoying the crispness of the dawn air on his naked skin. His sleep had been untroubled by dreams and the future was filled with the promise of gold. If the King of Legend adopted his horse-armour, all other fighting monarchs would follow and Ursus would retire to a palace in the Great River Valley with a score of concubines.

At twenty, Ursus had his future clearly mapped out. Although of the House of Merovee, he and Balan were but distant relatives of Meroveus and had no claim to the crown of the Long-Haired Kings. And the life of a soldier offered no delights to a man who had spent his youth in the pleasure palaces of Tingis.

He scrubbed himself dry with a soft woollen towel and donned a fresh black shirt under his oiled jerkin. From a small leather flask he poured a few drops of perfume to his palm, which he spread through his long dark hair. The stink of the stables was galling and he wandered to the open fields, enjoying the scent of the wild roses growing by the ancient circle of standing stones.

Prasamaccus joined him. The older man seemed nervous.

'What is wrong, my friend?' asked Ursus, sitting on the flat-topped altar stone.

'I drank like an old fool and now there is a hammer inside my head.'

'Too much honey,' said Ursus, trying not to smile.

'And too loose a tongue. I should not have spoken so about the King and his business.'

280

'Put your fears at rest, Prasamaccus; I cannot remember any of it. The wine went straight to my head also. As far as I recall, you spoke of Lord Uther as the finest king in Christendom.'

Prasamaccus grinned. 'Which he is. Thank you, Ursus.'

Ursus said nothing. He was staring at the ragged line of armed men cresting the far hills.

'I do hope they are ours,' he whispered.

Prasamaccus shielded his eyes, then swore. Pushing himself to his feet the older man hobbled towards the house, shouting at the top of his voice and pointing to the now charging line. Herdsmen and horse-handlers came running from the stables with bows in hand while the twenty regular legionaries, armed with swords and shields, formed a fighting line in the yard before the house. Ursus sprinted back to his room to gather his own bow and quiver. Adriana was crouching below the main window.

'Who are they?' asked Ursus, as the riders neared.

'Trinovante tribesmen,' she said.

An arrow flashed through the open window, slamming into the door-frame across the room. Ursus stepped back from view, notching an arrow to his bow.

The horsemen thundered into the yard, leaping from their mounts to engage the legionaries. Outnumbered four to one the line gave way, the garishly clad tribesmen hacking and cutting a path towards the house.

Ursus risked a glance through the window as a warrior with a braided beard leapt for the opening. Dragging back on the bowstring he released the shaft to slice into the tribesman's throat and the man fell back.

'I think we should leave,' said Ursus, seizing Adriana by the hand and hauling her to her feet. The door burst inwards and three warriors entered the room, swords red with the blood of the fallen legionaries.

'I hope the thought of ransom has occurred to you,' said Ursus, dropping the bow and spreading his arms wide.

'Kill him!' ordered a tall dark-haired warrior with a fading scar on his cheek.

'I am worth quite a lot . . . in gold!' said the prince, backing away.

The warriors advanced. Ursus stepped forward, twisted on the ball of his foot and leapt, his right heel cracking against a warrior's chin and somersaulting the man into his companion. The prince landed lightly, diving to his right to avoid a slashing cut from Scarface. Then rolling to his feet, he ducked under a second sweep and drove his fingers up under the tribesman's breastbone. The man gasped, his face turning crimson . . . then he fell. Ursus scooped up the fallen man's sword and plunged it through the chest of the first warrior, who had started to rise. Adriana hit the third man with a stool knocking him from his feet.

A trumpet blast echoed outside and the thunder of hooves followed. Ursus ran to the window to see Uther, Victorinus and a full century of mounted legionaries hammering into the bewildered tribesmen. Many of the Trinovantes threw down their weapons, but they were slain out of hand.

Within a few minutes the battle was over, the bodies being dragged from the yard.

The King entered the house, his pale eyes gleaming, all weariness gone from him.

'Where is Prasamaccus?' he asked, stepping over the bodies. The warrior hit by Adriana groaned and tried to stand. Uther spun, his great sword cleaving the man's neck. The head rolled to rest against the wall, the body slumping to pump blood to the floor. Adriana looked away.

'I said, 'Where is Prasamaccus?'

'Here, my lord,' said the cripple, stepping into view from the back room. 'I am unharmed.'

The King relaxed, grinning boyishly. 'I am sorry we were not here sooner.' He moved to the window. 'Victorinus! There are three more in here!'

A group of legionaries entered the lodge, dragging the bodies out into the sunshine.

Uther sheathed his sword and sat. 'You did well, Ursus. You fight as well as you talk.'

'Fortune favoured me, sire, and Adriana downed one with a stool.'

'Hardly surprising; she comes from fine stock.'

Adriana curtseyed and then moved to the cupboard, fetching the King a goblet and filling it with apple juice from a stone jug. Uther drank deeply.

'You will be safe now. Gwalchmai has isolated the main band and by tonight there will be not one rebel Trinovante alive from here to Combretovium.'

'Are your subjects always this unruly?' asked Ursus and a flash of annoyance showed on the King's face.

'We British do not make good subjects,' said Prasamaccus swiftly. 'It is the land, Ursus. All the tribes revere their own kings, their own war leaders and holy men. The Romans destroyed most of the Druids, but now the sect is back and they do not accept Roman authority.'

'But Britannia is no longer ruled by Rome,' said the prince. 'I do not understand.'

'To the tribes, Uther is a Roman. They care nothing that Rome is gone.'

'I am the High King,' said Uther, 'by right and by conquest. The tribes accept that but the Druids do not. Neither do the Saxons, the Jutes, the Angles or the Goths, and only in recent years have the Sicambrians become friends.'

'You suffer no shortage of enemies, Lord Uther. Long may you have strong friends! How will you deal with the problem of the Druids?'

'The way the Romans did, my boy. I crucify them where I find them.'

'Why not gather your own?'

'I would as soon take a viper to my bed.'

'What do they want, after all, but that which all men want – power, riches, soft women? There must be some amongst them who can be bought. It would at least sow dissension amongst your enemies.'

'You've a sharp mind, young Ursus.'

283

'And an enquiring one, sire. How was it you knew the attack would come here?'

'The land knew, and I am the land,' answered Uther, smiling.

Ursus pushed the question no further.

Cormac ran until his legs burned and his lungs heaved, but he knew he could not outrun the horsemen following on the narrow trail, nor outfight those who had cut across the stream to his left and were now moving to outflank him. He struggled to reach the high ground, where at least he felt he would be able to kill one, perhaps two, of the hunters. He prayed one of them might be Agwaine.

He tried to leap a rounded boulder in the trail, but his tired legs struck the stone – spilling him to the grass, his sword spinning from his fingers. He scrambled forward to retrieve it . . . just as a hand circled the hilt.

'An interesting blade,' said a tall, hooded man and Cormac dragged his knife clear and prepared to attack. But the stranger reversed the sword, offering the hilt to the startled boy. 'Come, follow me.'

The hooded man ducked into the undergrowth, pushing aside a thick bush to reveal a shallow cave. Cormac scrambled inside, and the man pulled the bush across the opening. Less than a minute later the Saxon hunters swept past the hiding-place. The stranger threw back his hood and ran his hands through the thick black and silver hair which flowed to his broad shoulders. His grey eyes were deep-set and his beard swept out from his face like a lion's mane. He grinned.

'I'd say you were outnumbered, young man.'

'Why did you help me?'

'Are you not one of God's creatures?'

'You are a holy man?'

'I understand the Mysteries. What are you called?'

'Cormac. And you?'

'I am Revelation. Are you hungry?'

'They will return. I must go.'

'I took you for a bright lad, a boy with wit. If you leave here now, what will happen?'

'I am not a fool, Master Revelation. But what will happen will still happen an hour from now, or a day. I cannot cross the entire South Saxon without being seen. And I do not want you to be slain with me. Thank you for your kindness.'

'As you will, but eat! It is the first rule of the soldier.'

Cormac settled his back against the wall and accepted the bread and cheese he was offered. The food was welcome, as was the cool water from the man's leather-covered canteen.

'How is it that you, a Saxon, have such a sword?'

'It is mine.'

'I am not disputing its ownership. I asked how you came by it.'

'It was my father's.'

'I see. Obviously a fine warrior. The blade is of a steel that comes only from Hispania.'

'He was a great warrior; he killed six men on the day I was born.'

'Six? Truly skilled. And he was a Saxon?'

'I do not know. He died that day and I was raised by . . . by a friend.' Grysstha's face leapt to Cormac's mind and for the first time since his death tears flowed. The boy cleared his throat and turned away. 'I am sorry, I . . . I am sorry.' Choking sobs fought their way past his defences; he felt a strong hand on his shoulder.

'In life, if one is lucky, there are many friends. You are lucky, Cormac. For you have found me.'

'He's dead. They killed him, because he spoke up for me.'

The man's hand moved to Cormac's forehead. 'Sleep now and we will speak later, when the danger is past.'

As Revelation's fingers touched his brow, a great drowsiness flowed over the boy like a warm blanket . . . And he slept without dreams.

He awoke in the night to find himself covered by a thick woollen blanket, his head resting on a folded cloak. Rolling over, he saw Revelation sitting by a small fire, lost in thought.

'Thank you,' said Cormac.

'It was my pleasure. How do you feel?'

'Rested. The hunters?'

285

'They gave up and returned to their homes. I expect they will come back in the morning with hounds. Are you hungry?' Revelation lifted a copper pot from the fire, stirring the contents with a stick. 'I have some broth, fresh rabbit, dried beef and herbs.' He poured a generous portion into a deep wooden bowl and passed it to the boy. Cormac accepted it gratefully.

'Are you on a pilgrimage?' he asked, between mouthfuls.

'Of a kind. I am going home.'

'You are a Briton?'

'No. How is the broth?'

'Delicious.'

'Tell me of Grysstha.'

'How do you know the name?'

The bearded man smiled. 'You mentioned it in your sleep. He was your friend?'

'Yes. He lost his right hand fighting the Blood King. After that he was a goatherd; he raised me and I was like his son.'

'Then you were his son; there is more to being parent than the ties of blood. Why do they hate you?'

'I don't know,' said Cormac, remembering Grysstha's dying words. 'Are you a priest?'

'What makes you think so?'

'I saw a priest of the White Christ once. He wore a habit like yours, and sandals. But he had a cross of wood he wore on his neck.'

'I am not a priest.'

'A warrior, then?' said Cormac doubtfully, for the man carried no weapons save a long staff that now lay beside him.

'Nor a warrior. Simply a man. Where were you heading?'

'Dubris. I could find work there.'

'For what are you trained?'

'I have worked in a smithy, a mill and a pottery. They would not let me work in the bakery.'

'Why?'

'I was not allowed to touch their food, but sometimes the baker would let me clean his rooms. Are you going to Dubris?'

'No. To Noviomagus to the west.'

'Oh.'

'Why not come with me? It is a pleasant walk and the company would be fine.'

'West is where my enemies are.'

'Do not concern yourselves with enemies, Cormac. They shall not harm you.'

'You do not know them.'

'They will not know you. Look!' From his backpack the man pulled a mirror of polished brass. Cormac took it and gasped, for staring back at him was a dark-haired youth, thin-lipped and round of face.

'You are a nigromancer,' he whispered, fear rising.

'No,' said the man softly. 'I am Revelation.'

Despite his shock. Cormac struggled to think through the choices facing him. The stranger had not harmed him, had allowed him to keep his sword and had treated him kindly. But he was a sorcerer and this alone was enough to strike terror into the boy's heart. Suppose he wanted Cormac for some ghastly blood sacrifice, to feed his heart to a demon? Or as a slave?

And yet if Cormac tried to reach Dubris alone, he would be hunted down and slain like a mad dog.

At least if the sorcerer had evil plans for him, they were not plans for today.

'I will travel with you to Noviomagus,' he stated.

'A wise choice, young Cormac,' said Revelation, rising smoothly and gathering his belongings. He scraped the pot and bowl clean with a handful of scrub grass and returned them to his backpack. Then, without a backward glance, he set off in the moonlight towards the west.

Cormac joined him, struggling to match the man's long stride as they walked out of the forested hills and across the dales of the South Saxon. At midnight Revelation stopped in a sheltered hollow and lit a fire, using an ornate tinder-box that fascinated Cormac. Of silver, it was embossed with a fire-breathing dragon. Revelation tossed it to the boy, then added twigs to the tiny blaze, feeding it to greater strength.

'It was made in Tingis, in the north of Africa, by an old Greek named Melchiades. He loves to create works of art around items we use every day. It is an obsession with him, but I love his work.' Cormac opened the box carefully. Inside was a sprung lever in the shape of a dragon's head; in the mouth was a sharp-edged flint. When the lever was depressed the flint ran along a serrated iron grille, causing a shower of sparks.

'It is beautiful.'

'Yes. Now make yourself useful and gather some wood.' Cormac handed back the box and moved among the trees, gathering wind-fall fuel. When he returned Revelation had spread ferns on the ground by the fire for a soft bed. The tall traveller built up the blaze and then lay down under his blanket; he was asleep within seconds. Cormac sat beside him for a while, listening to the sounds of the night.

Then he too slept.

Soon after dawn the travellers set off once more, after a breakfast of fresh bread and cheese. How the bread could be fresh worried Cormac not at all now that he knew his companion was a man of magic. Anyone who could alter another man's face and hair would have no difficulty with creating a tasty loaf!

The riders came into sight just before noon, behind a dog-handler with six leashed wolfhounds. As the dogs spotted the two travellers they bounded forward, baying furiously. Their strength dragged the handler from his feet and he was forced to release the ropes as they sped onwards.

'Stand still,' ordered Revelation. He raised his staff and waited as the hounds closed with ferocious speed, fangs bared for the attack.

'Down!' he bellowed and the hounds ceased their growling and halted before him. 'Down, I said!' Obediently the dogs dropped to their haunches as the five horsemen cantered forward. They were led by Agwaine, his brother Lennox behind him. The other three were carles from Calder's hall, grim-eyed men bearing hand-axes.

The red-faced, mud-spattered dog-handler gathered the trailing leashes and pulled the dogs back into line.

'Good day,' said Revelation, leaning forward on his staff. 'Hunting?'

Agwaine touched his heels to his horse and rode close to Cormac. 'We are seeking a boy around this lad's age, wearing a similar tunic.'

'A red-haired lad?'

'You have seen him?'

'Yes. Is he a runaway?'

'What he is is no business of yours,' snapped Agwaine.

'Come, boy,' Revelation told Cormac and walked on, threading his way through the riders. Cormac followed swiftly.

'Where do you think you're going?' shouted Agwaine as he hauled on the reins, turning his horse and cantering to block Revelation's path.

'You are beginning to irritate me, young puppy. Move aside.'

'Where is the boy?'

Revelation raised his hand suddenly and Agwaine's horse shied, tipping the youth to the grass. Revelation walked on.

'Take him!' yelled Agwaine and the three Saxon carles dismounted and ran forward.

Revelation swung to face them, once more leaning on his staff.

The men approached warily. The staff lanced upwards to connect with the nearest man's groin and with a strangled scream he dropped his axe and fell to his knees. Revelation blocked a wild-axe blow and his staff thundered against a bearded chin, pole-axing a second warrior. The third looked to Agwaine for orders.

'I would think twice before hunting the boy,' said Revelation. 'From what I have seen here, you would have trouble tackling a wounded fawn.'

'Ten gold pieces,' said Agwaine, lifting a leather pouch from his saddlebag and tipping the coins into his hand.

'Ah, now that is a different matter, young sir. The boy told me he was heading for Dubris. I last saw him yesterday, on the high path.'

Agwaine dropped the money back into his pouch and rode away.

'No more than I would expect from a Saxon,' said Revelation, smiling. He gathered up his pack and strolled towards the west with Cormac running alongside him.

'I thought you said you were no warrior?'

'That was yesterday. Who was that young man?'

'Agwaine, son of Calder.'

'I dislike him intensely.'

'So do I. Had it not been for him, Grysstha would still be alive.'

'How so?'

'He has a sister, Alftruda. She put her arms around me, so Agwaine and his brothers attacked me. That's why.'

'A childish squabble? How can that cause a man's death?'

'It is the law. I am not allowed to strike any villager, not even to protect myself.'

'A strange law, Cormac. Does it apply only to you?'

'Yes. How far is Noviomagus?'

'Three days away. Have you ever seen a Roman town?'

'No. Are there palaces?'

'I think for you there will be. And once there, I can purchase some clothes for you and a scabbard for your father's sword.'

Cormac looked up at the grey-haired traveller. 'Why are you being so kind to me?'

Revelation grinned. 'Perhaps it is because I dislike Agwaine. Then again, perhaps I like you. You choose.'

'Will you use me for sorcery? Will you betray me?'

Revelation stopped and laid his hand on Cormac's shoulder.

'In my life there are deeds never to be forgotten or forgiven. I have killed. I have lied. I have cheated. Once I even killed a friend. My word used to be a thing of iron . . . but I have broken even that. So how can I convince you I mean you no harm?'

'Just tell me,' said Cormac simply.

Revelation offered his hand and Cormac took it. 'I shall not betray you, for I am your friend.'

'Then that is good enough,' said the boy. 'When can I look like myself again?'

'As soon as we reach Noviomagus.'

'Is that your home?'

'No, but I am meeting someone there. I think you will like her.'

'A girl!' exclaimed Cormac, crestfallen.

'I am afraid so. But curb your disappointment until you have met her.'

4

Noviomagus was a thriving estuary town, growing rich on trade with the Sicambrians in Gaul, the Berbers of Africa and the merchants of Italia, Graecia, Thrace and Cappadocia. A mixture of older well-constructed Roman dwellings and inferior copies built of sandstone blocks and timber, Noviomagus contained more than six thousand inhabitants.

Cormac had never seen so many people gathered in one place as when he and Revelation threaded their way through cramped, choked streets, past bazaars and markets, shops and trading centres. To the lad the people were as splendid as kings in their cloaks of red, green, blue, orange and yellow. Glorious patterns of checks, stripes, swirls or pictures of hunting scenes were woven into tunics, shirts and capes. Cormac was dazzled by the opulence around him.

A full-breasted woman with dyed red hair approached Revelation. 'Come and relax with Helcia,' she whispered. 'Only ten denarii.'

'Thank you, I have no time.'

'A real man always has time,' she said, her smile fading.

'Then find a real man,' he told her, moving on.

Three more young women propositioned the travellers and one even ran her hand down Cormac's tunic, causing him to leap back, red-faced and ashamed.

'Ignore them, Cormac,' said Revelation, stepping from the street into an alley so narrow that the two of them could not walk side by side.

'Where are we going?' asked the youth.

'We are here,' answered Revelation, pushing open a door and stepping into a long room furnished with a dozen bench-tables and chairs.

The air was close and there were no windows. The two travellers sat down at a corner table, ignoring the other five customers. A thin hatchet-faced man approached, wiping his hands on a greasy rag.

'You want food?'

'Ale,' said Revelation, 'and some fruit for the boy.'

'There are oranges just in, but they are expensive,' said the innkeeper. Revelation opened his hand to show a shining silver half-piece. 'Will that be all? I've got some steak ready.'

'Some for my companion, then.'

'What about a woman? We've three here better than anything you've ever seen; they'll make you feel like a king.'

'Perhaps later. Now bring the ale and the fruit.'

The man returned with a leather-covered tankard and a bowl bearing three fist-sized spheres of yellow gold.

'Rip off the skin and eat the segments inside,' advised Revelation.

Cormac did so and almost choked on the sweet, acid juice. He devoured the fruit and licked his fingers.

'Good?'

'Wonderful. Oranges! When I am a man, I shall plant my own and eat them every day.'

'Then you will have to live in Africa, across the sea, where the sun burns a man's skin blacker than darkness.'

'Would they not grow here?'

'The winter is too cold for them. What do you think of Noviomagus?'

'It's very noisy. I wouldn't like to live here. People keep touching me, and that is rude. And those women – if they are so hungry for love, why don't they marry?'

'A good question, Cormac. Many of them *are* married – and they are not hungry for love, they are hungry for money. In towns like this, money is the only god. Without it you are nothing.'

The steak was thin and tough, but to Cormac it tasted magnificent and he finished it at a speed that surprised the innkeeper.

'Was it all right, sir?'

'Wonderful!' Cormac replied.

'Good,' said the man, studying Cormac's face for any sign of sarcasm. 'Would you like some more fruit?'

'Oranges,' Cormac said, nodding.

A second bowl of fruit followed the first. The inn began to fill with customers and the two travellers sat in silence, listening to the babble of voices around them.

Most conversations concerned the wars and their subsequent – or imagined – effect on trade. Cormac learned that the Northern Trinovantes had rebelled against the High King. In the south-east, a force of Jutes had sailed to Londinium, sacking the town before being crushed by Uther's fleet in the Gallic waters. Three ships had been sunk, two more set ablaze.

'They don't seem to fear an attack here,' said Cormac, leaning forward.

Revelation nodded. 'That is because of the dark side of business, Cormac. Noviomagus, as I said, treats money like a god. Therefore they trade with anyone who will pay. They send iron goods from the Anderida mines, swords, axes, spears, arrow-heads to the Goths, the Jutes and the Angles. The weapons of war are purchased here.'

'And the King allows this?'

'There is little he can do to stop it and they also supply him with weapons and armour. The finest leather breastplates are made in Noviomagus, as well as swords of quality and bronze shields.'

'It is not right to trade with your enemies.'

'Life is very simple when one is young.'

'How does the King survive, if even his own people support his enemies?'

'He survives because he is great. But think on this: these merchants supply the Jutes and earn great wealth. The King taxes them, which brings gold to his treasury. With this gold, he buys weapons to fight the Jutes. So, without the Jutes Uther would have less gold with which to oppose them.'

'But if the Jutes – and the others – didn't attack him, he would not need so much gold,' Cormac pointed out.

'Good! There is the seed of a debater within you. But if there were no enemies he would not need an army, and without an army we would not need a king. So, without the Jutes Uther would have no crown.'

293

'You are making my head spin. Can we go now? The air in here is beginning to smell.'

'A little while longer. We are meeting someone. You go outside – but do not wander far.'

Cormac eased his way out into the alley to see a young girl struggling with a burly warrior wearing a horned helm. On the ground beside them lay an elderly man with blood seeping from a wound to his head. The warrior pulled the struggling girl from her feet, his right hand clamped across her mouth.

'Stop!' shouted Cormac, dragging his sword from his belt. The warrior cursed, flinging the girl to the ground. Cormac rushed forward and, to his surprise and relief, the attacker turned and fled. The lad approached the girl, helping her to her feet. She was slim and dark-haired, her face oval, her skin ivory pale. Cormac swallowed hard and knelt beside the old man; he was clean-shaven and wearing a long blue toga. The boy lifted his wrist, feeling for a pulse.

'I am sorry, my lady, but he is dead.'

'Poor Cotta,' she whispered.

'Why were you attacked?'

'Is there an inn near here called The Sign of the Bull?' she asked, turning her head towards him. He looked then into her pale grey eyes and saw that she was blind.

'Yes, I will take you there,' he said, reaching out his hand. She did not move, so he took her arm.

'We cannot leave him like this,' she said. 'It is not right.'

'I have a friend nearby. He will know what to do.'

He led her into the inn, steering her carefully around the tables. The sudden noise of the interior alarmed her and she gripped his arm, but he patted her hand and led her to Revelation who stood swiftly.

'Anduine, where is Cotta?'

'Someone killed him, my lord.'

Revelation cursed, flicked the silver coin to the waiting innkeeper and then took the girl by the hand and led her outside. Cormac followed, a curious feeling of emptiness within him now that his charge was no longer in his care.

294

Outside, Revelation was kneeling by the old man. He closed the dead eyes and then stood. 'We must leave him here. Swiftly.'

'But Cotta . . .'

'If he could speak, he would insist on it. What did you see, Cormac?'

'A foreign man with a horned helm was pulling her away. I ran at him, and he fled.'

'Bravely done, lad,' said Revelation. 'Thank the Source you had a need for fresh air.' Dipping into the pocket of his coarse woollen habit Revelation produced a small golden Stone which he held over the girl. Her dark hair lightened to corn yellow and her simple dress of pale green wool became tunic and trews of rust-brown and beige.

Three men entered the alley. Two wore bronze helms, decorated with ravens' wings; the third was clothed all in black and carried no weapons.

'She's gone,' said one of the men, running past Cormac. The other two entered the inn. Revelation led Anduine back along the alley as the two Vikings emerged from the building.

'You there! Wait!' came the shout.

Revelation turned. 'Put your arms about her and treat her like your lover,' he whispered to Cormac. Then, 'Can I assist you brothers? I have no money.'

'The boy was seen with a girl in a green dress. Where is she?'

'The blind wench? A man came for her. He seemed greatly agitated; I think that is his friend lying dead back there.'

Behind them Cormac leaned in to Anduine, resting his arms on her shoulders. He did not know what to do, but had seen the village boys with the maidens. Softly he kissed her cheek, shielding her face from the three armed men.

'We are dead men!' hissed one of the warriors.

'Be silent, Atha! Girl, come here,' ordered the leader.

Just then a group of militia-men rounded the alley, led by a middle-aged officer.

'What's going on here?' he asked, sending two of his men to check the body.

'The old man was robbed,' said Revelation. 'A terrible thing in such a civilised town.'

'Did you see the attack?'

'No,' said Revelation, 'I was at the inn having a meal with my son and his wife. Perhaps these fine fellows can help you?'

'Are you carrying money?' the officer asked.

'No,' said Revelation with a sad smile, opening his arms for the search, which was swift and thorough.

'Do you have friends in Noviomagus?'

'I fear not.'

'Work?'

'Not at present, but I am hopeful.'

'Melvar!' called the officer and a young soldier ran up. 'Escort these . . . travellers from the town. I am sorry, but no one may stay who does not have means of support.'

'I understand,' said Revelation, taking Anduine by the arm and leading her from the alley. She stumbled and almost fell and the black-clad Viking leader cursed loudly. 'Blind! It's her!' He tried to follow, but the officer barred his way.

'Just a moment, sir. There are a few questions.'

'We are merchants from Raetia – I have documents.'

'Then let me see them, sir.'

Beyond the alley, the soldier Melvar led the trio to the western edge of Noviomagus. 'You might be able to get work on some of the farms north of here,' he said. 'Otherwise I'd suggest Venta.'

'Thank you,' said Revelation. 'You have been most kind.'

'What is happening?' asked Cormac when the officer had gone. 'Who were those warriors?'

'Wotan's Hunters – and they are seeking Anduine.'

'Why?'

'She is his Bride and he wants her.'

'But he is a god . . . isn't he?'

'He is a devil, Cormac – and he must not have her. Now let us begone, for the hunt has just begun.'

'Can you not work more magic?'

Revelation smiled. 'Yes, but now is not the time. There is a Circle of standing stones near here. We must reach them by nightfall and then . . . then you will need more courage than most men possess.'

'Why?' asked Cormac.

'The demons are gathering,' said Revelation.

The stones formed a Circle some sixty feet across, around the flat-topped crest of a hill eight miles from Noviomagus. Cormac led the weary Anduine to the centre of the hill, where he spread his blanket and sat beside her. The blind girl had borne the journey well, holding close to Cormac who steered her carefully away from jutting tree-roots and rocks.

Revelation had moved ever further ahead and when the tired youngsters reached the hill he was kneeling by an old alter stone, carefully notching his staff. Cormac approached him, but he waved the boy away, then began to measure the distance from the altar to the first standing stone – a massive grey-black monolith twice as tall as himself. Cormac returned to Anduine, gave her some water and wandered to the other side of the Circle. The huge stones were more jagged here and one of them had fallen, the base cracked like a rotten tooth. Cormac knelt beside it. Carved into the stone was a heart bearing letters in Latin. The boy could not read Latin, but he had seen such inscriptions before. Two lovers had sat here, looking to the future with hope and joy. There were other carvings, some recent, and Cormac wished he could read them.

'Where is Revelation?' asked Anduine. Cormac rose and, taking her hand, led her to the fallen stone where they sat in the fading sunshine.

'He is close, marking the ground with chalk and measuring the distance between the stones.'

'He is creating a spirit fortress,' said Anduine, 'sealing the Circle.'

'Will it keep the demons out?'

'It depends how much magic he holds. When he came to see me in Austrasie his Power-Stone was almost finished.'

'Power-Stone?'

'They are called Sipstrassi. All the Lords carry them; my grand-father had three.'

Cormac said nothing but watched as Revelation continued his esoteric work with the chalk, joining an apparently random series of lines, half-circles and six-sided stars.

'Why are they hunting you?' he asked Anduine. 'There must be other brides less troublesome?'

She smiled and took his hand. 'You were born in a cave and your life has been very sad. Your great friend was slain and your sorrow is as deep as the sea. You are strong, both in the body and the soul, and there is a small wound – like a gash – on your right arm, where you fell while being chased by the hunters.' Reaching out, she took his right hand, her fingers sliding softly along the skin of his arm until she reached the graze. 'And now,' she said, 'it is gone.'

He glanced down. All signs of the tear in the skin had vanished.

'You too are a sorceress?'

'And that is why they want me. They killed my father, but Cotta and the Lord Revelation rescued me. They thought I would be safe in Britannia, but there is no safe place. The Gates are open.'

Revelation joined them, his face streaked with sweat and dust, his grey eyes showing his fatigue. 'The power of the Stone is used up,' he said. 'Now we wait.'

'Why has Wotan left the Halls of Asgard?' asked Cormac. 'Is it Ragnorak? Has the end of the world come?'

Revelation chuckled. 'Three fine questions, Cormac! The most important, though, is the last. If we are all alive in the morning, I will answer it for you. But for now let us prepare. Take Anduine to the altar stone and lift her over the chalk-marks. None of them must be disturbed.'

The youth did as he was bid, then he drew his sword and plunged it in the ground beside him. The sun was dipping over the sea in red fire and the sky was streaked with glowing clouds.

'Come here,' said Revelation and Cormac squatted down beside him.

'Tonight you will be tested. I want you to understand that it will begin with deceit and they will want you to leave the Circle. But you must be strong — no matter what happens. Do you understand?'

'Stay within the Circle. Yes I understand.'

'If they break through, one of us must kill Anduine.'

'No!'

'*Yes*. They must not have her power. There is so much I wish I could explain, Cormac. You asked about Ragnorak. It will come soon if they take her — later, if they do not. But, believe me, it will be the better for her to die at our hands than theirs.'

'How can we fight demons?'

'You cannot. I can. But, if they fail, they will be followed by men. I wish I knew how many. Then you will fight. I hope Grysstha taught you well.'

'He did,' said Cormac. 'But I am frightened now.'

'As am I; there is no shame in that. Fetch your sword.'

Cormac turned and rose to see the maid Anduine kneeling by the blade, her hands slowly running down the length of the steel.

'What are you doing?' he asked.

'Nothing that will harm you, Cormac,' she replied, pulling the sword clear of the earth and offering it to him, hilt first.

The sun sank, the last glimmerings of light fading in the western sky. A cool wind rose, hissing through the long grass. Cormac shivered and took his sword to the waiting Revelation.

'Sit down and gaze upon the blade,' said Revelation. 'It is a part of you now. Your harmony, your spirit, your life flows through it. These three mysteries a warrior must understand: Life, Harmony and Spirit. The first is Life, sometimes called the Greek gift, for it is taken back day after day. What is it? It is breath, it is laughter, it is joy. It is a candle whose flame falls towards a tomb. The brighter the light, the shorter its existence. But one thing is certain — and this the warrior knows. All lives end. A man can hide in a cave all his days, avoiding war, avoiding pestilence, and still he will one day die. Better the bright flame, the great joy. A man who has never known sorrow can never appreciate joy. So the man who has not faced death can never understand life.

299

'Harmony, Cormac, is the second mystery. The tree knows harmony, and the breeze and the quiet stars. Man rarely finds it. Find it now, here on this lonely hill. Listen to the beating of your heart, feel the air in your lungs, see the glory of the moon. Be at one with the night. Be at one with these stones. Be at one with your sword and yourself. For in harmony is strength, and in strength there is life.

'Lastly there is Spirit. Tonight you will want to run . . . to hide . . . to escape. But spirit will tell you to stand firm. It is a small voice and easy to shut out. But you will listen. For spirit is all a man has against the Darkness. And only by following the voice of spirit can a man grow strong. Courage, loyalty, friendship and love are all gifts of spirit.

'I know you cannot understand now all that I am saying, but soak the words into your soul. For tonight you will see evil and know despair.'

'I will not run. I will not hide,' said the boy.

Revelation placed his hand on Cormac's shoulder. 'I know that.'

A swirling mist rose up around them like the smoke of a great fire, rolling tendrils questing across the Circle and recoiling as it touched the chalk-lines. Higher and higher it rose, closing over their heads in a grey dome. Cormac's mouth was dry, but sweat dripped into his eyes. He wiped it clear and stood with his sword at the ready.

'Be calm,' said Revelation softly.

A sibilant whispering began within the mist and Cormac heard his name being called over and over. Then the grey wall parted and he saw Grysstha kneeling at the edge of the Circle, the two arrows still jutting from his chest.

'Help me, boy,' groaned the old man.

'Grysstha!' yelled Cormac, moving towards him, but Revelation's hand gripped his arm.

'It is a lie, Cormac. That is not your friend.'

'It is! I know him.'

'Then how is he here – forty miles from where his body lay? No, it is a deceit.'

300

'Help me, Cormac. Why won't you help me? I spent my years helping you.'

'Be strong, boy,' whispered Revelation, 'and think on this: If he loved you, why would he call you to be slain by demons? It is *not* him.'

Cormac swallowed hard, tearing his eyes from the kneeling man. Then the figure rose, the flesh stripping away like the skin of a snake. It swelled and curved, dark horns sprouting from its brow, long gleaming fangs rimming its mouth.

'I see you!' it hissed, pointing a taloned finger at Revelation. 'I know you!' A black sword appeared in its hand and it rushed at the slender chalk-line. White fire blossomed, scorching its skin. It fell back, screaming, then attacked once more. Other bestial figures now appeared behind it, screeching and calling. Cormac hefted his sword, the blade gleaming white as captured moonlight. The mass beyond the Circle charged and a thunderous explosion roared from the ground. Many of the demonic beasts fell back, writhing and covered in flames, but three entered the Circle. Revelation raised his staff over his head and was instantly clothed in black and silver armour, the staff now a silver lance that split into two swords of dazzling brightness. He leapt to meet the attackers and with a wild scream Cormac rushed to aid him.

A demon with the face of a lion lunged at him with a dark sword. Cormac blocked the blow, rolled his wrists and sent his own blade hissing into the creature's neck. Green gore fountained into the air and the beast fell dying.

'The girl! Guard the girl!' screamed Revelation. Cormac swung his eyes from Revelation's battle with the two demons to see Anduine being dragged from the altar by two men. Without pause for thought, he leapt forward. The first of the men ran at him, and the boy saw his attacker's eyes were red as blood. As the man's mouth opened to reveal long curved fangs, fear struck Cormac like a physical blow and his pace faltered. But just as the creature bore down on him with terrifying speed, the boy's courage flared. The sword flashed up to block a blow from a slender dagger and then down, cleaving the demon's collarbone and exiting through the belly. With a hideous scream the beast died. Cormac hurdled the body and the creature holding Anduine threw her to one side and drew a grey sword.

'Your blood is mine,' it hissed, baring its fangs. Their swords met in flashing arcs and Cormac was forced back across the Circle in a desperate effort to ward off the demonic attack. Within seconds he knew he was hopelessly outclassed. Three times his enemy's sword was blocked within inches of his throat, and every counter of his own was turned aside with contemptuous ease. Suddenly he tripped over a jutting rock, tumbling to his back, the demon leapt for him, the sword slashing down . . . only to be blocked by the blade of Revelation. The silver-armoured warrior brushed aside a second blow, spun on his heel and beheaded his opponent.

As suddenly as it had come the mist disappeared, the stars and moon shining with pure light upon the stones.

'Are we safe?' whispered Cormac as Revelation pulled him to his feet. Beyond the Circle stood seven Viking warriors.

'Not yet,' said Revelation.

The black-clad man they had seen in Noviomagus stepped forward. 'Release the girl and you will live.'

'Come and take her,' offered Revelation and the warriors advanced in a grim line, some holding swords and other axes. Cormac stood rooted to the spot, waiting for Revelation to signal a move. When it came, it surprised the Vikings as much as it astonished Cormac.

Revelation charged.

His swords slashed down at the first men in the line and two were dead in that instant. In the chaotic mêlée that followed, Cormac screamed a wild battlecry and launched himself at the Vikings to Revelation's right, his sword hammering into a man's arm half-severing it. The attacker yelled in pain and leapt to his left, blocking his comrades' attack on Cormac. The boy lunged his sword into the man's suddenly unprotected belly, then shoulder-charged his way through them.

A sword sliced into his shoulder, but diving to the ground he rolled under a swinging axe, crashing into the axeman's legs.

The Viking tumbled to the ground and Cormack swung his sword viciously into his neck. Bright blood spurted over the blade. Rising to his feet, he saw that Revelation had killed the last of the warriors and the black-clad leader was sprinting away across the Circle. Revelation swept up a fallen axe and hurled it with terrifying force to take the leader in the back of the neck, almost severing the head. Cormac glanced around the Circle, but no fresh enemies could be seen. Then he looked towards Revelation and froze, his sword dropping from his fingers.

Gone was the beard and the lion's mane of silver hair. Instead, standing before him was the dark-haired warrior of his dream, the man who had leapt from the cliff on the day Cormac was born.

'What is the matter, boy? Is my real face so terrible?'

'It is to me,' said Cormac. Tell me your name – your true name.'

'I am Culain lach Feragh, once called the Lance Lord.'

'The Great Betrayer.'

Culain's grey eyes locked to Cormac's. 'I have been called that – and not without justification. But what is it to you?'

'I am the babe you left in the cave, the son you left to rot.'

Culain's eyes closed and he turned away momentarily. Then taking a deep breath, he turned to Cormac.

'Can you prove this?'

'I don't have to. I know who I am. Grysstha found me the day you . . . I was going to say died . . . but that is obviously not true. You helped my mother to the Cave of Sol Invictus. You told her you were sorry you had led her to this. Then you killed those men and went to the cliff-top. There you threw the sword into a tree, while the horseman and the cripple watched.'

'Even if you were the babe, you were too young to see all that,' said Culain.

Cormac lifted the Stone from around his neck and tossed it to the warrior. 'I didn't know any of it until the day I ran away, when I slept in the cave and saw a vision. But I was found in that cave, beside the warhound and her pups, and for all my life men have called me "daemon's son". Had it not been for Grysstha, I would have been slain then.'

'We thought you dead,' whispered Culain.

'For years I dreamt you would come for me . . . it gave me hope and strength. But you never did. Why did you not come back – even to bury your son?'

'You are not my son, Cormac. Would that you were!'

'But you were with her!'

'I loved her, but I am not your father. That honour goes to her husband, Uther, High King of Britain.'

Cormac stared at the strong, square face of the warrior who had been Revelation and searched in his own heart for hatred. There was nothing. In that moment of recognition something had died within the boy and its passing had been masked by his instant anger. Now that anger was gone, and Cormac was more truly alone than he had ever been.

'I am sorry, boy,' said Culain. 'Pick up your sword. We must go.'

'Go?' whispered Cormac. 'I'll not go with you.' He retrieved his blade, turned his back on Culain and Anduine and began to walk towards the south and Noviomagus. But just before he reached the edge of the Circle a blinding flash of light reared up before him and his vision swam. As swiftly as it had come, the brightness was gone and Cormac blinked.

Ahead of him was not the scene of recent memory, the sea glistening darkly beyond the white walls of Noviomagus. Instead mountains reared against the horizon, snow-capped and majestic, cloaked in forests of pine and rowan.

'We need to speak,' said Culain. 'And you are safer here.'

Suddenly Cormac's anger flared once more, this time as a berserk fury. Without a word he leapt at Culain, sword flashing for the man's head. Culain blocked the blow with dazzling speed, but was forced back by the ferocious, double-handed assault. Time and again Cormac came within scant inches of delivering the death-blow, but each attack was countered with astonishing skill. In the background, unable to see what was happening, Anduine stumbled forward with arms outstretched, calling their names. In his rage, Cormac did not notice the blind girl and his sword slashed in a wide arc, missing Culain and slicing towards the girl. Culain leapt feet-first at the boy, catapulting him from his feet, the swinging sword catching Anduine high in the shoulder. Blood spurted from the scored flesh and Anduine screamed but Culain ran to her, holding Cormac's Stone against the wound which sealed instantly.

From the ground Cormac viewed the scene with horror and deep shame. He sat up and, leaving his sword where it lay, approached the others.

'I am sorry, Anduine. I did not see you.'

She reached out and he took her hand. Her smile was as welcome as the sunshine after the storm.

'Are we all friends again?' she asked. Cormac could not reply and from Culain there was a grim silence. 'How sad,' said Anduine, her smile fading.

'I will find some wood for a fire,' said Culain. 'We will camp here tonight, and tomorrow we will journey into the mountains. I used to have a home here; it will afford us safety for a while at least.'

He stood and wandered from the Circle. Under the bright moonlight Cormac sat with Anduine, unable to find the words to approach her. But he held to her hand, as if it were a talisman.

She shivered. 'You are cold?'

'A little.'

Reluctantly he released her hand and fetched the blanket, which he wrapped around her slender frame. During the battle with the Vikings the spell of changing had vanished, and now she was as Cormac had first seen her – dark-haired and possessed of a fragile beauty. She held the blanket to her with both hands and Cormac felt the absence of her touch.

'Has your anger gone?' she asked.

'No, it is waiting deep inside me. I feel it like the winter chill. I wish I did not.'

'Revelation is not your enemy.'

'I know. But he betrayed me, he left me.'

'He thought you dead.'

'But I wasn't! All the years of my life have been filled with pain. Had it not been for Grysstha, I would have died. And no one would have cared. I never knew my mother; I never felt her touch, nor her love. And why? Because Culain stole her from her husband. From my father! It was wrong!'

'The story of the Betrayal is well known,' she whispered. 'Perhaps too well known. But there is nothing base about Revelation. I know. I think you should wait until you can speak with him. Hold your anger.'

'He was the King's closest friend,' said Cormac. 'The Queen's Champion. What can he say to lessen his shame? If he needed to rut like a bull, why did he not choose one of a thousand other women? Why my mother?'

'I cannot answer these questions. But he can.'

'That, at least, is true enough,' said Culain, dropping the bundle of dry wood to the grass. Once more he wore the brown woollen habit and carried the wooden staff of Revelation, though this time there was no beard, no lion's mane of grey hair.

'What happened to my mother?' asked Cormac, once the fire was lit.

'She died in Sicambria two years ago.'

'Were you with her?'

'No, I was in Tingis.'

'If you were so in love, why did you leave her?'

Revelation did not reply but lay back, his eyes fixed to the stars.

'This is not the time,' said Anduine softly, laying her hand on Cormac's arm.

'There will never be a time,' hissed the boy, 'for there are no answers. Only excuses! I do not know if Uther loved her, but she was his wife. The Betrayer knew that and he should never have touched her.'

'Cormac! Cormac!' said Anduine. 'You speak as if she was an object like a cloak. She was not – she was a woman and a strong one. She travelled with the Blood King across the Mist and fought the Witch Queen alongside him. Once, when he was a hunted child, she saved him by killing an assassin. Did she not have a choice?'

Revelation sat up and added wood to the fire. 'Do not seek to defend me, Anduine, for the boy is right. There are no answers,

306

only excuses. That is all there is to be said. I wish it were different. Here, Cormac, this is yours.' He tossed the Stone and the chain across the fire. 'I gave it to your mother a year before you were born; it was what saved you in the cave. It is Sipstrassi, the Stone from Heaven.'

'I do not want it,' said Cormac, letting it fall to the ground. He watched with satisfaction as the anger flared in Revelation's eyes, and saw the iron control with which the warrior quelled it.

'Your anger I can understand, Cormac, but your stupidity galls me,' said Revelation, lying down and turning his back to the fire.

5

The following morning the trio made their way deep into the Caledones mountains, far to the north of the Wall of Hadrian, arriving at a ruined cabin just after noon. The roof had given way and a family of pack-rats nested by the stone hearth. Revelation and Cormac spent several hours repairing the building and cleaning the dust of many years from the floors of the three-roomed dwelling.

'Could you not use magic?' asked Cormac, wiping sweat and dirt from his face as Revelation packed the roof with turves.

'Some things are better done with hands and heart,' Revelation answered.

These were the first words spoken by the two men since the clash in the Circle and once more an uncomfortable silence settled. Anduine was sitting beside the nearby stream, scrubbing at rusted pots and carefully removing various fungi from the wooden platters Cormac had found in a rotting cupboard. Late in the afternoon Revelation set traps in the hills above the cabin and, after a cool uncomfortable night on the floor of the main room, they breakfasted on roast rabbit and wild onions.

'To the north of here is a second cabin,' said Revelation, 'and close by you will find apple and pear trees. The game is also plentiful higher in the mountains – deer and mountain sheep, rabbits and pigeon. Can you use a bow?'

'I can learn,' said Cormac, 'but I am expert with the sling.'

Revelation nodded. 'It is wise also to learn what plants give nourishment. The leaves of marigold contain goodness, as do nettles, and you will find onions and turnips in profusion in the western valley.'

'You sound as if you are going away,' said Anduine.

'I must. I need to find a new Stone, for I have little magic left.'

308

'How long will you be away?' she asked and Cormac hated the edge of fear in her voice.

'Less than a week, if all goes well. But I will remain here for a while. There is much to be done.'

'We do not need you,' said Cormac. 'Go when you please.'

Revelation ignored him but later, as Anduine stripped and dressed the rest of the meat, took him out into the open ground before the cabin.

'She is in great danger, Cormac, and if you are to protect her you must make yourself stronger, faster, more deadly than you are now. As matters stand, an old milkmaid could take her from you.' Cormac sneered and was about to reply when Revelation's fist hammered into his chin. The youth hit the ground hard, his head spinning.

'The Romans call it boxing,' said Revelation, 'but it was refined by a Greek called Carpophorus. Stand up.' Cormac pushed himself to his feet, then dived at the taller man. Revelation swayed back, lifting his knee into Cormac's face, and the ground came up at him once more. Blood oozed from his nose and he had difficulty in keeping Revelation in focus. Still he rose and charged, but this time a fist crashed into his belly and he doubled over, all air smashed from his lungs, and lay on the ground battling for breath. After several minutes he struggled to his knees. Revelation was sitting on a fallen log.

'Here, in these high lonely mountains, I trained your father – and your mother. Here the Witch Queen sent her killers, and from here Uther set out to recapture his father's kingdom. He did not whine or complain; he did not sneer when he should have been learning. He merely set his sights on a goal and achieved it. You have two choices, child: leave or learn. Which do you make?'

'I hate you,' whispered Cormac.

'That is immaterial. Choose!'

Cormac looked up into the cold grey eyes and bit back the angry words crowding for release. 'I will learn.'

'Your first lesson is obedience – and it is vital. In order to be stronger, you must push yourself to the edge of your endurance. I shall ask you to do more than is necessary, though at times you will

309

feel I am being needlessly cruel. But you must obey. Do you understand, child?'

'I am not a child,' snapped Cormac.

'Understand this, *child*. I was born when the sun shone on Atlantis. I fought with the Israelites in the land of Canaan, I was a god to the Greeks, and a King among the tribes of Britannia. My days are numbered in tens of thousands. And what are you? You are the leaf that spans a season, and I am the oak that weathers the centuries. You are a child. Uther is a child. The oldest man in the world is a child to me. Now, if you must hate me – and I fear you must – at least hate me like a man and not like some petulant babe. I am stronger than you, more skilled than you. I can destroy you, with or without weapons. So learn – and one day you may beat me . . . though I doubt it.'

'One day I will kill you,' said Cormac.

'Then prepare yourself.' Revelation thrust a long stick into the ground, then a second a foot to the left. 'You see that stand of pine on the mountain?'

'Yes.'

'Run to it and return here before the shadow touches the second stick.'

'Why?'

'Do it or leave this mountain,' said Revelation, standing and wandering away towards the cabin.

Cormac took a deep breath, wiped the clotting blood from his nose and set off at an easy lope, the clean mountain air filling his lungs, his legs driving him easily up the mountain trail. Once in among the trees he could not see the stand of pine and he increased his pace. His calves began to burn, but he pushed himself on. As the gradient grew ever more steep, so his breathing grew faster. He emerged from the trees still a half-mile short of the target and staggered to a walk, sucking in great gulps of air. He was tempted to sit and recover his strength, or even to return to Revelation and tell him that he had reached the pine. But he did not. He struggled on and up. Sweat drenched his face and tunic and his legs felt as if candle-flames had been lit inside them when at last he staggered into the grove. Hanging from a branch was a clay jug of water. He drank deeply and set off back for the cabin. On the downhill run his tired legs betrayed him and missing his footing he stumbled, fell and rolled down the slope, coming up hard against a tree-root which gouged his side. Up once more, he continued his halting run until he came into the clearing before the cabin.

'Not good,' said Revelation, staring coolly at the red-faced youth. 'It is only two miles, Cormac. You will do it again this evening, and tomorrow. Look at your mark.'

The shadow was three fingers' breadth past the stick.

'Your arms and shoulders are strong, but it is strength without speed. How did you build them?'

Cormac, at last able to excel, moved to a tree and leapt to grab an overhanging branch. Swiftly he raised himself to touch his chin to the branch, over and over again with smooth, rhythmic movements.

'Keep going,' said Revelation.

At the count of one hundred Cormac dropped to the ground, the muscles of his arms burning, his eyes gleaming with triumph.

'That builds strength, but not speed,' said Revelation. 'It is worthwhile, but it must be complemented with other work. You are powerful for your age, but you are not supple. A swordsman must be lightning-swift.' He took a long whittled stick and held it horizontally between his fingers. 'Place your hand over the top of the stick, fingers straight, and when I release it – catch it.'

'Simple,' said Cormac, holding his hand over the wood and tensing for the strike. Revelation released the stick and Cormac's hand swept down, clutching at air.

'Simple?' echoed Revelation. Three times more Cormac attempted to catch the stick, and once almost made it, his fingers striking the wood and accelerating its fall.

'You are too stiff in the hips, and the muscles of your shoulders are tense and therefore immobile.'

'It is not possible,' said Cormac.

'Then you hold the stick.' The boy did so, and as his fingers parted Revelation's hand dropped like a striking snake when the stick had fallen less than a foot. 'Speed, Cormac. Action without thought. Do not concern yourself about catching the stick, merely do it. Empty your mind, loosen your limbs.'

After some thirty attempts, Cormac succeeded. Then followed another ten failures. It was galling for the boy, but his will to succeed carried him on. Before the morning was spent he had caught the wood seven times with his right hand, three times with his left.

Revelation lifted his hand to his face and his image shifted and blurred, becoming once more Culain of the Silver Lance.

For an hour more Culain and the tiring youth practised with swords. Cormac almost forgot his hatred of the tall warrior as he marvelled at the man's natural grace and superb reflexes. Time and again he would roll his wrists, his blade skimming over Cormac's to hiss to a halt touching the skin of the boy's neck, or arm, or chest.

Culain lach Feragh was more than a warrior, Cormac realised, he was a prince among warriors.

But as soon as the session was over Cormac's hostility returned. Culain read it in his eyes and sheathed his sword, creating once more the silver lance.

'Take Anduine up into the hills,' he said. 'Help her to identify the paths.' Turning on his heel the warrior strode into the cabin, bringing the girl out into the sunlight.

Cormac took her arm and led her into the trees.

'Where is the sun?' she asked. 'I cannot feel her heat.'

'Above the woods, shielded by the leaves.'

'Tell me about the leaves.' Bending, he lifted a fallen leaf from the ground and pressed it into her hand. Her fingers fluttered over the surface. 'Oak?'

'Yes. A huge, hoary oak, as old as time.'

'Is it a handsome tree?'

'Like a strong old man, grim and unyielding.'

'And the sky?'

'Blue and clear.'

'Describe blue – as you see it,' she said.

He stopped and thought for a moment. 'Have you ever felt silk?'

'Yes. I had a dress of silk for my last birthday.'

312

'Grysstha once had a small piece of silk and it was wondrous soft and smooth. Blue is like that. Just to look upon it fills the heart with joy.'

'A sky of silk,' she whispered. 'How pretty it must be! And the clouds. How do you see the clouds?'

'There are few clouds today, and they float like white honeycakes, far away and yet so clear you feel you could reach out and touch them.'

'A silk and honeycake sky,' she said. 'Oh, Cormac, it is so beautiful. I cannot see it, but I can feel it, deep in my heart.'

'I would cut off my arm to let you see it,' he said.

'Don't say that,' she said. 'Don't ever think that I am unhappy because I cannot share your visions. Take me further up the mountain. Show me flowers that I can touch and smell . . . and describe them to me in silks and honeycakes.'

Each morning, when his arduous training was completed, Cormac would take Anduine walking through the woods – into hidden glens and hollows and often to a small lake, cool and clear beneath the towering mountains. He would marvel at her memory, for once having walked a path and found landmarks she could touch – a rounded boulder with a cleft at the centre, a tree with a huge knot on the bark, a V-shaped root – she would walk it unerringly from then on. Sometimes she could judge the trails by the gradients or, knowing the hour, by the position of the sun as it warmed her face. Once she even challenged Cormac to a race and all but beat him to the cabin, tripping at the last over a jutting root.

The youth came to love these walks, and their conversations. He joyed in describing the flying geese, the hunting fox, the proud longhorn cattle, the regal stags. She in turn enjoyed his company, the warmth of his voice and the touch of his hand.

Only on the days when he had failed in tasks set him by Revelation did she find his presence unsettling, feeling his anger and his hatred charging the air around her with a tension she had no desire to share.

313

'He does it only so that you will improve,' she said one damp morning, as they sat beneath an oak waiting for a shower to pass.

'He wants to see me fail.'

'Not so, Cormac – and you know it. He trained your father here and I would imagine he felt as you do.'

Cormac was silent for a time and she felt the emotions soften. His fingers slid across her hand, squeezing it gently. She smiled. 'Are you feeling yourself again?'

'Yes. But I do not understand the man. In the Circle he told me to kill you should the demons break through. They did so – but he did not try to kill you. Then he brought us here in a flash of light. Why did he not do it at the start? Then we would not have had to fight the demons at all.'

'For me that is what makes him great,' said Anduine, leaning in to Cormac and resting her head on his shoulder. 'He was right. It would be better for me to die than to aid Wotan with my soul. But that is the *strategist* speaking. When it came to the battle, it was the *man* who fought it – and he would give the last drop of his blood before taking mine. As to coming here, he could not while the demons lived. All the enemies had to be slain, so that none could mark our passing. Had we run here at the start, then they would have followed. As it is, Cormac, one day they will find us.'

He put his arm around her, drawing her to him. 'I too would die, before allowing them to harm you.'

'Why?' she whispered.

He cleared his throat and stood. 'The rain is stopping. Let us find the orchard.'

They discovered the lake on Midsummer Day, disturbing a family of swans, and Cormac splashed into the water, hurling his tunic and leggings to a rock by the waterside. He swam for some minutes, while Anduine sat patiently beneath a towering growth of honeysuckle. Then he waded ashore and sat beside her, revelling in the warmth of the sun on his naked body.

'Do you swim?' he asked.

'No.'

'Would you like to learn?'

314

She nodded and stood, untying the neck of her pale green dress and slipping it over her shoulders. As it fell to the floor Cormac swallowed hard and looked away. Her body was ivory-pale, her breasts full, her waist tiny, her hips . . .

'Follow me into the lake,' he said, clearing his throat and turning from her. She laughed as she felt the cool water on her feet and ankles, then waded further.

'Where are you?' she called.

'I am here,' he answered, taking her hand. Turn to face the shore and lean back into my arms.'

'The water will go over my head.'

'I will support you. Trust me.'

She fell back into his arms, kicking out her legs and floating on the surface of the lake. 'Oh, it is beautiful,' she said. 'What must I do?'

Remembering the teachings of Grysstha in the river of the South Saxon, he said, 'Your lungs will keep you afloat, as long as their is air in them. Breathe in deeply, spread your arms and kick out with your feet.' His arms slid under her body, and he found himself gazing down at her breasts, her white belly and the triangle of dark hair pointing like an arrow to her thighs. Swinging his head, he fixed his gaze on her face. 'Take a deep breath and hold it,' he said. Gently he lowered his hands. For several seconds she floated and then, as if realising she was unsupported, she dropped her hips and her head dipped below the sparkling water. Swiftly he raised her as she flung her arms around his neck, coughing and spluttering.

'Are you all right?'

'You let me go,' she accused him.

'I was here. You were safe.' Leaning down he kissed her brow, pushing back the dark, wet hair from her face. She laughed and returned the kiss, biting his lip.

'Why?' she asked him, her voice husky.

'Why what?'

'Why would you die for me?'

'Because you are in my care. Because . . . you are my friend.'

315

'Your friend?'

He was silent for a moment, savouring the touch of her body against his. 'Because I love you,' he said at last.

'Do you love me enough to give me your eyes?'

'My eyes?'

'Do you?'

'I do not understand you.'

'If you say yes, you will be blind but I will be able to see. Do you love me that much?'

'Yes, I love you more than life.' Her hands swept up touching both sides of his face, her thumbs resting on his eyelids. Darkness enveloped him, a terrible, sickening emptiness. He cried out and she led him to the shoreline, where he stubbed his toe on a rock. She helped him to sit and fear swept over him. What had he *done?*

'Oh, Cormac, so that is the sky. How wonderful! And the trees, just as you described them. And you, Cormac, so handsome, so strong. Do you regret your gift?'

'No,' he lied, his pride overcoming his terror.

Her hands touched his face once more and his sight returned. He took her in his arms, pulling her to him as he saw the tears in her eyes.

'Why did you return my gift?' he asked.

'Because I love you also. And because you looked so lost and afraid. No one has ever done for me what you offered to do, Cormac. I will never forget it.'

'Then why are you crying?'

She did not reply. How could she tell him that until now she had never understood the loneliness of darkness?

'His anger towards you is very great,' said Anduine as she and Culain sat in the sunshine. Two months had passed and now the cooler breezes of Autumn whispered in the golden leaves. Every day Cormac and Culain would work together for many hours – boxing, wrestling, duelling with sword or quarter-staff. But when the sessions were over the youth would turn away, his feelings masked, his grey eyes showing no emotion.

316

'I know,' answered the warrior, shielding his eyes and watching the boy gamely running on towards the stand of pine, high up on the mountain's flank. 'He has reason to. But he likes you, he trusts you.'

'I think so, my lord. But I cannot heal the anger. As I touch it, it recoils like mist before me. Will he not speak of it?'

'I have not tried to speak to him, Anduine. There would be little to gain for either of us. I first met his father on this mountain and it was here that Uther learnt to love Laitha, my Gian Avur. Now the son follows. And still the world is at war, evil flourishes and good men die. I am sorry about your father. Had I come sooner . . .'

'He was an old warrior,' she said, smiling. 'He died as he would have wished with his sword in his hand, his enemies falling to him.'

'He was brave to refuse Wotan.'

'It was not bravery, my lord. He wanted a higher price for me. Wotan merely mistook greed for nobility.'

'You miss very little, Anduine, for one who cannot see.'

'You are leaving today?'

'Yes. You will be safe, I think, until I return. I am sorry that the cabin is so bare of luxury. It will be hard for you.'

'I may just survive,' she said, smiling. 'Do not concern yourself.'

'You are a fine woman.'

Her smile faded. 'And you are a good man, my lord. So why do you plan to die?'

'You see too much.'

'You did not answer me.'

'To ask the question means you know the answer, for the two are one.'

'I want to hear you say it.'

'Why, lady?'

'I want you to hear yourself. I want you to understand the futility.'

'Another time, Anduine.' He took her hand and kissed it softly.

'No, there will be no other time. You will not come back and I will never meet you again.'

317

For a while Culain was silent and she felt the tension in him ease away.

'All my life,' he said at last, 'all my long, long life I have been able to look at Culain and be proud. For Culain never acted basely. Culain was the true prince. My arrogance could have swamped mountains. I was immortal: the Mist Warrior, the Lance Lord from the Feragh. I was Apollo for the Greeks, Donner to the Norse, Agripash to the Hittites. But in all the interminable centuries I never betrayed a friend, nor broke a trust. Now I am no longer that Culain and I wonder if ever I was.'

'You speak of the Queen?'

'Uther's bride. I raised her – here where we sit. She ran in these mountains, hunted and laughed, sang and knew joy. I was a father to her. I did not know then that she loved me, for she was a child of the earth and my love was a goddess of eternal beauty. But then you know the tale of the Witch Queen and her deeds.' Culain shrugged. 'When the battle was over, I should never have gone back. Uther and Laitha thought me dead; they were married then and, I believed, happy. But I found the last to be untrue. He ignored her, treating her with shameful disdain. He took other women and flaunted them at his palaces, leaving my Gian desolate and a laughing-stock. I would have killed him, but she forbade it. I tried to comfort her. I pitied her. I loved her. I brought her happiness for a little while. Then they became reconciled and our love was put away. She conceived a child by him – and all the past torments seemed forgotten.

'But it did not last for his bitterness was too strong. He sent her to Dubris, telling her the sea air would help her in her pregnancy. Then he moved a young Iceni woman into his palace. I went to Gian.' He chuckled, then sighed. 'Foolish Culain; it was a trap. He had men watching the house. I was seen and they tried to take me. I killed three of them – and one was an old friend.

'I took Gian to Anderida and then further along the coast, having got a message to friends in Sicambria. A ship was due to meet us and we sheltered in an old cave, safe from all – even the magic of Maedhlyn, Uther's Lord Enchanter.'

318

'How did they find you?' she asked.

'Gian had a pet hound called Cabal. Uther's horse-master, a crippled Brigante called Prasamaccus, released the beast outside Dubris and it trailed us all the way to the cave. Gian was so pleased when it arrived, and I did not think – so great was her pleasure that it masked my intellect. The hound gave birth to a litter of five pups some time before Gian bore Cormac. A black and bitter day that was! The babe was dead, of that there is no doubt. But Gian left it with her Sipstrassi necklace and somehow the magic brought him back.

'But by then the hunters had found me. I killed them all and carried Gian to the cliff-top. Uther was already there, sitting on his war-horse. He was alone and I thought of killing him. Gian stopped me once more – and I looked to the sea. There in the bay was the Sicambrian ship. I had no choice; I took Gian in my arms and leapt. I almost lost her in the waves, but at last we were safe. But she never recovered her spirit. The Betrayal of Uther and the death of her son became linked in her mind as a punishment from God and she sent me away.'

'What became of her?' whispered Anduine.

'Nothing became of her. She was dead and yet living. She joined a community of God-seekers in Belgica and stayed there for thirteen years, scrubbing floors, growing vegetables, cooking meals, studying ancient writings and seeking forgiveness.'

'Did she find it?'

'How could she? There is no God in the Universe who would hate her. But she despised herself. She would never see me. Every year I journeyed to Belgica – and every year the gatekeeper would go to her, return and send me away. Two years ago he told me she had died.'

'And you, my lord? Where did you go?'

'I went to Africa. I became Revelation.'

'And do you seek forgiveness?'

'No. I seek oblivion.'

Culain sat opposite the young warrior in the watery sunshine, pleased with the progress Cormac had made in the last eight weeks.

The youth was stronger now, his long legs capable of running for mile upon mile over any terrain, his arms and shoulders showing corded muscle, taut and powerful. He had outgrown the faded red tunic and now wore a buckskin shirt and woollen trews Culain had purchased from a travelling merchant passing through the Caledones towards Pinnata Castra in the east.

'We must talk, Cormac,' said the Lance Lord.

'Why? We have not yet practised with the sword.'

'There will be no sword-play today. After we have spoken, I shall be leaving.'

'I do not wish to talk,' said Cormac, rising.

'Know your enemy,' said Culain softly.

'What does that mean?'

'It means that from today you are on your own – and Anduine's life is in your care. It means that when Wotan finds you – as he will – only you and your skill will be between Anduine and the Blade of Sacrifice.'

'You are leaving us?'

'Yes.'

'Why?' asked the youth, returning to his seat on the fallen log.

'I do not answer to you for my life. But before we part, Cormac, I want you to understand the nature of the enemy, for in that you may find his weakness.'

'How can I fight a god?'

'By understanding what a god is. We are not talking about the Source of All Creation, we are talking about an immortal: a man who has discovered a means to live for ever. But he is a man nonetheless. Look at me, Cormac. I also was an immortal. I was born when the sun shone over Atlantis, when the world was ours, when Pendarric the King opened the Gates of the Universe. But the oceans drank Atlantis and the world was changed for ever. Here, on this Island of Mist, you see the last remnants of Pendarric's power, for this was the northern outpost of the empire. The standing stones were gateways to journeys within and beyond the realm. We gave birth to all the gods and demons of the world. Werebeasts, dragons, blood-drinkers – all were set free by Pendarric.'

Culain sighed and rubbed at his eyes. 'I know there is too much to burden you with here. But you need to understand at least a part of a history that men no longer recall, save as legend. Pendarric discovered other worlds, and in opening the gates to those worlds he loosed beings very different from men. Atlantis was destroyed, but many of the people survived. Pendarric led thousands of us to a new realm – the Feragh. And we had Sipstrassi, the Stone from Heaven. You have seen its magic, felt its power. It saved us from ageing, but could not give us wisdom nor prevent the onset of a terrible boredom. Man is a hunting, competitive animal. Unless there is ambition, there is apathy and chaos. We found ambitions. Many of us returned to the world and with our powers we became gods. We built civilisations and we warred one upon another. We made our dreams reality. And some of us saw the dangers . . . others did not. The seeds of madness are nurtured by unlimited power. The wars became more intense, more terrifying. The numbers of the slain could not be counted.

'One among us became Molech, the God of the Canaanites and the Amorites. He demanded the blood sacrifices from every family. Each first-born son or daughter was consigned to the flames. Torture, mutilation and death were his hallmarks. The agonised screams of his victims were as sweet to him as the music of the lyre. Pendarric called a council of the Feragh and we joined together to oppose Molech. The war was long and bloody, but at last we destroyed his empire.'

'But he survived,' said Cormac.

'No. I found him on the battlements of Babel, with his guard of demons. I cut my way through to him and we faced each other, high above the field of the fallen. Only once have I met a man of such skill, but I was at the magical peak of my strength and I slew Molech, cut his head from his shoulders and hurled the body to the rocks below.'

'Then how has he returned?'

'I do not know. But I will discover the truth, and I shall face him again.'

'Alone?'

Culain smiled. 'Yes, alone.'

'You are no longer at the peak of your strength.'

'Very true. I was almost slain twenty-five – no, twenty-six years ago. The Sipstrassi restored me but since then I have not used its power for myself. I want to be a man again. To live out a life and die like a mortal.'

'Then you will not beat him.'

'Victory is not important, Cormac. True strength is born of striving. When you first ran to the pine, you could not return before the shadow passed the stick. Did you say, "Ah well, there is no point in running again?" No. You ran and grew stronger, fitter, faster. It is the same when facing evil. You do not grow stronger by running away. It is balance. Harmony.'

'And how do you win if he kills you?' said Cormac.

'By sowing the seed of doubt in his mind. I may not win, Cormac, but I will come close. I will show him his weakness and then a better man can destroy him.'

'It sounds as if you are merely going away to die.'

'Perhaps that is true. How will you fare, here alone?'

'I do not know, but I will protect Anduine with my life.'

'This I know.' Culain dipped his hand into the leather pouch at his side and produced the Sipstrassi necklace Cormac had dropped within the Circle of stones. The youth tensed, his eyes glinting with anger.

'I do not want it,' he said.

'It gave you life,' said Culain softly, 'and whatever you think of me, you should know that your mother never recovered from losing you. It haunted her to her dying day. Add this to the burden of your hate for me. But it was not *my* gift to you – it was hers. With it you can protect Anduine far more powerfully than with the sword.'

'I would not know how to use it.'

Culain leaned forward. 'Take it, and I will show you.'

'Give it to Anduine and I will think about it after you have gone,' said Cormac, rising once more.

'You are a stubborn man, Cormac. But I wish we could part as friends.'

322

'I do not hate you, Culain,' said the youth, 'for you saved me from Agwaine and fought off the demons for Anduine. But had it not been for you, I would not have known a life of pain and sorrow. I am the son of a King and I have been raised like a leper. You think I should thank you?'

'No, you are my shame brought to life. But I loved your mother and would have died for her.'

'But you did not. Grysstha once told me that men will always excuse their shortcomings, but to your credit you never have. Try to understand, Culain, what I am saying. I admire you. I am sorry for you. But you are the father of my loneliness and we could never be friends.'

Culain nodded. 'At least you do not hate me and that is something to carry with me.' He held out his hand and Cormac took it. 'Be on your guard, young warrior. Train every day. And remember the three mysteries: life, harmony and spirit.'

'I shall. Farewell, Revelation.'

'Farewell, Prince Cormac.'

6

In the months following the Trinovante uprising, Britannia enjoyed an uneasy peace. Uther paced the halls of Camulodunum like a caged warhound, eagerly watching the roads from his private apartments in the north tower. Every time a messenger arrived the King would hurry to the main hall, ripping the seals from despatches and devouring the contents, ever seeking news of insurrection or invasion. But throughout the Summer and into the Autumn peace reigned, crops were gathered, militiamen sent home to their families.

Men walked warily around Uther, sensing his disquiet. Across the Gallic Sea a terrible army had ripped into the Sicambrian kingdoms of Belgica and Gaul, destroying their forces and burning their cities. The enemy king, Wotan, was named Anti-Christ by the Bishop of Rome, but this was not unusual. A score of barbarian kings had been dubbed by the same name, and subsequently many had been admitted to the church.

Rome herself sent five legions to assist the Sicambrians. They were destroyed utterly, their standards taken.

But in Britain the people enjoyed the hot summer and the absence of war. Store-houses groaned under the weight of produce, the price of bread and wine plummeted. Only the merchants complained, for the rich export markets of Gaul had been disrupted by the war and few were the trade ships docking at Dubris or Noviomagus.

Each morning Uther would climb to the north tower, lock the door of oak and set the Sword of Power in its niche within the grey boulder. Then he would kneel before it and wait, focusing his thoughts. Dreams and visions would swirl in his mind, and his spirit would soar across the land from Pinnata Castra in the north to Dubris in the south, from Gariannonum in the east to Moriodunum in the west, seeking gatherings of armed men. Finding nothing, he would follow the coastline, spirit eyes scanning the grey waves for sign of long ships and Viking raiders.

But the seas were clear.

One bright morning he tried to cross the Gallic Sea, but found himself halted by a force he could neither see nor pass, like a wall of crystal.

Confused and uncertain, he returned to his tower, opening the eyes of his body and removing the Sword from the stone. Stepping to the ramparts, he felt the cool Autumn breeze on his skin, and for a while his fears slumbered.

His manservant Baldric came to him at noon, bringing wine, cold meat and a dish of the dark plums the King favoured. Uther, in no mood for conversation, waved the lad away and sat at the window staring out at the distant sea.

He knew Victorinus and Gwalchmai were concerned about his state of mind, and he could not explain the fear growing in his soul. He felt like a man walking a dark alleyway, knowing – without evidence, and yet with certainty – that a monster awaited him at the next turn: faceless, formless, yet infinitely deadly.

Not for the first time in the last ten years Uther wished that Maedhlyn was close. The Lord Enchanter would either have laid his fears to rest, or at worst identified the danger.

'If wishes were horses the beggars would ride,' muttered Uther, shutting his mind from the memory of Maedhlyn's departure. Harsh words, hotter than acid, had poured from Uther that day. They were regretted within the hour, but could not be drawn back. Once spoken they hung in the air, carved on invisible stone, branded into the hearts of the hearers. And Maedhlyn had gone . . .

As Laitha had gone. And Culain . . .

Uther poured more wine, seeking to dull the memories and yet enhancing them. Gian Avur, Fawn of the Forest, was the name Culain had given to Laitha – a name Uther had never been allowed to use. But he had loved her, and had been lost without her.

'Why then did you drive her into his arms?' he whispered.

There was no answer to be found in logic or intellect. But Uther knew where it lay, deep in the labyrinthine tunnels of dark emotion. The seeds of insanity were sown on that night in another world when the youth had first made love to the maid, only to have her whisper the name of Culain at the moment of Uther's greatest joy. The opposite of the alchemist's dream – gold become lead, light plunged into darkness. Even then he could have forgiven her, for Culain was dead. He could not . . . would not be jealous of a corpse. But the Lance Lord returned and Uther had seen the light of love reborn in Laitha's eyes.

Yet he could not send him away, for that would be defeat. And he could not kill him, for he owed everything to Culain. He could only hope that her love for the Lance Lord would be overcome by her marriage vow to the King. And it was so – but not enough. He tested her resolve time and again, treating her with appalling indifference, forcing her in her despair to the very act he feared above all others.

King of Fools!

Uther, the Blood King, the Lord of No Defeat! What did it matter that armies could not withstand him when he dwelt in loneliness in a chilly tower? No sons to follow him, no wife to love him. He turned to the bronze mirror set on the wall; grey roots were showing under the henna-dyed hair and the eyes were tired.

He wandered to the ramparts and stared down at the courtyard. The Sicambrian, Ursus, was strolling arm in arm with a young woman. Uther could not recognise her, but she seemed familiar. He smiled. The horse-armour had been a miserable failure, becoming sodden and useless in the rain, but Ursus had proved a fine cavalry commander. The men liked his easy manner and his quick wit, added to which he was not reckless and understood the importance in strategy of patience and forethought.

The King watched the easy way Ursus draped his arm over the woman's shoulder, drawing her to him in the shadows of a doorway, tilting her chin to kiss her lips. Uther shook his head and turned away. He rarely had women sent to his apartments these days; the act of loving left him with a deep sadness, a hollow empty loneliness.

His eyes scanned the green landscape, the rolling hills and the farms, the cattle herds and the sheep. All was at peace. Uther cursed softly. For years he had fostered the myth that he was the land, the soul and heart of Britannia. Only his trusted friends knew that the Sword gave him the power. Yet now, even without the aid of the mystic blade, Uther could feel a sinister threat growing in the shadows. The tranquillity around him was but an illusion, and the days of blood and fire were waiting to dawn.

Or are you getting old, he asked himself? Have you lied for so long about the myth that you have come to believe it?

A cold breeze touched him and he shivered.

What was the threat? From where would it come?

'My lord?' said a voice and Uther spun to find Victorinus standing in the doorway. 'I knocked on the outer door, but there was no response,' said the Roman. 'I am sorry if I startled you.'

'I was thinking,' said the King. 'What news?'

'The Bishop of Rome has agreed a treaty with Wotan, and has validated his claims to Gaul and Belgica.'

Uther chuckled. 'A short-lived Anti-Christ, was he not?'

Victorinus nodded, then removed his bronze helm. His white hair made him seem much older than his fifty years. Uther moved past him into the apartments, beckoning the general to sit.

'Still clean-shaven, my friend,' said the King. 'What will you do now the pumice-stones are no longer arriving?'

'I'll use a razor,' said Victorinus, grinning. 'It does not become a Roman to look like an unwashed barbarian.'

'That is no way to speak to your King,' said Uther, scratching at his own beard.

'But then your misfortune, sire, was to be born without Roman blood. I can only offer my deepest sympathies.'

'The arrogance of Rome survives even her downfall,' said Uther smiling. 'Tell me of Wotan.'

'The reports are contradictory, sire. He fought four major battles in Sicambria, crushing the Merovingians. Nothing is known of their King; some say he escaped to Italia, others that he sought refuge in Hispania.'

327

'The strategies, man. Does he use cavalry? Or the Roman phalanx? Or just a horde, overwhelming by numbers?'

'His army is split into units. There are some mounted warriors, but in the main he relies on axemen and archers. He also fights where the battle is thickest and, it is said, no sword can pierce his armour.'

'Not a good trait in a general,' muttered the King. 'He should stay back, directing the battle.'

'As you do, my lord?' asked Victorinus, raising an eyebrow.

Uther grinned. 'I will one day,' he said. 'I'll sit on a canvas stool and watch you and Gwalchmai sunder the enemy.'

'I wish you would, sire. My heart will not take the strain you put upon it with your recklessness.'

'Has Wotan sent emissaries to other kings?' asked Uther.

'Not as far as we know – only the Bishop of Rome and the boy emperor. He has pledged not to lead his armies into Italia.'

'Then where will he lead them?'

'You think he will invade Britain?'

'I need to know more about him. Where is he from? How did he weld the German tribes, the Norse and the Goths into such a disciplined army? And in so short a time?'

'I could go as an ambassador, sire. His court is now in Martius.'

Uther nodded. 'Take Ursus with you; he knows the land, the people and the language. And a gift; I will arrange a suitable offering for a new king.'

'Too fine a gift may be misread as weakness, sire, and you did have a treaty with Meroveus.'

'Meroveus was a fool, his army the laughing-stock of Europe. Our treaty was for trade, no more. You will explain to Wotan that the treaty was between the Kings of Sicambria and Britain, and that I acknowledge the agreement to remain active, even as I acknowledge his right to the throne.'

'Is that not dangerous, sire? You will be supporting the right of the conqueror against the right of blood.'

'It is a dangerous world in which we live, Victorinus.'

*   *   *

Ursus woke in a cold sweat, his heart hammering. The girl beside him slept on under the warm blankets, her breathing even. The prince slid out from the bed and walked to the window, pulling back the velvet hangings and allowing the breeze to cool his flesh. The dream had been so real; he had seen his brother pursued through the streets of Martius and dragged into a wide hall. There Ursus watched a tall blond-bearded warrior cut his brother's heart from his living body.

He moved to the table and found there was still a little wine in the jar. He poured it into a clay goblet and drained it.

Just a dream, he told himself, born of his concern over the invasion of Gaul.

A bright light flashed behind his eyes, filling his head with fiery pain. He cried out and stumbled, blind and afraid, tipping the table to the floor.

'What is it?' screamed the girl. 'Sweet Christos, are you ill?' But her voice faded back into the distance and a roaring filled his ears. His vision cleared and he saw once more the blond-bearded warrior, this time standing in a deep circular pit. Around him were other warriors, all wearing horned helms and carrying huge axes. A door above them opened and two men dragged a naked prisoner to a set of wooden steps, forcing him to climb down into the pit. With horror Ursus saw it was Meroveus, the King of Sicambria. His beard was matted, his hair encrusted with mud and filth; his slender body showed signs of cruel use, whip-marks criss-crossing the skin.

'Well met, brother king,' said the tall warrior, gripping the prisoner by his beard and hauling him upright. 'Are you well?'

'I curse you, Wotan. May you burn in the fires of Hell!'

'Fool! I am Hell, and I lit the fires.'

Meroveus was dragged to a greased and pointed stake and hoisted high in the air.

Ursus tore his eyes from the scene, but could not block the awful sounds as the monarch was brutally impaled. Once more the bright light flashed and now he was viewing a scene in a great wooden hall. Warriors surrounded a crowd – their lances aimed at men, women and children who stood in silent terror. Ursus recognised many faces: cousins, uncles, aunts, nephews. Most of the Merovingian nobles were gathered here. Warriors in mail-shirts began to throw buckets of water over the prisoners, jeering and laughing as the liquid splashed down. It was a ridiculous scene, yet tainted with a terrible menace. Once more the blond-bearded Wotan stepped forward, this time carrying a torch. Terrified screams sprang up from the prisoners as Wotan laughed and hurled the torch into the mass. Fire swept the group . . . and Ursus suddenly understood. It was not water they were drenched with . . . but oil. The lancers retired at speed as burning men ran like human torches, spreading the blaze.

The walls ran with flames and dark smoke settled over the scene . . .

Ursus screamed and fell back, weeping piteously, into the arms of the girl.

'Dear God,' she said, stroking his brow. 'What is it?'

But he could not answer. There were no words in all the world. There was only pain . . .

Two officers from the adjoining rooms entered, lifting Ursus to the wide bed. Other men gathered in the stone corridor. The surgeon was summoned and the girl quietly gathered her clothing, dressed and slipped away.

'What is the matter with him?' asked Plutarchus, a young cavalry officer who had befriended Ursus during the summer. 'There is no wound.'

His companion, Decimus Agrippa, a lean warrior of ten years' experience, merely shrugged and looked into Ursus' unblinking, unfocused eyes.

Gently he pressed the lids closed.

'Is he dead?' whispered Plutarchus.

'No, I think he is having a fit. I knew a man once who would suddenly go stiff and tremble with such a seizure. The great Julius was said to be so afflicted.'

'Then he will recover?'

Agrippa nodded, then turned to the men in the corridor. 'Off to your beds,' he ordered. 'The drama is over.'

The two men covered Ursus with the linen sheet and the soft woollen blankets. 'He does like luxury,' said Agrippa, grinning. It was not often that the man smiled and it made him almost handsome, thought Plutarchus. Agrippa was made for command – a cool, distant warrior whose skill and lack of recklessness led men to clamour to join his troop. In major engagements he lost fewer men than the more reckless of his brother officers, yet invariably achieved his objectives. He was known among the *Cohors Equitana* as the Dagger in the Night or, more simply, the Dagger.

Plutarchus was his second Decurion, a young man fresh from the city of Eboracum and yet to prove his worth on the battlefield.

The surgeon arrived, checked Ursus' pulse and his breathing and tried to rouse him, breaking the wax seal on a phial of foul-smelling unguent and holding it below the unconscious man's nose. There was no reaction from Ursus, though Plutarchus gagged and moved away.

'He is in a deep state of shock,' said the surgeon. 'What happened here?'

Agrippa shrugged. 'I was sleeping in the next room when I heard a man scream, then a woman. I came in with young Pluta to find the Sicambrian on the floor and the woman hysterical. I thought it was a fit.'

'I doubt it,' said the surgeon. 'The muscles are not in spasm and the heart is slow, but regular. You!' he said to Plutarchus. 'Bring a lantern to the bed.' The young officer obeyed and the surgeon opened the prince's right eye. The pupil had contracted to no more than a dot of darkness within the blue.

'How well do you know this man?'

'Hardly at all,' answered Agrippa, 'but Pluta has spend many days in his company.'

'Is he a mystic?'

'No, I do not believe so, sir,' said Plutarchus. 'He has never spoken of it. He did tell me once that the House of Merovee was renowned for its knowledge of magic, but he said it with a smile and I took him to be jesting.'

'So,' said the surgeon, 'no speaking in strange tongues, no divining, no reading of the portents?'

'No, sir.'

'Curious. And where is the woman?'

'Gone,' said Agrippa. 'I do not think she was desirous of more public scrutiny.'

'Whores should get used to it,' snapped the surgeon. 'Very well, we'll leave him resting for tonight. I will send my daughter here tomorrow morning with a potion for him; he will sleep most of the day.'

'Thank you, surgeon,' said Agrippa solemnly, aware of the spreading grin on Plutarchus' face.

After the surgeon had departed, the younger man began to chuckle.

'You will share the cause of your humour?' Agrippa asked.

'He called his own daughter a whore. Do you not think that amusing? Half the officers have tried to entice her to bed and the other half would like to. And here she was, alone and naked with the Sicambrian!'

'I am not laughing, Pluta. The Sicambrian has the morals of a gutter-rat, and the lady deserves better. Do not mention her name to anyone.'

'But she was seen by the other men in the corridor.'

'They will say nothing either. You understand me?'

'Of course.'

'Good. Now let us leave our rutting ram to his rest.'

Throughout the exchange between the two men Ursus had been conscious, though paralysed. After they had gone he lay unable to feel the soft sheet upon his body, his memory hurling the visions of death to his mind's eye over and over again.

He saw Balan's heart torn from his chest and heard the agonised scream, watching helplessly as the light of life died in his brother's eyes. Poor Balan! Sweet little brother! Once he had cried when he found a fawn with a broken leg. Ursus had ended its misery, but Balan was inconsolable for days. He should have entered the

332

priesthood but Ursus, using the power of an older brother's love, had talked him into the quest for riches.

Both men had grown used to the luxury of their father's palace in Tingis, but when the old man died and the size of his debts became clear, Ursus was unprepared for a life of near-poverty. The brothers had used the last of the family wealth to secure passage to Sicambria, there to introduce themselves to their influential relatives. The King, Meroveus, had granted them a small farm near Martius where the court resided, but the revenues were meagre.

Balan had been blissfully happy wandering the mountains, bathing in silver streams, composing poems and sketching trees and landscapes. But the life did not suit Ursus, for there were few women to be had and a positive dearth of wide silk-covered beds.

But Balan would have been happy at the Monastery of Revelation in Tingis, sleeping on a cot-bed and studying the Mysteries. Now he was dead, victim of a demonic king and a greedy brother.

Towards dawn Ursus' skin began to tingle and at last he could open his eyes. He stared for a long time at the rough-hewn ceiling, tears flowing, memories burning his soul – reshaping it, until the heat of anguish fled to be replaced by the ice of hatred.

'The Sicambrian has the morals of a gutter-rat. The lady deserves better.'

Balan also deserved better from his brother.

Feeling returned to his arms and shoulders and pushing back the bed-linen, he forced himself to a sitting position and massaged his legs until he felt the blood begin to flow.

He felt weak and unsteady and filled with a sadness bordering on despair. The door opened and Portia entered, carrying a wooden tray on which was a bowl of fresh water, a small loaf of flat baked bread, some cheese and a tiny copper phial stoppered with wax.

'Are you recovered?' she asked, placing the tray on the chest by the wall and pushing shut the door.

'Yes and no,' he said. She sat beside him, her small body pressed to his and her arms around him. He could smell the sweet perfume in her auburn hair and feel her soft breasts against his chest. He lifted her chin and kissed her gently.

333

'Are you sure you are recovered? Father has sent a sleeping draught; he says rest is needed.'

'I am sorry for your embarrassment last night. It must have been hard for you. Forgive me.'

'There is nothing to forgive. We love each other.'

Ursus winced at the words, then forced a smile. 'Love can mean different things to different people. Agrippa said I have the morals of a gutter-rat and he was quite correct. He said you deserved better; he was right in that also. I am sorry, Portia.'

'Do not be sorry. You did me no harm. Far from it,' she said, stiffening as the realization of his rejection struck her. But she was Roman and of proud stock and would not let him see her pain. 'There is food there. You should eat.'

'I must see the King.'

'I should dress first – and wash.' Pulling away from him, she walked to the door. 'You really are a fool, Ursus,' she said. And the door closed behind her.

The prince washed swiftly, then dressed in shirt, tunic and leggings of black under a pearl-grey cape. His riding-boots were also stained grey and adorned with silver rings. The outfit would have cost a British cavalry commander a year's salarium, yet for the first time it gave Ursus no pleasure as he stood before the full-length bronze mirror.

Despite his messages of urgency, the King refused to see him during the morning and the prince was left to wander the town of Camulodunum until the appointed hour. He breakfasted in the garden of an inn, then journeyed to the Street of Armourers, purchasing a new sword shaped after the Berber fashion with a slightly curved blade. These swords were becoming increasingly fashionable with Uther's cavalry, for their use from horseback. The curved blade sliced clear with greater ease than the traditional gladius, and being longer they increased the killing range.

The church bell tolled the fourth hour after noon and Ursus swiftly made his way to the north tower where Uther's manservant and squire, Baldric, bade him wait in the long room below Uther's apartments. There Ursus sat for a further frustrating hour before he was ushered in to the King.

Uther, his hair freshly dyed and his beard combed, was sitting in the fading sunshine overlooking the fields and meadows beyond the fortress town. Ursus bowed.

'You mentioned urgency,' said the King, waving him to a seat on the ramparts.

'Yes, my lord.'

'I heard of your seizure. Are you well?'

'I am well in body, but my heart is sickened.'

Swiftly and succinctly Ursus outlined the visions that had come to him, and the nauseating slayings he had witnessed.

Uther said nothing, but his grey eyes grew bleak and distant. When the young man had concluded his tale, the King leaned back and switched his gaze to the countryside.

'It was not a dream, sire,' said Ursus softly, mistaking the silence.

'I know that, boy. I know that.' Uther stood and paced the ramparts. Finally he turned to the prince. 'How do you feel about Wotan?'

'I hate him, sire, as I have hated no man in all my life.'

'And how do you feel about yourself?'

'Myself? I do not understand.'

'I think you do.'

Ursus looked away, then returned his gaze to the King. 'I get no pleasure from the mirror now,' he said, 'and my past is no longer a cause for pride.'

Uther nodded. 'And why do you come to me?'

'I want permission to return home – and kill the Usurper.'

'No, that you shall not have.'

Ursus rose to his feet, his face darkening. 'Blood cries out for vengeance, sire. I cannot refuse it.'

'You must,' said the King, his voice gentle and almost sorrowful. 'I will send you to Martius – but you will travel with Victorinus and a party of warriors as an embassy to the new king.'

'Sweet Mithras! To face him and not to kill him? To bow and scrape before this vile animal?'

'Listen to me! I am not some farmer, responsible only for his family and his meagre crop of barley. I am a king. I have a land to protect, a people. You think this Wotan will be content with Gaul and Belgica? No. I can feel the presence of his evil; I feel his cold eyes roaming my lands. Fate will decree we face each other on some bloody battlefield, and if I am to win I need knowledge – his men, his methods, his weaknesses. You understand?'

'Then send someone else, sire, for pity's sake.'

'No. Harness your hatred and keep it on a tight rein. It will survive.'

'But surely it will end his threat if I just kill him?'

'If it were that simple, I'd wish you God's luck. But it is not. The man uses sorcery and he will be protected by man and demon. Believe me! And if you failed, they would know from whence you came – and have legitimate cause to war upon Britain. And I am not ready for them.'

'Very well, sire. It shall be as you say.'

'Then swear it upon your brother's soul.'

'There is no need . . .'

'Do it!'

Their eyes locked and Ursus knew he was beaten. 'I so swear.'

'Good. Now we must have a new name for you – and a new face. Wotan has butchered the House of Merovee, and if you are recognised your death is assured. You will meet Victorinus at Dubris. You will be Galead, a Knight of Uther. Follow me.' The King led Ursus into the inner apartments and drew the Sword of Power from its scabbard. Touching the blade to the prince's shoulder, Uther's eyes narrowed in concentration.

Ursus felt a tingling sensation on his scalp and face and his teeth began to ache. The King removed the sword and led the warrior to the oval mirror on the wall.

'Behold the latest of Uther's knights,' he said with a wide grin.

Ursus stared into the mirror at the blond stranger with his close-cropped hair and eyes of summer blue.

'Galead,' whispered the new knight. 'So be it!'

336

7

The winter was fierce in the Caledones, snow-drifts blocking trails, ice forcing its way into the cracks in the wooden walls of the cabin. The surrounding trees, stripped of their leaves, stood bare and skel-etal, while the wind howled outside the sealed windows.

Cormac lay in the narrow bed with Anduine snuggled beside him and knew contentment. The door rattled in its frame and the fire blazed brightly, dancing shadows flickering on the far wall. Cormac rolled over, his hand sliding gently over Anduine's rounded hip, and she lifted her head and kissed his chest.

Suddenly she froze.

'What is it?' he asked.

'There is someone on the mountain,' she whispered. 'Someone in danger.'

'Did you hear something?'

'I can feel their fear.'

'Their?'

'Two people, a man and a woman. The way is blocked. You must go to them, Cormac, or they will die.'

He sat up and shivered. Even here in this bright, warm room, cold draughts hinted at the horror outside. 'Where are they?'

'Beyond the stand of pine, across the pass. They are on the ridge leading to the sea.'

'They are not our concern,' he said, knowing his argument would be useless. 'And I might die out there myself.'

'You are strong and you know the land. Please help them!'

He rose from the bed and dressed in a heavy woollen shirt, leather leggings, sheepskin jerkin and boots. The jerkin had a hood lined with wool which he drew over his red hair, tying it tightly under his chin.

'This is a heavy price to pay for your love, lady,' he said.

'Is it?' she asked, sitting up, her long dark hair falling across her shoulders.

'No,' he admitted. 'Keep the fire going. I will try to be back by dawn.'

He looked at his sword lying beside the hearth and considered carrying it with him, but it would only encumber him. Instead he slipped a long-bladed hunting-knife behind his belt and stepped out into the blizzard, dragging the door shut with difficulty.

Since Culain's departure three months before, Cormac had stuck to his training – increasing the length of his runs, working with axe and saw to build his muscles, preparing the winter store of wood which now stood six-feet high and ran the length of the cabin, aiding the insulation on the north wall. His body was lean and powerful, his shoulders wide, his hips narrow. He set off towards the mountain peaks at an easy walk, using a six-foot quarterstaff to test the snow beneath his feet. To hurry would mean to sweat; in these temperatures the sweat would form as ice on the skin beneath his clothes and that would kill him as swiftly as if he were naked. The straighter paths on the north side were blocked with drifts and Cormac was forced to find a more circuitous route to the pine, edging his way south through the woods, across frozen streams and ponds. Huge grey wolves prowled the mountains, but these kept clear of the man as he made his slow, steady progress. For two hours he pushed on, stopping to rest often, saving his strength, until at last he cleared the pine and began the long dangerous traverse of the ridge above the pass. Here the trail was only five feet wide, snow covering ice on the slanted path. One wrong or careless step and he would plummet over the edge, smashing himself on the rocks below. He halted in a shallow depression sheltered from the wind and rubbed at the skin of his face, forcing the blood to flow. His cheeks and his chin were covered by a fine red-brown down that would soon be a beard, but his nose and eyes felt pinched and tight in the icy wind.

The blizzard raged about him and vision was restricted to no more than a few feet. His chances of finding the strangers were shrinking by the second. Cursing loudly, he stepped out into the wind and continued his progress along the ridge.

338

Anduine's voice came to him, whispering deep in his mind: 'A little further, to the left, there is a shallow cave. They are there.'

He had long grown used to her powers. Ever since he had given her – albeit briefly – the gift of sight, her mystic talents had increased. She had begun to dream in vivid pictures of glorious colour, and often he would allow her the use of his eyes to see some strange new wonder – swans in flight, a racing stag, a hunting wolf, a sky torn by storms.

Moving on, he found the cave and saw a man huddled by the far wall, a young woman kneeling by him. The man saw him first and pointed – the woman swung, raising a knife.

'Put it away,' said Cormac, walking in and looking down at the man. He was sitting with his back to the wall and with his right leg thrust out in front of him, the boot bent at an impossible angle. Cormac glanced around. The shelter was inadequate; there was no wood for a fire, and even could he light one the wind would lash it to cinders.

'We must move,' he said.

'I cannot walk,' replied the man, his words slurred. There was ice in his dark beard and his skin was patchy and blue in places. Cormac nodded.

Reaching down, he took the man's hand and pulled him upright; then he ducked his head to let the body fall across his shoulders and heaved him up.

Cormac grunted at the weight and slowly turned. 'Follow me,' he told the girl.

'He will die out there,' she protested.

'He will die in here,' answered Cormac. He struggled to the ridge and began the long trek home: his burden almost more than he could bear, the muscles of his neck straining under the weight of the injured man. But the blizzard began to ease and the temperature lifted slightly. After an hour Cormac began to sweat heavily and his fear rose. He could feel the ice forming and the dreadful lethargy beginning. Sucking in a deep breath, he called to the young woman.

'Move alongside me.' She did so. 'Now talk.'

339

'I'm too tired . . . too cold.'

'Talk, curse your eyes! Where are you from?' He staggered on.

'We were in Pinnata Castra but we had to leave. My father broke his leg in a fall. We . . . we . . .' She stumbled.

'Get up, damn you! You want me to die?'

'You bastard!'

'Keep talking. What is your name?'

'Rhiannon.'

'Look at your father. Is he alive?' Cormac hoped he was not. He longed to let the burden fall; his legs were burning, his back a growing agony.

'I'm alive,' the man whispered.

Cursing him savagely, Cormac pushed on. They reached the pine after two torturous hours and then began the long climb downhill to the woods. The blizzard found fresh strength and the snow swirled about them, but once in the trees the wind dropped.

Cormac reached the cabin just as dawn was lightening the sky. He dropped his burden to the cot-bed, which creaked under his weight.

'The girl,' said Anduine. 'She is not with you.'

Cormac was too weary to curse as he stumbled from the cabin and back into the storm. He found Rhiannon crawling across a snow-drift and heading away from the cabin. She struggled weakly as he lifted her, then her head sagged on his shoulder.

In the cabin he laid her before the fire, rubbing warmth into her arms and face.

'Strip her clothes away,' ordered Anduine, but Cormac's cold fingers fumbled with the leather ties and she came to his aid. He removed his own clothes and sat by the fire wrapped in a warm blanket, staring into the flames.

'Move away,' Anduine said. 'Let the heat reach her.' Cormac turned and saw the naked girl. She was blonde and slim, with an oval face and a jaw that was too strong to be feminine. 'Help me,' asked Anduine and together they moved her nearer the fire. Anduine pulled the warm blanket from Cormac's shoulders and laid it over Rhiannon. 'Now let us see to the father.'

340

'You don't mind if I dress first?'

Anduine smiled. 'You were very brave, my love. I am so proud of you.'

'Tell me in the morning.'

Stepping to the bed, Anduine pulled the blanket clear of the injured leg which was swollen and purple below the knee. When Cormac was clothed once more she bade him twist the limb back into place. The injured man groaned but did not wake. While Cormac held it, Anduine placed her hands on either side of the break, her face set in deep concentration. After some minutes she began to tremble and her head sagged forward. Cormac released his hold on the man's leg and moved round to her, helping her to her feet.

'The break was jagged and splintered,' she said. 'It was very hard forcing it to knit. I think it is healing now, but you will need to cut some splints to support it.'

'You look exhausted. Go back to bed – I'll tend them.'

She grinned. 'And you, I take it, are back to the peak of your strength?'

'Assassins!' screamed the girl on the floor by the fire, sitting bolt upright. Slowly her eyes focused and she burst into tears. Anduine knelt beside her, holding her close and stroking her hair.

'You are safe here, I promise you.'

'No one is safe,' she said. 'No one!'

The wind howled outside the door, causing it to rattle against the leather hinges.

'They will find us,' whispered Rhiannon, her voice rising. Anduine's hand floated over the girl's face, settling softly on her brow.

'Sleep,' she murmured and Rhiannon sank back to the floor.

'Who is hunting them?' asked Cormac.

'Her thoughts were jumbled. I saw men in dark tunics with long knives; her father killed two of them and they escaped into the wilderness. We will talk to her when she wakes.'

'We should not have brought them here.'

'We had to. They needed help.'

341

'Maybe they did. But *you* are my concern, not them.'

'If you felt like that, why did you not drop your burden on the high mountain when you thought you were going to die?'

Cormac shrugged. 'I cannot answer that. But, believe me, if I thought they were a danger to you I would have slit both their throats without hesitation.'

'I know,' she said sadly. 'It is a side of you I try not to think about.' She returned to her bed and said nothing more about the strangers.

Cormac sat by the fire suddenly saddened and heavy of heart. The arrival of the father and daughter had cast a shadow over the mountain. The ugliness of a world of violence had returned, and with it the fear that Anduine would be taken from him.

Taking up his sword, he began to hone the edge with long sweeping strokes of his whetstone.

Anduine slept later than usual and Cormac did not wake her as he eased from the bed. The fire had sunk to glowing ashes and he added tinder until the flames leapt. Larger sticks were fed to the blaze and the warmth crept across the room. Cormac knelt beside the blonde-haired girl; her colour was good, her breathing even. Her father was snoring softly and Cormac moved to the bedside and stared down at the man's face. It was strong and made almost square by the dark beard, which glistened as if oiled. The nose was flat and twisted by some savage break in the past, and there were scars around the eyes and on the brow. Glancing down at the man's right arm, which lay outside the blankets, he saw that this too was criss-crossed with scars.

The snoring ceased and the man's eyes opened. There was no sign of drowsiness in the gaze that fastened on the young man.

'How are you feeling?' Cormac asked.

'Alive,' answered the man, pushing his powerful arms against the bed and sitting up. He threw back the covers and looked down at his leg, around which Cormac had fashioned a rough splint.

'You must be a skilled surgeon. I feel no pain. It is as if it were not broken at all.'

342

'Do not trust it overmuch,' said Cormac. 'I will cut you a staff.'

The man swung his head, staring down at his daughter by the fireside. Satisfied that she was sleeping, he seemed to relax and smiled, showing broken front teeth.

'We are grateful to you, she and I.' He pulled the blankets over his naked body. 'Now I will sleep again.'

'Who was hunting you?'

'That is none of your concern,' was the soft reply, the words eased with an awkward smile.

Cormac shrugged and moved away. He dressed swiftly in woollen tunic, leggings and sheepskin boots, then stepped out into the open. Icicles dripped from the overhanging roof and the slate-grey sky was breaking up, showing banners of blue. For an hour he worked with the axe, splitting wood for the store. Then he returned, as the smell of frying bacon filled the air.

The man was dressed and sitting at the table, the girl beside him wrapped in a blanket. Anduine was delicately slicing the meat, her blindness obvious. Her head was tilted, her eyes seeming to stare at the far wall.

She smiled as Cormac entered. 'Is it a beautiful day?'

'It will be,' he said, sensing the change in the atmosphere. The man was deep in thought, his face set and his eyes fixed on Anduine.

Cormac joined them at the table and they broke their fast in silence.

'What are your plans now, Oleg Hammerhand?' asked Anduine, as the meal was finished.

'How is it, lady, that you know my name?'

'How is it that you know mine?' she countered.

Oleg leaned back in the chair. 'All across the world men seek news of the Lady Anduine, the Life-Giver. Some say Wotan took her, others that she died. I met a man who was close by when her father was slain. He said that a man dressed as a monk, yet wielding two swords, cut his way through the assassins and rescued the princess. Was that man you?' he asked, switching his gaze to Cormac.

'No. Would that it were!'

Oleg swung back to face Anduine. 'Wotan has offered 1,000 gold pieces for news of your whereabouts. Can you imagine? 1,000 pieces! And there has been not a word. Not a sign.'

'Until now,' said Anduine.

'Yes,' he agreed. 'But we will not betray you, lady – not for ten times ten times that amount.'

'I know. It is not in your nature, Oleg.' Anduine leaned towards the girl and reached out, but the girl shrank back. 'Take my hand, Rhiannon.'

'No,' whispered the girl.

'Do it, girl,' ordered Oleg.

'She is a demon!'

'Nonsense!' Oleg roared.

Anduine leaned back, withdrawing her hand. 'It is all right; we all have our fears. How close behind were the hunters?'

'We lost them in the mountains,' said Oleg, 'but they will not give up the search.'

'They want Rhiannon,' said Anduine. 'For she too has a talent.'

'How did you know?' Oleg asked, his eyes fearful.

'She called me from the mountain; that is why Cormac came.'

'I am sorry we have caused you trouble. We will leave as soon as my leg is mended.'

'You think to escape Wotan?'

'I do not know, lady. All my life I have been a warrior – a wolf of the sea. I fear no man. And yet . . . this Wotan is not a man. His followers are crazed. They adore him – and those who are less than adoring are rooted out and slain. A kind of madness has infected the people of the Northlands. The God is returned. The grim, grey god walks among men. Can I escape him? I fear that I cannot.'

'Have you seen this Wotan?' asked Cormac.

'Indeed I have. I served him for three years. He is strong, which is all we ever asked in a leader. But he is more than this. He has power, in his voice and in his eyes. I have seen men cut their own throats on his order . . . and do it gladly for the honour of pleasing him. He is like strong wine – to listen to him is to be filled with a sense of glory.'

344

'You sound like a worshipper still,' whispered Anduine.

'I am lady. But I am a man also – and a father. The Brides of Wotan die. My Rhiannon is not for him.'

'How did you escape?' Cormac asked.

'I was told to deliver Rhiannon to his castle in Raetia. I said that I would, but instead we boarded a merchant trireme bound for Hispania. Strong winds and fear of the following storm made the captain seek shelter near Pinnata Castra, but the storm winds were Wotan's and his assassins attacked us outside the castle. I killed two and we fled, away into the blizzard.'

'How many hunters are there?' Cormac wanted to know.

'Only five attacked us, but there will be more. And he has other forces to do his bidding, though I will not speak of them before the Lady Anduine.'

'Do not fear for me, Oleg. I am aware of the demons; they have attacked me also.'

'How then did you survive?'

'Through the courage of others. Cormac saved my life, as did the monk you heard of.'

'Then the demons are not invincible?'

'Nothing is invincible. There is no evil that cannot be conquered, not even Wotan.'

'I would like – dearly like – to believe that. But he is now the king across the water, and all the nations pay him homage – even Rome sends gifts with ambassadors who bow and scrape.'

'Uther does not bow and scrape,' said Cormac. 'Wotan has yet to face the Blood King.'

'That I know. It is the whisper of the world, Cormac. In every tavern men wonder at the outcome. It is said Uther has a magic Sword, a gift from a god – that once it parted the sky like a tearing curtain and men saw two suns blazing in the heavens. I would like to see the day he and Wotan face each other.'

'And I,' agreed Cormac. 'Blood King and Blood God.'

Rhiannon tensed, her head jerking upright and her hands covering her face.

'What is it?' asked Oleg, his huge arm circling her shoulder.

345

'The hunters have found us,' she whispered.

In the silence that followed Cormac could feel his heart beating hard inside his chest. His fear rose as bile in his throat, and he felt his hands trembling. All his life he had been subject to the whims of others, lashed and beaten, allowed no opportunity to stand tall and learn the virtues of pride; no time to absorb the strength-giving qualities of defiance. With Culain his anger had carried him on, but now as the enemy approached he felt a terrible sense of despair crawling on his skin, bearing him down.

Anduine came round to stand beside him, her soft hand touching the skin of his neck, her fingers easing the knot of tension in his shoulders. Her voice whispered inside his mind.

'I love you, Cormac.' The depth of her emotion warmed him like a winter fire, the ice of his panic fleeing from it.

'How many are there?' he asked aloud.

'Three,' whispered Rhiannon.

'How close?'

'They are on the hillside to the south, approaching the cabin,' answered the girl.

'And I have no sword!' thundered Oleg, crashing his fist to the table.

'I have,' said Cormac softly. Standing, he took Anduine's hand and kissed the palm, then walked to the hearth where the sword of Culain stood by the far wall.

'I'll come with you,' Oleg said, gathering a carving-knife from the table and pushing himself to his feet.

'No,' said Cormac. 'Wait – and deal with any left alive.'

'You cannot defeat three men.'

Cormac ignored him and walked into the cold sunlight. He moved swiftly to the chopping-ring, laid his sword beside it and took up the axe. The six-pound blade hammered into a chunk of wood, splitting it neatly; he lifted another piece and carried on working. After several minutes he heard the hunters moving across the yard and turned. As Rhiannon had said, there were three men, tall and bearded, their hair braided beneath bronze helms.

Stooping, he lifted it, feeling the balance. Sheathing his own sword, the warrior faced Cormac.

'To be killed by your own blade . . . not a good way to die. The gods will mock you for eternity.'

Cormac's eyes narrowed, his rage returning, but he quelled it savagely. Hefting the axe, he launched a murderous swing and the Viking leapt back. But, halfway into the swing, Cormac released the haft and the axe flew from his hands, the six-pound head smashing into the Viking's face. The man stumbled back, dropping the sword, whereupon Cormac jumped forward, swept up the blade and hammered it into the Viking's chest. The man died without a sound. Dragging the sword clear, Cormac wiped it of blood and returned to the cabin.

'That was well done,' said Oleg. 'But you need to work on your grip; you held the sword too tightly.'

Cormac smiled. 'Next time I'll remember.'

'Next time it will not be so difficult, lad.'

'How so?'

'Next time the Hammerhand will be beside you. And then you will learn something.'

8

After many weeks of travel, Culain lach Feragh arrived at the ruined Stone Circle of Sorviodunum. At dawn, under a bright glowing sky, he approached the central altar and laid his silver staff upon it. The sun rose to bathe the monoliths in golden light, the staff shining like captured fire.

Culain closed his eyes and whispered three Words of Power. The air crackled around him, blue fire rippling over his cloak and tunic. Then the sky darkened and an emptiness smote him – a great, engulfing blackness that swallowed his soul.

He awoke feeling sick and dazed.

'You are a fool, Culain,' said a voice and he turned his head. His vision swam and his stomach heaved. 'No one should seek to pass the gateway without a Stone.'

'Still preaching, Pendarric?' he growled, forcing himself to a sitting position. He was lying in a soft bed, covered with sheets of silk. The sun blazed brightly in the violet sky beyond the arched window. His eyes cleared and he gazed at the broad-shouldered figure seated beside the bed.

'I rarely preach these days,' said the Atlantean king, a broad grin parting the square-cut golden beard. 'The more adventurous of my subjects have found various pursuits beyond the Mists, and those who remain are more interested in scholarly pursuits.'

'I have come for your help.'

'I did not doubt it,' said the King. 'When will you cease these games in the old world?'

'It is not a game – not to me.'

'That at least is welcome news. How is the boy?'

'Boy? Which boy?'

'Uther, the boy with the Sword.'

Culain smiled. 'The boy now has grey in his beard. They call him the Blood King, but he reigns wisely.'

'I thought that he would. And the child, Laitha?'

'Are you mocking me, Pendarric?'

The King's face became stern, the blue eyes cold. 'I mock no one, Culain – not even reckless adventurers like you and Maedhlyn who have ruined a world. What right have I to mock? I am the King who drowned Atlantis. I do not forget my past, and I condemn no one. Why do you ask?'

'You have not kept a watch on the old world?'

'Why should I? Goroien was the last danger and you disposed of her and her undead son. I don't doubt Maedhlyn is still meddling with kings and princes, but he is unlikely to destroy the world. And you? For all your recklessness, you are a man of honour.'

'Molech has returned,' said Culain.

'Nonsense! You beheaded him at Babel – the body was consumed by fire.'

'He is back.'

'Maedhlyn agrees with you on this?'

'I have not seen Maedhlyn in sixteen years. But believe me, the Devil has returned.'

'Let us walk in the garden – if you are strong enough. Some tales need to be told in bright sunlight.'

Culain eased himself from the bed and stood but dizziness swamped him. He took a deep breath and steadied himself.

'You will be weak for a day or so. Your body suffered terrible punishment in the journey and you were all but dead when you appeared.'

'I thought there would be sufficient power in the lance.'

'There might have been – for a younger man. Why is it, Culain, that you insist on growing old? What virtue is there in dying?'

'I want to be a man, Pendarric: to experience the passing of the seasons; to feel myself a part of the life of the world. I have had enough of immortality. As you said, I have helped to ruin a world. Gods, goddesses, demons, legends – each one contributing to a future of violence and discord. I want to grow old; I want to die.'

'The last, at least, is the truth,' said the King. He led Culain to a side door and then on down a short corridor, to a terraced garden. A young man brought them a tray of wine and fruit and the King sat on a curved seat by a bed of roses. Culain joined him.

'So, tell me of Molech.'

Culain told him of the vision in the monastery, and of the lightning bolt that seared his hand. He detailed the astonishing rise to power of the king, Wotan, and his conquests in Belgica, Raetia, Pannonia and Gaul. At last Culain sat back and sipped his wine, staring out over the gardens at the green hills beyond the city.

'You said nothing of Uther – or his lady,' said Pendarric.

Culain took a deep breath. 'I betrayed him. I became his wife's lover.'

'Did he kill her?'

'No. He would have, but we escaped to Gaul and she died there.'

'Oh, Culain . . . of all the men I have known, you are the last I would expect to betray a friend.'

'I offer no excuses.'

'I would hope not. So, then, Molech has returned. What is it you require of me?'

'As before – an army to destroy him.'

'I have no army, Culain. And if I did, I would not sanction a war.'

'You know of course that he desires to kill you? That he will attack Britain and use the Great Gate at Sorviodunum to invade the Feragh?'

'Of course I know,' snapped the King. 'But there is no more to be said about war. What will you do?'

'I shall find him – and . . . fight him.'

'For what purpose? The old Culain could have defeated him . . . did defeat him. But you are not the old Culain. What are you, in human terms – forty, fifty?'

'Somewhat more,' was the wry reply.

'Then leave him be, Culain, and return to your monastery. Study the mysteries. Live out your days – and your seasons.'

'I cannot,' Culain said simply.

For a while the two men sat in silence, then Pendarric laid his hand on Culain's shoulder. 'We will not talk again, my friend, so let

352

me say this: I respect you; I always have. You are a man of worth. I have never heard you blame another for your own mistakes, nor seek to curse fate, or the Source, for your misfortunes. That is rare . . . and a precious quality. I hope you find peace, Culain.'

'Peace . . . death . . . Perhaps they are the same,' whispered Culain.

Uther awoke in the night, his hand clawing at the air, the nightmare clinging to him in the sweat-dampened sheets. He threw them back and rolled from the bed. In his dreams dark holes had appeared in the walls of the castle, disgorging monsters with curved talons and dripping fangs, stinking of death and despair. He sucked in a deep breath and moved to the window; the battlements were deserted.

'Old men and children fear the dark,' whispered the Blood King, forcing a chuckle.

The breeze whispered along the castle walls and for a moment he thought he heard his name hissing softly in the night wind. He shivered. Calm yourself, Uther!

Then the sound came again, so low that he shut his eyes and craned his head towards the window. There it was . . .

'Uther . . . Uther . . . Uther . . .'

He pushed it from his mind as a trick of the night and returned to his bed. Glancing back at the window, he saw a flickering shape floating there.

In the moment that he identified it as a man, Uther reacted. His hand swept back to the Sword sheathed at the bedside and the blade flashed into the air. He leapt towards the window – and froze. Though the figure remained, it was wholly transparent and hung like trapped smoke against the moonlight.

'They are coming,' whispered the figure . . .

And vanished.

Confused and uncertain, Uther threw the Sword to the bed and wandered to the table by the far wall where stood a jug of wine and several goblets. As he reached for the jug he stumbled, his mind reeling. He fell to his knees, and only then saw the mist covering the floor of his room. His senses swam, but with one desperate heave he regained his feet and half-staggered, half-fell towards the bed. His hand scrabbled for the Swordhilt, closing around it just as the darkness seemed set to envelop him. The Sword of Power glowed like a lantern and the mist fled, snaking back to the wall and under the door. Naked, the King dragged open the door and stepped into the corridor beyond, where Gwalchmai slept on a narrow cot.

'Wake up, my friend,' said the King, nudging the sleeping man's shoulder. There was no response. He shook him harder. Nothing.

Fear touched the King and he moved slowly down the circular stair to the courtyard. Four sentries lay on the cobbles with their weapons beside them.

'Sweet Christos!' whispered Uther. 'The dream!'

A movement to his left and he whirled, the Sword slicing the air. The ghostly figure floated beside him once more – the face hooded, the figure blurred and indistinct.

'The Sword,' it whispered. 'He wants the Sword.'

'Who are you?'

Suddenly a hand of fire swept around the figure and the heat hurled the King from his feet. He landed on his shoulder and rolled. Dark shadows spread on the walls around him, black as caves, opening . . .

Uther ran to one of the sentries, dragging the man's sword from his scabbard. Then touching his own blade to the weapon, he closed his eyes in concentration. Fire blazed on the blades as the King staggered and stared down: in his hands were two Swords of Power, twins of shining silver steel.

The dark caves opened still further and the first of the beasts issued forth. Uther swung back the true blade and hurled it high into the air. Lightning blazed across the sky . . . and the Sword of Cunobelin disappeared.

The beast roared and stepped into the courtyard, its terrible jaws parted in a bestial snarl. Others crowded behind it, moving into the courtyard and forming a circle around the naked King. Men in dark cloaks came after them, grey blades in their hands.

'The sword,' called one of them. 'Give us the sword.'

'Come and take it,' said Uther.

The man gestured and a beast raced forward. Fully seven feet tall, it was armed with a black axe. Its eyes were blood-red, its fangs yellow and long. Most men would have stood frozen in terror, but Uther was not as most men.

He was the Blood King.

He leapt to meet the attack, ducking under the swinging axe, his sword ripping through the creature's scaled belly. A terrible scream tore aside the silence of the night and the other creatures howled in rage and pushed forward, but the dark-cloaked man ordered them back.

'Do not kill him!' he screamed and Uther stepped back, wondering at this change of heart. Then he glanced down at his sword to see that the beast's blood had stained the blade . . . and ended the illusion. Once more it was a simple gladius of iron, with a wooden hilt wrapped in oiled leather.

'Where is the Sword?' demanded the leader, his eyes betraying his fear.

'Where your master can lay no hand upon it,' answered Uther, smiling grimly.

'Damn your eyes!' screamed the man and he threw back his cloak and raised his sword of shimmering grey. The others followed his example. There were more than a dozen and Uther was determined to take a goodly number of them as company on the journey into Hell. They spread out around him . . . then rushed forward. Uther charged the circle, sweeping aside a frenzied thrust and burying his gladius in a man's heart. A cold blade pierced his back and he dragged the gladius clear and spun, his sword tearing through a warrior's neck. Two more blades hammered into him, filling his chest with icy pain, but even as he fell his sword lashed out and gashed open a man's face. Then numbness flowed through him and Death laid a skeletal finger on his soul. He felt himself floating upward and his eyes opened.

'Now you are ours,' hissed the leader, his cold grey eyes gleaming in triumph. Uther looked down at the body which lay at the man's feet; it was his own, and there was not a mark upon it. He watched as the attackers lifted their blades, and saw the swords swirl and disperse like mist in the morning breeze.

'Now you will learn the true meaning of agony,' said the leader. As he spoke the huge hand of fire appeared, engulfing the King's soul and vanishing into darkness. Leaving the body where it lay, the beasts and men returned to the shadows which closed behind them, becoming once more the grey stone of a silent fortress.

Galead, the blond knight who had been Ursus, prince of the House of Merovee, awoke in the chill of the dawn. The room was cool, the bed empty. He sat up and shivered, wondering if it was the cool breeze that prickled his skin or the memory of those ice-blue eyes . . .

For three weeks the embassy had been kept waiting in the city of Lugdunum, assured that the new King would see them at his earliest opportunity. Victorinus had accepted the delays with Roman patience, never giving public display to his increasing anger. The messages from Wotan had been delivered by a young Saxon called Agwaine, a tall warrior with yellow hair and a sneering manner.

The choice of Agwaine was a calculated insult, for the warrior was from the South Saxon, Uther's realm, and that made him a traitor in Victorinus' eyes.

But the Roman made good use of his enforced idleness, touring the city with Galead, listening to the talk in the taverns, watching the various regiments of Gothic warriors at maneouvres, gathering information that would aid Uther in the now inevitable war.

On their trip from the coast they had seen the massive triremes under construction and the barges that could land an army on the south coast, there to be swelled by dissenting Saxons and Jutes longing for a victory against the Blood King.

On the twenty-second day of their wait, Agwaine arrived in the hour just after dawn with a summons from Wotan. Victorinus thanked him courteously and dressed in a simple toga of white. Galead wore the leather breastplate, leggings and greaves of a *Cohors Equitana* commander, a gladius at his side; but over this was the

356

short white surplice of the herald, a simple red cross embroidered over the heart.

The two men were taken to the central palace and into a long hall, lined with lances on which severed heads were impaled.

Galead glanced at the rotting skulls, quelling his anger as he recognised one as Meroveus, the former King of the Merovingians. Swallowing hard, he marched slowly behind Victorinus towards the high throne on which sat the new God-King. Flanked by guards in silver armour Wotan sat and watched as the men approached, his eyes fixed on the white-clad Victorinus.

Reaching the foot of the dais, Victorinus bowed low.

'Greetings, my Lord King, from your brother across the water.'

'I have no brothers,' said Wotan, the voice rich and resonant. Galead gazed at him, awed by the power emanating from the man. The face was handsome and framed by a golden beard, the shoulders broad, the arms thick and powerful. He was dressed in the same silver armour as his guards and cloaked in black.

'My king,' said Victorinus smoothly, 'sends you a gift to celebrate your coronation.' He turned and two soldiers carried forward a square box of polished ebony. They knelt before the King and opened it. He leaned forward and lifted the silver helm from within. A gold circlet decorated the rim, the silver raven's wings were fixed to the sides as ear-guards.

'A pretty piece,' said Wotan, tossing it to a guard who set it down on the floor beside the throne. 'And now to the realities. I have given you three weeks to see the power of Wotan. You have used this time well, Victorinus, as befits a soldier of your rank and experience. Now go back to Britain and tell those in power that I will come to them, with gifts of my own.'

'My lord Uther . . .' began Victorinus.

'Uther is dead,' said Wotan, 'and you are in need of a king. Since there is no heir, and since my brother-Saxons have appealed to me for aid against your Roman tyranny, I have decided to accept their invitation to journey to Britannia and investigate their claims of injustice.'

'And will you journey with your army, my lord?' Victorinus asked.

'Do you think I will have need of it, Victorinus?'

'That, my lord, will depend on the King.'

'You doubt my word?' asked Wotan and Galead saw the guards tense, their hands edging towards their swords.

'No, sire. I merely point out – with respect – that Britain has a king. When one dies, another rises.'

'I have petitioned the Vicar of Christ in Rome,' said Wotan, 'and I have here a sealed parchment from him bestowing the kingdom of Britannia upon me, should I decide to accept it.'

'It could be argued that Rome no longer exercises sovereignty over the affairs of the west,' said Victorinus, 'but that is for others to debate. I am merely a soldier.'

'Your modesty is commendable, but you are far more than that. I would like you to serve me, Victorinus. Talented men are hard to find.'

Victorinus bowed. 'I thank you for the compliment. And now, with your leave, we must prepare for the journey home.'

'Of course,' said Wotan, rising. 'But first introduce your young companion; he intrigues me.'

'My Lord, this is Galead, a Knight of Uther.' Galead bowed and the King stepped down from the dais to stand before him. Galead swallowed hard and looked up into the ice-blue eyes.

'And what is your view, Knight of Uther?'

'I have no view, sire, only a sword. And when my King tells me to use it, I do so.'

'And if I was your King?'

'Ask me again, sire, when that day dawns.'

'It will dawn, Galead. Come the Spring, it will dawn. Tell me,' he said, smiling and raising his arms to point at the severed heads, 'what do you think of my ornaments?'

'I think they will attract flies, sire, when the Spring comes.'

'You recognised one of them, I think?'

Galead blinked. 'Indeed I did, sire, and your powers of observation are acute.' He pointed to the rotting head of Meroveus. 'I saw him once – when my father was visiting Gaul. It is the . . . former . . . King.'

'He could have served me. I find it strange that a man will prefer to depart this life in agony, rather than enjoy it in riches and pleasure. And for what? All men serve others . . . even kings. Tell me, Galead, what point is there in defying the inevitable?'

'I was always told, sire, that the only inevitability is death, and we do our best to defy that daily.'

'Even death is not inevitable for those who serve me well – nor is it a release for those who oppose me. Is that not true, Meroveus?'

The rotting head seemed to sag upon the lance, the mouth opening in a silent scream. 'You see,' said Wotan softly, 'the former King agrees. Tell me, Galead, do you desire me for an enemy?'

'Life, my lord, for a soldier, is rarely concerned with what he desires. As you so rightly say, all men are subject to the will of someone. For myself I would prefer no enemies, but life is not that simple.'

'Well said, soldier,' replied the King, turning and striding back to the throne.

The two men backed down the hall, then turned and walked in silence to their lodgings. Once there Victorinus slumped in a broad chair, head in hands.

'It may not be true,' said Galead.

'He did not lie; there would be no point. Uther is dead. Britain is dead.'

'You think Wotan will be King?'

'How do we stop him? Better that he is elected and the blood-letting minimised.'

'And you will suggest that course?'

'Do you have a better?'

As the younger man was about to answer he saw Victorinus' hand flicker, the fingers spreading and then closing swiftly into a fist. It was the scout's signal for silence in the presence of the enemy.

'No, sir, I think you are right,' he said.

Now, in the bright new morning, Galead rose and walked naked to the stream behind the lodgings. There he bathed in the cool waters that ran from the snow-covered mountains down into the valleys.

Refreshed, he returned to his room and dressed for the journey ahead. There were twelve men in the party, and they met to break their fast in the dining room of the inn. Victorinus, clothed once more as a warrior commander in bronze breastplate and bronze-studded leather kilt, sat in silence. The news of Uther's death had filtered to all the warriors, darkening their mood.

A young stable-boy entered and informed Victorinus that the horses were ready, and the group made their way to their mounts, riding from the city as the sun finally cleared the mountains. Victorinus waved Galead forward and the blond young warrior cantered his mount alongside the veteran.

The two men rode ahead of the following group, out of earshot, then Victorinus reined in and turned towards the young Merovingian.

'I want you to head for Belgica and take ship from there.'

'Why, sir?'

Victorinus sighed. 'Use your wits, young prince. Wotan may have been fooled by my words and the air of defeat I summoned. But he may not. Were I him, I would see that Victorinus did not reach the coast alive.'

'All the more reason to stick together,' said Galead.

'You think one sword can make the difference?' snapped the old general.

'No,' Galead admitted.

'I am sorry, my boy. I get irritated when people try to kill me. When you get back to Britain, find Prasamaccus – he's a wily old bird – and Gwalchmai. Both of them will offer sage counsel. I do not know who will have taken charge – perhaps Petronius, though he is ten years older than I. Or maybe Geminus Cato. I hope it is the latter; he at least understands war, and its nature. From the looks of the barges they will be ready to sail by the Spring, and that gives little time for adequate preparation. My guess is they will land near Anderida, but they may strike further north. Wotan will have allies at either end of the kingdom. Damn Uther to Hell! How could he die at a time like this?'

'And what will you do, sir?'

'I'll continue as expected – but I will leave the road come night-fall. Sweet Mithras, what I would not give for ten of the old legions! Did you see those Roman soldiers at Wotan's court?'

'Yes. Not impressive, were they?'

'No helmets or breastplates. I spoke to one of the young men and it seems the army voted to do away with them because they were so heavy! How did Rome ever rule the world?'

'A country is only as strong as its leaders allow it to be,' said Galead. 'The Goths could never have conquered without Wotan to bind them, and when he dies they will be sundered once more.'

'Then let us hope he dies soon,' said Victorinus. 'Once we are out of sight of the city, strike north – and may Hermes lend wings to your horse.'

'And may your gods bring you home, sir.'

Victorinus said nothing, but he removed his cloak and folded in across his saddle, a ritual all cavalry officers followed when riding into hostile territory.

'If I am not home by the Spring, Galead, light a lantern for me at the Altar of Mithras.'

Culain stood at the centre of the Stone Circle, his silver lance in his hand.

'Are you sure this is wise, my friend?' asked Pendarric.

Culain smiled. 'I was never wise, Lord King. A wise man understands the limits of his wisdom. But I believe it is my destiny to stand against the evil of Wotan. My swords may not be enough to sway the battle, but then again they may. Unless I try, I will never know.'

'I too will go against the dark one,' said Pendarric, 'but in my own way. Take this – I think you will have need of it.' Culain reached out and accepted a golden Stone the size of a sparrow's egg.

'I thank you, Pendarric. I do not think we will meet again.'

'In that you are correct, Lance Lord. May the Source of All Things be with you always.'

Pendarric raised his arms and spoke the Word of Power . . .

9

The city of Eboracum was in mourning when Revelation arrived at the south gate. The sentry, seeing the white-bearded stranger was a monk carrying no weapons, merely a long wooden quarterstaff, stepped aside and waved him through.

'Is the King in residence?' asked Revelation.

'You have not heard?' said the sentry, a young militia-man bearing only a lance.

'I have been on the road for three days. I have seen no one.'

'The King is dead,' said the sentry. 'Slain by sorcery.'

Other travellers waited behind Revelation and the guard waved him on. He moved under the gate tower and on into the narrow streets, his mind whirling with memories: the young Uther, tall and strong in the Caledones, the Blood King leading the charge against the enemy, the boy and the man so full of life. Revelation felt a terrible sadness swelling within him. He had come here to make his peace with the man he betrayed, to seek forgiveness.

He moved through the town like a dreamer, not seeing the shops and stores and market stalls, heading for the Royal Keep where two sentries stood guard, both in ceremonial black coats and dark-plumed helms.

Their lances crossed before him, barring the way.

'None may enter today,' said a guard softly. 'Come back tomorrow.'

'I need to speak to Victorinus,' said Revelation.

'He is not here. Come back tomorrow.'

'Then Gwalchmai or Prasamaccus.'

'Are you hard of hearing, old man? Tomorrow, I said.'

Revelation's staff swept up, brushing the lances aside. The men jumped forward to overpower him, but the staff cracked against the first man's skull, bowling him from his feet, then it hammered into

362

the second man's groin, doubling him over, where a second blow took him at the base of the neck.

Revelation walked on into the courtyard. Groups of men were sitting idly by, their faces set and their misery apparent.

'You!' said Revelation, pointing at a warrior sitting on a well wall. 'Where is Gwalchmai?' The man looked up and gestured to the north tower. Revelation mounted the steps and made his way up the circular stairwell to the King's apartments. There, on a bed covered with white linen, lay the body of Uther dressed in full armour and plumed helm. Beside the bed, holding the King's hand, was Gwalchmai, the Hound of the King. Tears stained his cheeks and his eyes were red-rimmed.

He did not hear Revelation approach, nor did he react when the man's hand touched his shoulder, but at the sound of the voice he jerked as if stung and leapt to his feet.

'How did it happen, Gwal?'

'You!' Gwalchmai's hand flew to his side, but there was no sword. The eyes blazed. 'How dare you come here?'

Revelation ignored him and moved to the bed. 'I asked how it happened,' he whispered.

'What difference does it make? It happened. A sorcerous mist filled the castle and all fell into a deep sleep. When we awoke, the King was lying dead in the courtyard beside the body of a scaled beast. And the Sword was gone.'

'How long ago?'

'Three days.'

Revelation lifted the King's hand. 'Then why no sign of stiffening?' He slid his fingers to the King's wrist and waited. There was no pulse, yet the flesh was warm to the touch.

From the pocket of his robe he produced Pendarric's Stone, which he touched to the King's brow. There was no discernible movement, but the pulse point under his fingers trembled.

'He is alive,' said Revelation.

'No!'

'See for yourself, man.' Gwalchmai moved to the other side of the bed and pressed his fingers to the King's throat, just under the jawline. His eyes brightened, but the gleam died.

'Is this more sorcery, Culain?'

'No, I promise you.'

'Of what worth are the promises of an Oath breaker?'

'Then you must judge, Gwalchmai. There is no stiffness in the body, the blood has not fallen back from the face and the eyes are not sunken. How do you read his condition?'

'But there is no breath, there is no heartbeat,' said the Cantii tribesman.

'He is at the point of death, but he has not yet passed the Dark River.'

Revelation put both hands to the King's face.

'What are you doing?' asked Gwalchmai.

'Be silent,' ordered Revelation, closing his eyes. His mind drifted, linking with Uther, drawing on the power of the Stone he carried.

Darkness, despair and a tunnel of black stone . . . A beast . . . Many beasts . . . a figure, tall and strong . . .

Revelation screamed and was hurled back across the room – the front of his habit ripped, blood welling from the talon tears on his chest. Gwalchmai stood transfixed as Revelation slowly rose to his feet.

'Sweet Mithras,' whispered Gwalchmai. Revelation took the Stone and held it to his chest and the wounds sealed instantly.

'They have Uther's soul,' he said.

'Who?'

'The enemy, Gwalchmai: Wotan.'

'We must rescue him.'

Revelation shook his head. 'That would take a power beyond mine. All we can do is protect the body. While it lives there is hope.'

'A body without a soul – what good is it?'

'The flesh and the spirit are linked, Gwalchmai, each drawing on the strength of the other. Wotan will know now that the body lives and he will seek to destroy it; that is a certainty. What is puzzling, however, is why the soul was taken. I can understand Wotan's desire to kill Uther, but not this.'

'I care nothing for his motives,' hissed Gwalchmai, 'but he will die for this. I swear it.'

'I fear he is too powerful for you,' said Revelation. He walked to the far wall and traced a line along it with the golden Stone, past the door, on to the north wall and on around the room until he reached his starting point. 'Now we shall see,' he said.

'Why have you come back?'

'I thought I had come to ask Uther to forgive me. But now I think the Source guided me here to protect the King.'

'Had he been . . . alive . . . he would have killed you.'

'Perhaps. Perhaps not. Fetch your weapons, Gwal, and armour. You will need them soon.'

Without a word Gwalchmai left the room and Revelation pulled up a chair and sat beside the bed. Why had the King been taken? Molech would not idly waste such power merely to torment an enemy. And the power drain on his Sipstrassi Stones would be enormous for such a venture. He had to believe there was something to gain; something worth the loss of magic. And the body – why leave it alive?

Revelation gazed down at the King. The armour was embossed with gold, the helm bearing the crown of Britain and the eagle of Rome, the breastplate fashioned after the Greek style and embossed with the symbol of the Bear. The brass-studded kilt was worn over leather leggings and thigh-high boots, reinforced with copper to protect the knees of the horsemen in the crashing together of mounts during a charge. The scabbard was jewel-encrusted, a gift from a rich merchant in Noviomagus, and made to house the Great Sword of Cunobelin.

It was a sickening thought that the Sword of Power was now in Wotan's hands. For once it had been Culain's, and he had watched it being fashioned from pure Silver Sipstrassi, the rarest form of the magical Stone – a hundred times more powerful than the gold pebble Culain now carried. Without the Sword Wotan was powerful enough – but with it, could any power on earth stand against him?

The door opened and Gwalchmai entered, in full armour and wearing two short swords scabbarded at the hips. Behind him came Prasamaccus, bearing his curved cavalry bow and a quiver of arrows.

'It is good to see you again,' said Revelation. Prasamaccus nodded and limped into the room, laying the bow and quiver by the wall.

'Somehow,' said the old Brigante, 'I did not think the fall from the cliff would kill you. But when you failed to reappear . . .'

'I travelled to Mauretania on the African coast.'

'And the Queen?'

'She stayed in Belgica. She died there some years ago.'

'It was all a terrible folly,' said Prasamaccus. He held out his hand to Revelation, who took it gratefully.

'You do not hate me then?'

'I never hated anyone in all my life. And if I were to begin, it would not be with you, Culain. I was there the first night when Uther made love to Laitha; it was in the land of the Pinrae. Later I saw the prince, as he then was, and he told me that during the love-making – when his emotions were at their highest point – Laitha whispered your name. He never forgot it . . . it ate at him like a cancer. He was not a bad man, you understand, and he tried to forgive her. The trouble is that if you can't forget, you can't forgive. I am sorry the Queen is dead.'

'I have missed you both during the years,' said Revelation. 'And Victorinus. Where is he?'

'Uther sent him to Gallia to discuss treaties with Wotan,' said Gwalchmai. 'There has been no word in a month.'

Revelation said nothing and Prasamaccus pulled up a chair and sat down beside the bed. 'When will they come?' he asked.

'Tonight, I think. Perhaps tomorrow.'

'How will they know the body lives?'

'I tried to reach Uther's soul. Wotan was there and one of the beasts attacked me. Wotan will know I traced the thread of Uther's life and they will follow it back.'

'Can we stop them?' asked the Brigante softly.

'We can try. Tell me everything of how the King was found.'

'He was lying in the courtyard,' said Gwalchmai. 'There was a nightmare beast beside him, gutted and dead, and rotting at a rate you would not believe. By nightfall, only the bones and the stench remained.'

'That is all that was there? Just a dead beast and the King?'

'Yes . . . no . . . There was a gladius by the body; it belonged to one of the guards.'

'A gladius? Did the guard drop it there?'

'I do not know. I'll find out.'

'Do it now, Gwal.'

'How important can it be?'

'If the King was using it, then believe me it is important.'

Once Gwalchmai had gone, Prasamaccus and Revelation walked together on the circular battlement around the north tower, staring out over the hills surrounding Eboracum.

'The land is so green and beautiful,' said Revelation. 'I wonder will it ever know a time without war?'

'Not so long as men dwell here,' replied Prasamaccus, pausing to rest his lame leg by sitting on the battlement wall. The wind was chill and he drew his green cloak around his slender frame. 'I thought you immortals never aged,' he said.

Revelation shrugged. 'All things have their seasons. How is Helga?'

'She died. I miss her.'

'Do you have children?'

'We had a boy and a girl. The boy died of the red plague when he was three, but my daughter survived. She is a handsome lass; she is pregnant now, and hoping for a boy-child.'

'Are you happy, Prasamaccus?'

'I am alive . . . and the sun shines. I have no complaints, Culain. You?'

'I think that I am content. Tell me, has there been any word of Maedhlyn?'

'No. He and Uther parted company some years ago. I do not know the rights and wrongs of it, but it began when Maedhlyn said his magic could not discover where you hid with Laitha. Uther believed it was his loyalty to you that prevented him giving aid.'

'It was not,' said Revelation. 'I used my stone to shield us.'

Prasamaccus smiled. 'I am sorry about the hound. I wished we had never discovered you. But Uther was my King, and my friend. I could not betray him.'

367

'I bear no ill-will, my friend. I just wish you had searched a little harder after we leapt from the cliff.'

'Why so?'

'Uther's son was waiting in the cave. Laitha bore the child there and it survived.'

The colour drained from the old Brigante's face. 'A son? Are you sure it was Uther's?'

'Without the slightest doubt. He was raised among the Saxons – they found him by the hound and her pups and they called him Daemonsson. Once you see him, there will be no doubt in your mind. He is the image of Uther.'

'We should fetch him here. He should be the new King.'

'No,' said Revelation sharply. 'He is not ready. Say nothing of this to Gwal or any other man. When the time is right, Uther himself will acknowledge him.'

'If the King lives,' whispered Prasamaccus.

'We are here to see that he does.'

'Two elderly warriors and an immortal seeking to die? Not the most awe-inspiring force to be mustered in this Land of Mist!'

Gwalchmai returned just as the sun was setting and Revelation and Prasamaccus joined him in the King's apartments.

'Well?' asked Revelation.

The white-haired Cantii shrugged. 'The guard said that when the mist struck, his sword was in its scabbard, but when he awoke it was beside the King. What of it?'

Revelation smiled. 'It means that Uther killed the beast with the guard's gladius. What does that suggest to you?'

Gwalchmai's eyes brightened. 'He did not have his Sword.'

'Exactly. He knew what they had come for and hid the blade where they could not find it. Therefore they took him alive . . . for torture.'

'Can you torture a soul?' asked Prasamaccus.

'Better than you can a body,' Revelation answered. 'Think of the inner pain you have suffered over the death of a loved one – is it not greater than any physical wound?'

368

'What can we do, Culain?' whispered Gwalchmai, his gaze resting on the still body of the King he had served for a quarter of a century.

'First we must protect the body, secondly find the Sword of Power.'

'It could be anywhere,' said Prasamaccus.

'Worse,' admitted Revelation, 'it could be *anything*.'

'I do not understand you,' the Cantii said. 'It is a sword.'

'It is fashioned from Silver Sipstrassi, the most potent source of power known to the ancient world. We built the Gateways with its power, fashioned the standing stones, created the old straight tracks your people still use. With it we left the Ancient Paths, stretching across many kingdoms, joining many sites of earth magic. If Uther wished, the Sword could become a pebble, or a tree, or a lance, or a flower.'

'Then for what do we search?' asked Prasamaccus. 'Can we send Uther's knights across the land in search of a flower?'

'Wherever it is, the Magic of the Sword will become apparent. Let us say it is a flower: in that region plants will grow as never before, crops will flower early and sickness will disappear. The knights must search for such signs.'

'If it is in Britannia,' said Gwalchmai.

'If it was easy to find, then Wotan would take it,' snapped Revelation. 'But think on this: When Uther was in peril, he had at best only moments to hide the Sword. Knowing the King as you both do, where do you think he would send it?'

Prasamaccus shrugged. 'The Caledones, perhaps, where he first met you and Laitha. Or the Pinrae, where he defeated the army of Goroien. Or Camulodunum.'

'All places Wotan will search, for the King's story is well known. Uther would not make it so easy,' said Revelation. 'Sweet Christos!'

'What?' asked Gwalchmai.

'There are two people in the Caledones that Wotan must not find. And I cannot reach them; I cannot leave here.' He rose from his seat, his face grey, his eyes haunted. Prasamaccus laid a gentle hand on his shoulder.

369

'The boy you spoke of?' Revelation nodded.

'And now you must choose between . . .' Prasamaccus left the sentence unfinished. He knew the torment raging inside him. Save the father or the son. Or, as Culain would see it, betray one to save the other.

Behind him Gwalchmai lit the lanterns and drew the first of his swords, which he honed with an old whetstone. Revelation took up his staff and closed his eyes. The brown woollen habit disappeared, to be replaced by the black and silver armour of Culain lach Feragh. The grey beard vanished and the hair on his head darkened. The staff became silver and Culain twisted the haft, producing two short swords of glistening silver.

'You have made your decision then?' whispered Prasamaccus.

'I have, may God forgive me,' said the Lance Lord.

The Spring was beautiful in the Caledones, the mountains ablaze with colour, the swollen streams glittering in the sunlight, the woods and forests filled with birdsong. Cormac had never been happier. Oleg and Rhiannon had found and renovated the old cabin higher in the mountains, leaving Anduine and Cormac to the solitude needed by young lovers. On most mornings Oleg would join Cormac on his training runs, and teach him the more subtle skills of sword-play. But once the sun passed noon Oleg would journey back to his cabin. Of Rhiannon Cormac saw little, but enough to know she was unhappy. She had not believed her father concerning Wotan, and was convinced he had prevented her from becoming a Queen over the Goths. Now she stayed in the high country, wandering the hills, seeking her own inner peace.

But thoughts of Rhiannon rarely entered Cormac's head. He was alive, surrounded by beauty and in love.

'Are you happy?' Anduine asked him, as they sat naked by the lake in the afternoon sunshine.

'How could I not be?' he countered, stroking her cheek and leaning in to kiss her softly on the mouth. Her arm looped around his neck, pulling him down until he could feel her soft breasts pressing against the skin of his chest. His hand slid down her hips,

370

and he marvelled anew at the silky softness of her skin. Then he drew back from her.

'What is wrong?' she asked.

'Nothing,' he replied, chuckling, 'I just wanted to look at you.'

'Tell me what you see?'

'What can I tell you, my lady?'

'You could flatter me mercilessly. Tell me I am beautiful – the most beautiful woman who ever lived.'

'You are the most beautiful I have ever seen. Will that suffice?'

'And do you love me only for my beauty, young sir? Or is it because I am a princess?'

'I am the son of a king,' said Cormac. 'Is that why you love me?'

'No,' she whispered. 'I love you for what you are as a man.'

They made love once more, this time slowly and without passion. At last they moved apart and Cormac kissed her softly on the brow. He saw the tears in her eyes and pulled her to him.

'What is the matter?'

She shook her head, turning away from him.

'Tell me . . . please.'

'Each time that we are together like this, I fear it is the last. And one day it will be.'

'No!' he said. 'We will always be together. Nothing will separate us.'

'Always?'

'Until the stars fall from the sky,' he promised her.

'Only until then?'

'Only until then, lady. After that, I might need someone younger!'

She smiled and sat up, reaching for her dress. He passed it to her, then gathered his own clothes and the sword he had worn since the attack.

'Give me your eyes, Cormac,' she asked.

He leaned towards her, allowing her hand to touch his closed eyelids. Darkness descended, but this time there was no panic.

'I'll race you home,' she shouted, and he heard her running steps. He grinned and walked forward six paces to the round rock, his hand feeling for the niche that pointed south. Lining himself with the niche, he began to run, counting the steps. At thirty he slowed and carefully inched forward to the lightning-struck pine, whose upper branch pointed down towards the cabin and the straight run into the clearing.

As he reached it he heard Anduine scream, a sound that lanced his heart and filled him with a terrible fear.

'Anduine!' he yelled, his torment echoing in the mountains. He blundered on, sword in hand, not noticing that he had left the path until he tripped over a jutting root. As he fell awkwardly, the sword slipped from his grasp and his fingers scrabbled across the grass, seeking the hilt.

He fought for calm and concentrated on the sounds around him, his fingers still questing. At last he found the blade and stood. The incline of the hill was to his left, so he slowly turned right and followed the hill downwards, his left hand stretched out before him. The ground levelled and he could smell the wood-smoke from the cabin chimney.

'Anduine!'

A movement to his right, heavy and slow. 'Who's there!'

There was no answer, but the sound increased as hurried steps moved towards him. Cormac waited until the last second, then swung the sword in a whistling arc; the blade hammered into the attacker and then slid clear. More sounds came to Cormac then – angry voices, shuffling feet. Gripping his sword double-handed, he held it before him.

A sudden movement to his left – and a hideous pain in his side. He twisted and slashed out with his sword, missing his attacker.

By the wall of the cabin, Anduine regained consciousness to find herself being held tightly by a bearded man. Her eyes opened and she saw Cormac, blind and alone within a circle of armed men.

'No!' she screamed, closing her eyes and returning his gift.

Cormac's vision returned just as a second attacker moved silently forward. The man was grinning. Cormac blocked a blow, then sent his own blade slicing through the Viking's throat. The remaining seven charged in and Cormac had no chance, but as he fell he

372

hacked and cut at the enemy. A sword-blade pierced his back, another tore a gaping wound in his chest.

Anduine screamed and touched her hand to her captor's chest. The man's tunic burst into flames that seared up to cover his face. Bellowing in pain he released her, his hands beating around his beard as the fire caught in his hair.

She fell, then stood and ran at the group surrounding Cormac, her hands blazing with white fire. A Viking warrior moved towards her with sword raised, but flames lanced from her hands, engulfing him. A second warrior hurled a knife that slammed into her chest. She faltered, staggered but still came on, desperate to reach Cormac. From behind her another warrior moved in, his blade piercing her back and exiting at her chest. Blood bubbled from her mouth and she sank to the ground.

Cormac tried to crawl to her, but a sword plunged into his back and darkness swept over him.

From the hill above, Oleg Hammerhand roared in anger. The Vikings turned as he raced into the clearing with two swords in his hands.

'I see you, Maggrin,' shouted Oleg.

'I see you, traitor,' hissed a dark-bearded warrior.

'Don't kill him!' yelled Rhiannon from the cabin doorway.

Oleg and Maggrin rushed at each other, their blades crashing, sparks flying from the contact. Oleg spun on his heel and rammed his second sword like a dagger into the man's belly. As Maggrin fell, the four survivors attacked in a group. Oleg ran to meet them, blocking and cutting with a savage frenzy they could not match. One by one they fell before the cold-eyed warrior and his terrible blades. The last survivor broke into a run to escape his doom, but Oleg hurled a sword after him which hit him hilt-first on the back of the head and he fell. Before he could rise, the Hammerhand had reached him and his head rolled from his shoulders.

Oleg stood in the clearing, his lungs heaving, the berserk rage dispelling. Finally he turned to Rhiannon.

Traitress!' he said. 'Of all the acts you could have committed to bring me shame, this was the worst. Two people risked their lives to save you . . . and paid for it with their own. Get out of my sight! Go!'

'You don't understand!' she shouted. 'I didn't want this to happen; I just wanted to get away.'

'You called them there. This is your work. Now go! If I see you after this day, I will kill you with my bare hands. GO!'

She ran to him. 'Father, please!' His huge hand lashed across her face, spinning her from her feet.

'I do not know you! You are dead,' he said. She struggled to stand, then backed away from the ice in his eyes and ran away down the hillside.

Oleg moved first to Anduine, pulling the sword clear from her back.

'You will never know, lady, the depth of my sorrow. May God grant you peace.' He closed her eyes and walked to where Cormac lay in a spreading pool of blood.

'You fought well, boy,' he said, kneeling. Cormac groaned. Oleg lifted him and carried him into the cabin where, stripping the youth's blood-drenched clothes, he checked his wounds. Two in the back, one in the side, one in the chest. All were deep and each one could see a man dead, Oleg knew. But all of them? Cormac had no chance.

Knowing it was useless, yet Oleg gathered needle and thread and stitched the wounds. When they were sealed, he covered Cormac with a blanket and built up the fire. Then with candles lit and the cabin warm, Oleg returned to the bed. Cormac's pulse fluttered weakly and his colour was bad – grey streaks on his face, purple rings below his eyes.

'You lost too much blood, Cormac,' whispered Oleg. 'Your heart is straining . . . and I can do nothing! Fight it, man. Every day will see you stronger.' Cormac's head sagged sideways, his breath rattling in his throat. Oleg had heard that sound before. 'Don't you die, you whoreson!'

All breathing ceased but Oleg pushed his hand hard down on Cormac's chest. 'Breathe, damn you!' Something hot burned into Oleg's palm and he lifted his hand. The Stone on the chain around

Cormac's neck was glowing like burning gold and a shuddering breath filled the wounded man's lungs.

'Praise be to all the gods there ever were,' said Oleg. Placing his hand once more on the Stone, he stared down at the wound in Cormac's chest. 'Can you heal that?' he asked. Nothing happened. 'Well, keep him alive anyway,' he whispered.

Then he rose and took a shovel from the back of the cabin. The ground would still be hard, but Oleg owed this at least to Anduine, the Life Giver, the Princess from Raetia.

10

As the night wore on, Gwalchmai slept lightly on his chair at the bedside, his head resting on the wall. Prasamaccus and Culain sat silently. The Brigante was recalling his first meeting with the Lance Lord, high in the Caledones when the dark-cloaked Vampyres sought their blood and the young prince escaped through the gateway to the land of the Pinrae. The boy, Thuro – as he then was – became the man Uther in a savage war against the Witch Queen. He and Laitha had wed there and she had brought him the gift of the Sword; two young people ablaze with the power of youth, the confidence that death was an eternity away. Now, after a mere twenty-six summers, the Blood King lay still, Gian Avur – the beautiful Laitha – was gone, and the kingdom Uther had saved faced destruction by a terrible foe. The words of the Druids echoed through Prasamaccus' mind.

'For such are the works of man that they are written upon the air in mist, and vanish in the winds of history.'

Culain was lost in thoughts of the present. Why had they not slain the King once his soul was in their possession? For all his evil, Molech was a man of great intellect. News of Uther's death would demoralise the kingdom, making his invasion plans more certain of success. He worried at the problem from every angle.

Wotan's sorcerer priests had come to kill the King and take the Sword. But the Sword was gone. Therefore they took Uther's soul. Perhaps they thought – not without justification – that the body would die.

Culain pushed the problem from his mind. Whatever the reason, it was a mistake and the Lance Lord prayed it would be a costly one. Though he did not know it, it had proved more than costly to the priest who made it, for his body now hung on a Raetian battlement – his skin flayed, crows feasting on his eyes.

A glowing ball of white fire appeared in the centre of the room and Prasamaccus notched an arrow to his bow. Culain stretched his sword across the bed and touched Gwalchmai's shoulder. The sleeper awakened instantly. Taking the golden stone, Culain touched it to both of Gwalchmai's blades, then moved to Prasamaccus and emptied his quiver, running the stone over each of the twenty arrow-heads. The glowing ball collapsed upon itself and a grey mist rolled out across the room. Culain waited, then lifted the Stone and spoke a single Word of Power. A golden light pulsed from him, surrounding the two warriors and the body of the King. The mist filled the room . . . and vanished. A dark shadow appeared on the far wall, deepening, spreading until it became the mouth of a cave. A cold breeze blew from the opening, causing the lanterns to gutter. Moonlight streamed through the open windows, and in that silver light Gwalchmai saw a beast from the Pit emerge from the cave. Scaled and horned, with long curved fangs, it pushed out into the room. But as it touched the lines of magic Culain had laid, lightning seared its grey body and flames engulfed it. It fell back into the cave, hissing in pain.

Three men leapt into the room. The first fell with an arrow in his throat. Culain and Gwalchmai darted forward and, within moments, the other assassins both lay dead upon the floor.

The two warriors waited with swords raised, but the cave-mouth shrank to become a shadow and faded from sight.

Gwalchmai pushed the toe of his boot at a fallen assassin, turning the body to its back. The flesh of the face had decomposed and only a rotting corpse lay there. The old Cantii warrior recoiled from the sight. 'We fought dead men!' he whispered.

'It is Wotan's way of gaining loyalty. The bravest of his warriors are untouched by death . . . or so they believe.'

'Well, we beat them,' said Gwalchmai.

'They will return, and we will not be able to hold them. We must take the King to a place of safety.'

'And where is safe from the sorcery of Wotan?' asked Prasamaccus.

'The Isle of Crystal,' Culain answered.

'We cannot carry the King's body halfway across the realm,' argued Gwalchmai. 'And even if we could, the Holy Place would not accept him. He is a warrior – they will have no dealings with those who spill blood.'

'They will take him,' said Culain softly. 'It is, in part, their mission.'

'You have been there?'

Culain smiled. 'I planted the staff that became a tree. But that is another story from another time. Nowhere on land is the earth magic more powerful, nor the symbols more obscure. Wotan cannot bring his demons to the Isle of Crystal. And if he journeys there himself it will be as a man, stripped of all majesty of magic. He would not dare.'

Gwalchmai stood and looked down at the seemingly lifeless body of Uther. 'The question is irrelevant. We cannot carry him across the land.'

'I can, for I will travel the Ancient Paths, the *lung mei*, the way of the spirits.'

'And what of Prasamaccus and me?'

'You have already been of service to your King and you can do no more for him directly. But Wotan's army will soon be upon you. It is not my place to suggest your actions, but my advice would be to rally as many men to Uther's banner as you can. Tell them the King lives and will return to lead them on the day of Ragnorak.'

'And what day is that?' Prasamaccus asked.

'The day of greatest despair,' whispered Culain. He stood and walked to the western wall. Here he knelt, Stone in hand, and in the near silence that followed both men heard the whispering of a deep river, the lapping of waves on unseen shores. The wall shimmered and opened:

'Swiftly now!' said Culain, and Gwalchmai and Prasamaccus lifted the heavy body of the Blood King and carried it to the new entrance. Steps had appeared, leading down into a cavern and a deep, dark river. A boat was moored by a stone jetty; gently the two Britons lowered the king into it. Culain untied the mooring-rope and stepped to the stern.

As the craft slid away, Culain turned. 'Get back to the turret as swiftly as you can. If the gateway closes, you'll be dead within the hour.'

As swiftly as the limping Prasamaccus could move, the two men mounted the stairs. Behind them they could hear weird murmurings and the scrabbling sounds of talons on stone. As they neared the gateway Gwalchmai saw it shimmer. Seizing Prasamaccus, he hurled him forward and then dived after him, rolling to his knees on the rugs of Uther's room.

Behind them now was merely a wall, bathed in the golden light of the sun rising above the eastern hills and shining through the open window.

Victorinus and the twelve men of his party rode warily but without incident during the first three days of their journey. But on the fourth, as they approached a thick wood with a narrow path, Victorinus reined in his mount.

His second aide, Marcus Bassicus – a young man of good Romano-British stock – rode alongside.

'Is anything wrong, sir?'

The sun above them was bright, the pathway into the woods shrouded by the overhanging trees. Victorinus took a deep breath, aware of the presence of fear. Suddenly he smiled.

'Have you enjoyed life, Marcus?'

'Yes, sir.'

'Have you lived it to the full?'

'I think so, sir. Why do you ask?'

'It is my belief that death waits, hidden in those trees. There is no glory there – no prospect of victory. Just pain and darkness and an end to joy.'

The young man's face became set, his grey eyes narrowed. 'And what should we do, sir?'

'You and the others must make your choice but I must enter those woods. Speak to the men, explain to them that we are betrayed. Tell them that any who wish to flee may do so, without shame; it is no act of cowardice.'

379

'Then why must you ride on, sir?'

'Because Wotan will be watching and I want him to know that I do not fear his treachery – that I welcome it. I want him to understand the nature of the foe. He has conquered Belgica, Raetia and Gaul and has the Romans on bended knees before him. Britannia will not be as these others.'

Marcus rode back to the waiting men, leaving the general staring at the entrance to his own grave. Victorinus lifted the round cavalry shield from the back of his saddle and settled it on his left arm. Then looping the reins of his war-horse around the saddle-pommel, he drew his sabre and without a backward glance touched his heels to his mount and loved on. Behind him the twelve soldiers took up their shields and sabres and rode after him.

Within a clearing, just inside the line of trees, two hundred Goths drew their weapons and waited.

'You say the King is alive,' said Geminus Cato, pushing the maps across the table and rising to pour a goblet of mixed wine and water. 'But you will forgive my cynicism, I hope?'

Gwalchmai shrugged and turned from the window. 'I can offer you only my word, general. But it has been considered worth respecting.'

Cato smiled and smoothed the close-cropped black beard which shone like an oiled pelt. 'Allow me to review the facts that are known. A tall man, dressed in the robes of a Christian, assaulted two guards and made his way unobstructed to the King's Tower. This man, you say, is the legendary Lancelot. He declared the body to be alive and used sorcery to remove it from the tower.'

'In essence that is true,' Gwalchmai admitted.

'But is he not also the King's sworn enemy? The Great Betrayer?'

'He is.'

'Then why did you believe him?'

Gwalchmai looked to Prasamaccus, who was sitting quietly at the table. The crippled Brigante cleared his throat.

'With the utmost respect, general, you never knew the Lance Lord. Put from your mind the interminable stories regarding his treachery. What did he do? He slept with a woman. Which of us has not? He alone saved the King when the traitors slew Uther's father. He alone journeyed to the Witch Queen's castle and killed the Lord of the Undead. He is more than a warrior of legend. And his word, on this matter, I believe utterly.'

Cato shook his head. 'But you also believe the man is thousands of years old, a demigod whose kingdom is under the great western sea.'

Prasamaccus swallowed the angry retort that welled within. Geminus Cato was more than a capable general; he was a skilled and canny soldier, respected by his men, though not loved and – with the exception of Victorinus – the only man capable of fielding a force against the Goths. But he was also of pure Roman stock, and had little understanding of the ways of the Celts or the lore of magic that formed their culture. Prasamaccus considered his next words with care.

'General, let us put aside for a moment the history of Culain lach Feragh. Wotan has tried – perhaps successfully – to assassinate the King. His next move will be to invade and when he does so he will not find himself short of allies – once it is known that Uther will not stand against them. Culain has given us time to plan. If we spread the word that the King lives – and will return – it will give the Saxons, Jutes and Angles a problem to consider. They have heard of the might of Wotan, but they *know* the perils of facing the Blood King.'

Cato's dark eyes fixed on Prasamaccus and for several minutes the silence endured, then the general returned to his seat.

'Very well, Horse-Master. Tactically I accept that it is better for Uther to be alive than dead. I shall see that the story is disseminated. But I can spare no knights to seek the Sword. Every officer of worth is out scouring the countryside for volunteers and all militia-men are being recalled.' He pulled the maps towards him and pointed to the largest, the land survey commissioned by Ptolemy hundreds of years before. 'You have both travelled the land extensively. It is not difficult to imagine where Wotan will land in the south, but he has several armies. Were I in his place I would be

381

looking for a double assault, perhaps even a triple. We do not have the numbers to cover the country. So where will he strike?'

Gwalchmai gazed down on the map of the land then called Albion. 'The Sea Wolves have always favoured the coastline here,' he said, stabbing his finger to the Humber, 'at Petvaria. If Wotan follows this course he will be below Eboracum, cutting us off from our forces in the south.'

Cato nodded. 'And if the Brigantes and Trinovantes rise to support him, the whole of Britain will be sliced into three war zones: from the wall of Hadrian to Eboracum, from Eboracum to Petvaria – or even Durobrivae, if they sail in by the Wash – and from there to Anderida or Dubris.

'At best we can raise another ten thousand warriors, bringing our total mobile force to twenty-five thousand. Rumours tell us that Wotan can muster five times as many men, and that is not to count the Saxon rebels or the Brigante in the north. What I would not give for Victorinus to return with reliable intelligence!' He looked up from the map. 'Gwalchmai, I want you to journey to Gaius Geminus in Dubris . . .'

'I cannot, general,' said Gwalchmai.

'Why?'

'I must seek the Sword.'

'This is no time for chasing shadows, seeking dreams.'

'Perhaps,' admitted the old Cantii warrior, 'yet still I must.'

Cato leaned back and folded his brawny arms across his leather breastplate. 'And where will you seek it?'

'In Camulodunum. When the King was a boy, he loved the hills and woods around the city. There were special places he would run to and hide from his father. I know those places.'

'And you?' said Cato, turning.

Prasamaccus smiled. 'I shall journey to the Caledones mountains. It was there he met his one love.'

Cato chuckled and shook his head. 'You Celts have always been a mystery to me, but I have learned never to argue with a British dreamer. I wish you luck on your quest. What will you do if you find the Blade?'

Gwalchmai shrugged and looked to Prasamaccus. The Brigante's pale eyes met the Roman's gaze. 'We will carry it to the Isle of Crystal, where the King lies.'

'And then?'

'I do not know, general.'

Cato was silent for a while, lost in thought. 'When I was a young man,' he said at last. 'I was stationed at Aquae Sulis, and often I would ride the country near the Isle. We were not allowed there, on orders from the King, but once – because it was forbidden – three officers and I took a boat across the lakes and landed by the highest hill. It was an adventure, you see, and we were young. We built a fire and sat laughing and talking. Then we slept. I had a dream there, that my father came to me and we spoke of many things. Mostly he talked of regret, for we had never been close after my mother died. It was a fine dream and we embraced; he wished me well, and spoke of his pride. The following morning I awoke refreshed. A mist was all about us, and we sailed back to where our horses were hobbled and rode to Aquae Sulis. We were immediately in trouble, for we had returned without our swords. None of us could remember removing them, and none had noticed we rode without them.'

'The Isle is an enchanted place,' whispered Prasamaccus. 'And when did your father die?'

'I think you know the answer to that, Prasamaccus. I have a son, and we are not close.' He smiled. 'Perhaps one day he will sail to the Isle.'

Prasamaccus bowed and the two Britons left the room.

'We cannot undertake this task alone,' said Gwalchmai as they emerged into the sunlight. 'There is too much ground to cover.'

'I know, my friend. But Cato is right. Against the power of Wotan he needs all his young men and only ancients like us can be spared.'

Prasamaccus stopped. 'I think that is the answer, Gwal. Ancients. You recall the day when Uther split the sky and marched out of the mist leading the Ninth?'

'Of course. Who could forget it?'

'The Legate of the Lost Legion was Severinus Albinus. Now he has a villa at Calcaria – less than half a day's ride from here.'

'The man is over sixty!' objected the Cantii.

'And how old are you?' snapped Prasamaccus.

'There is no need to ram the dagger home,' said Gwalchmai. 'But he is a rich Roman and probably fat and content.'

'I doubt it. But he will know the whereabouts of other survivors of the Ninth. They were Uther's legion, sworn to him by bonds stronger than blood. He brought them from the Vales of the Dead.'

'More than a quarter of a century ago. Most of them will have died by now.'

'But there will be some who have not. Maybe ten, maybe a hundred. We must seek them out.'

Severinus Albinus still looked every inch the Roman general he had been until a mere five years previously. His back was spear-straight, his dark eyes eagle-sharp. For him, the past twenty-five years had been like living a dream, for he and all his men of the Ninth Legion had been trapped in the hell of the Void for centuries before the young prince, Uther Pendragon, rescued them and brought them home to a world gone mad. The might of Rome – preeminent when Severinus had marched his men into the mist – was now but a shadow, and barbarians ruled where once the laws of Rome were enforced by legions whose iron discipline made defeat unthinkable. Severinus had been honour bound to serve Uther and he had done it well, training native British troops along imperial lines, fighting in wars for a land about which he cared nothing. Now he was at peace in his villa – reading works of ancient times that, for him at least, were reminders of a yesterday that had swallowed his wife and children and all that he knew and loved. A man out of his time, Severinus Albinus was close to contentment as he sat in his garden reading the words of Plutarch.

His personal slave, Nica, a Jew from the Greek islands, approached him.

'My lord, there are two men at the gate who wish to speak with you.'

'Tell them to come tomorrow. I am in no mood for business.'

'They are not city merchants, lord, but men who claim friendship.'

Severinus rolled the parchment and placed it on the marble seat beside him. 'They have names, these friends?'

'Prasamaccus and Gwalchmai.'

Severinus sighed. 'Bring them to me – and fetch wine and fruit. They will stay the night, so prepare suitable rooms.'

'Shall I heat the water, lord, for the guest baths?'

'That will not be necessary. Our guests are Britons and they rarely wash. But have two village girls hired to warm their beds.'

'Yes, lord,' answered Nica, bowing and moving away as Severinus stood and smoothed his long toga, his contentment evaporating. He turned to see the limping Prasamaccus shuffling along the paved walkway, followed by the tall, straight-backed Cantii tribesman known as the King's Hound. Both men he had always treated with respect, as the King's companions deserved, but he had hoped never to see them again. He was uncomfortable with Britons.

'Welcome to my home,' he said, bowing stiffly. 'I have ordered wine for you.' He gestured to the marble seat and Prasamaccus sank gratefully to it while Gwalchmai stood by, his powerful arms crossed at his chest. 'I take it you are here to invite me to the funeral?'

'The King is not dead,' said Prasamaccus. Severinus covered his shock well as the scene was interrupted by a servant bearing a silver tray on which were two goblets of wine and a pitcher of water. He laid it on the wide arm-rest of the seat and silently departed.

'Not dead? He lay in state for three days.'

'He is in the Isle of Crystal, recovering,' said Gwalchmai.

'I am pleased to hear it. I understand the Goths will be moving against us and the King is needed.'

'We need your help.' said Gwalchmai bluntly. 'And the men of the Ninth.'

Severinus smiled thinly. 'The Ninth no longer exists. The men took up their parcels of land and are now citizens – none less than fifty years old. As you well know, the King disbanded the Ninth, allowing them a retirement well-earned. War is a challenge for young men, Gwalchmai.'

'We do not need them for war, Severinus,' said Prasamaccus. 'The Sword of Power is gone – it must be found.' The Brigante told the general about the attack on the King and Culain's theory of the Sword. Through it all Severinus remained motionless, his dark eyes fixed on Prasamaccus' face.

'Few men,' said Severinus, 'understood the power of the Sword. But I saw it slice the air like a curtain to free us from the Mist, and Uther once explained the riddle of how he always knew where the enemy would strike. The Sword is as valuable as the King. Yet it is all very well to seek the Ninth, but there is no time to scour the land. You talk of a site where magic is suddenly powerful. In peace-time perhaps the quest would have some meaning, but in war? There will be columns of refugees, enemy troops, hardship, pain and death. No, a random search is not the answer.'

'Then what is?' asked Gwalchmai.

'Only one man knows where the Sword was sent. We must ask him!'

'The King lies in a state close to death,' said Prasamaccus. 'He cannot speak.'

'He could not when last you saw him, Prasamaccus. But if Culain took him to the magic Isle, perhaps he is now awake?'

'What do you suggest, general?'

'I will get word to the men of the Ninth. But do not expect a large gathering; many are now dead and others returned to Italia, hoping to find some link with their pasts. And we will start our journey tomorrow to the south-west.'

'I cannot travel with you, general,' said Prasamaccus. 'I must go to the Caledones.'

Severinus nodded. 'And you, Gwalchmai?'

'I will ride with you. There is nothing for me here.'

'There is nothing for any of us here,' said Severinus. 'The world is changing. New empires grow, old ones die. The affairs of a nation are like the life of a man; no man and no empire can for long resist decline.'

'You think the Goths will win?' stormed Gwalchmai.

'If not the Goths, then the Saxons or the Jutes. I urged Uther to recruit Saxon warriors for his legions, to allow them a degree of self-government. But he would not listen. In the South Saxon alone there are thirty thousand men of sword-bearing age. Proud men. Strong men. This realm will not long survive Uther.'

'We have not suffered a defeat in twenty-five years,' said Gwalchmai.

'And what is that to history? When I was young, in the days of Claudius, Rome ruled the world. Where are the Romans now?'

'I think age has weakened your courage.'

'No, Gwalchmai, four hundred years in the Mist strengthened my wisdom. There is a guestroom for each of you. Go now – we will talk later.'

The Britons retired to the villa, leaving the old general in the garden where Nica found him. 'Is there anything you need, lord?'

'What news from the merchants?'

'They say that a great army is gathering across the water and that Wotan will be here within weeks.'

'What do the merchants plan?'

'Most have hidden their wealth. Some have reinvested in Hispania and Africa. Still more are preparing to welcome the Goths. It is the way of the world.'

'And you, Nicodemus?'

'Me, lord? Why, I will stay with you.'

'Nonsense! You have not spent ten years building yourself a fortune merely to die as my slave.'

'I do not know what you mean, lord.'

'This is no time for denials. You risked my capital with Abrigus and he brought home a cargo of silks that netted me a handsome sum. You took a commission of one hundred silver pieces which you re-invested skilfully.'

Nica shrugged. 'How long have you known?'

'About six years. I am leaving tomorrow and I do not think I will return. If I do not come home within the year, then the villa is yours – and all my capital; there is a sealed parchment to that effect

387

lodged with Cassius. My slaves are to be freed and an amount set aside for the woman, Trista; she has been good to me. You will see all this is done?'

'Of course, lord, but naturally I hope you will have a long life and return speedily.'

Severinus chuckled. 'And still you lie, you rogue! Get ready my sword, and the armour of combat – not the ornamental breastplate, but the old leather cuirass. As to the mount, I will take Canis.'

'He is getting old, lord.'

'We are all getting old, Nica. But he's wily and fears nothing.'

The boat slid through the dark waters, Culain sitting silently at the tiller, until at last the tunnel widened into a cavern hung with gleaming stalactites. The waters bubbled and hissed and the walls gleamed with an eldritch light. Culain steered the craft through a maze of natural pillars and out on to a wide mist-smeared lake. The stars were bright, the moon shining over the distant tor on which stood a round tower. The air was fresh and cool and the Lance Lord stretched and drew in a deep breath as the peace of the Isle swept over him. His eyes roamed the landscape, seeking the once-familiar forms of the Sleeping Giants, the Questing Beast, the Centaur, the Dove, the Lion. Hidden for two thousand years, but potent still.

The craft moved on into the tree-shadowed bay, towards the campfire that twinkled in the distance like a resting star. As the boat neared the land, seven hooded figures rose from around the fire and advanced in a line towards the shore.

'Why have you called us?' asked a woman's voice.

'I have a friend here, in need of your help.'

'Is your friend a man of peace?'

'He is the King.'

'Is that an answer?'

'He is the man who declared the Isle of Crystal to be sacred, and he has protected its sanctity and its freedom.'

'The Isle needs no *man* to declare it sacred, nor swords to protect its freedom.'

'Then look upon him simply as he is, a man whose soul has been stolen and whose body is in peril.'

'And where would you have us take him?' asked the woman.

'To the Round Hall in the Circle of the Great Moon, where no evil may dwell, where the two worlds join in the sign of the Sacred Fish.'

'You know much of our Mysteries.'

'I know *all* of your Mysteries . . . and more besides.' Without another word the women moved forward and effortlessly lifted the King from the craft. In two lines, the body almost floating between them, the hooded women set off into the shadows with Culain following. A figure in white emerged from the trees, a hood drawn over her face.

'You cannot travel further, warrior.'

'I must remain with him.'

'You cannot.'

'You think to stop me?'

'You will stop yourself,' she told him, 'for your presence weakens the power that will keep him alive.'

'I am not evil,' he argued.

'No, Culain lach Feragh, you are not evil.'

'You know me, then? That is good, for you must also know that I planted the Thorn and began the work you now continue.'

'You began it, yes, but not in faith; it was but one more of your games. You told the Sisters that you know all their Mysteries and more besides. Once that was the truth, but it is no longer. You think you chose this place, Culain? No. It chose you.'

'Forgive my arrogance, lady. But let me stay. I have much to atone. And I am lost and have nowhere to go.'

Moonlight bathed the bay, making the white-robed priestess almost ethereal, and the warrior waited as she considered his words. Finally she spoke.

'You may stay on the Isle, Culain – but not at the Round Hall.' She pointed up at the great Tor and the tower that stood there. 'There you may rest, and I will see that food is brought to you.'

'Thank you, lady. It is a weight lifted from my heart.'

389

She turned and was gone. Culain climbed the ancient path that circled the Tor, rising higher and higher above the land and lakes below. The tower was old, and had been old when he was a child in Atlantis. The wooden floors had rotted and only the huge stones remained, carefully fashioned with a precision now lost to the world and interlocked without the aid of mortar. Culain lit a fire with some of the rotten wood and settled down to sleep beneath the stars.

11

Cormac awoke to a barren landscape of skeletal trees and dusty craters. Beside him lay his sword, and behind him was a tunnel that rose up through a mountain. Sitting up, he looked into the tunnel. At the far end, high in the heart of the mountain, he saw a flickering glow and yearned to walk towards it and bathe in the light.

But just then he became aware of another figure and swung, sword in hand, to see an old man sitting on a flat rock; his beard was white and he was dressed in a long grey robe.

'Who are you?' asked Cormac.

'No one,' answered the man with a rueful smile. 'Once though, I was someone and I had a name.'

'What is this place?'

The man shrugged. 'Unlike me, it has many names and many secrets. And yet, like me, it is nowhere. How did you come here?'

'I . . . there was a fight . . . I . . . cannot remember clearly.'

'Sometimes that is a gift to receive with gratitude. There is much I would like to un-remember.'

'I was stabbed,' said Cormac, 'many times.' Lifting his shirt, he examined the pale flesh of his chest and back. 'But there are no scars.'

'The scars are elsewhere,' said the man. 'Did you fight well?'

'No. I was blind . . . Anduine! I must find her.' He stood and moved towards the tunnel.

'You will not find her there,' said the man softly, 'for that way lies blood and fire and life.'

'What are you saying, old man?'

'I am stating the obvious, Cormac, son of Uther. Your lady has gone before you on this long grey road. Do you have the courage to follow?'

'Courage? You are making my head spin. Where is she?'

The old man rose and pointed to the distant mountains beyond the black river that wound across the foot of the valley below. 'She is there, Cormac, where all new souls gather. The Mountains of the Damned.'

'I ask you again, old man, what is this place?'

'This, young prince, is the place of nightmares. Here only the dead may walk. This is the Void and here dwells Chaos.'

'Then . . . I . . .'

'You are dead, prince Cormac.'

'No!'

'Look around you,' said the old man. 'Where is life? Is there grass, or any living tree? Is there sign of any animal or bird? Where are the stars that should grace the sky?'

'And yet I still think and feel, and I can wield my sword. This is a dream, old man; it does not frighten me.'

The man rose and smoothed his grey robe. 'I am journeying to those mountains. Do you wish me to give a message to your lady?'

Cormac looked back at the tunnel and the beckoning light. Every emotion in him screamed to run towards it, to escape the pitiless grey of the land around him. But Anduine was not here. He looked to the mountains.

'You say she is there, yet why should I believe you?'

'Only because you do. I would not lie to you, young prince. I served your father and his father and grandfather. I was the Lord Enchanter.'

'Maedhlyn?'

'Yes, that was one of my names in the Light. Now I am no one.'

'So, you also are dead?'

'As dead as you, prince Cormac. Will you travel with me on the grey road?'

'Will I truly find Anduine?'

'I do not know. But you will walk her path.'

'Then I will join you.'

Maedhlyn smiled and walked down the hillside to the dark river. He raised his arms and called out and a black barge came into sight, steered by a monstrous figure with the head of a wolf and eyes that

392

gleamed red in the pale half-light of eternal dusk. Cormac raised his sword.

'You will not need that,' whispered Maedhlyn. 'He is only the Ferryman, and will offer no harm to you.'

'How can he harm a dead man?' asked Cormac.

'Only your body has died. Your spirit can still know pain and, worse, extinction. And there are many beasts here, and Once-men who will seek to harm you. Keep your sword ready, Cormac. You will have need of it.'

Together they climbed into the barge, which moved out on to the river under the skilled silent poling of the Ferryman.

The boat came to rest against a stone jetty and Maedhlyn climbed clear, beckoning Cormac to follow him. The Ferryman sat still, his red eyes fixed on the youth and his hand extended.

'What does he want?'

'The black coin,' said Maedhlyn. 'All travellers here must pay the Ferryman.'

'I have no coin.'

The old man was troubled. 'Search your pockets, young prince,' he ordered. 'It must be there.'

'I tell you I have nothing.'

'Search anyway!'

Cormac did as he was bid, then spread his arms. 'As I said, I have nothing but my sword.'

Maedhlyn's shoulders sagged. 'I fear I have done you a terrible injustice, Cormac.' He turned to the Ferryman and spoke in a language the youth had never heard. The beast seemed to smile, then he stood and turned the barge, poling it back on to the river.

'What injustice?'

'You are not, it seems, dead, though how you have come here is a mystery. All souls carry the black coin.'

'There is no harm done. He carried us over.'

'Yes, but he will not take you back – and that is the tragedy.'

'It is not wide, Maedhlyn. If necessary I can swim across.'

'No! You must never touch the water; it is the essence of Hell itself. It will burn what it touches and the pain will last an eternity.'

393

Cormac approached the old man, placing his arm over Maedhlyn's shoulder.

'It is no tragedy. I have no wish to live without Anduine, and she has already passed the river. Come, let us walk. I wish to reach the mountains before dark.'

'Dark? There is no dark here. This is how the Void is, and always will be. There is no sun and no moon, and the stars are a distant memory.'

'Let us walk anyway,' snapped Cormac. Maedhlyn nodded and the two set off.

For many hours they continued on their way until at last weariness overcame the prince. 'Do you never tire?' he asked the Enchanter.

'Not here, Cormac. It is another sign of your bond to life. Come, we will sit up there on the hillside; I will light a fire and we will talk.'

They camped within a circle of boulders. Maedhlyn gathered dead wood and the small fire blazed brightly. The Enchanter seemed lost in thought, and Cormac did not disturb him. After a while, Maedhlyn stretched and smiled grimly.

'It would have been better, young prince, to have met under the sun, in the woods around Eboracum or in the palace at Camulodunum. But men must make of events what they can. I taught your father when he was your age, and he was swift in learning. He became a man who could bend almost any situation to his will. Perhaps you also are such a man?'

Cormac shook his head. 'I was raised as a demon's son, shunned by all. The man who was a father to me was slain, and I fled. I met Culain and he saved me. He left me to protect Anduine and I failed. That is the story of Cormac. I do not think I am as Uther was.'

'Do not judge yourself too harshly, young prince. Tell me all of the story – and I will be your judge.'

As the fire flickered to glowing ash, Cormac told of his early life with Grysstha, of the kiss from Alftruda that led to Grysstha's murder, of the meeting with Culain and the battle with the demons to protect Anduine. Lastly he outlined the rescue of Oleg and his daughter, and the fight with the Vikings that ultimately caused the attack on the cabin.

Maedhlyn listened quietly until the story was complete, then he added fresh fuel to the fire.

'Uther would have been proud of you, but you are too humble, prince Cormac; I would guess that has much to do with the tribulations of your childhood. Firstly, when Alftruda's brothers attacked you, you defeated them all – the act of a warrior and a man of courage. Secondly, when the demons came, you fought like a man. And when you carried Oleg from the mountain, you once more showed the power of your spirit. And yes, you failed; the forces against you were too powerful. But know this, child of Uther, to fail is not so terrible. The real act of cowardice is never to try.'

'I think, Maedhlyn, I would sooner have been less heroic and more successful. But there is no point now in worrying at it. I will have no opportunity to redeem myself.'

'Do not be too sure of that,' said the Enchanter softly. 'This world, damnable as it is, has many similarities with the one you have left.'

'Name them?'

'The Lord of this world is Molech, once a man but now a demon. You know him better as Wotan. This was his realm for nigh two thousand years.'

'Wotan? How is that possible?'

'Through one man's stupidity. My own. But let me tell the story in my own time. You know, of course, of the Feragh, the last living fragment of Atlantis?'

'Yes, Culain told me.'

'Well, in those glorious days there were many young men who yearned for adventure. And we had the power of the Stones and we became gods to the mortals. One such young man was Molech. He revelled in dark emotions and his pleasures would turn most men's stomachs; torture, pain and death were as wine to him. He turned his world into a charnel-house. It was too much for any of us to bear and the Feragh turned against him. Our King, Pendarric, led a war that saw Molech humbled. Culain fought him on the towers of Babel and killed him there, beheading him and hurling the body to the rocks to be burned.'

'Then how did he return?'

'Be patient!' snapped Maedhlyn. 'Molech, like all of us, could use the Stones to become immortal. But he went one step further than we had; he took a ring of Silver Sipstrassi and embedded it in his own skull, under the skin, like an invisible crown. He became Sipstrassi, needing no Stone. When Culain killed him, I took the head. No one knew what I had done. I burned the flesh from it and kept it as a talisman, an object of great power. It aided me through the centuries that followed. I knew Molech's spirit still lived and I communed with it, and with the dead of his realm, learning much and using the knowledge well. But, in my arrogance, I did not realise that Molech was also using me and his power was growing.

'Some years ago, just after you were born, Uther and I suffered a parting of the ways. I journeyed to the lands of the Norse, and there met a young woman who wished to be my student. I allowed her into my house and into my heart. But she was a servant of Molech and she drugged me one night and placed the skull on my head. Molech took my body and my spirit was sent here. Now he torments me with my own stupidity, and the murderous excesses we fought so hard to destroy are returned to plague the world. And this time he will not be defeated.'

'Culain still lives. He will destroy him,' said Cormac.

'No, Culain is a shadow of the man that once was. I thought that Uther and the Sword of Power might just be strong enough, but Wotan out-thought me there also. He has taken the Blood King.'

'Killed him?'

'No. Would that he had!'

'I do not understand you,' said Cormac.

'Uther is here, Prince Cormac, in the Void. Held in chains of soulfire.'

'I care only for Anduine,' said Cormac. 'While I can admire the strength and skills of the man who sired me, all I know is that he hounded my mother to her eventual death. I do not care for his suffering.' He rose smoothly to his feet. 'I have rested enough, Maedhlyn.'

'Very well,' whispered the Enchanter. His hand floated over the fire and the blaze died instantly. 'It is a long walk and a road fraught with perils. Keep to the path. No matter what happens, Cormac, keep to the path.'

Together they set off on the wide road. On either side the pitiless landscape stretched to a grey horizon, the land broken only by ruined trees and jutting black boulders, jagged and stark. Dust rose about their feet, drying Cormac's throat and stinging his eyes.

'This is a soulless place,' he said, bringing a wry chuckle from Maedhlyn.

'That is exactly the opposite of the truth, young man. All that lives here *are* the souls of the departed. The problem we face is that the majority of those condemned here are evil. And here a man's true nature is what is seen. Take the Ferryman. He was a man once, but now he has the shape of the beast he hid in life.'

'Anduine has no place here,' said Cormac. 'She is gentle and kind; she harmed no one.'

'Then she will pass on along the road. Do not fear for her, Cormac. There is a cosmic balance to this place and not even Molech could disturb it for long.'

As they rounded a bend in the road, they saw a young girl whose foot was caught in a snare. 'Help me!' she called and Cormac stepped from the road to where she lay, but as he reached her a towering figure loomed from behind a rock.

'Look out!' yelled Maedhlyn and Cormac spun, his sword slashing in a murderous arc that clove through the side of the scaled beast.

With a hissing scream that sprayed black blood over Cormac's shirt, the monster vanished. Behind him the girl rose silently, fingers extended like claws. Maedhlyn hurled a slender dagger that took her between the shoulder-blades and Cormac whirled as she fell to her knees. Her eyes were red as blood, her mouth lined with pointed fangs, a serpent's tongue slid between her blue lips. Then she too vanished.

'Get back to the road,' ordered Maedhlyn, 'and bring my dagger.' The blade lay in the dust. Cormac scooped it up and rejoined the Enchanter.

'What were they?'

'A father and daughter. They spent their lives robbing and killing travellers on the road between Verulamium and Londinium. They were burnt at the stake twenty years before you were born.'

'Does nothing good live here?'

'A man finds good in the most unlikely places, prince Cormac. But we shall see.'

They journeyed on for what could have been an eternity. Without stars or moon to judge the hours, Cormac lost all sense of passing time, yet eventually they reached the mountains and followed the path to a wide cave where torches blazed.

'Be on your guard here, for there is no protection,' warned Maedhlyn.

Inside the cave scores of people were sitting, or sleeping, or talking. The newcomers were ignored and Maedhlyn led the prince down a series of torchlit tunnels, packed with souls, halting at last in a central cavern where a huge fire burned.

An elderly man in a faded brown habit bowed to the Enchanter. 'God's peace to you, brother,' he said.

'And to you, Albain. I have here a young friend in need of goodness.'

Albain smiled and offered his hand. He was a frail, short man with wispy white hair framing his bald head like a crown above his ears. 'Welcome, my boy. What you seek is in short supply. How may I help you?'

'I am searching for my wife; her name is Anduine.' He described her to the old monk who listened attentively.

'She was here, but I fear she was taken away. I am sorry.'

'Taken? By whom?'

'The Loyals came for her. We had no time to hide her.'

'Molech's guards,' explained Maedhlyn. 'They serve him here as they served him in life, for the promise of a return to the flesh.

'Where did they take her?'

Albain did not answer, but looked at Maedhlyn.

'She will be at The Keep – Molech's fortress. You cannot go there, Cormac.'

'What is there to stop me?' he asked, grey eyes blazing.

'You truly are Uther's son,' said Maedhlyn, caught between sorrow and pride.

Several figures moved from the shadows.

'Uther's son?' said Victorinus. 'And is that you, Maedhlyn?'

'So the war has begun,' Maedhlyn whispered.

'Not yet, wizard, but soon. Tell me – is he truly Uther's son?'

'Yes. Prince Cormac, meet Victorinus, Uther's ablest general.'

'I wish I could say well met, prince Cormac' He turned once more to Maedhlyn. 'Albain told us the King's soul is held at the Keep . . . that they are torturing him. Can it be true?'

'I am sorry, Victorinus, I know you were his friend.'

'Were? Death does not change my friendship, Maedhlyn. There are thirteen of us here and we will find the king.'

'The open ground before the Keep,' said Maedhlyn, 'is patrolled by hounds of great size. They have teeth like daggers and skin like steel; no sword will slay them. Then within the first wall live the Loyals, two hundred at least – all formidable warriors during their lives. Beyond the second wall I have never seen, but even the Loyals fear to go there.'

'The King is there,' said Victorinus, his face set, his eyes stubborn.

'And Anduine,' added Cormac.

'It is madness! How will you approach the Keep? Or do you think your thirteen swords will cut a path for you?'

'I have no idea, Maedhlyn; I am only a soldier. But once you were the greatest thinker in all the world – or so you told me.'

'Hell is no place for flattery,' said the Enchanter. 'But I will think on it.'

'Does Molech have no enemies?' Cormac asked.

'Of course he has, but most of them are like he is: evil.'

'That does not concern me. Are they powerful?'

'Believe me, Cormac, this is not a course to pursue.'

399

'Answer me, damn you!'

'Yes, they are powerful,' snapped Maedhlyn. 'They are also deadly, and even to approach them could cost you your soul. Worse, you could end up like your father – wrapped in chains of fire and tortured until you are naught but a broken shell, a mewling ruined thing.'

'Why should they do this to me?'

'Because you are your father's son. And Molech's greatest enemy here is Goroien, the Witch Queen defeated by Uther – and her lover-son Gilgamesh, slain by Culain. Now do you understand?'

'I understand only that I want to meet her. Can you arrange it?'

'She will destroy you, Cormac.'

'Only if she hates me more than she desires to defeat Molech.'

'But what can you offer her? She has her own army, and slave-beasts to do her bidding.'

'I will offer her the Keep – and the soul of Wotan.'

'Talk to them, Albain,' said Maedhlyn, as the small group sat in a corner of the stalactite-hung cavern. 'Explain what they are risking.' The old man looked at Victorinus, his face showing his concern.

'There are many here who will pass no further on the road. They exist as beasts in this terrible twilight. Others are drawn on towards what some believe is a beautiful land with a golden sun and a blue sky. I myself believe in that land and I encourage people to travel there. But to do so, you must hold to the path.'

'Our King is held here,' said Victorinus. 'We have a duty towards him.'

'Your duty was to give your lives for him and you did that. But not your souls.'

'I will not speak for the others, Albain, only for myself. I cannot journey further while the King needs me – not even for the promise of paradise. You see, of what worth would paradise be to me if I spent it in shame?'

Albain reached across and took Victorinus by the hand. 'I cannot answer that for you. All I know is that here – in this land of death and despair – there is still the promise of hope for those who travel on. Some cannot, for their evil has found a home here. Others will not, for their fears are very great and it is easier, perhaps, to hide in the eternal shadows. But this ghastly world is not all there is, and you should not deny yourself the journey.'

'Why have you not journeyed on?' asked Cormac.

Albain shrugged. 'One day perhaps I will. For now there is work for me among the haunted and the lost.'

'As indeed there is work for us,' said Cormac. 'I am not a philosopher, Albain, but my love is here and you say she is held by Molech. I will not allow that. Like Victorinus, I could not live in any paradise with that on my conscience.'

'Love is a fine emotion, prince Cormac, and there is precious little of it here. Let me argue from another standpoint. To defeat Molech, you seek the aid of Goroien – she who was as evil as the man you desire to destroy. Can a man wed himself to the powers of evil and remain untouched by it? What will happen when the fire of your purity touches the ice of her malice?'

'I do not know. But Molech's enemies should be my friends.'

'Friends? How much do you know of Goroien?'

'Nothing, beyond Maedhlyn telling me she was an enemy to Uther.'

'She was an Immortal who held her eternal beauty by sacrificing thousands of young women, watching as their blood ran over her Magic Stone. She brought her dead son back to life – and made him her lover. His name was – and is – Gilgamesh, the Lord of the Undead. That is what you are seeking to ally yourself with.'

Cormac shook his head and smiled. 'You do not understand, Albain. You speak of my purity? I would sacrifice a world to free Anduine; I would see a million souls writhe in agony to see her safe.'

'And would she desire this, young prince?'

Cormac looked away for a moment. 'No, she would not,' he admitted, 'and perhaps that is why I love her so deeply. But I will seek Goroien.'

401

'She will destroy you – and that is only if you *can* reach her. To do so, you must leave the road and journey across the Shadowlands. Here the most vile of creatures dwell and they will haunt your every step.'

Victorinus raised his hand and all eyes turned to him. 'I appreciate your advice, Albain, and your warnings. But the prince and I will leave the road to seek the Witch Queen.' He turned to his aide, Marcus. 'Will you travel with me?'

'We died with you, sir,' said the young man. 'We'll not leave you now.'

'Then it is settled. What of you, Maedhlyn?'

'The Witch hates me more than any of you, but yes – I will go. What else is there for me?'

Albain rose and gazed sadly at the fifteen men. 'I wish you God's luck. There is no more to say.'

Cormac watched the little man weave his way through the crowded cavern. 'How did he come to be here, Maedhlyn?'

'He followed the right god at a time when Rome was ruled by the wrong one. Let us go.'

402

12

Three invasion fleets landed on the coasts of Britannia in the fourth week of the Spring. Eleven thousand men came ashore at Segundunumn near the easternmost fortress of the near-derelict wall of Hadrian. The town was sacked, hundreds of citizens put to the sword.

The second fleet – led by Wotan's ablest general, Alaric – disgorged eight thousand men at Anderida on the south coast, and this army was further swelled by two thousand Saxons recruited by the renegade Agwaine. Refugees packed the roads and tracks towards Londinium as the Goths swept along the coastline towards Noviomagus.

The third fleet beached at Petvaria, having sailed unchallenged along the mouth of the Humber. Twenty-two thousand fighting men came ashore, and the British defence force of twelve hundred men fled before them.

In Eboracum, less than twenty-five miles away, the city was in panic.

Geminus Cato, left with little choice, gathered his two legions of ten thousand men and marched to engage the enemy. Fierce storms lashed the legions and, during the first night of camp, many men swore they had seen a demonic head outlined against the thunder-clouds and lit by spears of lightning. By morning, desertions had reduced Cato's fighting force by more than a thousand.

His scouts reported the enemy closing in just after dawn and Cato moved his men to the crown of a low hill, half a mile to the west. Here trenches were hastily dug and spiked and the horses of the officers were removed to a picket line in a nearby wood, behind the battle site.

The storm-clouds disappeared as swiftly as they had come, and the Goths came into sight in brilliant sunshine which blazed from their spear-points and raised axes. Cato felt the fear spread along the line as the sheer size of the enemy force made its impact on the legions.

'By all the Gods, they're a pretty bunch,' shouted Cato. A few men sniggered, but the tension did not break.

'A young soldier dropped his gladius and stepped back. Tick it up boy,' said Cato softly. 'It'll gather rust lying there.' The youth was trembling and close to tears. 'I don't want to die,' he said.

Cato glanced at the Goths who were gathering for the charge and then walked to the boy, stooping to gather his sword. 'Nobody does,' he said, pushing the hilt into the soldier's hand and guiding him back into line.

With a roar that echoed the previous storm, the Goths hurled themselves at the line.

'Archers!' bellowed Cato. 'Take your positions!' The five hundred bowmen in their light leather tunics ran forward between the shield-bearers and formed a line along the hilltop. A dark cloud of shafts arched into the air and down into the charging mass. The Goths were heavily armoured and the casualties were few, yet still the charge faltered as men fell and tripped those following.

'Retire and take up spears!'

The bowmen pulled back behind the shield-wall, dropped their bows and quivers and, in pairs, took up the ten-foot spears lying in rows behind the heavily armoured legionaries. The first man in each pair knelt hidden behind a shielded warrior, holding the spear three feet from the point. The second man gripped the shaft at the base, awaiting the order from Cato.

The charging Goths were almost at the line when Cato raised his arm.

'Now!'

As the spearmen surged forward, the hidden spears – directed by the kneeling men at the front – lashed between the shields, plunging into the front ranks of the attacking warriors, smashing shields to shards and cleaving through chainmail. The unbarded spears were dragged back, then rammed home again and again.

The slaughter was terrifying and the Goths fell back, dismayed.

Three times more they charged, but the deadly spears kept them at bay. The ground before the line was thick with enemy dead, or wounded writhing in agony with their ribs crushed, their life-blood oozing into the soft earth.

An officer moved across the Goth's front line and spoke to the waiting warriors. Five hundred men flung aside their shields and advanced.

'What are they doing, sir?' asked Cato's aide, Decius. Cato did not reply. It did not become an officer in the midst of a battle to admit he had no idea.

The Goths surged up the hill, screaming the name of Wotan. The spears plunged into them but each stricken warrior grabbed the shaft of the weapon that was killing him, trapping the spear in his own body. The main army attacked once more, this time crashing against the British shield wall with tremendous force.

For a moment the wall split and several warriors forced their way into the line. Cato drew his gladius and rushed at them; he was joined by a young legionary and together they closed the breach. As the Goths fell back, Cato turned to the legionary and saw it was the boy who earlier had dropped his sword.

'You did well, lad.' Before the boy could reply, a terrifying roar went up from the Gothic ranks and the enemy surged towards the line.

The battle lasted the full day, with neither side triumphant, yet at dusk Cato had no choice but to pull back from the hill. He had lost two hundred and seventy-one men, with another ninety-four wounded. The enemy losses, he calculated, were around two thousand. In military terms it was a victory, but realistically, Cato knew it gained the Britons little. The Goths now knew – if they were ever in doubt – that Uther's army was not as poorly led as the Merovingian forces across the water. And the Britons knew the Goths were not invincible. Apart from those two points nothing had been gained from the day, and Cato marched his men back along the road towards Eboracum, having already chosen the site for the next battle.

'Is it really true, sir?' asked Decius as the two men rode ahead of the legions. 'Is the King alive?'

'Yes,' answered Cato.

'Then where is he?'

Cato was weary, and not for the first time wished he had another aide. But Decius was the son of a rich merchant and had paid for the appointment with a beautiful villa outside Eboracum.

'The King will let us know his plans when he is ready. Until then, we will do what he asks of us.'

'But several men saw the corpse, sir. And the funeral arrangements were being made.'

Cato ignored the comment. 'When the night camp is made, I want you to tour the fires. The men fought well today. Make yourself known among them – compliment them; tell them you have never seen such bravery.'

'Yes, sir. For how long should I continue to do this?'

Cato bit back his anger and thought of his villa. 'Never mind, Decius. You set up my tent and I'll talk to the men.'

'Yes, sir. Thank you.'

Galead's dreams were dark and filled with pain. Awaking in the cold dawn, he stared at the ashes of the last night's fire. He had seen in his dreams Victorinus and his twelve warriors ride into the wood, to be surrounded by the Goths – led by the traitor Agwaine – and had watched the old general die as he had lived, with cold dignity and no compromise.

Shivering, he rekindled the fire. His news was of little worth to Britain now. The invasion fleets would sail within days, the King was dead, the power of Wotan beyond opposition. Yet he could feel no hate, only a terrible burden of sorrow dragging down his spirit.

Beside him lay his sword and he stared at it, loth to touch it. What was it, he wondered, that led men to desire such weapons, that filled them with the need to use them against their fellows, hacking and cutting and slaying?

And for what? Where was the gain? Few soldiers grew rich. Most returned to the same poor farms and villages they had grown

406

up in, and many lived out their lives without limbs, or with terrible scars that served as grim reminders of the days of war.

A sparrow landed beside him, pecking at the crumbs of the oatcake he had eaten at dusk the day before. Another joined it. Galead sat unmoving as the birds hopped around the scabbarded sword.

'What do they tell you?' asked a voice.

Galead looked across the fire to see a man seated there, wrapped in a cloak of rich rust-red. His beard was golden and heavily curled and his eyes were deep blue.

'They tell me nothing,' he answered softly, 'but they are peaceful creatures and I am happy to see them.'

'Would they have fed so contentedly beside Ursus, the prince who desired riches?'

'If they had, he would not have noticed them. Who are you?'

'I am not an enemy.'

'This I already knew.'

'Of course. Your powers are growing and you are rising above the sordid deeds of this world.'

'I asked who you were, stranger.'

'My name is Pendarric.'

Galead shivered as he heard the name, as if deep inside himself the name echoed in a distant hall of memory. 'Should I know you.'

'No, though I have used other names. But we walk the same paths, you and I. Where you are now I once stood, and all my deeds seemed as solid as morning mist – and as long-lasting.'

'And what did you decide?'

'Nothing. I followed the heart's desire and came to know peace.'

Galead smiled. 'Where in these lands can I find peace? And were I to try, would it not be selfish? My friends are about to suffer invasion and my place is with them.'

'Peace does not rest within a realm, or a city, or a town or even a crofter's hut,' said Pendarric. 'But then you know this. What will you do?'

'I will find a way to return to Britain. I will go against the power of Wotan.'

'Will it give you satisfaction to destroy him?'

Galead considered the question. 'No,' he said at last. 'Yet evil must be countered.'

'With the sword?'

Galead looked down at the weapon with distaste. '*Is* there another way?'

'If there is, you will find it. I have discovered a wonderful truth in my long life: those who seek with a pure heart usually find what they are looking for.'

'It would help me greatly to *know* what I am looking for.'

'You talked about countering evil, and in essence that is a question of balance. But the scales are not merely linear. A great amount of evil does not necessarily require an equivalent amount of good to equalise the balance.'

'How can that be true?' Galead asked.

'An angry bear will suffer a score of arrows and still be deadly . . . but a touch of poison, and it falls. Sometimes an apparently meaningless incident will set in motion events that will cause either great suffering or great joy.'

'Are you saying there is a way to bring down Wotan without the sword?'

'I am saying nothing that simple. But it is an interesting question for a philosopher, is it not? Wotan feeds on hatred and death and you seek to combat him with swords and shields. In war, a soldier will find it all but impossible not to hate the enemy. And so, do you not give Wotan even more of what he desires?'

'And if we do not fight him?'

'Then he wins, and brings even more death and despair to your land and many others.'

'Your riddle is too deep for me, Pendarric. If we fight him, we lose. If we do not, we lose. Yours is a philosophy of despair.'

'Only if you cannot see the *real* enemy.'

'There is something worse than Wotan?'

'There always is, Galead.'

'You speak as a man of great wisdom, and I sense you have power. Will you use that power against Wotan?'

'I am doing exactly that at this moment. Why else would I be here?'

'Are you offering me a weapon against him?'

'No.'

'Then what is the purpose of your visit?'

'What indeed?' answered Pendarric. His image faded and Galead was alone, once more. The birds were still feeding by the sword and the knight turned to look at them but as he moved they fluttered away in panic. He stood and strapped the blade to his side, covered the fire with earth and saddled his horse.

The coast was a mere eight miles through the woods and he hoped to find a ship that might land him on the shores of Britain. He rode the narrow trails through the forest, lost in thought, listening to the birdsong, enjoying the sunlight that occasionally lanced through the gaps in the overhanging trees. His mood was more tranquil following Pendarric's appearance, though the sorrow remained.

Towards the middle of the morning he met an elderly man and two women, standing alongside a hand-cart with a broken wheel. The cart was piled with possessions – clothes, chests and a very old chair. The man bowed as he approached, the women standing nervously as Galead dismounted.

'May I offer assistance?' he asked.

'That is truly kind,' said the man, smiling. His hair was long and white, though darker streaks could still be seen in his forked beard. One of the women was elderly, the other young and attractive with auburn hair streaked with gold; her right eye was bruised and her lip cut and swollen. Galead knelt by the cart and saw that the wheel had come loose and torn away from the joining-pin at the axle.

He helped them to unload the cart, then lifted it so that the wheel could be pushed back in place. Using the back of a hatchet blade, he hammered the joining-pin home and then reloaded the cart.

'I am very grateful,' said the man. 'Will you join us for our midday meal?'

409

Galead nodded and sat down by the roadside as the young woman prepared a fire. The older woman busied herself taking pans and plates from the back of the cart.

'We do not have much,' said the old man, seating himself beside Galead. 'Some oats and salt. But it is filling and there is goodness in the food.'

'It will suffice. My name is Galead.'

'And I am Caterix. That is my wife Oela, and my daughter Pilaras.'

'Your daughter seems in pain.'

'Yes. The journey has not been kind to us, and I pray to the Lord that our troubles may now be over.'

'How was she hurt?'

Caterix looked away. 'Three men robbed us two days ago. They . . . assaulted my daughter and killed her husband, Doren, when he tried to aid her.'

'I am sorry,' said Galead lamely.

The meal was eaten in silence, after a short prayer of thanks from Caterix. Galead thanked the family for their hospitality and offered to ride with them to the coast, where they had friends. Caterix accepted the offer with a bow and the small group followed slowly as Galead rode ahead.

As dusk flowed into evening Galead, rounding a bend in the trail, saw a man sitting with his back to a tree. He rode forward and dismounted. The man was bleeding heavily from a wound in his chest and his face was pale, the eyelids and lips blue from loss of blood. Ripping open the dirty tunic, Galead staunched the wound as best he could. After several minutes Caterix came upon the scene; he knelt beside the wounded man, lifting his wrist and checking his pulse.

'Get him to the cart,' he said. 'I have some cloth there for bandages, and a needle and thread.' Together they half-lifted, half-dragged the man to a rounded clearing by a silver stream. The two women helped to clean the wound and Caterix expertly sewed the jagged flesh together. Then they wrapped the man in blankets warmed by the fire.

'Will he live?' asked Galead.

Caterix shrugged. 'That is in the Lord's hands. He has lost much blood.'

In the night Galead awoke to see the girl, Pilaras, kneeling by the wounded man. Moonlight glinted from the knife in her hand.

She sat motionless for a long moment, then raised the knife, resting the point on the sleeping man's neck. Suddenly her head sagged forward and Galead saw that she was weeping. She lifted the knife and replaced it in the sheath at her side, returning to her blankets by the cart.

Galead lay back and returned to his dreams. He watched as the invasion ships landed on the coasts of Britain, saw the Goths begin their march towards the cities and, over it all, two visions that haunted him: a demonic head filling the sky, surrounded by storm-clouds and lightning, and a Sword shining like a midnight lantern.

Despite his dreams, he awoke refreshed. The wounded man was sleeping still, but his colour was better. Galead washed in the stream and then approached Caterix, who was sitting beside the victim.

'I must leave you,' said Galead. 'I need to find a ship to take me home.'

'May the Lord guide you and protect you on your journey.'

'And you on yours, Caterix. It was a fine deed to save the man's life.'

'Not fine at all. What are we if we do not aid our fellows in their times of trial?'

Galead rose and walked to his horse, then on impulse he returned to Caterix.

'Last night your daughter held a knife to this man's throat.'

He nodded. 'She told me this morning. I am very proud of her.'

'Why did she do it?'

'This is the man who raped her and killed her husband.'

'And you saved him? Sweet Mithras, he deserves death!'

'More than likely,' answered Caterix, smiling.

'You think he will thank you far saving him?'

'His thanks are not important.'

411

'Yet you may have saved him only to allow him to butcher other innocent people – to rape more young girls.'

'I am not responsible for his deeds, Galead, only my own. No man willingly allows those he loves to suffer hurt and pain.'

'I do not disagree with that,' said Galead. 'Love is a fine emotion. But he is not someone you love.'

'Of course he is. He is a brother.'

'You know him?'

'No, I do not mean a brother of the flesh. But he – like you – is my brother. And I must help him. It is very simple.'

'This is no way to deal with an enemy, Caterix.'

The old man looked down at the wounded robber. 'What better way is there of dealing with enemies than making them your friends?'

Galead walked back to his horse and stepped into the saddle. He tugged on the reins and the beast began to walk along the trail. Pilaras was gathering herbs at the wayside and she smiled as he passed.

Touching his heels to the horse's sides, he rode for the coast.

Culain sat beneath the stars on his sixteenth night at the Isle of Crystal. Every morning he would wake to find food and drink on a wooden tray outside the tower; every evening the empty dishes would be removed. Often he would catch a glimpse of a shadowy figure on the path below, but always he would walk back inside the tower, allowing his nocturnal visitors the solitude they so obviously desired.

But on this night a moon shadow fell across him as he sat and he looked up to see the woman in white, her face shrouded by a high hood.

'Welcome, lady,' he said, gesturing her to seat herself. As she did so, he saw that beneath the hood she wore a veil. 'Is there need for such modesty even here?' he asked.

'Especially here, Culain.' She threw back the hood and removed the veil and his breath caught in his throat as the moonlight bathed the pale face he knew so well.

412

'Gian?' he whispered, half-rising and moving towards her.

'Stay where you are,' she told him, her voice stern and lacking all emotion.

'But they told me you were dead.'

'I was tired of your visits, and I was dead to you.' There were silver streaks in her hair and fine lines about the eyes and mouth, but to Culain the Queen had lost none of her beauty. 'And yet now you are here once more,' she continued, 'and once more you torment me. Why did you bring *him* to me.'

'I did not know you were here.'

'I have spent sixteen years trying to forget the past and its tragedies. I thought that I had succeeded. You, I decided, were a young girl's fantasy. As a child I loved you – and in so doing destroyed my chance for happiness. As a lonely Queen, I loved you – and in so doing destroyed my son. For several years I hated you, Culain, but that passed. Now there is only indifference – both to you and to the Blood King my husband became.'

'You know, of course, that your son did not die?'

'I know many things, Lance Lord. But what I desire to know most is when you will leave this Isle.'

'You have become a hard woman, Gian.'

'I am not Gian Avur, not your little Fawn of the Forest. I am Morgana of the Isle, though I have other names I am told. You should know how that feels, Culain – you who were Apollo, and Aeneas, and Cunobelin the King and so many valiant others.'

'I have heard the leader of this community called the Fey Witch. I would never have dreamt it was you. What has happened to you, Laitha?'

'The world changed me, Lance Lord, and I care no longer for it nor for any creature that lives in it.'

'Then why are you here in this sacred place? It is a centre for healing and peace.'

'And so it remains. The Sisters are spectacularly successful, but I and others spend our time with the true Mysteries: the threads that link the stars, the patterns that weave through human lives, criss-crossing and joining, shaping the world's destiny. I used to call it

413

God, but now I see it is greater than any immortal dreamt of by man. Here in this – '

'I have heard enough, woman. What of Uther?' cut in Culain.

'He is dying,' she hissed, 'and it will be no loss to the world when he passes.'

'I never thought to see evil in you, Gian; you were always a woman of exquisite beauty.' He laughed grimly. 'But then evil comes in many guises and it does not have to be ugly. I have sat here in silent penance for many nights, for I believed that when I began this community it was for selfish motives. Well, lady, perhaps they were selfish. Yet the Isle was still fashioned with love and for love, and you – with your search for Mysteries I knew a thousand years before you were born – you have perverted it. I'll stay on this Tor no longer . . . nor wait your bidding.' He rose smoothly, gathered his staff and began the long climb down towards the circle of huts.

Her voice rang out behind him, an edge of cold triumph in her words.

'Your boat is waiting, Culain. If you are on it within the hour, I may not allow the Blood King to die. If you are not, I will withdraw the sisters from him and you may take the corpse where you will.'

He stopped, suffering the taste of defeat. Then he turned.

'You were always wilful and never one to admit an error. Very well, I will go and leave Uther to your tender mercies. But when you pause in your studies of the Mysteries, think on this: I took you in as a tiny child and raised you as a father. I offered nothing to make you feel there should be more. But you it was who whispered my name as you lay with Uther. You it was who bade me stay at Camulodunum. It is there that my guilt begins – and I will carry it. But perhaps when you look down from your gilded tower, you will see that tiny scrap of your own guilt – and find the courage to lift it to your eyes.'

'Are you done, Lance Lord?'

'I am done, Morgana.'

'Then leave my Isle.'

414

13

'We leave the road here,' said Maedhlyn, as the party crested a low dusty hill. 'And there is the realm of Goroien,' he continued, pointing to a distant range of forbidding mountains.

The landscape was pitted and broken, but many shadows moved furtively between the dead trees and the cracked boulders. Some slunk on all fours, others flew on black wings, still more slithered or ran.

Cormac took a deep breath, willing himself to step from the sanctuary of the road. He glanced at Victorinus, who smiled and shrugged.

'Let us go,' said the prince, drawing his sword. The fifteen men, weapons ready, moved off into the gloom and at once the shadows converged on them. There were beasts with slavering jaws, men with hollow fangs and red-rimmed eyes, wolves whose faces shifted and changed like mist . . . becoming human, then bestial. Above them flew giant bats, wheeling and diving, their leather wings slicing the air over the heads of the marchers. But none came within range of the bright swords.

'How far?' asked Cormac, walking beside Maedhlyn at the head of the column.

'Who can judge time here?' replied the former Enchanter. 'But it will take long enough.'

Grey dust rose about their feet as they walked on, flanked by an army of shadows drawing ever more close.

'Will they attack us?' Victorinus whispered.

Maedhlyn spread his hands. The man at the rear of the column screamed as taloned claws wrenched at his cloak, pulling him from his feet.

Victorinus whirled. 'Sword circle!' he called and their blades held high, the warriors leapt into the ranks of the beasts and surrounded their fallen comrade.

415

The creature holding him vanished as a gladius clove its heart. 'Marching formation,' said Victorinus, and as the small group of warriors formed in two lines the shadows moved back.

On and further on they marched, until the road could no longer be seen and the dust hung around them like a storm-cloud, blurring their vision, masking the distant mountains.

Twice more the shadows moved in, but each time the bright swords of the Britons forced them back.

At last they came to higher ground on which stood an ancient stone circle, blackened and ruined. The shadows ringed the foot of the hill and it was with a sense of relief that the weary group sat down amongst the stones.

'Why will they not come here?' asked Victorinus.

'I am not the fount of all human knowledge,' snapped Maedhlyn.

'You always claimed you were.'

'I would like you to know, Victorinus, that of all Uther's followers you were the one whose company I enjoyed least.'

'Cutting words, Enchanter,' answered Victorinus, grinning. 'Perhaps now you'll have an eternity in my company.'

'Hell, indeed,' commented Maedhlyn.

'This must have once been a living land,' said Cormac. There were trees, and we have crossed a score of dried-out stream-beds. What changed it?'

'Nothing changed it, Cormac,' Maedhlyn replied. 'For it does not exist. It is an echo of what once was; it is a nightmare.'

'Does our presence not prove its existence?' asked Marcus Bassicus, moving to sit alongside them.

'Did you ever dream you were somewhere where you were not?' countered Maedhlyn.

'Of course.'

'And did that dream prove the existence of the dreamscape?'

'But we are all sharing this dream,' Marcus argued.

'Are we? How can you know? Perhaps we are just figments of your nightmare, young Marcus. Or perhaps you are all appearing in mine.'

Victorinus chuckled. 'I knew it would not be long before you began your games.' He turned to the other men sitting by, listening intently. 'I once saw this man spend two hours arguing the case that Caligula was the only sane man ever to walk the earth. At the end, we all believed him and he laughed at us.'

'How could you not believe me?' asked Maedhlyn. 'Caligula made his horse a senator and, I ask you, did the horse ever make a wrong decision? Did it seek to seize power? Did it argue for laws that robbed the poor and fed the rich? It was the finest senator in Roman history.'

Cormac sat listening to the chatter and a slow, burning anger began to seize him. All his life he had lived with fear – of punishment, of humiliation, of rejection. These chains had held him in thrall since his first memories, but the fire of his anger cut through them. Only two people had ever loved Cormac Daemonsson – and both were dead. From deep inside him, a new Cormac rose and showed him his life from another viewpoint. Maedhlyn had been right, Cormac Daemonsson was not a failure, nor a loser. He was a man – and a prince, by right and by blood.

Power surged in his heart and his eyes blazed with its heady strength.

'Enough!' stormed Cormac, rising. 'This talk is like the wind in the leaves. It achieves nothing and is merely a noise. We are here and this place is real. Now let us move on.'

'He would have made a good king,' whispered Victorinus, as he and Maedhlyn followed Cormac down the hill.

'This is a fine place to learn arrogance,' agreed the Enchanter.

At the foot of the hill Cormac advanced on the shadow horde. 'Back!' he ordered and they split before him, creating a dark pathway. He marched into it, looking to neither left nor right, ignoring the hissing and the gleaming talons. Then sheathing his sword he strode on, eyes fixed on the mountains.

A tall figure in black breastplate stepped into his path. The man was wearing a winged helm that covered his face – all but the eyes which gleamed with a cold light. In his hands were two short swords, about his waist a kilt of dark leather and on his shins were black greaves. He stood in perfect balance on the balls of his feet, poised to attack.

417

Cormac continued to walk until he stood directly before the warrior.

'Draw your sword,' said the man, his voice a metallic echo from within the helm. Cormac smiled and considered his words with care, and when he spoke it was with grim certainty.

'If I do, it will be to kill you.'

'That has been done before, but not by the likes of you.'

Cormac stepped back and the sword of Culain flashed into his hand. The warrior stood very still, staring at the blade. 'Where did you come by that weapon?'

'It is mine.'

'I am not questioning its ownership.'

'And I am weary of this nonsense. Step aside or fight!'

'Why are you here?'

'To find Goroien,' answered Maedhlyn, pushing forward to stand between the warriors.

The man sheathed his blades. 'The sword earns you that right,' he told Cormac, 'but we will speak again when the Queen is done with you. Follow me.'

The tall warrior led them across the arid valley to a wide entrance carved into a mountain. Here torches blazed and guards stood by, bearing silver axes. Deep into the heart of the mountain they walked until they came to a huge doorway, before which stood two massive hounds. The warrior ignored them and pushed open the doors. Inside was a round hall, richly carpeted and hung with rugs, curtains and screens. At the centre, lounging on a divan, lay a woman of exquisite beauty. Her hair was golden, highlighted by silver; her eyes pale blue, matching the short shift she wore; and her skin was pale and wondrous smooth. Cormac swallowed hard as the warrior advanced to the divan and knelt before her. She waved him aside and summoned Cormac.

As he approached he saw her shimmer and change to a bloated, scaled creature, diseased and decaying, then back to the slim beauty he had first seen. His steps faltered, but still he came on.

'Kiss my hand,' she told him. He took the slender fingers in his own and blanched as they swelled and disgorged maggots in his

418

palm. His thoughts fixed on Anduine, he steeled himself as his head bent and his lips touched the writhing mass.

'A brave man indeed,' she said. 'What are you called?'

'Cormac Daemonsson.'

'And are you the son of a demon?'

'I am the son of Uther, High King of Britain.'

'Not a name to conjure friendship here,' she said.

'Nor is he a friend to me; he hounded my mother to her death.'

'Did he indeed?' Her gaze wandered to the figure of Maedhlyn at the back of the hall. 'And there is my old friend, Zeus. You are a long way from Olympus . . . such a very long way. I cannot tell you how pleasant it is to see you,' she hissed.

Maedhlyn bowed gravely. 'I wish I could echo the sentiment,' he called.

She returned her gaze to Cormac. 'My first thought is to watch you scream, to listen to your howls of torment, but you have aroused my curiosity. And events of interest are rare for Goroien now. So speak to me, handsome prince – tell me why you sought the Queen.'

'I need to assault the Keep,' he said simply.

'And why should that interest me?'

'Simply because Wotan – Molech – is your enemy.'

'Not enough.'

'It is said, my lady, that he has the power to return his followers to a life of flesh and blood. Could it not be that were you to control the Keep, you would also have that power?'

As she lay on the divan, she stretched out once more. Cormac longed to tear his eyes from the shimmering figure of beauty and decay.

'You think I have not tried to defeat him? What do you bring me that could make the difference?'

'First, let me ask what prevents you from taking the Keep?'

'Molech's power is greater than my own.'

'And if he were not here?'

'Where else would he be?'

'In the world of flesh, my lady.'

419

'That is not possible. I was among those who destroyed him at Babel; I saw Culain cut the head from the body.'

'Yet he is returned, thanks to the man Maedhlyn. The same could be done for you.'

'Why are you offering me this, when your very blood should scream its hatred for me?'

'Because the woman I love was murdered on account of this Molech, and even now he has her soul at the Keep.'

'But there is something else, yes? Something that brings Maedhlyn to me – and those other men of Uther's.'

'He also has the King's soul in chains of fire.'

'Now I see. And you want Goroien to free Uther? You are mad.' She raised one hand and guards moved in from all around the hall.

'Molech is alive,' said Cormac softly. 'He calls himself Wotan now and he plans to invade Britain. Only Uther has the power to destroy him. If, when that happens, you are in control of the Keep, will Molech's soul not come unwittingly to you?'

She waved back the guards. 'I will consider the questions you have raised. Maedhlyn! Join the prince and myself in my chambers. The rest of you may wait here.'

For an hour in the Queen's private chambers, as she lay on a silk-covered bed, Maedhlyn talked of the return to life of the man Molech. Cormac noted that the tale was slightly different from the story Maedhlyn had told him. In this version, Maedhlyn was far less at fault and only defeated by an act of treachery. Cormac himself said nothing as the Enchanter spoke, but watched the shimmering Queen, trying to gauge the emotions in her ever-changing face.

As Maedhlyn finished speaking, Goroien sat up. 'You always were an arrogant fool,' she said, 'and at last you pay the price. But then there was no Culain to save you this time. Wait in the outer rooms.' Maedhlyn bowed and left the chamber. 'Now you, prince Cormac.'

'Where should I begin?'

'How did the son of Uther come to be known as the son of a demon?'

And he told her. Her eyes blazed as he spoke of Culain's love for the Queen, but she remained still and silent until, at last, he spoke of the day on the mountain when the Vikings had come and Anduine was slain.

'So,' she whispered, 'you are here for love? Foolish, Cormac.'

'I never claim to be wise, my lady.'

'Let us test your wisdom,' she said, leaning forward with her face close to his. 'You have given me all that you have, is that not correct?'

'It is.'

'So you are of no further use to me?'

'That is true.'

'Did not Maedhlyn tell you I was not to be trusted? That I was evil?'

'Yes.'

'Then why did you come here?'

'He also said Culain lach Feragh once loved you.'

'And what difference does that make?' she snapped.

'Perhaps none. But I love Anduine and I know what that means. She is part of me, and I of her. Apart from her, I am nothing. I do not know if evil people can love – or if they do, how they can remain evil. But I do not believe Culain would love anyone who did not possess a measure of goodness.'

'As you say, prince Cormac, you are not wise. Culain loved me for my beauty and my wit. And he betrayed me, just as he betrayed Uther. He wed another . . . and I killed her. He had a daughter, Alaida; he tried to save her by allowing her to marry the King of Britain, but I found her and she too died. Then I tried to kill her son, Uther, but there I failed. And now, you tell me, he is a prisoner and facing death . . . and *his* son sits in my fortress asking a favour. What do you offer me so that I will grant you aid? Think carefully, Cormac. A great deal rests on your answer.'

'Then I am lost, my lady, for I can offer you nothing else.'

'Nothing,' she echoed. 'Nothing for Goroien? Leave me and join your friends. I will have an answer for you in a little while.'

He looked into her gleaming eyes and his heart sank.

*　　*　　*

421

The fishing-boat beached in the moonlight in the shelter of a rounded bay close to Anderida. Galead thanked the skipper, gave him two small golden coins and clambered over the side, wading through the calf-deep water to the rocky beach. He climbed a narrow path to the cliff-top, then turned to watch the boat bobbing out on the Gallic Sea.

The night air was cool, the sky clear. Galead pulled his long cloak about his shoulders and sought the shelter of the trees, halting in a hollow where the light from his fire could not be observed from more than a few yards in any direction. He slept uneasily and dreamt of a sword floating over water, and of a light in the sky like a great glowing, silver sphere speeding across the heavens. Waking at midnight, he added fuel to the fire; he was hungry and finished the last of the smoke-dried fish the boatman had supplied.

It had been twelve days since Caterix had rescued the robber and Galead found his thoughts constantly straying to the little man. He rubbed at the bristles on his chin and pictured a hot bath with scented water, and a slave girl to dry him and oil his body, soft hands easing the tension from his muscles. Groaning as desire surged in him, he quelled it savagely.

Gods, it was an age since he had last felt soft flesh beneath him and warm arms encircling his back. For several minutes the prince Ursus returned, haunting his mind.

'What are you doing in this forsaken land?' Ursus asked him.

'I am honour bound,' Galead told him.

'And where is the profit in it, fool?'

He transferred his gaze to the flames, unable to answer. He wished Pendarric would appear and sat quietly waiting until the dawn. But there was nothing.

The day was overcast and Galead set off in the direction the fisherman had indicated, heading west along the coast. Three times he saw deer, and once a large buck-rabbit, but with no bow there was no opportunity for swift hunting. Once he had known how to set a snare, but his lack of patience would never allow him to sit for hours in silent hope.

Throughout the morning he walked until he saw, slightly to the north, smoke curling into the air. He turned towards it and, cresting a hill, saw a village in flames. Bodies littered the ground and Galead sat down staring at the warriors in their horned helms as they moved from home to home, dragging out women and children, looting and killing. There were maybe fifty raiders and they stayed for more than an hour. When at last they moved off to the north, nothing stirred in the village save the snaking smoke from the gutted homes.

Galead rose wearily and made his way to the Saxon hamlet, halting by each of the bodies. None lived. A smashed pot still contained dried oats and these Galead scooped into a linen cloth, knotting it and tying it to his belt. Further on, in the centre of the devastated settlement, he found a ham charred on one side; with his knife he cut himself several slices and ate them swiftly.

Glancing to his right, he saw two children lying dead in the doorway of a hut, their arms entwined, their dead eyes staring at him. He looked away.

This was war. Not the golden glory of young men in bright armour carving their names in the flesh of history. Not the Homeric valour of heroes changing the face of the world. No, just an awful stillness, a total silence and an appalling evil that left dead children in its wake.

Carving several thick sections from the ham, he threw the joint aside and walked from the settlement, once more heading west. At the top of a rise he looked back. A fox had stolen in to the village and was tugging at a corpse. Above the scene the crows were circling . . .

Something in the bush to his right moved and Galead swung, his sword snaking out. A child screamed and the knight threw away his weapon.

'It's all right, little one,' he said softly, as the girl covered her face with her hands. Leaning in to the bush he lifted her out, cradling her to his chest. 'You are safe.' Her arms circled his neck and she clung to him with all her strength. Stooping, he lifted his sword and sheathed it, then turned from the village and continued on his way.

The child was no more than six years old, her arms painfully thin. Her hair was yellow, streaked with gold, and this he stroked as he walked. She said nothing, scarcely moving in his arms.

By mid-afternoon Galead had covered some twelve miles. His legs ached with walking, his arms were weary with carrying the child. As he topped a short rise he saw a village below: eighteen rounded huts within a wooden stockade. There were horses in a paddock and cattle grazed on the slopes. Slowly he made his way down the hill. A young boy saw him first and ran into the village, then a score of men armed with axes strode out to meet him. The leader was a stocky warrior with an iron-grey beard.

The man spoke in the guttural language of the Saxon.

'I do not speak your language,' Galead answered.

'I asked who you are,' said the man, his accent thick and harsh.

'Galead. This child is Saxon; her village was attacked by the Goths and all were slain.'

'Why would the Goths attack us? We share the same enemies.'

'I am a stranger here,' said Galead. 'I am a Merovingian from Gaul. All I know is that warriors with horned helms slaughtered the people of this child's village. Now can I bring her in – or shall we move on?'

'You are not an Uther-man?'

'I have said what I am.'

'Then you may enter. My name is Asta. Bring her to my home; my wife will take care of her.'

Galead carried the child to a long hall at the centre of the village where a sturdy woman tried to prise the child from his arms. She screamed and clung on and although Galead whispered gentle words to her, she would not leave him. The woman just smiled and fetched warm milk in a pottery cup. As Galead sat at a broad table, the girl in his lap drinking the milk, Asta joined them.

'You are sure it was the Goths?'

'There were no Romans in the attack.'

'But why?'

'We cannot talk now,' said Galead, indicating the silent child, 'but there were many women in the settlement.'

424

Asta's blue eyes gleamed with understanding and his face darkened. 'I see. And you observed this?'

'Unfortunately, yes.'

The man nodded. 'I have sent one rider to scout the village and follow the raiders, and three other to settlements close by. If what you say is true, then the Goths will rue this day.'

Galead shook his head. 'You do not have the men, and any attempt you make to fight will result in more slaughter. If I may advise you, have scouts out and when the Goths approach – hide in the hills. Does your king not have any forces here?'

'Which king is that?' snapped Asta. 'When I was a young warrior the Blood King crushed our forces, allowing the boy – Wulfhere – the title of King of the South Saxon. But he is no king; he lives like a woman – even to having a husband.' Asta spat his contempt. 'And the Blood King? What would he care that Saxon women are . . . abused?'

Galead said nothing. The child in his arms had fallen asleep, so he lifted her and carried her to a cot by the far wall near the burning log-fire, where three warhounds lay sleeping on the hay-strewn floor. He covered the child with a blanket, and kissed her cheek.

'You are a caring man,' said Asta as he returned to the table.

'Tell me of the Goths?' said Galead.

Asta shrugged. 'Little to tell. Around eight thousand landed here, and they destroyed a Roman legion. The main part of the army has headed west; around a thousand remain.'

'Why west? What is there for them?'

'I do not know. One of our young men rode with them for a while and he said their general wanted to know the best route to Sorviodunum. My man did not know. That is across the country.'

'Was the King, Wotan, with them?'

Once more the Saxon shrugged. 'What is your interest?'

'Wotan destroyed my whole family in Gaul and my interest is to see him die.'

'They say he is a god. You are mad.'

'I have no choice,' Galead answered.

425

14

'The south is virtually ours, sire,' said Tsurai, his flat brown eyes staring at the marble floor. Wotan said nothing as he watched the man, seeing the tautness in his flat Asiatic face, the tension in the muscles of his neck. Sweat was beading the man's brow and Wotan could almost taste his fear.

'And the north?'

'Unexpectedly, sire, the Brigantes have risen against us. A small group of our men strayed to one of their holy sites where there were some women dancing.'

'Did I not say there was to be no trouble with the tribes?'

'You did, sire. The men have been found and impaled.'

'Not enough, Tsurai. You will take their officers and impale them also. What regiment were they?'

'The Balders, sire.'

'One in twenty of them will be beheaded.'

'Lord, I know you are all-wise, but permit me to say that men at war are subject to many views of the passions . . .'

'Do not preach to me,' said Wotan softly. 'I know all the deeds men are capable of. It is nothing that a few women are raped, but obedience to my will is the paramount duty of all my people. A Saxon village was also attacked yesterday.'

'It was, lord?'

'It was, Tsurai. The same punishment must be exacted there – and very publicly. Our Saxon allies must see that Wotan's justice is swift and terrible. Now tell me of Cato in the middle lands.'

'He is a skilful general. Three times now he has fought holding actions, and our advance on Eboracum is not as swift as we had hoped. But still,' he continued hurriedly, 'we are advancing and the city should fall within days.'

426

'I did not expect the assault of Eboracum to succeed as swiftly as my generals thought it would,' said Wotan. 'It is of no matter. What have you discovered as to the whereabouts of the Blood King's body?'

'It is on the Isle of Crystal, my lord – close to Sorviodunum.'

'You are certain?'

'Yes, lord. Geminus Cato has an aide called Decius and he in turn has a mistress in Eboracum. He told her that a man called the Lance Lord took the King's body to the Isle to restore it.'

'Culain,' whispered Wotan. 'How I long to see him again!'

'Culain?' I do not understand, sire.'

'An old friend. Tell Alaric to proceed on Sorviodunum, but to send two hundred men to the Isle. I want the head of Uther on a lance; that body should have been cut into pieces on the first attack.'

'The enemy is saying, lord, that the king will come again.'

'Of course they are. Without Uther and the Sword, they are like children in the dark.'

'Might I ask, lord, why you do not slay his spirit? Would that not solve any problem of his return?'

'I desire the Sword and he alone knows where it lies. As long as his body lives, he has hope burning in his heart and defies me. When it dies, he will know and I will milk his despair. Go now.'

Alone once more, Wotan locked the door of his windowless chamber and settled back on the broad bed. Closing his eyes, he forced his spirit to plummet into darkness . . .

His eyes opened in a torchlit room of cold stone and he rose from the floor and took in his surroundings – the empty-eyed statues, the colourless rugs and hangings. How he hated this place for its pale shadow of reality. In the corner was a jug and three goblets. During the long centuries he had passed here he had often poured the red, tasteless liquid, pretending it was wine. Everything here was a mockery.

He strode to the outer hall. Everywhere men leapt to their feet in surprise, then dropped to their knees in fear. Ignoring them all, he walked swiftly to the dais on which stood the Throne of Molech. For some time he listened to the entreaties of those who served him here: the pleas for a return to the flesh, the promises of eternal obedience. Some he granted, most he refused. At last he left the throne-room and walked down the curved stairwell to the dungeons. A huge beast with the head of a wolf bowed as he entered, its tongue lolling from its long jaws and dripping saliva to the stone floor.

Wotan moved past him to the last dungeon where Uther hung by his wrists against the far wall. Tongues of flame licked at his body, searing and burning – the flesh repairing itself instantly, only to be burnt again. Wotan dismissed the flames – and the King sagged against the wall.

'How are you faring, Uther? Are you ready to lie to me again?'

'I do not know where it is,' whispered Uther.

'You must. You sent it.'

'I had no time. I just hurled it, wishing it gone.'

'The man who first saw you said he heard you call a name. What was that name?'

'I do not remember, I swear to God.'

'Was it a friend? Was it Culain?'

'Perhaps.'

'Ah, then it was not Culain. Good! Who then? Who could you trust, Blood King? It was not Victorinus. Whose name was on your lips?'

'You'll never find it,' said Uther. 'And if I was free from here, I could not find it either. I sent the Sword to a dream that can never be.'

'Tell me the dream!'

Uther smiled and closed his eyes. Wotan raised his hand and once more fire surged over Uther, forcing a blood-curdling scream of agony. The flames disappeared, the blacked skin replaced instantly.

'You think to mock me?' hissed Wotan.

'Always,' said Uther, tensing himself for the next torture.

'You will find that always is a very, very long time, Uther. I am tired of fire. You should have some company.' As Wotan stepped back to the doorway, holes appeared in the dungeon walls and rats poured out, swarming over the helpless King to bite and tear at his flesh.

Wotan strode from the dungeon, screams echoing behind him in the corridor.

He moved back to the upper levels and found the captain of his Loyals waiting by the throne. The man bowed as he entered.

'What do you want, Ustread?'

'I have something for you, lord. I hope it will make amends for my failure in Raetia.'

'It needs to be something rather greater than you can find here,' said Wotan, still angry from his talk with the stubborn King.

'I hope you will find I do not exaggerate, lord.' Ustread clapped his hands and two soldiers entered, holding a girl between them.

'A woman? What use is that here? I can –' Wotan stopped as he recognised the princess. 'Anduine? How?' He walked forward, waving away the guards and she stood silently before him.

'What happened to you, princess?'

'Your men killed me. I was in the mountains of the Caledones and they stabbed me.'

'They will pay. Oh, how they will pay!'

'I do not wish them to pay. What I wish is to be released. I am no longer of value to you; there is nothing left to sacrifice.'

'You misunderstood me, Anduine. You were never for sacrifice. Come with me.'

'Where?'

'To a private place, where no harm will come to you.' He smiled. 'In fact, quite the reverse.'

The child screamed in the night and Galead awoke instantly. Rising from his blankets by the dying fire he went to her, lifting her to his arms.

'I am here, little one. Have no fear.'

'*Mudder tod,*' she said, repeating the words over and over. Asta's wife crossed the hall, a blanket round her shoulders. Kneeling by the bedside, she spoke to the child for some minutes in a language unknown to the Merovingian. The girl's face was bathed in sweat and the woman wiped it clear as Galead laid her down once more. Her tiny hands gripped the front of Galead's tunic, her eyes fearful. *'Vader! Vader!'*

'I won't leave you,' he said. 'I promise.' Her eyes closed and she slept.

'You are a gentle man; very rare for a warrior,' said the woman. She stood and moved to the fire, adding wood and fanning the blaze to life. Galead joined her and they sat together in the new warmth.

'Children like me,' he said. 'It is a good feeling.'

'My name is Karyl.'

'Galead,' he replied. 'Have you lived here long?'

'I came from Raetia eight years ago when Asta paid my father. It is a good land, though I miss the mountains. What will you do with the child?'

'Do? I thought to leave her here, where she will be looked after.'

Karyl gave a soft, sad smile. 'You told her you would not leave her. She believed you and she is much troubled. No child should suffer the torment she has endured.'

'But I cannot look after her. I am a warrior, in the midst of a war.'

Karyl ran her hands through her thick, dark hair; her face in profile was not pretty, but there was a strength that made her a handsome woman.

'You have the Sight, have you not, Galead?' she whispered, and a shiver touched him.

'Sometimes,' he admitted.

'As do I. The men here were going to join the Goths, but I bade Asta wait, for the signs were strange. Then you came; a man who wears a face that is not his own, but who cares for a Saxon child. I know you are an Uther-man, but I have not told Asta. Do you know why?'

'No.'

'Because Asta will also be an Uther-man before this is over. He is a good man, my husband; a strong man. And these Goths are seduced by evil. Asta will summon the Fyrrd when he learns that what you said is true. And the Saxon warriors will rise.'

430

'There are no swords,' said Galead. 'Uther forbade any Saxon to bear arms.'

'What is a sword? A cutting tool. We Saxons are an ingenious people and our warriors now are skilled in the use of the axe. They will rise — and aid the Blood King.'

'You think we can win?'

She shrugged. 'I do not know. But you, Galead, you have a part to play in the drama . . . and it will not be with a sword.'

'Speak plainly, Karyl. I was never good at riddles.'

'Take the child with you. There is a woman you must meet: a cold, hard woman. She is the gateway.'

'The gateway to what?'

'As to that, I can help you no further. The child's name is Lectra, though her mother called her Lekky.'

'Where can I take her? You must know somewhere.'

'Take her to your heart, warrior. She is now your daughter, and that is how she sees you — as her father. Her mother's husband went to Raetia to serve Wotan while she was still pregnant and Lekky has waited long years to see him. In her tortured mind you are that man, come home to look after her. Without you, I do not think she will survive.'

'How do you know all this?'

'I know because I touched her, and you know I do not lie.'

'What was she saying when she woke?'

'Mudder tod? Mother dead.'

'And *Vader?* Father?'

Karyl nodded. 'Give me your hand.'

'Then you would know all my secrets.'

'Does that frighten you?'

'No,' he said, stretching out his arm, 'but it will lessen me in your eyes.'

She took his hand, sat silently for several moments and then released it.

'Sleep well Galead,' she said, rising.

'And you, lady.'

'I will sleep better now,' she told him, smiling. He watched her walk back to the far end of the hall and vanish into the shadows of

431

the rooms beyond. Lekky whimpered in her sleep and Galead took his blanket and lay down alongside her. She opened her eyes and cuddled into him.

'I am here, Lekky.'

'Vader?'

'Vader,' he agreed.

Goroien was alone in her mirrorless room, her mind floating back to the days of love and glory. Culain had been more than a lover, more than a friend. She remembered her father forbidding her to see the young warrior, and how she had trembled when he told her he had ordered his young men to hunt him down and kill him. Thirty of her father's finest trackers had set off into the mountains in the Autumn. Only eighteen returned; they said they had cornered him in a deep canyon, and then the snows had blocked the passes – and no man could live in that icy wilderness for long.

Believing her lover dead, Goroien had refused all food. Her father had threatened her, whipped her, but he could not defeat her. Slowly she lost her strength and death was very close on that midwinter night.

Semi-delirious and bed-ridden, she had not seen the drama that followed.

During the Feast of Midwinter the great door had opened and Culain lach Feragh had strode down the centre of the hall to stand before the Thane.

'I have come for your daughter,' he said, ice clinging to his dark beard.

Several men had leapt to their feet with swords ready, but the Thane waved them back.

'What makes you believe you can leave here alive?' the Thane asked.

Culain had stared around the long tables at the fighting men; then he laughed, and his contempt stung them all.

'What makes you think I could not?' he countered. An angry roar greeted the challenge, but once more the Thane quelled it.

'Follow me,' he said, leading the warrior to where Goroien lay. Culain knelt by the bedside, taking her hand, and she had heard his voice.

'Do not leave me, Goroien. I am here; I will always be here.'

And she had recovered, and they were wed. But that was in the days before the Fall of Atlantis, before the Sipstrassi made them gods. And in the centuries that followed each had taken many lovers, though always returning at the last to the sanctuary of each other's arms.

What had changed them, she wondered? Was it the power, or the immortality? She had borne Culain a son, though he never knew it, and Gilgamesh had inherited almost all of his father's skill with weapons. Unfortunately, he also inherited his mother's arrogance and amorality.

Now Goroien's thoughts turned to the last years. Of all obscenities, she had brought Gilgamesh back from the dead and taken him for her lover. In doing so she had doomed herself, for Gilgamesh suffered a rare disease of the blood that even Sipstrassi could not cure. And her immortality could no longer be assured by Sipstrassi alone. Blood and death kept her in the world of the flesh. In that period, as she had told Cormac, she had grown to hate Culain, killing his second wife and his daughter.

But at the very end, when Culain lay dying after his battle with Gilgamesh, she had given her own life to save him – dooming herself to this limitless hell.

Now her choice was simple. Did she aid Cormac or destroy him? All that formed the intellect of the former Witch Queen screamed at her to destroy this boy who was the seed of Uther who in turn was the seed of Culain through his daughter Alaida. The seed of her destruction! But her heart went out to the young man who had walked into the Void for the woman he loved. Culain would have done that.

For Goroien . . .

What had the boy said? A chance to return to the flesh? Did he think that would attract her? How could he know it was the last gift she would consider?

433

Gilgamesh entered and removed his helm. His face was scaled and reptilian; gone was the beauty he had known in life.

'Let me have the boy,' he said. 'I yearn for his life.'

'No. You will not have him, Gilgamesh. We will journey together to the Keep and then we will storm it. You will fight alongside Cormac and, regardless of the danger to yourself, you will keep him alive.'

'No!'

'If you love me – if you ever loved me – you will obey me now.'

'Why, Mother?'

She shrugged and turned away. 'There are no answers.'

'And when we have taken the Keep? If indeed we can.'

'Then we will free Uther also.'

'In return for what?'

'In return for nothing. That is the prize, Gilgamesh: Nothing. And I cannot think of anything I would rather have.'

'You make no sense.'

'Did you ever love me?'

He lifted his helm, his head bowing. 'I loved nothing else,' he said simply. 'Not life, not combat.'

'And will you do this for me?'

'You know I will do whatever you ask.'

'Once I was a queen among the gods,' she said. 'I was beautiful and men thought me wise. I stood with Culain at Babel and we brought down Molech and believed we had defeated a great evil, and men said they would sing of me throughout the ages. I wonder if they still do.'

Gilgamesh replaced his helm and backed from the room.

Goroien did not see him go. She was remembering that fine Spring day when she and Culain had wed by the Great Oak, when the world was young and the future limited.

15

For five days the dwindling force of Germinus Cato's two legions had withstood the ferocious charges of the Goths, retreating under cover of darkness and taking up fresh positions further back along the road to Eboracum. The men were weary to the point of exhaustion and Cato called his commanders to a meeting on the fifth night.

'Now,' he told them, 'is the time for courage. Now we attack.'

'Insanity!' said Decius, his disbelief total. 'Now is the time to retreat. We have less than six thousand men, some of whom are too tired to lift their shields.'

'And to where shall we retreat? Eboracum? It is indefensible. Further north to Vinovia? There we will meet a second army of Goths. No. Tonight we strike!'

'I will not be party to this!' said Decius.

'Then go back to Eboracum!' snapped Cato. 'Ten villas could not make me keep you here another moment.'

The young man rose and left the group and Cato switched his attention to the remaining eight officers. 'Anyone else?' No one moved. 'Good. Now, for five days we have offered the Goths the same strategy: hold and withdraw. They will be camped between the two rivers and we will come at them from both sides. Agrippa, you will lead the right column. Strike though to the tent that bears Wotan's banner. His generals will be at the centre. I will move from the left with sword and fire.'

Agrippa, a dark-eyed young man with ten years of warfare behind him, nodded. 'Decius did have a point,' he said. 'It will still be six thousand against twice that number. Once we attack, there can be no retreat. Win or die, general.'

'Realistically, our chances are slim. But the divine Julius once destroyed an army that outnumbered him by a hundred to one.'

'So his commentaries tell us,' said Agrippa.

'Come in on a wide front and re-form inside their camp. Once you have despatched the generals, try to forge a link with my column.'

'And if we cannot.'

'Then take as many of the bastards with you as you can.'

Cato dismissed the group and the officers roused their men. Silently the Roman army broke camp, leaving in two columns for the march.

Three miles away, the Goths had spread their tents across a wide flat area between two stretches of water. There were scores of fires, but few men were still awake. Sentries had been posted, but most of them were dozing at their posts or asleep behind bushes. No one feared an army that moved backwards day by day.

In the tent of the general, Leofric, the Gothic commanders sat on captured rugs of silk swilling wine and discussing the fall of Eboracum and the treasure that lay there. Leofric sat beside a naked young British girl, captured earlier that day by outriding scouts; her face was bruised from a blow one of the riders had given her before they raped her. But she was still pleasing to Leofric; he had taken her twice that day and planned to return for one more bout before passing her on to the men tomorrow. His hand cupped her breast, squeezing hard. She winced and cried out and Leofric grinned. 'Tell me how much you love me,' he said, his grip tightening.

'I love you! I love you!' she screamed.

'Of course you do,' he said, releasing her, 'and I love you – at least for tonight.' The men around him laughed. 'Tomorrow,' he said, 'there will be women for all of us – not village peasants like this wench but high born Roman cows with their pale skin and tinted lips.'

'You think Cato will retreat to the city?' asked Bascii, Leofric's younger brother.

'No, he cannot hold the walls. I think he will split his force and make for Vinovia, trying to gather men from among the Trinovante, but he will not succeed. We will have a hard job chasing him down, but he will fall. He has nowhere to go.'

'Is it true there are walls covered with gold in Eboracum?' Bascii asked.

'I doubt it, but there is treasure there and we will have it!'

'What kind of treasure?'

'The kind you find here,' he said forcing the girl back and opening her legs. She closed her eyes as to shouts of encouragement from the men around him. Leofric opened his breeches and mounted her.

Her torment continued interminably as first Leofric, then Bascii and then the others took her by turn. Pain followed pain ... followed humiliation. At last she was hurled aside and the men returned to their own tents.

Suddenly a trumpet blast pierced the night. Drunk and staggering, Leofric stumbled to the entrance to see Roman warriors streaming into his camp. Dumbfounded he fell back, scrabbling for his sword.

All was chaos as in tight, disciplined formations the Romans surged into the camp. Men ran from their tents, only to be ruthlessly cut down. Without preparation or organisation the Goths, most of them without armour, fought desperately in isolation.

Cato's men, moving from the left flank, put the torch to the tents – the wind fanning the flames to an inferno that swept across the open ground.

On the right Agrippa's force sliced through the Gothic ranks, forming a wedge that cut like a spear towards Leofric's tent. For all his drunkenness, the general was a warrior of great experience; he saw at once the desperate gamble Cato had taken and knew he could turn the tide. His battle-trained eye swept the scene. There! Bascii's men had formed a shield-wall, but what they needed was to strike against the Roman wedge, blocking it and the advance. The flames would stop the Romans from linking, and sheer weight of numbers would destroy them. Poor Bascii would never think of such a stratagem. Leofric stepped from the tent . . . and something struck him a wicked blow in the back. He stumbled and fell to his knees, his head spinning as he rolled to his back.

437

The British girl knelt over him, a blood knife in her hand, a wide smile of triumph on her mouth as the blade hovered over Leofric's eyes.

'I love you,' said the girl.

And the knife plunged down.

Cato stood over the body of Leofric, the dagger-hilt still jutting from the eye. 'The last of them are fleeing towards Petvaria,' said Agrippa. 'Lucius and three cohorts are harrying them.'

'I wonder what happened here,' Cato said.

'I do not know, sir. But, my congratulations on a famous victory!'

'Why congratulate me? You did your part, as did every man who served under me. By the gods, this place is beginning to stink!' Cato's dark eyes swept the field. Everywhere lay corpses – some burnt black by the inferno that roared over the tents, others lying where they had fallen, cut down by the swords of the legions. The British dead had been carried to a hastily dug ditch; the Goths, stripped of their armour and weapons, were being left for the crows and the foxes.

'Twelve thousand of the enemy were slain,' said Agrippa. 'The survivors will never re-form into an army.'

'Do not say *never*. They will return one day. Now we have to consider whether to march the men south to reinforce Quintas, or north to prevent the Goths marching on Eboracum.'

'You are tired, sir. Rest today and make your decision tomorrow.'

'Tomorrow may be too late.'

'My old commander used to say: "Weary men make mistakes." Trust his judgement, sir, and rest.'

'Now you quote my own words to me. Is there no respect left?' asked Cato, grinning.

'I have ordered your tent to be set up beyond the hill. The stream narrows in a hollow there, surrounded by oaks.'

Prasamaccus reined in his horse. To the north was the semi-ruined Wall of Antoninus, and before it a great battle was being fought. Thousands of Brigante warriors had encircled an army of Goths and the carnage was awesome. Neither side fought with any strategy – merely a savage and chaotic frenzy of slashing swords, axes and knives.

He steered his mount away from the scene; his practised eye could see there would be no victors today and both sides would withdraw from the field bloodied and exhausted. As a Brigante himself, he knew what would happen then. Tomorrow the tribesmen would renew their assault and continue to attack until the enemy was perished or victorious.

Moving west, he passed through the turf wall at a place where it had collapsed alongside a ruined fort. He shivered, whispered a prayer to the ghosts that still walked here and rode on towards the north-west and the mountains of the Caledones.

His journey had been largely without incident, though he had seen many refugees and heard terrifying stories of the atrocities committed by the invading army. Some had been exaggerated, most were stomach-turning. The elderly Brigante had long since ceased to be surprised at the horrors men could inflict on their neighbours, yet he thanked his gods that such stories could still inspire both horror and sorrow within him.

That night he camped by a fast-moving stream and moved out at first light on the steady climb to the cabin where he had first met Culain lach Feragh. It had not changed, and the welcoming sight of smoke from the short chimney lifted his spirits. As he dismounted a huge man stepped from the cabin, bearing a sword.

Prasamaccus limped towards him, hoping that his advanced years and obvious infirmity would sway the stranger into a more relaxed stance. 'Who are you, old man?' asked the giant, stepping forward and pressing the point of the blade to Prasamaccus' chest.

The Brigante gazed down at the blade, then up into the pale eyes of the warrior.

'I am not an enemy.'

'Enemies come in many guises.' The man looked weary, dark rings circling his eyes.

'I am looking for a young man and a woman. A friend said they were here.'

'Who was that friend?'

'His name is Culain; he brought them here to keep them safe.'

The man laid down the sword, turned and walked inside the cabin. Prasamaccus following. Within, he saw a wounded man lying on a narrow bed. The Brigante stood over him and saw that the wounds had sealed well, but there was a deathly pallor to his skin and he seemed to be barely breathing. On his chest lay a black Stone with hairline streaks of gold.

'He has been like that for weeks. I can do nothing more.'

'And the girl?'

'Buried outside. She died trying to save him.'

Prasamaccus stared at the wounded man's face – seeing the image of Uther, the same high cheekbones and strong jaw, the same long straight nose and thick brows.

'The magic is almost gone,' he said.

'I guessed that,' said the man. 'At the beginning it was gold streaked with black, but as the days passed the black lines grew. Will he die?'

'I fear that he will.'

'But why? The wounds are healing well.'

'Recently I saw another warrior in a like condition,' said Prasamaccus. 'They said his spirit was gone from his body.'

'But that is the same as being dead,' argued Oleg, 'and this boy is alive.'

Prasamaccus shrugged and lifted Cormac's wrist. 'The pulse is very weak.'

'I have some broth here, if you are hungry,' said Oleg, moving to the table. Prasamaccus limped to a chair and sat.

After they had both eaten, Oleg told the Brigante of the fight outside the cabin and how his own daughter, Rhiannon, had betrayed them. Prasamaccus listened in silence, reading the pain in Oleg's eyes.

'You love your daughter very much,' he remarked.

'Not any more.'

'Nonsense. We raise them, we hold them, we understand them, we weep at their weaknesses and their sorrows. Where is she now?'

'I do not know, I sent her away.'

'I see. I thank you, Oleg, for helping the prince.'

'Prince?'

'He is the son of Uther, High King of Britain.'

'He did not talk like a nobleman.'

'No, nor did life allow him to live like one.'

'Is there nothing we can do?' asked Oleg.

'If we could, I would take him to where his father lies, but it is too far; he would not survive the journey.'

'Then all we can do is sit and watch him die? I will not accept that.'

'Nor should you,' said a voice from the doorway and both men swung towards the sound, Oleg lurching upright and reaching for the sword.

'That will not be necessary,' said the stranger, pushing shut the door and moving into the room. He was tall and broad-shouldered, with hair and beard of spun gold. 'Do you remember me, Prasamaccus?'

The old Brigante sat very still. 'The day Uther found his Sword . . . you were there, helping Laitha. But you have not aged.'

'I was there. Now I am here. Put down your sword, Oleg Hammerhand, and prepare for a journey.'

'Where are we going?'

'To the Isle of Crystal,' replied Pendarric.

'This man says it is the length of the realm,' said Oleg. 'It will take weeks.'

'Not by the roads he will travel,' Prasamaccus told him.

'What roads are these?' Oleg asked as Pendarric moved into the clearing before the cabin.

'The Spirit Paths,' answered the Brigante. Swiftly Oleg made the sign of the Protective Horn and followed his limping companion to the clearing. Pendarric now held a measuring rod and was carefully chalking a series of interlocking triangles around a central circle. He looked up from his knees.

'Make yourselves useful,' he said. 'Dress the boy in warm clothes and then carry him out here. Be careful not to tread on the chalk-lines, or in any way disturb them.'

'He is a sorcerer,' whispered Oleg.

'I think that he is,' agreed Prasamaccus.

'What shall we do?'

'Exactly what he says.'

Oleg sighed. They dressed the unconscious Cormac and Oleg lifted him carefully from the bed, carrying him outside to where Pendarric waited in the centre of what appeared to be a curious star. Oleg trod carefully across the lines and laid the body down beside the tall sorcerer. Prasamaccus followed, bringing Oleg's sword and another blade.

When all were inside the Circle, Pendarric raised his arms and sunlight glinted from a golden Stone in his right hand. The air cracked around them, and a shimmering light began that suddenly blazed so bright that Prasamaccus shielded his eyes. Then it was gone . . .

And the trio stood within a stone circle on the crest of a hill crowned with trees.

'This is where I leave you,' said Pendarric. 'May good fortune attend you at the end of your journey.'

'Where are we?' asked Oleg.

'Camulodunum,' said Pendarric. 'It was not possible to move straight to the Isle. From here you will appear at the centre of the settlement, for it has been designed to imitate the setting of the stones. An old friend awaits you, Prasamaccus. Give her my love.'

Pendarric stepped from the circle and gestured. Once more the air shimmered and the next sight to greet their eyes was of three astonished women sitting in a roundhall, watching over the body of Uther.

'Our apologies, ladies,' said Prasamaccus, bowing. Oleg lifted Cormac and carried him to the large round table on which the King lay, where gently he laid him down beside his father. Prasamaccus approached and gazed at the two bodies with great tenderness.

'Such a tragedy that they have never met until now.'

One of the women left the room, the others remaining deep in prayer.

The door opened and a tall figure dressed in white entered. Behind her came the woman who had left.

Prasamaccus limped forward. 'Lady, once more I must apolo—' He stumbled to a halt as Laitha approached.

'Yes, Prasamaccus, it is I. And I am becoming increasingly angry about being haunted by shadows from a past I would as soon forget. How many more bodies do you intend to bring to the Isle?'

He swallowed hard and could find no words as she swept past him and looked down on the face of Cormac Daemonsson.

'Your son, Gian,' whispered Prasamaccus.

'I can see that,' she said, reaching out and stroking the soft beard. 'How like his father he is.'

'Seeing you makes me very happy,' he told her. 'I have thought of you often.'

'And I you. How is Helga?'

'She died. But we were very contented together and I have no regrets.'

'Would that I could say the same! That man,' she said, pointing at Uther, 'destroyed my life. He robbed me of my son, and any happiness I could have had.'

'In doing so he robbed himself,' said the Brigante. 'He never stopped loving you, lady. It is just . . . just that you were not meant for each other. Had you known Culain was alive, you would not have wed him. Had he been less proud, he could have put Culain from his mind. I wept for you both.'

'My tears dried a long time ago,' said Laitha, 'as I lay on a ship bound for Gaul with my son dead behind me – or so I thought.' She was silent for a moment. 'Both you and your companion must leave the Isle. You will find Culain camped on the hillside across the lake; there he waits for news of the man he betrayed.'

Prasamaccus looked into her eyes. Her hair was still dark though a silver streak showed at one temple, and her face was beautiful and curiously ageless. She did not look like a woman in her forties, but her eyes were flat and lifeless and there was a hardness to her that Prasamaccus found disturbing.

443

She looked down at the bodies once more, her face expression-less, then transferred her gaze to the Brigante.

'There is nothing of me in him,' she said. 'He is Uther's get and will die with him.'

They found Culain sitting cross-legged on the top of a hill. Behind him was a narrow causeway that led back to the Isle, clearly visible now the tide was low. He rose and embraced Prasamaccus.

'How did you come here?'

'I brought Cormac.'

'Where is he?'

'Alongside the King.'

'Sweet Christos!' whispered Culain. 'Not dead?'

'Close to it. Like Uther. Only a fading Stone keeps his heart beating.'

Prasamaccus introduced Oleg, who outlined once more the drama that had seen the death of Anduine. Culain sank back to the earth, staring to the east. The Brigante placed his hand on Culain's shoulder. 'It was not your doing, Lance Lord. You are not responsible.'

'I know – and yet I might have saved them.'

'Some things are beyond even your great powers. At least Uther and his son are still alive.'

'For how long?'

Prasamaccus said nothing.

'There are other matters to concern us,' said Oleg softly, pointing to the east where a large group of armed men could be seen riding at speed towards the hill.

'Goths!' said Prasamaccus. 'What can they want here?'

'They are here to kill the King,' said Culain, rising smoothly and taking up his silver staff. Twisting it at the centre, he produced two short swords, then spun and ran towards the causeway. Halfway down the hill, he turned and called to Prasamaccus.

'Hide, man! This is not place for a cripple.'

'He's right,' said Oleg, 'though he could have been less blunt. There are some bushes down there.'

'What of you?'

'I owe Cormac my life. If those men seek to kill the King, I don't doubt they'll also butcher the boy.' Without another word he sped down the hill to the mud-covered causeway; it was a mere six feet wide and the footing was treacherous. Carefully Oleg made his way some thirty feet along it to where Culain stood waiting.

'Welcome,' said Culain. 'I applaud your courage – if not your wisdom.'

'We cannot hold this bridge,' said Oleg. 'Weight of numbers will force us back, and once we are on level ground they will over-whelm us.'

'Now would be an exceptionally good time to think of a second strategy,' observed the Lance Lord as the Goths drew rein at the end of the causeway.

'I was just making conversation,' replied Oleg. 'Do you object to me taking the right side?'

Culain smiled and shook his head. Oleg moved warily to the right as the Goths dismounted and several of them moved on to the causeway.

'They do not appear to have any bowmen in their ranks,' said Oleg. An arrow sliced through the air and Culain's sword flashed up, swatting it aside just before it reached Oleg's chest.

A second followed, then a third. Culain ducked the one, then blocked the other with his sword.

'You are very skilled,' said Oleg. 'Perhaps you can teach me that trick on another day.'

The Goths charged before Culain could reply. They could only come two abreast. Culain moved forward, blocking a slashing cut and disembowelling the first man. Oleg ducked under a wild slash and hammered his fist to the other warrior's jaw, spinning him unconscious to the water where he sank without a struggle, his heavy armour dragging him to the bottom.

Culain's swords were shimmering arcs of silver steel as he wove a terrible web of death among the warriors pushing forward. Beside him Oleg Hammerhand fought with all the skill he could muster. Yet both men were forced inexorably towards the Isle.

The Goths fell back momentarily and Culain, breathing hard, steadied himself. Blood was flowing from a shallow cut to his temple and a deeper wound in his shoulder. Oleg had suffered wounds to his thigh and side. Yet still they stood.

From the hillside Prasamaccus could only watch in sad admiration as the two men defied the impossible. The sun was sinking in glory behind them and the water shone red in the dusk. Once more the Goths surged forward, only to be met by cold steel and courage.

Culain slipped and a sword pierced his side, but his own blade swept up through the enemy's groin and the man screamed and fell back. Scrambling to his feet, Culain blocked another blow and slashed his second sword in a vicious cut through his attacker's throat. Oleg Hammerhand was dying. One lung was pierced and blood frothed over his beard; a swordblade jutted from his belly, the wielder dead from an instinctive riposte.

But with a bellowing roar of rage and frustration Oleg charged into the Goths' ranks, his great weight smashing men from their feet. Swords cut at him from every side, and even as he died his fist crashed into a man's neck to snap it instantly. As he fell Culain rushed into the fray, his blades cleaving and killing. Dismayed, the Goths fell back once more.

Prasamaccus closed his eyes, tears streaming down his cheeks. He could not bear to watch the death of the Lance Lord, nor did he have the courage to turn away. Then a sound came from his right: marching men. Prasamaccus drew his hunting-knife and limped into their path, ready to die. The first man he saw was Gwalchmai, walking beside Severinus Albinus. Behind them came the survivors of Uther's Ninth Legion – grey-haired veterans long past their prime, yet still with the look of eagles. Gwalchmai ran forward.

'What is happening, my friend?'

'Culain is trying to hold the causeway. The Goth's seek the body of the King.'

'Ninth to me!' shouted Severinus, his gladius snaking clear of its bronze scabbard. With a roar the eighty men gathered alongside him, taking up positions as if the years of retirement had been but a midsummer dream.

'Wedge formation!' called Albinus and the soldiers at the outer edges fell back, forming the legendary spearpoint. 'War pace! Forward!' The wedge moved out on to open ground before the causeway, where the great mass of the Goths still waited a chance to mount the mud-covered bridge. Enemy warriors saw the approaching force and gazed in disbelief. Some even smiled at the sight of the greyhaired veterans, but their smiles vanished as the iron swords clove into their ranks, the wedge plunging on to the causeway itself.

A giant Goth hurled himself at Albinus, only to find his wild cut neatly blocked and a gladius slicing into his neck. 'Horns!' shouted Albinus. The veterans swung the line into the feared bull's horns and half-encircled the dismayed Goths. They fell back in disorder, seeking to regroup on higher ground. 'At them!' shouted Albinus and the men at the centre of the line charged. It was too much for the Goths, who broke and ran. On the causeway Culain, bleeding from a dozen wounds, saw the men facing him leap into the water rather than encounter the veterans of the Ninth. Despite their struggles to reach the shore, many of them were hauled below the surface by the weight of their armour. Culain fell to his knees, a terrible weariness sweeping over him.

His swords slipped from his hands.

Gwalchmai ran to him, catching him even as he toppled towards the water.

'Hold the causeway. They will return,' Culain whispered.

'I will carry you to the Isle, they'll heal you.'

Gwalchmai's huge arms gathered him up and the old Cantii warrior staggered along the causeway to where several women were watching the battle.

'Help me!' he said and they came forward hesitantly, taking his burden. Together they carried the dying man to the round hall.

Laitha watched them come, her face without expression as they laid him down on the mosaic floor with a rolled cloak under his head.

447

'Save him,' said Gwalchmai. A woman opened Culain's tunic, looked at the terrible wounds and closed it again. 'Magic! Use your magic!'

'He is beyond magic,' said another woman softly. 'Let him pass peacefully.'

Prasamaccus joined them, kneeling by Culain's side.

'You and Oleg killed thirty-one of them. You were magnificent,' he said. 'And Albinus has his men guarding the causeway and others patrolling the lake. More are coming every day; we will protect the King and his son.'

Culain's eyes opened. 'Gian?'

'She is not here,' said Prasamaccus

'Tell her . . .' Blood bubbled from his ruptured lungs.

'Culain? Dear God! Culain?'

'He is gone, my friend,' said Gwalchmai.

Prasamaccus closed the dead eyes and pushed himself wearily to his feet. In the doorway he saw Laitha, her eyes wide.

'He asked for you,' he said, his voice accusing. 'And you could not grant him even that. Where is your soul, Gian? You wear the robes of a Christian. Where is your love?'

Without a word, she turned and was gone.

16

Lekky, her hair washed and her thin body scrubbed by Karyl, sat on a horse gazing down from a great height at the countryside around her. Behind her sat her father, the tallest and strongest man in the world. Nothing could harm her now. She wished her father had not forgotten how to speak the language of the People; but even so his smile was like the dawn sun, and his hands were soft and very gentle.

She glanced down at her new tunic of grey wool, edged with black thread. It was warm and soft, just like the small sheepskin boots Karyl had given her. She had never worn footwear of any kind, and the sensation was more pleasant than she could ever have imagined as she wriggled her toes against the soft wool. Her father tapped her shoulder and pointed into the sky.

Swans were flying in a V-formation, their long necks straight as arrows.

The horse Asta had given them was an elderly mare of sixteen hands, sway-backed and slow. But Lekky had never ridden a horse, and to her it was a charger of infinite strength that could outride any of the war-horses of the Goths.

They stopped for a meal when the sun was at its height and Lekky ran around the clearing in her new boots, never having to worry about sharp stones beneath her feet. And her father played a silly game, pointing at obvious objects like the trees and sky and roots and giving them strange names. They were easy to remember, and he seemed pleased when she did so.

In the afternoon, close to dusk, she saw Goths in the distance riding towards them on the road. Father steered the mare into the trees and they dismounted until the Goths had passed. But she was not frightened; there were fewer than twenty of them and she knew Father could kill them all.

Later they camped in a shallow cave and he wrapped her in blankets and sat with her, singing songs in his strange, melodious language. He was not a good singer – not like Old Snorri – but she lay calmly in the firelight, staring up at the most wonderful face in the world, until at last her eyes drifted closed and she slipped into a dreamless sleep.

Galead sat and watched her for a long time. Her face was oval and pretty. One day she would be a beauty and boys would come from miles around to pay court at her door – especially if she kept the habit of tilting her head and smiling knowingly, as she had when he tried to teach her the basics of his language.

His smile faded. 'What are you thinking of, you fool?' he asked himself. The country was at war, and even if by some miracle the Goths were beaten back the Saxons would rise, or the Jutes, or the Angles, or any of the multitude of tribesmen. What chance would Lekky have of living a gentle life?

He settled down beside her, banked up the fire and rested his head on his arm. Sleep came swiftly, but with it dreams . . .

He saw a giant figure outlined against the stars, clouds swirling around its knees. The head was terrible, with eyes of fire and teeth of sharp iron, and its hand was reaching slowly for a great Sword that floated blade downwards in the sky. On the other side of the blade, turned away from it, was a beautiful woman. Then above the scene appeared a blazing, moving star, like a great silver coin racing across the heavens. The giant warrior cowered away from the star and the Sword seemed to shrink. The scene shifted and he watched the Blood King, naked and alone in the courtyard at Eboracum. As the beasts issued from the yawning tunnel, he hurled his Sword into the air and called out a single word.

Then Galead found himself sitting in a terraced garden, the sense of peace and tranquillity total. He knew who would be there.

'Welcome,' said Pendarric.

'I could stay here for ever,' Galead said and Pendarric smiled.

'I am glad you can feel the harmony. What have you learned, young knight?'

'Little that I did not know. What became of the old man, Caterix?'

'He found his friends and is safe.'

'And the robber?'

'Returned to the forest.'

'To kill again?'

'Perhaps, but it does not lessen the deed. You are journeying to the Isle of Crystal?'

'Yes.'

'Uther is there.'

'Alive?'

'That is yet to be established. You must find the lady Morgana and tell her to follow once more the advice of Pendarric. Do you understand your dreams?'

'No, save that the giant is Wotan and the Sword is Uther's.'

'The star is a comet that moves across the heavens once in every man's lifetime. It is made of Sipstrassi, and when it comes close it draws its magic back to its heart. A long time ago a piece of that comet crashed into our world, giving birth to magic. Now, as it passes once more, it will draw some of that magic away. There will be a moment, Galead – and you will know it – when the fate of the worlds hangs in balance. When that moment comes, tell the Sword-wielder to give you his blade. Raise it high and wish for whatever you will.'

'Why is it that you never speak plainly? Is this all a game to you?'

Pendarric shook his head. 'Do you not think I would gladly give you the wisdom to help the world? But that is not the way the Mystery is passed on. It never was. For each man, life is a journey towards knowledge and answers to the eternal questions: Who am I? Why am I here? If I tell you to go to a certain place and speak a Word of Power, what have you learned save that Pendarric is a sorcerer? But if I say to you, go to a certain place and say what is in your heart, and that proves to be a Word of Power, then you have learned something far greater. You will have stepped to the Circle of Mystery and you will progress to its centre. Caterix understood this when he aided the robber, though his heart urged him to let the man die. You also may come to understand.'

'And if I do not?'

451

'Then evil will be triumphant and the world will remain the same.'

'Why must that responsibility be mine?'

'Because you are the one least able to cope with it. You have journeyed far, prince Ursus – from the grasping, lecherous prince to the Knight Galead who rescues a child. Continue on your journey.'

Galead awoke soon after dawn. Lekky slept on and he prepared a bowl of hot oats, mixed with honey from the food-store Karyl had supplied. After breakfast, he saddled the mare and they set off towards the north west.

In the middle of the morning as he rode into a small wood he found himself facing a dozen riders, all wearing the horned helms of the Goths. He drew rein and stared at the cold-eyed men while Lekky shrank against him, shivering with fear.

The leader rode forward and spoke in Saxon.

'I am from Gaul,' answered Ursus in the Sicambrian tongue. The man looked surprised.

'You are a long way from home,' he said. The other riders moved closer, swords in their hands.

Galead prepared to hurl Lekky from the saddle and fight to the last.

'Indeed I am. But then so are you.'

'Who is the child?'

'An orphan. Her village was destroyed and her mother slain.'

'Such is war,' said the man, shrugging. He rode still closer. Lekky's eyes were wide with terror as he leaned in towards her and Galead tensed, his hand edging towards his sword.

'What is your name, little one?' the rider asked in Saxon.

'Lekky.'

'Do not be frightened.'

'I am not frightened,' she said. 'My father is the greatest of killers and will slay you all if you do not go away.'

'Then I think we had better go away,' he said, smiling. Straightening in the saddle, he returned his gaze to Galead.

'She is a brave girl,' he said, switching to Sicambrian. 'I like her. Why does she say you are her father?'

452

'Because I now have that honour.'

'I am Saxon myself,' said the man, 'so I know what an honour it is. Be good to her.'

Waving his arm, the man led the riders past the astonished Galead and continued on his way. The Goths rode on for several hundred yards, then the leader reined in once more and stared back at the single rider.

'Why did we not kill him?' asked his second-in-command. 'He was not Saxon.'

The leader shrugged. 'Damned if I know! I left this cursed country seven years ago and swore I would never come back. I had a pregnant wife here. And I have been thinking of finding her – and my son. I was just thinking of her when the rider appeared and it caught me off my guard.'

'We could always ride back and kill him?'

'No, let him go. I liked the child.'

Wotan led Anduine through a maze of corridors to a small group of rooms deep in the heart of the fortress. At the centre of the main room was a dark, round table on which sat a skull, a circlet of what appeared to be silver embedded in the bone of the brow. He pulled a chair close to the table.

'Sit!' he commanded and placed one hand on the skull, the other on Anduine's head. She felt a great drowsiness seeping over her and in a moment of panic fought against it, but the need to sleep was overpowering and she faded into it.

Wotan closed his eyes . . .

. . . and opened them in his tent outside Vindocladia, less than a day's march from the Great Circle at Sorviodunum.

'Tsurai!' he called. At once the tent-flap opened and his aide stepped into view, his swarthy features taut with fear. Wotan smiled.

'Fetch the girl Rhiannon.'

'Yes, lord.'

Minutes later two men ushered the girl into the tent, where Wotan now sat on the wooden throne. He dismissed the guards and gazed down on her face as she knelt before him.

'You led my guards to the traitor, Oleg,' he said, 'but he escaped?'

'Yes, my lord.'

'And his companions were slain?'

She nodded dumbly, aware of the glint in his eye and the chilling sibilance of his words.

'But you did not mention the names of his companions.'

'They were not traitors, lord, merely Britons.'

'You lie!' he hissed. 'One of them was the princess from Raetia.'

Rhiannon scrambled to her feet, desperate to escape the burning eyes. He lifted his hand and as she reached the tent entrance she felt a numbing force close around her waist, dragging her back.

'You should not have lied to me, pretty one,' he whispered as she was hurled to the ground at his feet. His hand descended to touch her brow and her eyes closed.

He lifted the sleeping body and laid it on the silk covers of the bed beyond the throne. His hands covered her face, his eyes closed in concentration. When he opened them and removed his hands, the features of Rhiannon had disappeared to be replaced by the oval beauty that had been Anduine. He drew a deep breath, calming himself for the Call, then placed his thumbs gently on the eyes of the sleeping woman. A shuddering breath filled her lungs and her hands twitched.

He stood back. 'Awake, Anduine,' he said.

She sat up and blinked, then rose from the bed, moving to the tent-flap and staring in silent wonder at the sky. When she turned back there were tears in her eyes.

'How did you do this?' she asked.

'I am a god,' he told her.

Deep in the abyss of the Void, Rhiannon also opened her eyes . . .

And her screams were pitiful.

Galead and Lekky arrived at the lake at sundown two days after the veterans of the Ninth had secured the causeway, which was now under water as the tide was at its height. As was the Roman way, a temporary fort had been established within the clearing: earth walls had been thrown up, patrolled by straight-backed warriors of the deadliest fighting force ever to march into battle.

Galead was stopped at the entrance by two sentries, one of whom fetched Severinus Albinus. The general had twice met Ursus, but had never seen the blond warrior the Merovingian had become. Dismounting, Galead explained that he had been with Victorinus in Gaul. Then he was led to a timber structure and told to wait for Gwalchmai. Lekky was given some soup and Galead settled down beside her at a rough-hewn table. After an hour, Gwalchmai entered with Prasamaccus alongside him. Lekky was asleep in Galead's lap, her head resting on his chest.

'Who is it you say you are?' asked the tall Cantii.

'I was Ursus, but the King used his power to change my face – in order that I would not be recognised as a Merovingian noble. My name is now Galead. I was sent with Victorinus.'

'And where is he?'

'He feared treachery and bade me make my own way. I think he is dead.'

'And how do we know you are no traitor?'

'You do not,' he said simply. 'And I would not blame you for your fears. A man appeared to me and told me to come to the Isle; he said I should seek the woman who ruled here. I think it is important that I at least meet her; you can have me guarded.'

'Who was this man?' Gwalchmai asked.

'He said his name was Pendarric.'

'What did he look like?' asked Prasamaccus.

'Golden hair, around thirty years old, maybe more.'

'And what were you to say to the lady?' continued the Brigante.

'I was to urge her to once more follow the advice of Pendarric.'

'Do you know what was meant?'

'No.'

Prasamaccus sat down and both Britons questioned Galead at length about his journey, and the instructions he had received from Uther. At last satisfied, they led him to a shallow-hulled boat and, with Lekky still asleep in his arms, Galead sat at the stern and felt the peace of the Isle sweep over him.

They beached the boat in a tree-shadowed bay and walked up to the settlement. Galead saw that it was constructed as a great circle of twelve huts built in a ring about a round hall. The perimeter was walled with timber – though not as a fort, more as a high fence. Several women in dark robes moved across the clearing, ignoring the newcomers who walked to a hut on the western side of the circle. Inside there were rugs and blankets, pottery jugs and a small iron brazier glowing with coals. Galead laid Lekky down and covered her with a blanket.

'Your sword,' said Gwalchmai, as Galead straightened. Pulling it clear, he handed it hilt-first to the Cantii. Prasamaccus then searched Galead swiftly and expertly for any concealed weapons.

'Now you may see the King,' Prasamaccus told him.

The three men made their way to the hall and Galead stood silently looking down on the two bodies lying side by side on the round table.

Three women sat close by, their heads bowed in prayer. Galead turned to Prasamaccus.

'Is there nothing we can do?'

The Brigante shook his head. The far door opened and Laitha entered. Prasamaccus and Gwalchmai both bowed and she approached Galead.

'Yet another wanderer,' she said. 'And what do you desire?'

'You are the Lady of the Isle?'

'I am Morgana.'

He gave her Pendarric's message and saw her smile. 'Well,' she said, 'that is a simple matter, for he once told me to raise my hand high in the air and grasp whatever I found.' She lifted a slender arm, clenched her fist and brought it down to hold it before Galead's face. Her fingers opened. 'There! Nothing. Do you have any other messages?'

'No, my lady.'

'Then go back to your little war,' she snapped. He watched her depart, and noticed she had not even glanced at the bodies.

'I do not understand,' he said.

Prasamaccus moved to his side. 'A quarter of a century ago, in a world that was not this one, she stood on a hilltop and raised her arm. Her hand seemed to disappear, and when she withdrew it she held the Sword of Power. With it she rescued Uther and the Ninth Legion from the Void and brought about the downfall of the Witch Queen. And Uther won back his father's kingdom.'

Then she is the Queen?'

'She is.'

'Pendarric was wrong, it seems. Who is the young warrior beside the King?'

'His son, Cormac. Are you a man given to prayer?'

'I am beginning to learn.'

'This is a good place to practise,' said the Brigante, lowering his head.

Lekky awoke in the hut; it was dark, and wind whistled in the thatch above her.

'Vader?' Fear sprang in her heart; the last thing she remembered was eating the soup the soldier had given her. She threw back the blanket and ran outside, but there was no one in sight; she was alone. *'Vader?'* she called again, her voice starting to tremble. Tears flowed and she ran into the clearing, where suddenly a tall figure in white appeared before her like a spirit of the dark.

Lekky screamed and stepped back, but the woman knelt before her. 'Do not be afraid,' she said, her Saxon heavily accented but her voice warm. 'No harm can come to you here. Who are you?'

'My name is Lekky. Where is my father?'

'First let us go inside, away from the cold.' She held out her hand and Lekky took it, allowing herself to be led into a second hut where a warm fire glowed in an iron brazier. 'Would you like some milk?' Lekky nodded and the woman poured the liquid into a pottery goblet.

'Now, who is your father?'

Lekky described him, in wondrous glowing terms.

'He is with his friends and will come for you soon. How is it that a small girl like you rides with such a warrior? Where is your mother?'

Lekky turned away, her lips tightening, her eyes filling with tears. Morgana reached out and took her hand. 'What happened?'

457

The child swallowed hard and shook her head. Morgana closed her eyes and stroked the girl's blonde hair. Drawing on the power of the Mysteries, she linked with the child and saw the raiders, the slaughter and the terror. She saw also the man, Galead.

She drew the child to her, hugging her and kissing her brow. 'It is all right. Nothing can harm you here, and your father will soon return.'

'We will always be together,' said Lekky, brightening. 'And when I am big, I shall marry him.'

Morgana smiled. 'Little girls do not marry their fathers.'

'Why?'

'Because . . . by the time you grow up, he will be very old and you will desire a younger man.'

'I won't care how old he is.'

'No,' whispered Morgana, 'neither did I.'

'Do you have a husband?'

'No . . . yes. But I was like you, Lekky. I lived in a village and it was . . . attacked. A man rescued me too, and raised me and taught me many things. And . . .' Her voice faltered, her vision blurring.

'Don't be sad, lady.'

Morgana forced a smile. 'We must see about getting you settled down – otherwise your father will come back to his hut and be worried.'

'Did you marry him?'

'In a way. Just like you, I loved him as a child does. But I never grew up and he never grew old. Now I'll take you home.'

'Will you sit with me?'

'Yes, of course I will.' Hand in hand they returned to the hut. The fire had almost died and Morgana added fuel, shaking out the ash-pan to allow air to the flames. Lekky snuggled down in her blanket.

'Do you know any stories?'

'All my stories are true ones,' said Morgana, sitting beside her, 'and that means they are sad. But when I was young I found a fawn in the forest. It had a broken leg. My . . . father was going to kill it, but he saw that I was very unhappy, so he set the leg and bound it

458

with splints. Then he carried it home. For weeks I fed the fawn and one day we took off the splints and watched it walk. For a long time the fawn lived near our cabin, until it grew into a strong stag. Then it went away into the mountains where, I am sure, it became the prince of all stags. From that time he always called me Gian Avur, Fawn of the Forest.'

'Where is he now?'

'He . . . went away.'

'Will he come back?'

'No, Lekky. Go to sleep now. I will stay here until your father returns.'

Morgana sat quietly by the brazier hugging her knees, her memory replaying the events of her youth. She had loved Culain in just the way Lekky loved Galead, with the simple all-consuming passion of the child whose knight has come for her. And now she knew it was not Culain who was wholly at fault. He had sacrificed many years to raise her and had always acted nobly. But she, from the moment he had arrived at Camulodunum, had used all her wiles to pierce his loneliness. She it was who had drawn him into betraying his friend. Yet Culain had never reproached her, accepting all the guilt.

What had he said that day on the Tor? 'The scrap of guilt' at her feet. Well, she had raised it to her face and taken it to her heart.

'I am sorry, Culain,' she whispered. 'I am sorry.'

But he was dead now and could not hear her.

And her tears melted the years of bitterness.

Goroien stepped into the audience hall, dressed in armour of blazing silver with two short-swords strapped to her slender hips. Cormac, Maedhlyn and the Romano-Britons all stood.

'I will aid you, Cormac,' she said. 'In a while, Gilgamesh will come to you and tell you that the army of the Witch Queen is ready to march.'

Cormac bowed deeply. 'I thank you, lady.'

The Queen said no more and left the hall without a backward glance.

'What did you say to her?' asked Maedhlyn.

Cormac waved away the question. 'How can we be sure that Wotan will be absent from the Keep? You said the men there are called Loyals, but they would not be loyal to something they never saw.'

'Very shrewd, prince Cormac,' said the Enchanter.

'Leave the empty compliments,' snapped Cormac. 'Answer the question.'

'We cannot be sure, but we know he lives in the world of flesh and that will take most of his time. We have all seen both worlds. In which would you choose to live, Cormac?'

'I mean to keep faith with Goroien,' said Cormac, ignoring the question, 'and that means that I need to know what you plan. You have been wonderfully helpful, Maedhlyn. You were there when I arrived in this forsaken land . . . as if you were expecting me. And that nonsense with the coin – you knew I was not dead.'

'Yes,' admitted Maedhlyn, 'that is true, but my loyalty was to Uther – to bring him back.'

'Not true. Not even close,' said the prince. By now Victorinus and the other Britons were listening intently and Maedhlyn was growing increasingly nervous. 'What you desire, Wizard, is to regain your body. You can only do that if we take Wotan's soul.'

'Of course I wish to return to the flesh. Who would not? Does that make me a traitor?'

'No. But if Uther is released and returns to the world, he will attempt to kill Wotan. And that would doom you here for ever, would it not?'

'You are building a house of straw.'

'You think so? You did not wish us to come to Goroien; you argued against attacking the Keep.'

'That was to save your souls!'

'I wonder.'

Maedhlyn stood, his pale eyes scanning the group. 'I have aided those of your blood, Cormac, for two hundred years. What you suggest is shameful. You think I am a servant of Wotan? When Uther was in danger, I managed to escape this world briefly and warn him. That is why he still lives, for he managed to hide the Sword of Power. I am no traitor, nor have I ever been.'

'If you wish to come with us, Maedhlyn, then convince me of it.'

'You are right, I knew you were not dead. Sometimes I can breach the Void and glimpse the world of flesh. I saw you fall in the Caledones woods, and I also saw the huge man with you carry you into the hut and lay you on the bed. You wore a Stone, and its power was unwittingly unleashed by your companion. He told it to keep you alive. It did – and it does. But I knew you were on the point of death and I travelled to the Gateway to await you. And, yes, I want to return to the world, but I would not sacrifice Uther's life to achieve it. There is nothing more that I can say.'

Cormac swung on Victorinus. 'You know this man, so you choose,' he said.

Victorinus hesitated, his gaze locked on Maedhlyn's. 'He always had his own game, but he is right when he says there is no treachery in him. I say we should take him with us.'

'Very well,' said Cormac, 'but watch him carefully.'

The door opened and Gilgamesh entered. He was fully armoured in black and silver, a dark helm once more covering his face. He approached Cormac and as their eyes met Cormac felt his hatred like a blow.

'The army is assembled and we are ready to march.'

Cormac smiled. 'You do not like this situation, do you?'

'What I like is of no consequence. Follow me.' He turned on his heel and strode from the room.

Outside the mountain entrance a vast horde of men and shadow-beasts were gathered, red-eyed creatures with sharp fangs, monsters with wings of leather, scaled men with pallid faces and cruel eyes.

'Mother of Mithras!' whispered Victorinus. 'These are our allies?'

Goroien stood at the centre of the mass, surrounded by a score of huge hounds with eyes of fire.

'Come, Prince Cormac,' she called. 'March with Athena, goddess of war!'

461

17

The Keep loomed like a black tomb over the landscape of the Void, a vast single-towered fortress with four crenellated battlements and a gateway shaped like the mouth of a demon, rimmed with fangs of dark iron.

Around it loped huge hounds, some as large as ponies, but of Molech's army there was nothing to be seen.

'I do not like the look of that gateway,' said Victorinus, standing beside Cormac at the centre of the shadow horde.

'Well you might not,' said Goroien. 'The teeth snap shut.'

'Is there a mechanism that operates them?' Cormac asked.

'There is,' said Maedhlyn. 'Molech based that design on one I created for him at Babel; there are a series of wheels and levers behind the gateway.'

'Then some of us must scale the walls,' Cormac said.

'No,' said Goroien, 'it will not be necessary to climb them.' Raising her hand, she called out in a language unknown to the Britons and the beasts around her made way for a group of tall men – their skins ivory pale, dark wings growing from their shoulders. 'These will bear you to the battlements.'

'Do they know we are here, do you think?' whispered one of the Britons.

'They know,' said Goroien.

'Then let us waste no more time,' said Cormac. Goroien threw back her head and a high-pitched chilling howl issued from her throat. Her own hounds leapt forward, hurtling across the dark plain. From the Keep came an answering howl and the beasts of Molech ran to meet them.

'If you cannot keep the gate open, we are lost,' Goroien told Cormac and the prince nodded. Winged creatures with cold eyes moved behind the Britons, looping long arms around their chests. Dark wings spread and Cormac felt himself sag into the creature's arms as it rose into the air. Dizziness struck him, and the beating of the wings sounded like a coming storm in his ears. High above the Keep they soared, and now Cormac could see the armoured warriors of Molech's Loyals manning the battlements. Arrows flew up towards him, arcing away as the winged beast rose above their range. Again and again the beast dropped within range, only to soar once more as the shafts were loosed. Around him Cormac could see the other winged carriers following the same tactic.

Then, without warning, they dropped together and Cormac heard several screams from among the Britons as the Keep rushed towards them. The bowmen on the walls let fly with their last shafts, but hit nothing, and men scattered as the diving beasts spread and beat frantically to slow their fall. Cormac felt the arms around him loosen as he was still ten feet above the battlements. Bracing himself and bending his knees, he was ready when the creature released him and landed lightly, his sword sliding into his hand. Around him the other Britons gathered themselves, and alongside him appeared the dark-armoured Gilgamesh.

The winged carriers departed and for a moment there was no movement on the battlements. Then, seeing how few were the attackers, the Loyals charged. With a wild cry Gilgamesh leapt to meet them, his swords a blur that clove into their ranks. Cormac and the Britons rushed to his aid and the battle was joined. There were no wounded or dead to encumber the fighting men. Mortal wounds saw the victim fall . . . and disappear. No blood, no screams of agony, no snaking entrails on which to slip and fall.

Victorinus fought, as ever, coolly and with his mind alert – missing nothing. He saw with wonderment the incredible skills of the warrior Gilgamesh, who seemed to float into action without apparent speed. This, Victorinus knew, was the mark of greatness in close combat: the ability to create space in which to think and move. Alongside him Cormac hacked and slashed in a frenzy, his passion and his recklessness achieving the same result as the more graceful Gilgamesh; warriors falling before him like leaves before an Autumn storm. Slowly the Loyals were pushed back along the narrow battlement.

Out on the plain the shadow horde had reached the gateway – and the teeth snapped shut. Once again Goroien sent up the shadow-beasts who harried the defenders on the battlements, swooping and diving, cold knives sweeping across unprotected throats.

Cormac despatched an opponent, then leapt to the parapet and sprinted along the wall above the shadow-horde a hundred feet below. A defender slashed at him but he hurdled the blade, landing awkwardly and swaying out over the edge. Recovering his balance he ran on, clambering up the outside wall of the gate tower and over the top to a second battlement. There were two warriors stationed there, both with bows. Cormac dived to one side as an arrow hissed by him. Dropping their bows, the archers drew short, curved swords and together they rushed him. He parried the first lunge, his blade cleaving through the man's neck, but the second man lashed out with his foot, spilling Cormac to the stone floor. His sword spun from his hand. Desperately he struggled to rise, but a curved sword touched his neck.

'Are you ready for death?' the man whispered.

A knife appeared in the warrior's throat and he vanished from sight as Gilgamesh leapt lightly down to join Cormac. 'Tool!' hissed Gilgamesh.

Cormac gathered his sword and looked around him. A stairwell led down to the gateway and he moved on to it and began the descent. Below the battlement was a room, and – as Maedhlyn had said – it was filled with interlocking wheels and levers. Three men sat by the mechanism. Gilgamesh touched Cormac's shoulder and moved silently ahead. The men saw him, dragged their swords free . . .

. . . and died.

'You are very skilled,' said Cormac.

'Just what I needed,' responded Gilgamesh. 'Praise from a peasant! How does this mechanism operate?'

Cormac gazed at the interlocking wheels, seeking the obvious – and finding it. 'I would say it was this,' he said, pointing to the dark handle that jutted from the smallest wheel. Gripping it with both hands, he began to turn it from right to left.

'How do you know that is the right way?' asked Gilgamesh.

'It does not move the other way,' said Cormac, smiling. 'Does that not tell you something?'

Gilgamesh grunted and ran to a second door. 'As soon as they see the fangs begin to rise, they will gather here more swiftly than flies on a wound.'

Even as he spoke, the pounding of feet could be heard upon the stairs. Cormac turned the handle as swiftly as he could, his muscles bunching and straining. The door burst open and several men rushed in; Gilgamesh despatched them swiftly, but others forced him back.

At last Cormac reached the point where the wheel would turn no more, and picking up a fallen sword, he rammed it into the mechanism and jammed it between the spokes of two larger wheels. Then he ran to aid the beleaguered Gilgamesh and together they halted the advance.

From below them came the clash of sword on sword. The Loyals fought desperately now, sensing their doom was close. Shadow-beasts appeared behind them on the stairs and the battle was ended.

Cormac pushed past the creatures and forced his way down to the Gateway tunnel. Inside the walls all was chaos. He saw Goroien battling desperately against three warriors and raced to her side, his sword crushing the skull of the man to her left. Spinning on her heel, Goroien plunged one blade into an attacker's belly while blocking a slashing blow from the second man. Cormac killed him with a disembowelling thrust.

Everywhere the Loyals were falling back. Victorinus and the eight surviving Britons ran to join Cormac.

'The King!' said Victorinus. 'We must find him.'

Cormac had thoughts only for Anduine, but he nodded and the group forced their way into the central tower, finding themselves in a long hall. Men and women fled past them, desperate to find places to hide. One of them ran to Cormac, grabbing his arm. He shook himself free but then recognised Rhiannon.

'What are you doing here?' he asked, pulling her clear of the mêlée. The Britons gathered around them both in a sword circle.

'Wotan sent me here,' she sobbed. 'Please help me!'

'Have you seen Anduine?'

'No. One of the guards said Wotan has taken her back to the world.'

'Back? I do not understand.'

'It is a promise he makes to his Loyals. He has a way of returning them to life.'

Cormac's heart sank and a terrible rage began to grow. What more must he do? He had come beyond the borders of death, only to find that fate had tricked him even here.

'The King!' Victorinus urged him.

'Lead us to the dungeons!' Cormac ordered Rhiannon and the blonde girl nodded and set off across the hall to a wide stairwell. They followed her down into a narrow torch-lit, shadow-haunted tunnel.

Suddenly a taloned hand flashed out, encircling Rhiannon's neck. There was a hideous snap and the girl disappeared. Cormac hurled himself forward and a beast with the head of a wolf stepped into view, roaring with rage. Cormac rammed his sword deep into its belly and it faded from sight.

Dungeon doors stood open through the length of the tunnel, except one at the very end. Cormac lifted the locking bar and pulled open the door. Within was a shocking sight: a man covered in rats that tore at his flesh. Raising his sword, Cormac severed the chains of fire that bound him; the body fell and the rats fled as the Britons came forward. The flesh of the man's body healed instantly, but his eyes were vacant and saliva drooled from the slack jaw.

'His mind has gone,' said Cormac.

'Who could blame it?' hissed Victorinus as with great gentleness they lifted the man to his feet.

'Don't know,' said Uther. 'Don't know.'

'You are with friends, sire,' whispered Victorinus. 'With friends.'

'Don't know.'

Slowly they led him from the tunnel and up into the throne hall, where Goroien now sat with Gilgamesh standing alongside her. The hall was thronged with shadow-beasts, who parted to make way for the small group of Britons and the naked man at their midst.

Goroien rose from the throne and walked slowly to stand before Uther, gazing into the empty eyes.

'There was a time when I would have been happy to see him this way,' she said, 'but not now. He was a mighty man and a fine enemy. When I was a child, my father used to say "May the gods give us strong enemies. For they alone will keep us powerful." Uther was the strongest of enemies.' She turned to Cormac, seeing the pain in his eyes. 'And what of your lady?'

'Wotan . . . Molech . . . has taken her back to the world with him.'

'Then you must return there, Cormac.'

He laughed, but there was no humour in the sound. He spread his hands. 'And how shall I do that?' She looked down and her eyes widened.

'However you do it, it must be done swiftly,' she said, pointing to his right hand. A dark shadow nestled there, round and semi-transparent.

'What is it?' he asked.

'It is the black coin, and once it is solid there will be no return.'

Maedhlyn waited within Molech's private chambers with a slender dagger in his hand. A light flared over the silver-crowned skull and a man's shape formed in the air. As it became solid Maedhlyn stepped behind it, his dagger plunging towards the back. With astonishing speed the man whirled, his powerful hand closing on Maedhlyn's wrist.

'Almost, Maedhlyn,' hissed Wotan, twisting the dagger from his grasp and pushing the white-bearded Enchanter from him. Wotan moved to the doorway and stood in the corridor; then stepping back, he shut the door.

'So,' he said, 'one empire falls. Well done, Lord Enchanter!'

467

'Kill me!' pleaded Maedhlyn. 'I can stand this no longer.'

Wotan laughed. 'Give it time. You sent me here two thousand years ago and now it is your turn to enjoy the unimaginable wonders of the Void: food with no flavour, women but no love, wine but no joy. And if you become so weary, you can always end your own life.'

'Take me back. I will serve you.'

'You have promised that already. You said that the boy, Cormac, might know the whereabouts of the Sword. But he did not.'

'I could still find it. They have rescued the King and he trusts me.'

'You will not find much left of your King, unless I misjudge the many talents of the companions I left with him.'

'Please, Molech . . .'

'Goodbye, Maedhlyn. I will pass on your kind regards to Pendarric.'

Wotan shimmered and was gone. Maedhlyn stood for a while staring at the silver-ringed skull, then lifted it and made his way to the hall.

He knelt before Goroien. 'Here, my Queen, is a gift worth more than worlds. It is the spirit-twin of the one Molech has in life. With it you can breach the world above and return yourself – and others – to the flesh.'

Goroien accepted the skull, then tossed it to Gilgamesh. 'Destroy it!' she ordered.

'But, Mother!'

'Do it!'

'No!' screamed Maedhlyn as Gilgamesh dashed the skull to the stone floor, where it shattered into hundreds of tiny shards. The glowing silver band rolled across the floor and Maedhlyn stumbled after it, but smoke began to issue from the circle and the band vanished. The Enchanter fell to his knees. 'Why?' he shouted.

'Because it is over, Maedhlyn,' she told him. 'We had thousands of years of life, and what did we do? We set mankind on a road of madness. I do not want life. I desire no more titles. The Witch Queen is dead; she will remain so.' She moved to Gilgamesh, placing her hands upon his shoulders. 'Now is the time for goodbyes, my dear. I have decided to travel the road to see where it ends. I ask one thing more of you.'

'Anything.'

'See Cormac and the King across the Dark River.'

'I will.'

'Goodbye, Gilgamesh.'

'Farewell, Mother.' Stooping, he kissed her brow, then stepped from the throne dais and stood before Cormac. 'Say goodbye to your friends. You are going home, peasant.'

'We will journey with you,' said Victorinus.

'No,' Cormac told him, taking his hand in the warrior's grip. 'You have your own journey ahead – may your gods accompany you.'

Victorinus bowed and walked to Maedhlyn. 'Come with us,' he said. 'Perhaps Albain was right . . . there *might* be a paradise.'

'No!' said Maedhlyn, backing away. 'I will return to the world. I will!' Turning, he stumbled from the hall and out into the Void.

Cormac bowed to Goroien. 'I thank you, lady. There is nothing more I can say.' She did not reply and he took the King's hand and led Uther from the hall, following the tall armoured figure of Gilgamesh.

Through the long journey Gilgamesh said nothing. His eyes were distant, his thoughts secret. Cormac's fears grew along with the coin that was now a dark and almost solid shape in his hand.

At last they reached the river and saw the barge waiting at the ruined jetty. The beast on it rose as it saw Cormac, its red eyes gleaming in dark triumph.

Gilgamesh stepped to the barge with his sword extended. The beast seemed to smile and spread its arms, offering its chest; the sword plunged home and it disappeared. Cormac helped the King to the craft, then climbed in alongside Gilgamesh.

'Why did it not fight?'

Gilgamesh removed his helm and threw it out into the water. Then he stripped himself of his armour, hurling it from him. Taking the pole, he steered the barge to the far side of the river, holding it against the shore.

Once more Cormac aided Uther. Ahead of them was the cave-mouth and Cormac turned.

'Will you come with us?'

Gilgamesh laughed softly. 'Come with you? The Ferryman cannot leave his craft.'

'I do not understand.'

'You will one day, peasant. There must always be a Ferryman. But we will meet again.' Turning, he poled the craft away into the shadows.

Cormac took the King's hand and climbed to the cave. High above the light still twinkled, like a faraway camp-fire.

Slowly the two men walked towards it.

Cormac awoke to feel a gnawing pain in his back and an aching emptiness in his belly. He groaned and heard a woman's voice say, 'Praise be to God!' He was lying on something hard and tried to move, but his limbs were stiff and cramped. Above his head was a series of high rafters supporting a thatched roof. A woman's face appeared above him, an elderly woman with kind eyes who smiled.

'Lie still, young man.' He ignored the advice and forced himself to sit up. She supported his arm and rubbed at his back when he complained of pain. Beside him lay the Blood King in full armour; his red hair had grown and white showed at the roots and the temples.

'Does he live?' asked Cormac, reaching for the King's hand.

'He lives,' she told him. 'Calm yourself.'

'Calm? We have just walked from Hell, woman.' The door opposite opened and a figure in white entered. Cormac's eyes flared as he recognised her as the woman in the Cave of Sol Invictus – the mother who had left her child.

His mother.

Emotions surged over him, each battling for supremacy: anger, wonder, love, sorrow. Her face was still beautiful and there were tears in her eyes. She reached for him and he went to her, his arms pulling her to him.

'My son,' she whispered. 'My son.'

470

'I brought him back,' said Cormac, 'but still he sleeps.'

Gently she pulled away from his embrace, her hand rising to stroke his bearded cheek. 'We will talk in a little while. There is so much to say . . . to explain.'

'You have no need to explain to me. I know what happened in the cave – and before it. I am sorry your life has brought you such pain.'

'Life brings us nothing,' she told him. 'Ultimately we choose our paths, and when they fail the blame rests with us. And yet I have regrets, such terrible regrets. I did not see you grow, we did not share the wonders.'

He smiled. 'Yet still I saw them.'

Uther moaned softly and Laitha turned to him, but Cormac's hand took her arm. 'There is something you should know,' he said. 'His mind has departed; they tortured him in ways I shall not speak of.'

Laitha moved to the King's side as his eyes opened. Tears welled and ran back into his hair.

'Don't know,' he said.

Her hands cupped his face. 'There is no need to know, my love. I am here; Laitha is here.' His eyes drifted closed and he slept once more.

Cormac felt a cool breeze touch his back and heard the approach of several men. Glancing back, he saw a young knight with short-cropped blond hair and two old men; one was tall, his long white hair braided in the fashion of the southern tribes, the other was thin and slight and walked with a pronounced limp. The three stopped and bowed to Cormac.

'Welcome back,' said the man with the braided hair. 'I am Gwalchmai, and this is Prasamaccus and Ursus, who calls himself Galead.'

'Cormac Daemonsson.'

Prasamaccus shook his head. 'You are the son of Uther, High King of Britain. And our hope for the future.'

'Do not armour me with your hopes,' he told them. 'When this is done I shall return to the Caledones mountains. There is nothing for me here.'

471

'But you were born to be King,' said Gwalchmai, 'and there is no other heir.'

Cormac smiled. 'I was born in a cave, and raised by a one-armed Saxon who knew more of nobility than any man I have met since. It seems to me that a king needs certain skills – and not just in war. I do not possess these skills and, more, I do not wish to possess them. I have no desire to rule the lives of others. I do not wish to be the Blood King's heir. I have killed men, and slain demons; I have despatched souls to the dark and walked across the Void. It is enough.'

Gwalchmai was about to argue further, but Prasamaccus lifted his hand.

'You must always be your own man, Prince Cormac. You mentioned the Void. Tell us of the King.'

'I brought him back – much good may it do you.'

'What does that mean?' snapped Gwalchmai.

'His mind . . .'

'Enough!' said Laitha. 'The King will return. You have seen him, Cormac, as he would wish no man to see him. But you do not know him as I do; he is a man of iron strength. The rest of you, leave us. Cormac, I have a hut prepared for you; there is food there and Galead will show you to it. Do not overexert yourself; your wounds are healing well, yet still your body will be weak for a while. Now go, all of you.'

For several hours Laitha sat beside the King, stroking his brow or holding his hand. Women came and lit candles, but she did not notice them, and as she gazed down on the careworn face and the greying hair she saw again the boy Thuro who had fled to the mountains to escape the assassins who had killed his father. He was a sensitive boy who did not know how to start a fire or hold a sword. In those far-off days of innocence, he had been gentle and kind and loving.

But the world had changed him, brought out the iron and the fire, giving birth to the Blood King of legend, taught him to fight and to kill and, worse, to hate.

And what a fool she had been. This young man had loved her with all his passion, and she had spurned him for a child's dream.

472

If there was one event in her life that she could reach back and change, it would be the night in Pinrae when the young Uther had come to her and they had made love beneath the two moons. Her feelings had soared, her body had seemed more alive than at any other time of her youth and as the blood had pounded within her, and her body trembled in the ecstasy of the moment, she had whispered the name of Culain. The whisper flew into Uther's heart like an arrow of ice, lodging there for ever. And yet – though she knew it not then – it was not the thought of Culain which had lifted her to such breathtaking heights but the love of Uther.

And she had destroyed it. No, she realised, not destroyed – but altered . . . corrupted with the acid of jealousy.

Culain had once loosed the same arrow at her when they had been asleep together in a cabin near the Queen's palace at Camulodunum. He had moved in his sleep and she had kissed him.

'Are you there, my love?' he had whispered dreamily.

'I am here,' she had told him.

'Never leave me, Goroien.'

Oh how that had hurt! How she had wanted, in that moment, to strike him, to tear at his handsome face. And was it not that one moment alone which had allowed her, later in Raetia, to spurn him, to send him from her? Was it not that whispered arrow which had caused her to be so cruel upon the Tor?

Uther stirred beside her. Once more his eyes opened and he whispered the two words over and over.

'What are you trying to tell me?' she asked, but his eyes were without focus and she knew he could not hear her. Footsteps sounded behind her, and the shadow of Galead fell upon the King's face.

'Cormac is asleep,' said Galead. 'May I join you?'

'Yes. Is Lekky well?'

'She is, my lady. She spent the afternoon with two of your women drawing unfathomable creatures on a flat stone, using up a great store of charcoal in the process. Now she is asleep beside Cormac. Is the King recovering?'

'He keeps saying, "Don't know." What is it that he does not know?'

'They tortured him to find the Sword and I would guess that he does not know where it lies. If he did, he would have told them.'

'Yet he must know,' she said, 'for it was he who sent it.'

'I saw his last fight in a dream. He hurled the blade high and screamed a name.'

'What name?'

'Yours, my lady.'

'Mine? Then where is the Sword.'

'I have thought much on that,' he said, 'and I think I may have the answer. Uther could not have sent the sword to you, for he thought you dead. When Pendarric appeared to me, he spoke in what I took to be riddles, but in fact his words were plain enough. He talked of good and evil, and I thought he meant Wotan. He said that I should identify the real enemy and then I would know how to fight it.'

'And who is the real enemy?'

'Hatred is the enemy. When I saw the Goths destroy that Saxon village, I hated them. And it seemed such a small matter to find Lekky and take her with me. But bringing her here allowed her to meet you and, as you told me last night, it allowed you to see without bitterness. And now, as it should be, you are here with the man you love. And that is the key.'

'Now you are speaking in Pendarric's riddles.'

'No, my lady. Uther did not send the Sword to a dead Laitha. He sent it to his love, thinking that it would never arrive and therefore no enemy would ever find it.'

'What are you saying?'

'It is waiting, my lady. It could not come to Morgana of the Isle, only to the woman who has the King's love.'

The Queen took a deep breath and raised her arm, her fingers open. A burning light grew around them, bathing the room in echoes of fire. Galead shielded his eyes as the brightness swelled, streaming from the windows and doorway and up through a hole

474

in the thatched roof – a straight bar of golden light rising through the clouds.

In his hut, Prasamaccus saw the glow outside the doorway and heard the shouts of the Sisters who had gathered outside the Round Hall. Stumbling out into the night, he saw the Hall pulsing with bars of flame. Fearing for the King's life he limped towards the light, his arm before his eyes. Gwalchmai and Cormac joined him.

On the causeway the men of the Ninth stood in awed silence as the light spread, bathing the Isle of Crystal in gold.

Fifty miles away, in Vindocladia, the Goths also observed the phenomenon and Wotan himself came from his tent to stand on a lonely hillside and stare at the burning light that smote the sky.

Back in the Round Hall, blinded by the brilliance, Laitha reached up and felt her fingers curling round the hilt of the great Sword. Slowly she pulled it down and the light faded. By the doorway Prasamaccus and Gwalchmai fell to their knees.

'He sent it to his love,' whispered Laitha, tears flowing as she laid the Sword beside the King, curling his hand around the hilt. 'I have the Sword, and now I must seek the man,' she said. 'Sit with me a while, Galead.' Her head drooped and her eyes closed, her spirit flying to a dreamscape of tall trees and proud mountains. Beside a lake sat a young boy with fair hair and a gentle face.

'Thuro,' she said and the boy looked up and smiled.

'I was hoping you would come,' he said. 'It is beautiful here; I shall never leave it.'

She sat beside him and took his hand. 'I love you,' she said. 'I always have.'

'Nobody can come here. I won't let them.'

'And what do you hope for?' she asked the boy.

'I never want to be king. I just want to be alone – with you.'

'Shall we swim?' she asked.

'Yes, I would like that,' he said, standing and removing his tunic. As he ran naked into the water and dived below the surface, she rose and let slip the simple dress she wore. Her body was young and she stared at her reflection in the water. No lines, no years of pain and disappointment had yet etched their tracks in her virgin beauty.

The water was cool and she swam to where Thuro floated on his back, staring up at the impossibly blue sky.

'Will you stay here with me for ever?' he asked, standing upright in the shallow water.

'If you want me to.'

'I do. More than anything else.'

'Then I will.'

They waded back to the shoreline and sat in the hot sunlight. He reached out to touch the skin of her shoulder and as she moved closer, his fingers slid down over the curve of her breast. His face flushed. Closer still she came, her arm slipping behind his neck and pulling his head towards her. Lifting her face she kissed him gently, softly. Now his hand roamed free across her body. Pushing her back to the grass he moved on top of her, entering her smoothly as her legs slid over his hips.

Laitha was floating on the rhythms of pleasure, and she felt those rhythms quicken and heighten.

'Thuro! Thuro! Thuro!' she moaned. She kissed his mouth and his cheek, feeling the beard that grew there. Her hands stroked the broad back of the man above her, caressing the corded muscle and the many scars.

'Uther!'

'I am here, lady,' he said, kissing her softly, and moving to lie alongside her. 'You have found me.'

'Forgive me,' she said.

'You shame me,' he told her. 'I treated you with disdain and I forced you and Culain together. And for all your suffering, I am sorry.'

'Forgive me anyway?' she asked him.

'I do. You are my wife. And I love you now, as I have always loved you.'

'Do you still wish to stay?'

He smiled sadly. 'What is happening back there?'

'Wotan's army is approaching Sorviodunum – and the Sword came to me.'

'To you?' he said, astonished. 'Then this is no dream? You are alive?'

'I am alive and waiting for you.'

'Tell me all.' Simply and without embellishment, she told him of Culain's saving of his body, and Uther's son journeying across Hell to rescue his soul. She spoke also of the terrible victories won by the Goths, and lastly of the gathering of the Ninth.

'Then back there I have no army?'

'No.'

'But I have the Sword – and my wife and son.'

'You do, my lord.'

'It is more than enough. Take me home.'

18

Prasamaccus, Gwalchmai, Cormac and Galead waited at the foot of the Tor, for the King had gone there soon after waking and had vanished from sight. Laitha told them to wait for his return and for two hours now the men had sat in the bright sunshine, eating bread and wine. They were joined by Severinus Albinus who sat apart from the group, staring to the south-east.

'Where is he?' said Gwalchmai suddenly, pushing himself to his feet.

'Be calm,' Prasamaccus told him.

'He is back from the dead but now he is lost to us once more. How can I be calm? I know him. Whatever he is doing entails great risk.'

As the afternoon faded, Laitha approached them. 'He wishes to see you,' she told Cormac.

'Alone?'

'Yes. You and I will speak in a little while.'

Cormac trudged the winding path, not knowing what to say when he reached the summit. This man was his father, yet he had never known him save as a mindless, wrecked creature rescued from the Void. Would the man embrace him? He hoped that he would not.

As he reached the crown of the Tor, he saw Uther in full armour sitting by the round tower with the great Sword lying beside him. The King looked up and stood and Cormac felt his heart beating faster, for this was no broken man – this was the Blood King, and he wore his power like a cloak upon his broad shoulders. The eyes were blue and chill as a winter wind, the stance that of the warrior born.

'What do you wish of me, Cormac?' he asked, his voice resonant and deep.

'Only what you have always given me,' said Cormac. 'Nothing.'

'I did not know of you, boy.'

'But you would have, had you not hounded my mother into fleeing to the cave.'

'The past is dead,' said Uther wearily. 'Your mother and I are reunited.'

'I am happy for you.'

'Why did you risk your life to save me?'

Cormac chuckled. 'It was not for you, Uther; I was seeking the woman I love. But you were there and, perhaps, blood called me. I do not know. But I want nothing of you or your kingdom – what is left of it. I want only Anduine, and then you will hear from me no more.'

'Harsh words, my son. But I will not argue with the judgement. I know the errors I have made, and no one can make the hurt less – or more. I would be glad if you would spend a little time with me, so that I can know you and be proud. But if you choose another path, so be it. Will you shake hands, man to man, and accept my thanks?'

'That I will do,' said Cormac.

Cormac walked back down the hill to the group, more light of heart than when he had climbed the Tor.

Gwalchmai and Prasamaccus were the next to be summoned, and after them Severinus Albinus.

He bowed to the King. 'I had thought to enjoy my retirement,' he said accusingly.

'Then you should have refused the call,' said the King.

Albinus shrugged. 'Life was tedious without you,' said the Roman.

Uther nodded and the two men smiled and gripped hands. 'Would that I could rely on other men as I can on you,' said the King.

'What now, Uther? I have three hundred old men guarding the causeway. The latest arrivals tell me there are more than twelve thousand Goths. Do we attack them? Do we wait?'

'We go to them with sword and fire.'

'Fine. It should earn us a splendid page in history.'

"Will you come with me this last time?"

Albinus grinned. 'Why not? There is nowhere else to run.'

'Then prepare the men, for we will travel as we did once before.'

'There were almost five thousand of us then, Lord King. And we were young and reckless.'

'You think twelve thousand Goths are a match for the legendary Ninth?' mocked Uther, grinning.

'I think I should have stayed in Calcaria.'

'We will not be alone, old friend. I have journeyed far, and I can promise you a day of surprises.'

'I do not doubt that, sire. And I am no fool; I know where you had to go, and I am surprised they let you walk away alive.'

Uther chuckled. 'Life is a grand game, Albinus, and should be treated as such.' His smile faded and his eyes lost their humour. 'But I have made promises other men may come to rue.'

Albinus shrugged. 'Whatever you have done, I am with you. But then I am old and ready for a tranquil life. I have a crooked servant in Calcaria who is even now praying for my death. I would like to disappoint him.'

'Perhaps you will.'

Galead was the last to be called, and the sun was setting as he found the King.

'You have changed, Ursus. Would you like your old face returned to you?'

'No, my lord. It would confuse Lekky and I am content as Galead.'

'You found the Sword. How can I repay you?'

Galead smiled. 'I seek no payment.'

'Speaking of swords, I see that you are no longer carrying a weapon,' said Uther.

'No, I shall never bear arms again. I had hoped to find a small farm and breed horses. Lekky could have had a pony. But . . .'He spread his hands.

'Do not abandon that hope, Galead. We are not finished yet.'

'Where will you raise an army?'

480

'Come with me and find out.'

'I will be no use to you. I will never be a warrior again.'

'Come anyway. The good Sisters will look after Lekky.'

'I have lost my appetite for blood and death. I do not hate the Goths, nor do I desire to see them slain.'

'I need you, Galead. And leave your sword behind; another will take its place at the appointed time.'

'You have spoken to Pendarric?'

'I do not need to. I am the King and I know what is to come.'

Lastly, Laitha came to him on the hilltop and they stood arm in arm, gazing out at the Sleeping Giants in the bright moonlight.

'Tell me you will come back,' she said.

'I will come back.'

'Have you used the Sword to see Wotan's power?'

'Yes – and I have seen the future. It is not all bad, though there will be hardship ahead. Whatever may happen tomorrow, the realm is finished. We fought hard to keep it alive, like a candle in the storm. But no candle lasts for ever.'

'Are you sad?'

'A little, for I have given my life to Britain. But the men who will come after I am gone are strong men, good men, caring men. The land will receive them, for they will love the land. My realm will not be missed for long.'

'And what of you, Uther? Where will you go?'

'I will be with you. Always.'

'Oh, dear God! You are going . . .'

'Do not say it,' he whispered, touching his finger to her lips. 'I will come back to the Isle tomorrow. You will stand on this hillside and you will see my boat. And from that moment we will never be parted, though the world ends in fire and the stars vanish from memory.'

'I will wait for you,' she said, and tried to smile . . .

But the tears came anyway.

Wotan rode at the head of his army, ten thousand fighting men who had tasted only victory since he had first walked amongst

481

them. The Saxons had deserted during the night, but they were not needed now. Ahead lay the Great Circle of Sorviodunum, and Wotan could remember the days of its construction and the Mystery contained in its measurements.

'I am coming for you, Pendarric,' he whispered into the breeze. And joy swept through him.

Slowly the army moved across the plain.

Suddenly there was a blaze of light from the Circle and Wotan reined in his horse. Sunlight gleamed from armour and he saw several hundred Roman soldiers ringing the stones. Then a tall man strode from the Circle to stand before the Goths. On his head was a great winged helm and in his hands the Sword of Cunobelin.

Wotan touched his heels to his mount and cantered forward.

'You are a stronger man than I thought,' he said. 'My compliments on your escape.' His pale eyes scanned the warriors. 'I have always believed you cannot beat a veteran for experience and strength under siege. But this . . .? This is almost comic.'

'Look to your right, you arrogant son of a whore,' said Uther, raising the Sword of Cunobelin and pointing it to the north. White lightning leapt from the highest hill, the air around it shimmering. From out of nowhere came Geminus Cato, leading his legion. Behind the disciplined British ranks streamed thousands of Brigantes, riding war-chariots of bronze and iron.

'And to your left,' hissed the King and Wotan swung in the saddle. Once more the air shimmered and parted and thirty thousand Saxon warriors, led by the forked-bearded Asta, marched to form a battle-line. Grim-eyed men bearing long-handled axes, they stood silently awaiting the order to take their revenge on the Goths.

'Where is your smile now?' asked the Blood King.

The Goths, outnumbered six to one, fell back into a huge shield-ring and Wotan shrugged.

'You think you have won? You believe those men are all I can call on?'

He removed his helm and Uther saw a glow begin beneath the skin of his brow, a pulsing red light that shone like a hidden crown.

482

The skies above darkened and in the clouds the King could see a demonic army of taloned creatures – wheeling and diving, tearing at some unseen barrier.

Without warning Wotan's horse shied before the King – scales appearing on its flanks, its head becoming long and wedge-shaped, fire exploding from its mouth. Even as the beast reared Uther raised his Sword, deflecting the fire to scorch the grass at his feet. The blade hissed down through the scaled neck and the creature fell writhing to the grass. Wotan leapt clear, his sword snaking into his hands.

'As it should be,' he said. 'Two kings deciding the fate of a world!'

Their swords clashed together. Wotan was a warrior of immense power and confidence, unbeaten in combat since his resurrection. But Uther was also a man of great strength and he had been trained by Culain lach Feragh, the greatest warrior of the age. The battle was evenly balanced; their swords hissed and sang and the watching men marvelled at the skill of the fighters. Time had no meaning, for neither man tired. Nor was there any evidence of supremacy as the battle continued. Only the demons moved, striving to break through the invisible barrier, while the warriors of all armies stood silently awaiting the outcome.

Uther's blade cut into Wotan's side, but a savage riposte sliced the flesh of the King's thigh. Now both men were bleeding from many cuts and the battle slowed. Uther staggered as Wotan's blade clove beneath his ribs. For a moment only, Wotan's eyes gleamed with triumph – but the King fell back and the great Sword of Cunobelin swung in a high, vicious arc. Wotan, his own blade trapped in Uther's body, could only scream as the blade smashed into his skull, slicing under the Sipstrassi crown and smashing the bone to crimson-streaked shards.

The Gothic King staggered back, calling on the power of Sipstrassi, but Uther rolled to his knees and hurled himself at the enemy, his sword ripping up through Wotan's belly and splitting his heart in two. Wotan fell, his body twitching, and with one stroke Uther cut the head from the torso. But the Sipstrassi still glowed on the skull and above the heads of the army the barrier was giving way. Uther tried to raise the Sword but his strength was failing.

A shadow fell across him as he knelt in the grass.

'Give me your Sword, my king,' said Galead.

Uther surrendered it and toppled forward to lie beside his enemy as Galead raised the blade over his head.

'Begone!' he called and a great wind grew, the clouds bunching in on themselves as lightning forked the sky. A beam of light shone from the Sword, cleaving the clouds.

The demons vanished.

High in the heavens a shining light appeared, like a silver coin trailing fire. Galead saw the Stone set in the sword shimmer and pale. This was the comet spoken of by Pendarric, the moving star that could draw Sipstrassi magic . . . and Galead knew then what to wish for.

'Take it all!' he screamed. *'All!'*

The sky overhead tore like a curtain and the comet seemed to swell. Closer and closer it came, huge and round like the hammer of the gods descending to destroy the earth. Men flung themselves to the ground, covering their heads. Galead could feel the pull of the comet – dragging the power from the Sword, drawing the magic from the Stone and pulling the life from his own frame. His strength wilted, his arms becoming thin and scrawny; his knees gave way and he fell, but still he held the blade high above his head.

As suddenly as it had come the comet was gone, and a great silence settled on the field. Cormac and Prasamaccus ran to the King, ignoring the broken, ancient man who lay on the grass with his bony hand still clutching the Sword of Cunobelin.

From the Great Circle there was a blaze of light and Pendarric stepped into sight. Kneeling beside Galead he touched a Stone to his brow, and youth flowed once more into his veins.

'You found the Words of Power,' said Pendarric.

'Has the evil gone?'

'There is no more Sipstrassi on the face of your planet. Far below the sea perhaps, but none where men will find it for a thousand years. You achieved it, Galead. You have ended the reign of magic.'

'But you still have a Stone.'

'I have come from the Feragh, my friend. The comet was not seen there.'

'The King!' said Galead, struggling to rise.

'Wait. Gather your strength.' Pendarric moved to where Uther lay. The King's wounds were grievous and blood was streaming from the injured side. Prasamaccus was doing his best to staunch the flow while Gwalchmai and Severinus Albinus supported the body and Cormac stood close by.

Pendarric knelt beside the King and made to press the Stone to his side.

'No!' whispered Uther. 'It ends here. Bring the leaders of the Goths and the Saxons to me, Prasamaccus. Do it swiftly!'

'I can save you, Uther,' said Pendarric.

To what end?' Blood stained the King's beard and his flesh was deathly pale. 'I could not be anything less than I am. I could not live on a farm. I love her, Pendarric, I always did. But I could never be just a man. You understand? If I stay, it will be to fight the Saxons and the Brigante and the Jutes – trying to keep the candle aflame just a little longer.'

'I know that,' Pendarric said sadly.

Prasamaccus returned with a tall fair-haired Goth, who knelt before the King.

'Your name?'

'Alaric,' answered the man.

'You want to live, Alaric?'

'Of course,' replied the warrior smoothly.

'Then you will lay down your weapons and I promise you that you will be allowed to return to your ships.'

'Why would you do this?'

'I am tired of blood and death. Your choice, Alaric: live or die. Make it now.'

'We will live.'

'A good choice. Severinus, see that my orders are obeyed, there is to be no more killing. Where is Asta?'

'I am here, Blood King,' said Asta, crouching before the dying monarch.

'And I will be true to the promise I made to you yesterday. I give you the land of South Saxon, to rule and to govern. This I say before witnesses.'

'Not as a vassal?'

'No, as a king, answerable only to your own people.'

'I accept. But this may not end the wars between my people and your own.'

'Not a man alive can end war,' said Uther. 'See that the Goths reach their ships.'

'Is that an order, Blood King?'

'It is a request, such that one king might make to another.'

'Then I agree. But you should have those wounds treated.'

Uther raised his blood-covered hand and Asta took it in the warrior's grip, wrist to wrist. Then he rose and walked back to his host.

'Get me to the Isle,' said Uther. 'There is someone waiting for me.'

With great care the men around him lifted the King and carried him back into the Great Circle where they laid him upon the altar. Pendarric stood by and the King called Cormac forward. 'We did not have time to know one another, my son. But do not think of me with bitterness. All men make mistakes, and most suffer for them.'

'No bitterness, Uther. Just pride . . . and regret.'

The King smiled, 'Galead,' he whispered, his voice fading.

'I am here, my lord.'

'When we come through the Gateway, you will see a boat. Carry me to it and sail to the Isle. A woman will be waiting there, who knows that I lied. Tell her my last thoughts were of her.' Uther sagged back on the stone.

Pendarric moved forward swiftly, raising his arm and the King and Galead disappeared.

Prasamaccus cried out in his anguish and stumbled away. Gwalchmai stood dry-eyed, his face set.

'He will return. I know that he will . . . when our need is great.'

No one spoke. Then Severinus Albinus placed his hand on Gwalchmai's shoulder.

486

'I do not know all your Celtic beliefs,' he said, 'but I believe also that there is a place for men like Uther, and that he will not die.'

Gwalchmai turned to speak, but the tears could not be held back, he nodded stiffly and walked away to stand alone at the altar, staring up at the sky.

Cormac stood by, his heart heavy. He had not really known Uther, but he was blood of his blood and he was proud. Turning he saw a young woman running across the field, her hair flowing behind her.

'Anduine!' he cried. 'Anduine!'

And she heard him.

Epilogue

Goroien lifted her silver helm and laid it on the throne, her gauntlets and breastplate beside it. Her swords she kept. Then she walked down to the hall, through the silent ranks of the shadow-beasts and out onto the plain before the Keep.

She could see the grey ribbon of the road wending its way into the distance, and upon it stood a shrouded figure. Slowly she walked to the hooded man, her hand upon the hilt of a silver sword.

'Are you a servant of Molech?' she asked.

'I am no one's servant, Goroien, save maybe yours.' He pushed back the hood and she gasped, hiding her face in her hands.

'Do not look at me, Culain. You will see only decay.'

Gently he took her hands and stared down at her unsullied beauty.

'There is no decay. You are as beautiful now as the day I first saw you.'

She looked at her hands and saw that he spoke the truth.

'Can you still love me after all I have done to you?' she asked him. He smiled and lifted her hand to his lips.

'No man knows where the road leads,' she said. 'You think there is a paradise?'

'I think we have already found it.'

Acknowledgements

Last Sword of Power, as with all my other novels, is the result of many months of hard work from a gifted team. Without them, my poor spelling, lousy punctuation, and my talent for split infinitives would be far more widely known. To my editor, Liza Reeves, and my copy-editor, Jean Maund – many thanks. I am also more than grateful to my 'readers', Edith Graham and Tom Taylo, and my proofreader Stella Graham. Thanks also to my father-in-law, Denis Ballard, for supplying the research on Roman Britain.

About the author

David Gemmell's first novel, *Legend*, was published in 1984. He has written many bestsellers, including the Drenai Saga, the Jon Shannow novels and the Stones of Power sequence. Widely acclaimed as Britain's king of heroic fantasy, David Gemmell died in 2006.

Find out more about David Gemmell and other Orbit authors by registering for the free monthly newsletter at www.orbitbooks.net.